# Cruel Vintage

This is a work of fiction. Names, characters, places, and incidents either are the product of the author's imagination or used fictitiously, and any resemblance to actual persons, living or dead, events, or locales is entirely coincidental. The publisher does not have control over and does not assume any responsibility for third-party websites, or their content, not owned by the publisher. Trademarks used herein are incidental and used specifically in a descriptive capacity.

Cover design by Brandi Doane-McCann

Formatting and interior design by Billington Creative

Print edition ISBN 978-0-9973024-7-9
e-Book edition ISBN 978-0-9973024-6-2

Library of Congress Control Number: 2020904492

# Cruel Vintage

## A BEN KAYE CASE

A Novel By

# Huston Michaels

Gold Miner Books

"[I]t is the wine that leads me on...
It even tempts [me] to blurt out stories never told."

Homer

*For Julie*

# DAY 1

The heel of the heavy boot tapped out a soft, staccato beat on the parking lot asphalt as the rider took another hit off the yomogi-laced joint. The weed helped keep the anticipation in check, the yomogi kept the senses sharp.

It was the perfect combination for the day of a kill, especially when the target controlled the timing. For the rider, it was now a simple waiting game.

The morning crept toward noon. The riding leathers were hot, and twice the rider moved to find better shade under the lollipop-trimmed trees in the landscaped strip between the sidewalk and the lot.

Still no sign of the target, and still the heel kept time.

For the hundredth time the rider caressed the squat, cylindrical canister tucked inside the black leather jacket and considered the irony of the day. Not a subtle dose, as irony goes, but certainly appropriate given the target's history.

The rider would have preferred a blade, but not today. The Lord had considered close combat too much of a risk.

"The man is dangerous," the Lord had warned. "Were he Japanese, he would be *Bushi*. You must not lose."

Had anyone else implied the weakness, the rider would have taken their head. The rider had never lost. The rider would not lose today. The beauty of the falling sun was eternal.

The heel continued its unconscious countdown to the target's death.

The cell phone in the rider's inside pocket buzzed, then connected to the Bluetooth ear piece.

"He's on the move," a voice said.

"*Hai. Arigato,*" the rider acknowledged and disconnected.

Twenty minutes later a silver Bentley Continental rolled down Wilshire Boulevard from the west and pulled to a stop at the curb in front of the showroom. The target got out of the passenger side, bent over for a moment to talk to the driver, then turned and headed for the door as the Bentley pulled away.

A beautiful, smiling woman in a Ferrari-red dress stepped outside and held the door open in welcome. Even from the rider's vantage point there was no hint in the target's movements that his lower left leg was a prosthesis.

From the Wilshire side, the showroom was little more than a storefront and a sign. The rider knew that vehicle access was from the one way, west-to-east street one block south. Relocation to the rear was necessary. The rider stubbed out the joint, started the bike and dropped the helmet's tinted visor. The heel stilled at last as the toe of the boot found the gear shift lever.

The delivery took longer than anticipated. The joint was briefly re-lit.

The rider heard the new Ferrari before it rolled into view. Its top was down.

The rider prepared while the target made a left and went to the light at Wilshire.

To the rider's surprise, the target stayed in the through lane instead of entering the left turn stacking lane.

*He's not going back to the office*, the rider realized, quickly evaluating the new variables.

When the light changed the Ferrari crossed Wilshire and headed north. The rider timed the light perfectly and was the last vehicle to get through on green, settling into early afternoon traffic two cars back and one lane over.

The target went east on Santa Monica Boulevard to La Cienega, made a left, went to Sunset and turned east again.

The heel began to bounce in the air below the peg.

Where the hell is he going?

When the Ferrari turned left onto Crescent Heights, the rider smiled behind the visor. There was no need to follow now.

Crescent Heights is four lanes before becoming Laurel Canyon Road. The rider hit the throttle hard, passed the beautiful red sports car and started the winding climb to Mulholland Drive.

At the summit the rider turned right at the light, went east a couple hundred yards to a point beyond Woodrow Wilson Drive, made a u-turn and waited at the curb.

It wasn't long before the Ferrari rolled up to the light at Laurel Canyon and Mulholland, its left turn signal blinking.

*"Ima, watashi wa anata o koroshimasu,"* the rider said aloud and

started the slow roll back down toward Laurel Canyon. Now, I will kill you.

"*Chui shite,*" the Lord whispered. Use caution.

It was a weekday, outside normal sightseeing hours, and all the northbound uphill traffic on Laurel Canyon except the Ferrari continued on down to The Valley on the other side.

Again, the rider's timing was perfect, goosing the powerful bike just as the westbound light turned red, dodging a car making a late left turn and speeding after the accelerating Ferrari. When the gap closed to about two hundred feet the rider could hear the unmistakable Italian aria of the car's exhaust as the target began to push the car.

At the top of the first steep climb there was a hard left. The rider focused on the Ferrari, oblivious to the spectacular views.

From the first turn and lookout, Mulholland rides the shoulders and crest of the hills, with no cross streets or houses at grade until Bowmont.

It now depended on oncoming traffic and how hard the target was willing to drive his new toy.

The opportunity came after the next overlook.

The rider saw one eastbound car approaching, gauged the speed and distance, and rolled hard on the throttle. The powerful engine screamed as the bike started to close on the Ferrari.

Just as the oncoming car passed by, the road straightened. The rider checked the rearview mirror. No following traffic.

The motorcycle leapt forward, quickly overtaking the Ferrari. As the rider leaned into the left lane the target looked in his rearview mirror, straight at the rider's visor.

The rider slowed alongside the Ferrari and shouted, "*Utsukushi kuruma!*" Beautiful car.

"What?" the target yelled back, glancing from the road to the rider and back.

The rider reached into the riding jacket and pulled out the canister. "*Okurimono!*" the rider shouted. A gift.

The rider lobbed the canister just above and in front of the target's head. It hit the passenger seat back and bounced into the footwell.

"Hey!" the target shouted, lifting off the gas as the rider rolled on the throttle and rapidly pulled away.

In the rearview mirror the rider could see the target trying to steer the car with one hand while he leaned over and groped for the canister with the other.

When the gap was about fifty feet, the rider pushed the bike's horn button.

The passenger compartment of the Ferrari instantly erupted into a ball of flame. The fiercely burning car careened back and forth across the road twice before slamming nose-first into the embankment on the uphill side.

Just before the intersection of Mulholland and Coldwater Canyon the rider pulled to the right shoulder and stopped as a fire truck and ambulance screamed by, heading for the plume of black smoke now rising rapidly into the sky to the east.

The rider waited for the fire truck to get some distance away before swinging a u-turn and heading east.

Time to confirm the kill.

"You served me well," the Lord said to the rider.

"*Arigatou gozaimasu, Shukun*," the rider said inside the helmet. Thank you, my Lord.

"Now you will seek our common enemy."

The rider's pulse quickened. "His presence is strong. He is near."

"Your *tengu* will guide you."

The rider pulled to the shoulder not far from the police car blocking the road. The fire had burned fiercely and the rider saw nothing that hinted that the target had survived. Pulling the cell phone from the jacket pocket, the rider surreptitiously took two pictures and messaged them to the number that had called earlier. 'It's done' was the caption.

Pleased, the rider again swung around and headed west. In a way, though, it seemed like such a shame that the target had waited almost a year for a $400K car, then died in a crash the first time he drove it.

# DAY 2
Tuesday Week 1

The last time Ben Kaye had walked into the West Bureau Detectives squad room he'd intended to sign his separation papers and clean out his desk. Then Captain Thompson had tempted him with a call for help from an old colleague, convincing him to instead take a leave of absence.

Kaye had gone to Colorado, stepping into the strangest case he'd ever worked.

A case that some nights still kept him awake, wondering.

The Squad had changed. Many desks were empty and there wasn't another detective to be seen. Kaye hung the Big Boar MC jacket, the twin, double-tusked boar always watching, over the end of the cubicle panel and took stock.

A phone atop a desk calendar pad and not much else. He pulled open the top drawer and found the same motley assortment of pens, pencils, push pins, paper clips and pads of paper that had been there when he left. His cork board was gone, as was the radio charger he habitually kept tucked into one corner of the space. He could find replacements.

The door to Thompson's office and the blinds covering the glass were both closed.

Kaye knew his Captain was expecting him.

He knocked.

"Come," Thompson's familiar voice boomed through the door.

Kaye entered. Thompson was a large, lumbering man, much taller than Kaye and nearly as heavy. He was on the phone. He put one hand over the mouthpiece and said, "Sit" before removing the hand and saying, "Yes, sir, I understand. We're doing the best we can with the available resources."

The Captain listened.

"Yes, sir," he said again after a moment. "We'll do our best."

Thompson hung up, stared venomously at the phone and muttered, "Go fuck yourself," before looking up at Kaye and smiling.

"Hi," he said with forced joviality. "Sorry you had to hear that."

"That's okay. I've heard it before."

"Thanks. But, seriously, welcome back Detective. You are back, right? You haven't changed your mind since you called?"

"I'm back," Kaye acknowledged. "Never thought I'd hear myself say that, but, yeah, I'm back."

"Thank God," Thompson said, then raised his eyebrows. "Paperwork?"

"Took care of it downtown yesterday."

"Excellent. I can sure use you."

"I see you're down a few bodies."

"A few? I've lost over a hundred years of combined detective experience in the last month, and the department is down hundreds of officers."

"What happened?"

"The plague happened."

"I thought the plague didn't make it to L.A."

"Let me rephrase," Thompson said. "The panic over the plague happened. People quit."

"Hire them back."

Thompson made a face and grunted in disgust.

"I wish," he said. "But the brain trust, and I use the term loosely, downtown is dragging their feet on that."

"Why?"

"The official word is that everyone that quit demonstrated a lack of commitment to the Department and the community, and doesn't deserve to wear the badge."

"And in the meantime," Kaye said, "you're too short-handed to handle the load."

"Hadn't really been a problem until last week," Thompson said. "Things were real quiet after the panic subsided, but now the bad guys are getting back up to speed and we're getting behind. Which is why I'm glad to see you and won't ask why you're back."

"I'm not sure I know why I'm back," Kaye admitted.

"Then we'll just go with it. And there is an upside to my manpower shortage, at least for you."

"What would that be?" Kaye asked.

"I don't have a partner for you."

"I'm good with that."

"I knew you would be."

"Where do I start?"

"All the major cases have been going downtown because of the manpower situation. I didn't know if you'd be ready to go today, or not, so I didn't rock the boat. I'll call down and see if there's a case or two they want to kick back. Otherwise, you're up for whatever comes in next."

"That works for me, " Kaye said, getting up to leave. "Thanks, Captain."

Kaye was twisting the door knob when Thompson said, "Oh, hey, there is something you can do for me to get you started."

"What's that?" Kaye said, turning around.

Thompson was rummaging through the piles of paper on his desk and came up with a small sheaf of reports with a note clipped to the top sheet.

"Call this guy and find out what his deal is."

Kaye took the papers and looked at the note. It was only a name and phone number.

"Who's Mark Edler?" he asked.

"He's a firefighter at a station up on Mulholland," Thompson said. "He's been pestering me since about the time you went to Colorado."

"About what?"

"Some guy crashed his brand new Ferrari and died. Edler insists it wasn't an accident and wants an investigation."

"Based on...?"

"I don't know. He's not an arson guy. In fact, I think he's still a Probie. He just happened to respond to the call."

"What did LAFD and our guys find?"

"Those are the reports," Thompson said. "Official finding all around was accidental death due to a motor vehicle crash. But this kid is making me crazy. He calls at least twice a week."

"Think he's crazy?" Kaye asked. "You know, a conspiracy nut or something?"

"I don't know. If he wasn't LAFD..." Thompson shrugged.

Kaye looked at the note again.

"Got it. I'll give him a call."

It took Kaye all of three minutes to settle back in at his old desk. That included finding a radio charger at one vacant desk and reclaiming a cork board from another.

He spent another ten minutes making the rounds, catching up with the other officers and staff in the Bureau and letting them know he was back. He was stunned by how deserted the place was for a weekday during business hours.

On the way back to his desk he turned a corner and almost ran over Patty Phillips, his favorite Police Assistant.

"Detective Kaye!" she shrieked, then hugged him. "I heard you were here. I was just coming to look for you. Are you back?"

"I'm back."

She beamed. "That's good news. We can sure use your help."

"I see that," Kaye said. "What happened? The Captain was pretty vague."

"Cops just gave up," Patty said. "It was crazy. It was anarchy. We couldn't keep up, not even close. On one shift when things were the worst, two patrol officers were beaten to death by mobs and there wasn't anybody to send to help them."

"Wow," Kaye said solemnly. "I had no idea."

"Yeah. Within days of that happening officers resigned in droves. The job is dangerous enough already and the odds just got so bad, well, it just wasn't worth it to them. They chose their families."

"Can't blame them for that," Kaye said. "Thompson said they aren't hiring people back."

"That's right," Patty said. "Officially they're saying it's because a lack of commitment or something, but unofficially I hear that the Police Commission wants to leverage this situation to clean out and rebuild the Department."

"Interesting," Kaye said. "Is your family okay?"

"Yes, everybody's fine, thank you."

"But you stayed."

"I did."

"Good for you," Kaye said, then added, "I guess."

She smiled.

"You know," Kaye went on, "you could probably move to patrol right now just by asking. You might need to do Law Week and pass the self-defense test, but you'd have no trouble with that."

Kaye had long tried to convince Patty to apply for a sworn officer position. She was smart, capable, and had great investigative instincts.

"I'm thinking about it." She smiled cryptically.

"Good. Let me know if you need a recommendation."

"Thank you, Detective. I'd better get back to work. Again, I'm sure glad you're back."

"Thanks, Patty."

Back at his desk, Kaye grabbed the papers and note Thompson had given him. He was going to read the reports, but had second thoughts. Better to talk to this Edler guy first and maybe save some time.

He dialed the number.

"Los Angeles Fire Department, Mulholland Crest Station," a male voice answered. "Lieutenant Schuyler. How may I help you?"

"Lieutenant, this is Detective Kaye, LAPD. I'm trying to reach a Mark Edler."

"Yeah, Edler works here, but he's off until oh-eight hundred tomorrow morning."

"Okay, thanks. I'll call back."

"Can I ask what this is about?"

"Something about a guy crashing his new Ferrari."

"Are you kidding me?" Schuyler said. "I told him to leave that alone. When did he call you?"

"He didn't call me. He's been calling my Captain. I just came back to work today from over a month off and my Cap threw this at me."

"I got it," Schuyler said. "But trust me, there's nothing to it. Our guys and your guys both concluded it was an accident."

"Is Edler a conspiracy kind of guy? You know, always looking for some weird angle?"

"No, he's not. He's still on probation, but he's doing well and has a solid career ahead of him. But he is a total Ferrari freak."

"What's that mean?" Kaye asked.

"The kid's obsessed with them," Schuyler said. "Knows everything about the cars, the history of the company, all that stuff. You name it, if it has the word Ferrari even near it, he knows it."

"Would you rather I didn't call him?"

Schuyler hesitated before answering.

"That's not my call. It's your time. If you want to waste it, that's up to you."

"I would like to talk to him," Kaye said. "If nothing else, interdepartmental courtesy. Plus, I can keep my boss happy."

"That I understand."

"Thanks, L.T."

Kaye hung up, leaned back in his chair and thought about Schuyler's description of Edler. Something about the kid being crazy about Ferraris might make it worth the time to talk to him.

After all, if you have a question, ask an expert, right?

He walked over and grabbed the Dailies off the board. Every day the Department distributed summary sheets of major crimes and suspects for posting in all the stations. Everything was available digitally on the Department intranet, but for some reason the old paper practice simply refused to die.

He soon realized Thompson was right. There was a deep dip in activity during the time that corresponded with the End of Days Plague panic, but over the previous week things had started to pick up. Among others, a serial rapist in The Valley was back in action, as was a crew that specialized in hitting grocery stores just before their armored car pickups. Pros, Kaye thought. Amateurs rob banks. Grocery stores aren't FDIC insured, so no FBI.

Other than that, what stood out to Kaye was the number of missing persons cases from the days of the panic. He knew that most of them would eventually turn up, but that some never would.

"Kaye," he heard Thompson's voice and turned to see the Captain headed his way. "Got something for you."

"What's up?"

"Patrol's requesting a detective at the Paloma Canyon Country Club. A shooting, two victims down."

"Paloma Canyon County Club?" Kaye asked, thinking he'd heard wrong.

"That's what they said. And they requested a coroner, too, so…"

"On the way," Kaye said, standing up. He grabbed the Big Boar jacket and slid into it.

Thompson saw the colors and stared at his detective with a look of resignation on his face. Then he turned and headed for his office.

He wasn't about to look a gift horse in the mouth. At least not today.

*** 

It took Kaye 45 minutes to make his way from the station across town and into the hills above Westwood, even though he pushed the new Road King hard and used every traffic-beating trick he knew.

It made him miss the one-block walk from the Hotel Jerome to the Aspen PD.

Almost.

He turned off Paloma Canyon Road and rolled down the driveway to the guard shack.

"Can I help you?" the young attendant asked, eyeing Kaye closely.

Kaye pulled the Big Boar jacket aside to reveal his badge.

"Detective Kaye, LAPD."

The kid's eyes widened and he pushed the button to open the gate.

"The clubhouse is to the left and down the hill about a hundred yards."

"Got it," Kaye said. "Thanks."

Paloma Canyon Country Club opened in 1938 and immediately became a haven for Hollywood's elite. Mayer, Capra, Bogart, Gable, Astaire, Tracy and Hepburn, they all came. Getting in was based on two simple precepts. One, a membership had to be for sale and, two, you had to have the money to pay the going rate. Memberships now traded for over a hundred times what the charter members had paid way back when. If you weren't a member, or standing next to one when you showed up, you didn't get through the gate no matter who you were.

Two LAPD patrol units and a Coroner's van were parked in the valet drop-off area, but Kaye couldn't see any activity.

"Detective Kaye?" he heard a woman's voice as he swung off the bike. He turned and saw a casually dressed, dark-haired woman about thirty.

"That would be me," Kaye said.

"Carol Soares," she said, stepping forward and extending her hand. "Assistant club manager. I was also told to expect some crime scene people. Are they with you?"

"No."

"Do you mind if we wait for them?"

"I'd rather not."

"I understand," Soares said, but her eyes told Kaye she didn't. "Follow me."

She led Kaye through the clubhouse and out the back. On the way she radioed someone named Johnny and told him to stand by with another cart for the crime scene people.

"Wow," Kaye said, stopping to soak in the view.

Verdant grass, flanked by dense trees, stretched down the hill in front of them. In the distance the buildings of UCLA and Wilshire Boulevard, and beyond them the Los Angeles Basin, provided an impressive backdrop.

"This is the first tee," Soares said. "A lot of very famous people have teed up here, and they were all nervous. Are you a

11

golfer, Detective?"

"No."

"Too bad. You could probably hit a golf ball a half-mile. Come with me, please." She turned and headed toward a golf cart parked off to the side of the tee box.

They set off down the hill, Soares navigating carefully on the often steep terrain.

"May I make a request?" she asked, glancing sideways.

"Never hurts to ask," Kaye replied.

"Beyond justice for the victims, of course, my primary concern is maintaining the club's reputation and our members' privacy. I hope I can count on the LAPD's cooperation in doing so."

*Back in Tinseltown* was what Kaye thought.

But what he said was, "I'm in no position to speak for the entire Los Angeles Police Department, Ms. Soares. All I can tell you is that I don't care for press conferences or the media in general, so you can cross me off the publicity hound list. Some case information goes to a department that handles media relations. After that it's beyond my control."

"I understand," Soares said, and this time her eyes told Kaye she meant it. "Thank you."

Soares stuck to the cart path, which struck Kaye as odd.

"Isn't there a more direct route?"

"Not really," she said. "The course is very up and down. We even have an elevator. We also re-opened not long ago after a major course reconfiguration. The club pro and head groundskeeper would both want my head on a platter if I drove a caravan of carts across the fairways."

They didn't encounter anyone else, and Soares finally turned off the path. Through the trees Kaye could make out a group of people up ahead. As they got closer he picked out the uniformed officers that went with the units parked back at the clubhouse. Soares skirted a tee box, its sign proclaiming it to be Number 7, a 209 yard par 3, before passing through a narrow gap in the trees.

From about a hundred feet away Kaye got his first glimpse of the crime scene.

A golf cart, facing the direction of the 7th tee box, sat on the path not far from the mouth of a tunnel that disappeared into the steep hillside. The driver was slumped in the seat, and even at that distance Kaye could see blood on the man's shirt. Another body sprawled face-down outside the cart and a jump-suited deputy coroner, his back to Kaye, knelt beside the body.

Another cart was parked off to one side.

"Stop here," Kaye said.

Soares stopped immediately and Kaye got out.

"You don't want to get closer?" Soared asked.

"This is fine. I want to look around."

"Oh, okay. I'll have the rest of your people here as soon as I can."

"Thank you."

As Soares pulled away, Kaye surveyed the surroundings.

Were it not for the tunnel, he would have been in a box canyon.

Looking up, he saw carefully groomed landscaping near the ridge top, which to him meant houses. A band of native vegetation, its width varying greatly as it snaked along the hillside, separated the mown grass and strategic plantings of the golf course from the landscaping of the houses above.

The trees were thick in places, non-existent in others. Kaye surmised it had to do with golf course design, but that was unknown territory for him. What mattered to him were sight lines and he checked them carefully as he slowly made his way toward the scene.

A uniform saw him coming and started up the slight hill to meet him.

"Well I'll be goddamned," Officer Teresa Hensley said, grinning widely as she got closer.

"Hey, Terry," Kaye said, also grinning.

Only a few months ago Hensley had been first-on-scene at Dr. Steven Birnbaum's office.

"What the hell are you doing here?" Hensley asked. "I heard you took extended leave, and nobody thought you'd be back, especially with all the shit flowing out of downtown."

"Well, I'm back. Today, as a matter of fact."

"No shit? Welcome back to the circus."

"Thanks, Terry. But we've got to stop meeting like this."

"I'm with you on that. Too many dead people."

"Tell me what we've got."

They started toward the scene as Hensley ran it down.

"Two vics. One middle-aged man and one woman young enough to be his daughter, maybe even a granddaughter, but…" She raised her eyebrows and made a face.

"Hey," Kaye said. "It is Hollywood."

13

"Yeah," Hensley snorted. "Anyway, looks like the guy took two to the chest. We haven't rolled the woman yet, but there are a couple small exit wounds on her back."

Kaye focused on the bodies as they got closer. About fifty feet from the cart they stopped. Kaye grabbed his cell phone and took pictures.

"Looks like she tried to run," he said.

"I agree," Hensley said. "But she didn't get far. The shooter must've been quick."

"Who found them?"

"There was a foursome behind them. The tunnel comes through from the sixth green, and when the group finished there they could see this cart blocking the exit."

"So they drove up on it?"

"Not initially," Hensley said. "One of them doesn't like small spaces and didn't want to go into the tunnel without being able to see a clear way out. They just thought somebody was being rude, but after a few minutes they got pissed."

"And drove through."

"One cart did, yeah. The others waited."

"And somebody called 9-1-1."

"Not exactly," Hensley said. "The club doesn't allow cell phones on the course."

"Seriously?"

"Yeah. Slows down play. Plus, down in these canyons service sucks."

"Okay," Kaye said. "So somebody had to drive back to the clubhouse for help."

"Correct."

"Please tell me they did not move the victims' cart."

"They did not, they managed to get around," Hensley said. "But what's funny is why."

"It wasn't the claustrophobia?"

"No. They're all in the movie business," Hensley said. "I recognized three of them instantly, and the guy who does action movies was smart enough to know not to do that. He told me 'Rule number one, don't disturb a crime scene'."

"Good for them," Kaye said. "You asked them to wait at the clubhouse, right?"

"I asked."

"I sense a 'but'…"

"They all said the same thing; they didn't hear or see anything. They provided personal information, but declined to wait around to be interviewed." Hensley reached into her pocket and extracted a piece of paper. "Contact information for all four," she said, handing the paper to Kaye.

He scanned the list, recognizing two of the names.

"Did they hear shots?" he asked.

"Nobody heard a thing. They were on the other side of the tunnel."

"Makes sense."

"Based on what they told me, the time gap was maybe fifteen minutes, tops," Hensley said. "They said our victims had cleared the green and entered the tunnel before they hit in, finished the hole and then waited for the cart to move before coming through and finding… this."

"Okay," Kaye said again, looking around some more. "What about the group in front of them? Did they hear anything?"

"According to the lady manager there wasn't a group right ahead of the vics, but I haven't verified that. She also told me she cleared the course behind the witnesses so nobody else could come through."

"I'll check for a group in front, just in case."

"Do you still need us?" Hensley asked. "We've got calls backing up."

"Go ahead and clear," Kaye said. "Thanks. And, hey, I still owe you that drink from the Birnbaum case. Name the place and time."

Hensley smiled and said, "You're off the hook. Debt cancelled."

"That's not the Terry I know."

"The Terry you knew wasn't engaged."

Kaye stared at her for a second before saying, "Engaged? Good for you. Do I know the guy? Is he on the job?"

"No, thank God," Hensley said. "He's a computer guy, and you don't know him."

"Must've happened fast."

"It did," she said. "I never really believed all that bullshit about knowing right away when you meet the right person, but I do now."

Kaye instantly remembered the day when Amy had walked in to Harley Charlie's bike shop. It was right at closing time, the beer was cold, and he'd insulted her by dismissing her, a beautiful woman dressed in a skirt, thinking she couldn't be a serious customer. Charlie had reamed him up one side and down the other right in front of her, and he instantly regretted it. He hung around the store every day for weeks, praying she'd come back.

Thankfully, she had.

The right person.

"Good for you. I'm happy for you."

"Thanks, Kaye. We're outta here. Welcome back, be safe."

"Always."

She shook her head and laughed as she turned to leave. Kaye watched as she signaled the other uniform, who met her at the cart parked away from the scene.

As they drove away, he headed for the cart and the detritus of the human condition that silently waited for him.

\*\*\*

When Kaye was twenty feet from the victims' cart the deputy coroner stood up, and he was surprised to see Dr. Jaime Archuleta.

Arch was equally surprised to see Kaye.

"I'll be damned," Arch said. "I heard you quit."

"Glad to see you, too, Arch. I took a leave of absence, but as of today, I'm back. You got here fast."

"Today?" Arch said, spreading his arms to take in the scene. "Nice welcome back, eh? And I was close."

"What can you tell me?"

"Let's start with this guy." Arch pointed to the man slumped in the cart. "Two entry wounds to the left chest, either one of which would have been fatal. No exit wounds. I peeked. Time of death hasn't been established, but I think it was pretty contemporaneous with the discovery of the bodies."

"Age?"

"Mid-fifties, plus or minus five."

"Did you find ID?"

"If he has it, he's sitting on it and I wasn't about to pull him off the cart before a detective showed up."

"What about the woman?"

"Don't know yet," Arch said. "Only the two visible wounds on her back, both small, which I'm guessing were caused by bullet fragments exiting. She's only about half as thick as the man. But we'll find out when we turn her over. I'd guess her age at twenty to twenty-five, maybe older, maybe younger, but I found no ID on her."

"Any signs of powder residue or contact burns?"

"None," Arch said. "The lab boys can test, but I'm betting they don't find anything. I think – but this is just speculation, okay? – they were shot from long range. The entry wounds look small caliber to me, and no exit wounds tells me I'll probably find fragmented military-style bullets when I open them up."

"You mean like a .223 or 5.56?"

"Exactly. But again, speculation. I won't know for sure until I recover what's in there. Odds are, though, with that caliber, probably no ballistics."

"Got it," Kaye said absently. He was studying the cart, and a couple of things seemed off. There was only one set of clubs in the rack, and there was no blood transfer or damage to the right side seat from pass-through bullet fragments.

"Hey, Arch, did Hensley by chance go back through the tunnel?"

"She did," Arch replied. "Said she was looking for another set of clubs. I told her not to bother, but she went anyway."

"What am I missing?"

"I don't think the woman was here to play golf, and I don't think she's his daughter."

"I would certainly hope not," Kaye said.

"But you gotta wonder if he was getting up and down and if she was counting strokes," Arch said, grinning broadly.

Movement in his peripheral vision caught Kaye's eye and he turned to see another cart headed their way. Carol Soares was driving and had two passengers.

Soares pulled up and the windbreaker-clad crime scene techs piled out. Kaye didn't recognize either one.

"Hang on a minute," he said to Soares before turning to the techs. "Two dead by GSW. Get what you can, but it probably won't be much. Doctor Archuleta thinks they were shot from a distance, so the chance of trace is probably about zero. Another foursome found them, but did not walk into the scene. Two uniforms, Archuleta and I have tromped around."

"Okay," one of the techs said. "We'll get what we can."

"Thanks," Kaye said. "Call me if you get anything unusual or probative. Otherwise, just e-mail me the report and the photos."

"Will do, Detective," the second tech said.

Kaye turned back to Soares.

"Ms. Soares, do you recognize the victims?"

"I haven't really seen them," she replied. "The woman officer kept me away."

"She was just protecting the crime scene. Are you up to taking a look?"

"I…I suppose I could do that."

"Thank you. Leave the cart here."

The techs had already started taking pictures and consulting with Arch by the time Kaye and Soares got to the mouth of the tunnel.

"Oh, my God," Soares whispered as soon as she was close enough to get a look at the male victim.

"Do you recognize him?" Kaye asked.

"Avi Geller."

"Is he a member?"

"Of course," Soares said. "Only members and accompanied guests are allowed on the course."

Kaye guided her around to the other side of the cart.

The female victim was face down, her head toward the mouth of the tunnel, right side on the cart path and left side on the grass. Her right arm was caught beneath her, her left splayed out to the side.

"Do you recognize her?" he asked Soares.

Soares studied the woman for a moment, then said, "I don't recognize her like that, but I don't think I've ever seen her before."

Kaye took Soares's elbow and steered her away from the cart.

"What can you tell me about Avi Geller?" he asked. "Has he been a member for long?"

"Quite a few years, I think. I've been here almost four years, and he was a member when I started."

"What does…did… he do?" Kaye asked.

"I think he's a producer," Soares said. "You know, movies and TV."

"Are members required to sign in their guests?"

"Yes. There's a log at the Starter's desk. You have full access, of course."

"Thank you. Officer Hensley said you told her there wasn't a group right ahead of the victims. Is that right?"

"That's what I understand, but you can check that with the Starter, too."

Soares's gaze went past Kaye and he turned to see Arch standing a few feet away.

"What do you need, Arch?"

"Actually," Arch said, "I have a request for Ms. Soares."

"What can I do for you, Doctor?" Soares asked.

"I'm assuming the club groundskeepers have some of those carts that are like little pickup trucks?"

"They do," Soares said.

"I'll need one…no, make that two, please," Arch said. "I'll need to transport the victims back to my van, and the techs will need a ride out."

"I'll have them brought down," Soares said. "Will you need to keep the cart Avi was using?"

"I don't think so," Kaye spoke up. "I'll bring it back when I'm done."

"Thank you," Soares said. "Now, if you'll excuse me." She turned and headed back to her cart.

***

Carol Soares's mind raced as she headed toward the clubhouse.

When she rounded the shoulder of the canyon near the 8th hole dogleg, where she knew there was cell service, she stopped in the shade of a large eucalyptus and pulled out her cell phone.

"It's done, I saw the body," she said without preamble when the call was answered. "But what the hell happened? Both of them?"

She listened.

"This is going to cause a lot of trouble," she said a second later. "I didn't sign —"

Obviously interrupted, she listened again.

"Okay, but you'd better keep your end —" She stopped and stared angrily at her phone. The other end of the conversation had hung up on her.

***

Kaye watched and waited while the techs worked.

They were thorough, but there wasn't much to find. After a fairly short time, one of them approached.

"Detective, we need to know how far out you want us to go," he said.

"I think you're good," Kaye said. "I'm with Arch on this one. I

19

don't think our shooter was ever close and I don't expect you to process the entire great outdoors."

"Thanks," the tech said, clearly relieved. "Can we move the bodies?"

"Hey, Arch," Kaye called out. "Okay to move the bodies?"

"I've been waiting on you," Arch replied. "They're all yours."

Kaye started with Avi Geller. He went to glove up, and rummaged around in Arch's box of tricks.

Arch saw him. "Sorry, I don't think I have the super-giant size gloves in stock today. I don't think it will matter if you go without just this once."

Kaye nodded, walked over and stood next to the cart, reached around Geller's shoulders, pushed his hands under the dead man's armpits and lifted him out of the cart like he was weightless.

Arch was waiting with a body bag and laid it out on the ground. Then he grabbed Geller's ankles and together they gingerly lowered the body onto the bag, face up.

Kaye quickly took a close-up of Geller's face, then rolled the body onto its side, felt the back pockets, and extracted a wallet. He opened it and came face to face with 56-year old Aviram Lemuel Geller of Bel Air on a much better day than he was having today.

The wallet wasn't thick. It held the driver's license, some cash, a couple of the same credit cards Kaye carried, a few photos Kaye assumed were of family and several business cards proclaiming Avi Geller the President of AZG Productions. He patted the other pockets looking for a cell phone or car keys and found nothing.

"I'm going to keep this," Kaye said, holding up the wallet for Arch and the techs to see.

"It's your case," Arch said. "Keep whatever you want to keep."

"You want to verify the cash?"

Archuleta almost burst out laughing, but stifled his reaction. He knew Kaye was loaded thanks to his late wife's ongoing book and film royalties and residuals.

"Like you need the money badly enough to steal it?"

"Procedure," Kaye said. "Normally a job for a partner, but, as you can see, no partner."

"How much is there?"

"One hundred and twenty-one dollars."

"Consider it verified," Arch said, still grinning as he leaned over and did a quick gross examination of the body now that it was out of the cart.

"Like I expected," he told Kaye. "No injuries or trauma other than the gunshot wounds. I think this smells like a hit."

"Thanks, Arch. I already got that."

"That must be why you're the detective and I'm just the country doctor." Arch smiled. "Okay, on to the little lady."

The techs began the process of fingerprinting and photographing Geller while Kaye and Arch moved on to the female vic.

There was no wallet, keys or phone in the back pockets of the shorts she wore. Kaye rolled her over and the cause of death was immediately evident: One round to the center chest. Her front pockets were also empty.

"If she got out to run, how'd she get shot in the chest?" Kaye asked, more of himself than Arch.

"Good question," Arch responded. "Two shooters, maybe?"

"I don't think so. Look at the terrain. If there was another shooter he, or she, would've had to be in the tunnel to hit her from that direction, and given the witnesses' accounts, I doubt that."

"Yeah, I think you're right," Arch said. "But remember, even with the wound location she would have still had several seconds mobility, more than enough to swing off the cart and try to run before she went down for good. The bad news is one entrance wound and two exits. The bullet broke up. No ballistics even if we found the fragments."

Just as they laid the corpse onto the second body bag and Kaye got his photo the groundskeepers showed up with the two mini-trucks. Kaye dealt with them while Arch did a quick gross.

"Just like Geller," Arch said when Kaye returned. "No other damage other than the fatal wound. But no ID on this one."

"I'll get Geller's keys from the valet," Kaye said. "If there are phones or a purse, they're probably in the car."

"I never would have thought of that," Arch said.

"That's why I'm the detective, Arch." He smiled.

Twenty minutes later there was a consensus that the crime scene work was done. Arch had wiped all of Avi Geller's bodily fluids from the golf cart seat and put the rags in the body bag with the corpse. He turned to Kaye.

"You coming back with us?" Arch asked.

"No," Kaye said. "I'm going to hang here for a bit. I want to check a couple things."

"Okay. I'll let you know if I find anything unusual when I do the posts. Otherwise I'll just e-mail you the final reports."

"Thanks, Arch. And, hey, good to see you again. Glad you didn't bail during all the trouble."

"That's why I'm the doctor," Arch deadpanned, then broke out laughing.

Kaye watched the little caravan disappear around the shoulder of the canyon beyond the 8th tee, then walked back to the mouth of the tunnel and slid into the seat formerly occupied by Avi Geller.

The shooter, by definition, had to be able to see his targets. He, or she, Kaye reminded himself, might have risked a timed, pre-sighted shot through the trees if Geller had been partially visible, but nobody can hit a running target they can't see without laying down a withering field of fire, and he still thought the woman had been trying to escape. Based on the fact that she'd only made it a few feet, Kaye presumed the shooter had eyes-on the entire time.

He studied the surrounding terrain and sight lines for nearly ten minutes, sketching a rudimentary map and marking reference points before sliding out of the cart and heading for the hillside.

Might as well take the easiest one first.

On the way, he turned frequently to maintain his location reference, traversing the hillside as he climbed. After ten minutes of slow climbing, during which he saw nothing useful, he reached an elaborate wrought iron fence, beyond which was a swimming pool and meticulously landscaped back yard.

It was only five minutes back down. After a quick visit to the cart to confirm landmarks he started up again on another line.

About two-thirds of the way up he rounded a large clump of native vegetation and almost tripped over a rock about the size of a suitcase.

Looking down, he noticed that the top of the rock was dirt-free, but had a rim of crusted dirt on its edges. Below that the rock was still lightly coated with soil.

He looked around. About seven feet away he saw the spot where the rock had been pulled from the dirt beneath a clump of tall native grass.

He studied the ground around the rock closely. The smaller grasses had been trampled. Just to make sure, he sat down on the rock's relatively flat surface. The sight line to the tunnel mouth was clear and the surrounding brush was tall and dense enough to shield him from view from either side or above.

He hefted the rock. For him it was an easy lift, but he knew the shooter had to be reasonably stout to get the rock out of its resting place and move it.

Next, hoping for either a lazy, nicotine-addicted shooter or a stroke of luck, he carefully searched the surrounding area looking for anything that might have been left behind.

Nothing.

Convinced he'd found the shooter's perch, he looked around and asked himself out loud, "Okay, so how did you get here?"

Kaye was no outdoorsman, but his father had been an avid deer hunter and had introduced Kaye to the chase at an early age. Hunting hadn't captivated him, but he still remembered a lot of his Dad's lessons.

On the climb he'd watched for, but not seen, any signs of recent passage. The ground was mostly covered with grasses, either untended native or mown as part of the golf course, and the ground on all but the steepest pitches was firm enough to hold even his weight without crumbling. Climbing the steeper spots, though, had caused small dirt slides when the slope gave way and his foot slid slightly downhill.

That was what he looked for now.

Almost immediately he was able to pick out the shooter's path down and back up the twenty feet above where he stood before it disappeared around another clump of vegetation.

It was easy to follow, even when he entered the densely planted buffer between the native plants and the house above.

It didn't take long for him to reach a stacked block retaining wall that reached about ten feet in height. Above that he could see the elaborate pointed gold tips of yet another wrought iron fence.

He went up the wall with ease, looking through the fence at another swimming pool and an expansive back yard that looked like a miniature version of the gardens of Versailles.

He scanned up and down the fence and saw a gate. It was latched, but not locked, which he thought was strange.

"Hello in the house!" Kaye shouted. "LAPD. Anybody home?"

No response.

He waited for a minute, watching for movement, before trying again.

Again, no response.

He debated letting himself in and decided against it. Not only were the odds of a random encounter with a citizen pissed off that the cops were in his back yard high, it would also probably negate the evidentiary value of anything he might come up with.

He made careful note of the house's roofline and the few trees visible on the front side of the property, knowing he could find it again from the street.

He didn't climb down, he jumped. Just as he stepped off the top of the wall he caught a glimpse of something metallic in the plantings below.

It was a padlock. And it had been cut.

Kaye carefully put the padlock in his pocket and made his way back down the hill to the now forlorn looking golf cart. Always thorough, he checked the two other possible sight lines, but found nothing.

When he was finished he turned the cart over to the attendant outside the clubhouse.

"Hey, can you point me to the Starter's Desk?" he asked the kid.

"Sure can."

Lon Burridge was easy to find. Half a foot taller than Kaye, fit, with a golfer's tan that didn't include his forehead, Burridge sat at a shaded kiosk between the clubhouse and first tee.

"Mr. Burridge, Detective Kaye, LAPD."

"Carol told me to expect you," Burridge said. "What can I do for you?"

"I need to see your log from earlier today. I'm interested in the woman who was with Avi Geller."

Burridge laid a ledger on the counter and pointed at the 11:15 a.m. start time. It had Geller's name in the member's column. Kaye noted that the most recent start time before Geller was 10:30 a.m.

"Really?" Kaye asked, putting his finger on the name next to Geller's in the guest column. "Jane Smith?"

"I know," Burridge said. "But you have to understand. Mr. Geller is…was…a member and members can bring guests. I don't check identification or ask questions."

"Did you have questions?"

"Of course I had questions. I'm not stupid. That girl wasn't even half Geller's age and she wasn't carrying clubs. Besides, Mr. Geller is a married man."

"Married?" Kaye asked, not remembering a ring on Geller's hand. "Are you sure?"

"Absolutely," Burridge said. "He always came to club functions with the same woman since I've been here and she was… What's the term? Age appropriate?"

"Had you ever seen Jane Smith before?"

"Never."

"What can you tell me about Geller?"

"Not a lot," Burridge said. "Decent golfer, probably a fifteen handicap, and a good tipper. More so lately."

"Why do you think that was?"

"He must've had a big deal coming together. It's almost predictable around here, based on the tips."

"Did he tell you what the deal was?"

Burridge laughed. "Detective, I'm an employee here. They, the members I mean, don't talk business with us. To most of them, we're furniture."

"But you hear things, right?"

Even through the deep tan Kaye saw Burridge blush as the starter looked away.

"So," Kaye prodded, "what did you hear?"

"I could lose my job."

"Lon, somebody shot Avi Geller in the chest, twice, a couple hours ago, and they shot the young woman, whoever she is, when she tried to run. It's my job to find out who did that to them, and if you can think of anything that might help me do that, I need to know."

"Off the record?" Burridge asked, looking around nervously.

"Sure."

"Okay," Burridge said. "Carol told me what happened, you know, and it made me think. I don't know if it means anything, but, yeah, I did hear Mr. Geller arguing with another guy a while back, before all the plague shit."

"Who was the other guy?" Kaye asked.

"I don't remember. He wasn't a member."

"A guest?"

"Yeah, but not Mr. Geller's. He was with someone else, I think, and there was another guest, too, but they all ended up playing together because Mr. Geller's usual partner had to cancel."

"What were they arguing about?"

"I don't know," Burridge said. "But when Mr. Geller and the other guy came out of the clubhouse they were really going at it. Not loud, you understand, but very intense. Mr. Geller was really pressing the guy. I heard him say something about 'give me a number' or something like that, a couple of times."

"So there was a deal?"

Burridge just shrugged.

"What did the other guy do?"

"That's just it," Burridge said. "He just said 'not for sale' or something, and when Mr. Geller kept after him I could tell he got pissed, because he grabbed Mr. Geller by the front of the shirt and got in his face."

"Did you hear what he said?" Kaye said.

"I couldn't make it out, exactly, but I think the other guy threatened Mr. Geller, and I could tell it scared Mr. Geller because he got real quiet and just kind of wilted."

"Then what happened?"

"Right then the member the two guests were with came out of the clubhouse and the guy holding Mr. Geller's shirt noticed me paying attention. He let go and said something like, 'C'mon Avi, let's just play golf.' Must've worked, because by the time they finished warming up and teed off, they were laughing and slapping like old war buddies."

"And that's all you heard?" Kaye asked.

"Yeah," Burridge said. "I don't even know if it means anything, but, you know, I remembered it after Carol told me what happened."

"But you don't know the other guy, the one who grabbed Geller?"

"No, never saw him before and haven't seen him since, and I can't remember the member's name, either. I think he was new. Oh, wait... His tee time had to be close to Mr. Geller's. It should be in the log."

Burridge grabbed the log and started flipping back through the pages.

"Shouldn't be hard to find," he said. "Today was only Mr. Geller's third time back since that day, what with all the problems going on. And we haven't exactly been over-booked lately."

Kaye waited.

"Aha, here it is," Burridge said after a few moments. He spun the log around so Kaye could read it and pointed to the line containing the entry. It was dated before Kaye had gone to Aspen.

Geller's name was down for the 11:15 a.m. tee time along with another member named Gleason, but there were no guests listed. All the other times between 10:00 a.m. and noon listed members and, if any, guests. Much of what was on the log for guests was just initials. Kaye wrote down all the information.

"You said that this Gleason didn't show up to play?" Kaye asked.

"Right," Burridge said. "The other guys were early, so I made some spots by making them a foursome."

"Can you describe the man Geller argued with?" Kaye asked.

"Sure," Burridge said. "White guy, late twenties, maybe early thirties. Maybe five eight or nine, dark hair, and a little heavy."

"Thanks, Lon," Kaye said. "Appreciate the cooperation."

"No problem. I always thought Mr. Geller was a nice guy."

Kaye's next stop was the parking valet stand.

"I need the keys to Avi Geller's car," he told the young woman on duty, his tone making it clear he wasn't making a request.

"Space seventeen," she said, handing him the keys.

It was a Mercedes-Benz key fob, and in space seventeen he found a white, AMG S63 cabriolet. It took only a minute to determine that neither Geller nor Jane Smith had left phones or anything else in the car.

For Kaye, that definitely moved Jane Smith to the Jane Doe column.

He next checked the registration for an address, expecting to find the car registered to AZG Productions. Instead, he found the names Aviram and Ziva Geller and an address not far away.

Instead of returning the keys to the valet he took them into the clubhouse and searched for Carol Soares.

He found her in her office and gave her the keys.

"Did Geller have a locker on the premises?" he asked.

"Of course," Soares said. "All our members do. Why?"

"Well, he didn't have a cell phone on him, and there wasn't one in the car. I can't imagine somebody in his business being without one, and thought a locker would be the next best bet."

"Come with me."

Five minutes later Kaye had Avi Geller's cell phone in his pocket. Fat lot of good it'll do me, he thought ruefully. Six digit pass code. There had been no purse or other cell phone in the locker.

He checked the time. It was getting late and he still wanted to find the house overlooking the course.

And he needed to talk to Mrs. Ziva Geller.

He decided to look for the house first.

\*\*\*

It wasn't as easy to find as he'd expected. Between the winding roads, the confusing terrain and the high walls and gates lining the street, it turned into a frustrating guessing game.

He got lucky when a red Porsche stopped in the road to wait while a gate opened. With a quick roll on the throttle he pulled the big Harley up next to the gate, swung off, and held up his badge for the driver to see.

She stopped before going through the gate and rolled her window down.

"I hope you're not looking for me," she said.

"No, ma'am. Detective Kaye. I need some help."

Without going into detail Kaye quickly sketched out what he was looking for.

She laughed.

"Don't feel bad. I've lived here for two years and sometimes still drive right by my own gate. Got any details?"

Kaye described the house and back yard, especially the pool and gardens.

"Sounds like the house three doors, or gates, down," she said, pointing. "It's had a for sale sign on it for the last several months. I think it's empty."

Kaye thanked her, made a tight u-turn and went down to the third gate.

The Porsche driver was right. A For Sale sign, most of it taken up by the smiling face of a forty-ish blonde with glasses and Hollywood smile, was affixed to the elaborate gate, and even at this time of day the ornate lights flanking the gate were on.

He wanted to make sure, so he jumped up, wrapped his hands over the top of the gate and pulled himself up.

It was the right house.

He pulled out his cell phone and called the number on the realty sign.

"Classic Realty," a woman answered. "Megan Sullivan. How may I help you?"

"Ms. Sullivan, my name is Ben Kaye. I'm a detective with the LAPD. I'd like to ask you some questions about your listing at," he gave her the address.

There was a brief silence.

"Is this a joke?" Sullivan said at last. "The asking on that house is just under eighteen million. Nineteen five if you want the furnishings. Minus the art, of course. If you really are who you say you are, I'm guessing that's out of your price range."

"I'm not interested in buying the house. I'm calling on police business. I'd be happy to give you my Captain's name and number if you'd like to call him."

"Is everything okay at the house?"

Kaye gave her a basic rundown, mentioning only that there had been an incident on the golf course and he thought a person of interest might have gone through the property.

"Why do you think that?" Sullivan asked.

"The padlock on the back fence gate was cut. I have reason to believe someone went up and down from there."

"Was anything vandalized?" Sullivan asked, and Kaye heard a tinge of anxiety in her voice.

"Not that I could see from the back fence," Kaye said. "I did not enter the yard."

"Thank God," Sullivan said. "Can you wait there until I get there? Probably close to an hour, maybe more depending on traffic."

"Sorry, no. I have somewhere else I need to be. Would you mind answering just a couple quick questions while I've got you?"

"You're kidding! You won't wait?"

"I can't," Kaye said. "If there's a problem when you get here, call the police and an officer will come out. Is the house occupied?"

"No," Sullivan said. "The owners anticipated a fairly quick sale, so they went ahead and moved. Didn't exactly turn out that way. The house is vacant, but furnished, if that makes sense."

"Where did the owners move to?"

"Northern Italy, near Lake Como."

"Does the house have a security system?" Kaye asked.

"Of course. State of the art, monitored, with armed response."

"Have there been any problems recently?"

"Not that the security company has made me aware of, and I'm the designated contact."

"Who's the security company?"

"SecureLife Security," she replied.

He recognized the name as reputable.

"Who else has access to the property?" Kaye asked.

"Licensed realtors, of course, if they have a showing. But I assure you, Detective, at this price point deals are almost always cash and nobody gets in without their financials being checked."

Kaye flashed back to when he and Amy had first looked at their house overlooking the Pacific. They'd had a very difficult time getting a showing because their credit reports showed their occupations as cop and teacher.

But Amy had pestered the agent relentlessly until he finally agreed to a showing just to get rid of her.

They loved the house and location and told the agent they wanted to make an offer. When the agent gently chided them for their lack of knowledge about how real estate worked, Amy had had enough. She bluntly told the agent that she was legally Amy Kaye, but her professional name was Kaye Shaeffer, she was a writer, and possibly the agent was aware that her latest book had been Number One on the best-seller list for eighteen straight weeks and that her agent had just optioned the movie rights for considerably more than the asking price of the house.

Kaye had thought the agent was going to faint.

"Yeah, been there," he mumbled.

"Excuse me," Sullivan said. "I missed that?"

"Not important. Who else has access?"

"The landscape and pool maintenance people," Sullivan said. "They contract with our agency for all our listings. They're licensed, insured and bonded. I trust them completely."

Kaye asked for, and got, the name of the company.

"Anybody else?" Kaye asked.

"Well, there's a cleaning service that comes once or twice a week and it's usually during the night," she replied, and gave him the name of the company.

"Thank you, Ms. Sullivan. I'm sorry I can't wait for you. I'll call if I need to get into the house, but I doubt that will be necessary. If it is, I'll have a warrant so there'll be no questions from the owners."

"I appreciate that. Thanks for letting me know about the gate." She hung up.

He checked the time again, although he knew exactly what time it was.

It was time to talk to Ziva Geller.

It took Kaye only a few minutes to get to the Geller house.

It was an elaborate French Country place on at least two acres and, unlike the houses lower down the hill, it was visible from the street.

Not that it wasn't fenced and gated. It was, and as Kaye rolled up to the gate he idly thought that the guy with the wrought iron fence business in the neighborhood must be doing well.

He punched the intercom call button and held his badge up to the camera mounted on the gate post.

"How may I help you?" a woman's voice asked.

"Detective Kaye, LAPD. I need to speak with Ziva Geller."

"What about?"

"I need to speak with Mrs. Geller privately."

"I'm Ziva Geller," the voice said. "And if this is about Avi's murder, there's nothing I can tell you."

Kaye was taken aback.

"Mrs. Geller, how and when did you find out about your husband's death?"

"Well, I wasn't there, if that's what you're asking," she said. "This is Hollywood. News travels fast. I've already spoken with my attorney, who advised me that I don't have to let the police in unless you have a warrant and that I am not required to make a statement."

"Sounds like you've got your bases covered," Kaye said. "Is there anything you'd like to tell me?"

There was a long pause, but the intercom light stayed on, so Kaye waited.

"Let's just say I'm not disappointed that the miserable, cheating bastard is dead. Saves me a trip to the courthouse to file the divorce papers."

The intercom light went out.

Kaye rolled the Harley back and out of camera range and pondered his next move.

He definitely wanted a face-to-face with Ziva Geller, but he knew he'd be better off giving her some time to calm down and absorb the reality of her husband's death.

He called Captain Thompson and left a voice mail to let his boss know he planned on going to talk to the fireman about the Ferrari in the morning, so not to look for him first thing.

Then he headed down to Sunset before turning west toward the beach and home.

\*\*\*

Kaye sat on the mat, feet spread almost to a full split, back straight and arms extended overhead with palms together, and took a moment to soak in the view.

In the deepening dusk he could just make out the swell marching toward the beach down the canyon beyond Pacific Coast Highway.

South swell. The surfers would be out in force tomorrow.

Refocusing, he lowered his hands and placed them flat on the mat, shoulder-width apart, directly in front of his legs. Keeping his back straight, he leaned forward until all his weight was on his hands, lifted himself from the mat and, still maintaining the split, rotated up into a handstand.

It was a move worthy of an Olympic gymnast. For a man scraping six foot one and almost three hundred pounds it was an amazing display of strength and flexibility. Kaye's unusual build, with a short torso and overly-long legs and arms, helped.

He held the handstand splits for ten slow, controlled breaths before raising his feet to the traditional handstand position. Another ten breaths, focusing on them and not his body. With a slow, controlled movement he raised his head to look toward the sea as he arched his back, bent his knees, and slowly lowered his feet toward the back of his head in a variation of Vrischikasana, the Scorpion Pose.

Then he started doing handstand push-ups, lowering himself until his chin touched the mat and pushing back up until his arms were straight.

His target was not a number, it was failure, and he grunted with the effort of the last five before stopping and slowly lowering his feet until he was in the arching bridge of Chakrasana. He held the position for ten breaths, then bent his elbows to ninety degrees, pushed mightily, and rose to stand in Tadasana.

Kaye possessed amazing, almost preternatural, strength, but flexibility had always been an issue. During physical therapy for a shoulder injury suffered in the Marine Corps he'd discovered that the exercises he was doing were yoga positions. He immediately became an adherent, and while he knew that his bulk would preclude ever attaining some asanas – try as he had, he'd never touched the back of his head with his feet during Scorpion -- his level of accomplishment was significant.

Yoga led him to Eastern philosophy and, to the great dismay of his fervently Christian mother, eventually to Zen Buddhism. While he didn't consider himself a practicing Buddhist; his mind was simply too Western to go there; it was the philosophy he'd found that most closely matched his world view.

He held Tadasana for twenty breaths, slowly relaxing.

He took a drink of water from the bottle on the patio table, fetched a cushion, sat down, and assumed the half-Lotus position. After his recent return from Colorado, his first task had been to visit Kyokoku-Dera monastery to see for himself that Roshi, his teacher, was okay after everything that had gone on during the End of Days plague panic. The two had spent hours discussing Kaye's experiences in Aspen, but, as usual, Roshi had offered few answers to Kaye's questions, instead reflecting them back upon his pupil so that Kaye could find those answers for himself.

"Your questions are insightful, Benkei," Roshi told him. The old monk was convinced Kaye was the reincarnation of the legendary 12th Century Japanese warrior-monk renowned for his strength and purpose. "I believe it is time for you to move on to *shikantaza zazen* to maintain your progress."

"What's that?"

"It is a more advanced meditation technique than what you have practiced until now. I have observed you during *zazen*, and your concentration and thought processes when we discuss the koans tell me you are ready."

"I'll try," Kaye said. "What do I do?"

Roshi laughed.

"You 'do' nothing, Benkei. It is zazen. But rather than concentrating inwardly or puzzling out a koan, which you have learned leads only to another question, your attention is now devoted outward to your surroundings. The goal is to see and hear your environment without letting it distract you from your Self, from your concentration."

"Is there a trick to it?"

Roshi laughed again.

"No tricks, Benkei! Hear the wind. Hear the jet flying overhead even if you cannot, and feel the wind from the wings of the birds in the garden. Hear the wind chimes if they ring, or their silence if they do not. Expand your Self to encompass all, and be in the moment. That is the success of *shikantaza*."

"How will I know if I'm successful?" Kaye asked.

"There is no formula," Roshi said patiently. "When you become one with the moment, you will feel it."

Since that day, Kaye had tried to follow Roshi's instructions almost every day, with limited success. Time to try it again.

He stretched the crown of his head upward and let his gaze drift downward. He'd never tell Roshi, but he'd found his meditation to be more successful with his eyes closed. With *shikantaza*, though, he had to leave his eyes open to observe his surroundings.

Maybe that's it, he thought. Maybe if I almost close my eyes and just concentrate on what I can hear, I can build into this.

He allowed his eyelids to droop and focused his mind on the sounds around him. His first realization was that there was a lot more noise than he usually heard, and he let his ears drink it in. He felt himself getting into sync with his environment.

When he walked into the kitchen he was astonished to see that he had been meditating for over an hour, twice the length of his normal sessions.

He showered and ate a small dinner, lingering at the table and putting together his schedule for the next day.

It was good to be back in the groove.

# DAY 3
Wednesday Week 1

The Los Angeles Fire Department has a string of stations spread along the length of Mulholland Drive between the 101 freeway and Mulholland's western terminus in the Santa Monica Mountains. Brush fires are the scourge of California and these stations are the first line of defense.

Kaye rolled his 1961 Harley Duo-Glide into the station parking lot just after the 8:00 a.m. shift change. It was a warm morning and the station's front and back overhead doors were up, allowing the slight breeze to blow through.

Two firefighters walked out to meet him.

"Nice bike," one said. "How can we help you?"

Kaye pulled his jacket back to show his badge.

"Ben Kaye. I'm looking for a Mark Edler."

The second firefighter turned around and shouted, "Edler, the cops are looking for you. Get your ass out here."

Kaye saw another firefighter look around the back of a pumper truck, wipe his hands on the rag he carried, and head his way.

"This is about that Ferrari, isn't it?" the shouter asked Kaye.

"It is."

"Dumb ass kid," the first guy said. "Just can't let it go."

"I'll see if I can straighten it out," Kaye said. "Thanks, guys."

"About time," Edler said when he stood in front of Kaye.

The kid was tall, thin, red-headed and still had a slight case of acne.

"Excuse me?" Kaye said.

"I said it's about time. I called you weeks ago."

"You didn't call me," Kaye said. "I just heard about this yesterday, and I'd suggest you stow the attitude if you want me to listen to what you have to say."

Edler stared at Kaye and gulped.

"Okay," he said after a moment. "I'm sorry. I'm just frustrated because nobody will listen to me about a murder."

"Are you an arson investigator or accident reconstructionist?"

35

"No," Edler said, then stared at Kaye. "Then why did you come?"

"Courtesy, I guess."

"So this is a jerk off visit? Come talk to me so you can file a report that you did, then do nothing? Thanks, but no thanks."

Edler turned to walk away.

"Wait," Kaye said. "That's not the only reason I'm here."

Edler turned back around.

"Your lieutenant said something that piqued my curiosity," Kaye went on. "He said you were a Ferrari freak. Knew everything about them there is to know."

"I'll take that as a compliment."

"You should," Kaye said. "And, truth be told, I'm the same way about Harleys. Have been since my Marine Corps days."

"So you think I might know what I'm talking about?"

"Exactly," Kaye said. "If I saw something that I believed contained a faulty conclusion about a Harley, they'd never convince me I was wrong. Because I'd know I wasn't."

"Thank you."

"Now, tell me why you're convinced it wasn't an accident."

"Follow me," Edler said. "I'll show you."

Kaye followed Edler into the station, where Edler showed him to a chair in the dining space and asked him to wait, then disappeared. A minute later he returned with a large pad of paper in his hands and took the seat next to Kaye.

"Okay," Edler said, opening the pad and extracting several sheets.

To Kaye they first looked like schematics, but then he realized they were technical drawings of a car. They were good.

"Did you do these?" he asked.

"Yes, and no," Edler replied. "A couple of them are from the Internet, but I use those for reference to put together what I want."

"I'm impressed. Now, convince me."

Edler launched into an explanation of how the Ferrari, like all cars, is really a collection of different systems designed and engineered to perform specific tasks. Each has its own function, but also needs to work in conjunction with the other systems for the car to be a car. The biggest challenge for the engineers was fitting all the necessary systems into the desired shape and size.

He showed Kaye his drawings of the three-segment 488 chassis, the braking system and the engine to bolster his argument.

"The engine," Edler said, "is really a collection of a huge number of sub-systems, but –"

"Whoa," Kaye interrupted. "Mark, you're telling me things I already know. Tell me why you don't think that crash was an accident."

"Okay, sorry," Edler said. "The four eighty-eight is a mid-engine car. The engine is behind the driver and the engine compartment is separated from the passenger compartment by a firewall. And there's a very good reason they call it a firewall.

"In the four eighty-eight there are only a few systems that function both behind, and in front of, that firewall. Penetrations are small, and few, as you might imagine. The systems I looked at were wiring, ducting and undertrays. I also looked at the tunnel, what you'd probably call the center console if you were in the car. It doesn't extend behind the firewall, but it runs longitudinally from the firewall almost to the front of the car."

"Why those?"

"The impact was to the nose of the car. The driver lost control, swerved several times – we know that from the tire scuff marks -- then crossed the oncoming traffic lane and hit the road cut embankment on the south side of Mulholland almost directly head-on."

"Okay. So?"

"Detective Kaye," Edler said, "there is absolutely no way that kind of impact should have caused that car to burn, especially where it burned."

"Was the impact enough to rupture the gas tank?"

"Absolutely not," Edler said. "There are actually two interconnected tanks on the car, mounted behind the firewall inside the rear quarter panel flares on both sides. Kind of like saddlebags on a motorcycle. There was no evidence of a fuel spill at the scene, and obviously no explosion behind the firewall. Which is important."

"Back to the systems," Kaye said. "You picked those because they gave you fore and aft damage comparisons, right?"

Edler smiled and said, "Very good. Yes, that's exactly right."

"What did you find?"

"Long story short, I think that fire started in the passenger compartment, somewhere under the dash on the passenger side, and that makes absolutely no sense."

"Maybe an electrical short, or brake fluid. Brake fluid is flammable."

"I don't think so," Edler said. "There could've been a short, but the fire was way too fast and way too hot for it to be brake fluid. Given our response time, the body was really burned. Plus, there were other things."

"Like what?"

"The undertrays on the passenger side, and the tunnel, were…wrong."

"Wrong? What does that mean?"

"Out of place," replied Edler. "Bent, but not in ways consistent with the impact. Like another force had acted on them prior to the car striking the embankment."

Kaye leaned back and studied Edler. The kid's knowledge base was impressive, but, still, what he was saying contradicted the findings of two trained professionals.

"You do know that the official conclusions by both your department and mine were accidental death as a result of a vehicle crash."

"I do," Edler said, nodding. "But they're wrong. The damage to the tunnel beneath the passenger side dash was inconsistent with a frontal impact. The degree of melt of the ducting was much higher in front of the firewall than behind it, which is totally wrong if the fire started in the engine compartment and somehow breached the firewall. Same with the wiring, and the wiring was totally gone near the passenger dash, but still intact at the front of the car and behind the firewall. Typically, where the wiring is most burned up is where the fire started."

"How long did you spend inspecting the car?" Kaye asked.

"I only had about forty minutes," Edler said. "We stayed on scene until the car cooled off enough to extract the victim and the tow truck could hook it up."

"You've made all these conclusions based on a forty minute eyeballing of a wreck too hot to touch?"

"Yeah, pretty much," Edler said, staring directly at Kaye.

Kaye pondered what Edler was telling him, then said, "Look, no disrespect, because you obviously know a lot about Ferraris and a lot more about accident reconstruction than I expected, but you're fixated on the cause of the fire and ignoring the fact that the driver was driving down the road all by himself, and with no help from anybody else managed to crash his car. The fire was an unfortunate by-product of the crash that, sadly, killed him. It's still an accident."

"That's just it," Edler said. "I think he did have help."

Here comes the conspiracy theory, Kaye thought. But he said,

"Help in what way?"

"I mentioned the undertray and the tunnel, right?"

"You did."

"It was really the tunnel that convinced me," Edler said. "As expected, it was crumpled from absorbing the impact. But the right side, under the dash, was totally obliterated. I mean, it was just…gone. Not so on the driver's side. Put that together with the bowed undertray and all the other indicators, and I think the conclusion is obvious."

"And what would that be?" Kaye asked.

Edler shrugged and said, "A bomb."

"A bomb?" Kaye asked. "Seriously? The guy just drove the car off the dealer's lot less than an hour before the crash. How could there be a bomb in the car?"

"I don't know," Edler said. "But everything I saw was consistent with an explosion under the passenger side dashboard. Not a big bomb, probably an incendiary device as opposed to high explosives, but believe me, Detective. There was a bomb in that car."

"Look," Kaye said. "I haven't even had a chance to take a really close look at the reports. But I'll check into this, okay?"

"As a courtesy?" Edler said, and Kaye heard the sarcasm in the firefighter's voice.

"No," Kaye said, reaching out and picking up the drawings and looking at them. "You've made me just skeptical enough, and you obviously know what you're talking about. I think there's a statistically measurable chance this could be more than an accident."

"Thank you."

"Don't thank me yet," Kaye said. "It could be, in fact probably is, nothing."

"If it's nothing, then it's nothing," Edler said. "All I want is for somebody with skills and the access I don't have to take a closer look."

"I'll do that, and I'll start by asking you a couple questions."

"Go right ahead."

"Was there anything unusual about the call out?" Kaye asked. "Anything you remember as being different?"

Edler was silent for a moment, thinking.

"One thing's been nagging me," he said at last. "We had a lookie-loo."

A lookie-loo was someone who stands and watches a fire from a sense of fascination. Kaye also knew it wasn't unusual for arsonists to stick around the scene to watch their handiwork, which is why photos of the crowd were always taken. For some it was a source of sexual excitement and gratification.

"That's not all that unusual."

"I know," Edler said. "But this was...different."

"How so?"

"I was riding in the engine cab. I first noticed the guy pulled over on the westbound shoulder, you know, being a good citizen and getting out of the way."

"He watched from there?"

"No, that's just it," Edler said. "We passed the guy when we were only about a third of the way to the call. But not long after we arrived on scene, there he is again, watching from the eastbound shoulder, as close as he could get without getting inside your guys' traffic perimeter. It didn't take us long to knock down the fire, and when I looked, the bike was gone."

"Bike?" Kaye asked. "Bicycle or motorcycle?"

"Moto," Edler said. "White Hayabusa. Looked almost new."

Kaye did some quick calculations in his head.

Edler must have read his mind, because he said, "You're trying to reconcile timing, right? Trust me, it doesn't fit."

"No, it doesn't," Kaye said. "How could the biker be eastbound and not make it past the station by the time you got the call, saddled up, rolled out and covered only a third of the distance?"

"I haven't been able to figure that out, either, unless..."

"Unless," Kaye said, "he was behind the Ferrari and passed it after it happened."

"Or caused it," Edler added.

"Did you identify the reporting party?"

"Yeah. It was the guy whose back fence was about thirty feet uphill from the Ferrari. His place would've been the first to burn if the fire had gotten into the brush."

"Did you tell your arson investigator everything you just told me?" Kaye asked.

"I did."

"And?"

"She didn't seem impressed, or interested."

"What else do you remember about the rider?"

"Gosh," Edler said. "Not much. Full leathers and helmet. Tinted face shield. I really couldn't even swear it was a guy."

"Not too many women ride 'Busas," Kaye said. "Okay, one last question, kind of off topic."

"Ask away."

"I don't want to offend you, but what the hell are you doing working in a fire station?"

Edler laughed heartily. "No offense taken. My Grandfather and my Dad were firefighters. I never wanted to be anything else."

"You've got other talents," Kaye said, pointing at the drawings.

"Oh, I'm using them," Edler said. "I've been LAFD for about six months and I've already seen ways I can improve the equipment. I'm working on three patent applications now."

"Then what? Get rich and retire?"

Edler's expression changed.

"I'm a firefighter, Detective Kaye. That's what I do."

Kaye looked at Edler and recognized a kindred spirit.

"Okay," he said, standing. "I'll let you know what I come up with."

Right then, the station alarm sounded.

\*\*\*

Kaye stayed out of the way until the responding equipment had cleared the station.

He checked the time. It was only just past 9:00 a.m. and he figured the morning commute had likely run it's clogged course. He'd be able to make the Bureau before 10:00 a.m.

He traced the Ferrari's likely route back down into the Basin. On the way he plotted his next moves on the Ferrari wreck and Avi Geller's murder.

It was good to be back in the saddle, in more ways than one.

\*\*\*

Traffic cooperated and Kaye rolled into the Bureau parking lot just after 9:40 a.m.

He found a note from Captain Thompson to see him ASAP, but the office door was closed and the room was dark behind the blinds.

The message light on his desk phone was lit.

"Detective Kaye, my name is Howard Feinmann. I represent Ziva Geller. She asked me to call you and apologize on her behalf for her being rude yesterday. She would also like to talk to you about her husband's death. I have an opening in my schedule for four o'clock this afternoon, and we will come to you. Please call me and let me know if that works for you." Feinmann recited a number, said, "Thank you," and hung up.

The call could mean one of two things: Either Mrs. Geller had a clear conscience and just wanted to get past her husband's death, or she was hiding something and wanted to get ahead of the curve.

Kaye much preferred meeting people connected to a case, particularly homicides, face-to-face with no advance warning. He'd long ago learned that catching people flat-footed got better results. Lies took time to construct, and the quicker they were constructed, the faster they were to tear down.

But sometimes you had to take what you were given.

He punched in the number.

"Howard Feinmann," a gruff voice answered.

"Counselor, Detective Ben Kaye, LAPD."

"Thanks for calling back, Detective."

"No problem. Four o'clock would be fine. Have you been here before?"

"Actually, no," Feinmann replied. "My practice hasn't included criminal defense for quite some time."

Kaye gave the lawyer the address and some landmarks, and Feinmann assured him he'd be able to find it.

"Just ask for me at the front desk," Kaye said.

"Thank you, Detective. We'll see you this afternoon."

He needed to make paper on the Geller case, but no sooner had he swung around to his desk to get started when Captain Thompson pushed through the squad room doors.

Thompson was a large, ponderous man. His time riding a Captain's desk had not been kind to his weight or general physical condition. The irony was that his dedication to being possibly one of the best Captain's in the department would likely keep him from ever getting promoted. He was topped out, he knew it, and Kaye knew that knowledge sometimes rankled the man.

The two had long had a contentious relationship, but it was mostly one way.

Thompson didn't like Kaye's penchant for bending the rules, riding a motorcycle on duty, or the Big Boar MC colors his detective habitually wore, but he tolerated those things because Kaye was the best investigator he had. Kaye made arrests and closed cases, and that was the business they were in.

Good numbers keep bosses happy, no matter what the business.

"In my office, now," Thompson growled as he walked past Kaye.

"What did I do now?" Kaye asked after taking the chair across from Thompson. "One day back. I think that's a new personal best."

Thompson stared at him, clearly not appreciating Kaye's attempt at humor.

"Does the name Megan Sullivan mean anything to you?"

Kaye started to answer 'no', but suddenly the name clicked.

"I talked to a realtor named Megan Sullivan on the phone yesterday," Kaye said, then gave Thompson the quick and dirty on the murders at Paloma Canyon and recounted the circumstances of his conversation with Sullivan.

Thompson's mood improved as Kaye ran it down.

"Okay," he said when Kaye was done. "I get it, and I agree with your choices under the circumstances."

"What's the problem?"

"Unfortunately for you, and for me because I just got my ass chewed by the Bureau Commander, this Sullivan woman is friends with Stella Smithers."

"Smithers, as in Deputy Chief Smithers?"

Thompson nodded. "She called Smithers last night and told him you refused to take a crime report and left the scene."

"Crime?" Kaye asked. "What crime?"

"Apparently the house in question was broken into at some point and was vandalized. I guess there's a lot of damage."

"I had no way of knowing that. In fact, I made the conscious decision not to go through the gate without a warrant because it might bring into question anything I found."

"I agree," Thompson said. "I also agree that going to talk to Geller's wife trumped you cooling your heels for an hour or more waiting for Sullivan when there was no indication a crime had been committed."

"So we're good?"

"We're good," Thompson nodded. "But I need you to put what you just told me in writing; an e-mail is fine; so I can give it to the Commander, who can then take it to Smithers."

"I'll do it right now," Kaye said. "Oh, and I talked to your Ferrari-crazy firefighter this morning."

"And?"

Kaye ran it down, and he could tell his Captain's curiosity was piqued.

"You think this kid might actually be on to something?"

"I think if I don't run it down I'm not doing my job."

"You gonna talk to our traffic guys and the LAFD arson investigator?"

Kaye thought about it for a moment.

"I don't think so, at least not yet," he replied. "I don't want to start off by stepping on toes, and I think it'd be better if I went at it like it was a new case, no preconceptions, and see what I come up with."

"Sounds good to me," Thompson said. "But it's low priority, okay? Focus on the Geller murder for now."

"It wasn't just Geller. A young woman was killed, too."

"I know, I know. But she's not on the news, okay?"

"Yes, sir," Kaye said, rising. "I'm meeting with Geller's wife and her lawyer this afternoon."

"Let me know how that goes."

Kaye went back to his desk and spent five minutes writing an e-mail about his telephone conversation with Megan Sullivan and the surrounding circs, then sent it to Thompson. Then he spent an hour making updates to the Geller file. As yet he had no forensics information from either Arch or the crime lab, so the file contained a lot of fluff, but not a whiff of progress.

\*\*\*

When he'd dotted the last 'i' and crossed the last 't', Kaye checked the time. He was hungry, and basically had time to kill until his meeting with Feinmann and Ziva Geller.

He grabbed the reports on the Ferrari crash, scanned through them quickly to find what he needed, grabbed his jacket and headed out.

After stopping for a quick bite on San Vicente, he headed for Beverly Hills.

As many times as he'd been to and through Beverly Hills he'd never noticed the Ferrari dealership. There was no on-street parking in front of the place and he circled the block three times before finding a place to park the Harley.

The nondescript store front on the street side was compensated for by the wide bank of overhead doors facing the street the next block over, two of which were up to take advantage of the Chamber of Commerce weather.

Kaye walked in and stopped to stare at the millions of dollars worth of rolling sculpture on display. Many of the cars were collectibles protected behind glass walls, others were surrounded by red velvet cordons strung between golden stanchions. He'd never been an exotic car devotee, even though he could afford any of the cars he could see. When he wasn't riding one of the Harleys in his collection he drove a newer model crew cab pickup that served his needs. It had very low mileage.

"Good afternoon," a voice said from behind him. Kaye turned to see a man dressed in a stylish navy blue suit, accented by a red tie, standing a few feet away with hands clasped expectantly.

"Welcome to Ferrari. My name is Anthony. How may I be of service today?"

"Detective Kaye, LAPD." He pulled back his jacket to show his badge. "I'd like to see a four eighty-eight Spider, please."

Anthony had obviously learned not to judge a potential customer by occupation or dress, because he simply said, "Of course. Follow me," and headed for the front of the store.

Kaye could immediately see the appeal of the car. Sleek, sexy, and the distinctive Ferrari red color guaranteed it wouldn't go unnoticed.

Anthony launched into his very low-key, soft-pedal sales presentation describing the features and performance of the car.

"I assume you can put on a roof panel," Kaye said when Anthony asked if he had questions.

"Of course," Anthony replied. "One push of a button and the car becomes weather tight."

"It's onboard?"

"Yes, it stows beneath the tonneau cover. Up and down in only seconds."

"I'm impressed," Kaye said. "Is this one available?"

"No, I'm sorry," Anthony said. "This one is waiting for the owner to come take delivery. We're currently taking orders for delivery eight to twelve months out."

"Business is good, eh?"

"Very, but I wouldn't recommend the four eighty-eight for you."

"Why is that?"

"With your size, Detective, I doubt you would find it comfortable."

"That's kind of what I thought when I saw it, too," Kaye admitted. "I'm really not here to buy a car."

"I assumed that," Anthony said. "You're here to talk about Mr. Howell's unfortunate crash and demise."

"I am."

"Frankly, I expected someone much sooner. Let's go sit down."

Kaye followed Anthony into a lavishly appointed office unlike anything he'd ever seen at a car dealership. It looked to him more like the drawing room of an Italian palazzo.

"So, how can I help you?" Anthony asked when they were seated.

"I'm taking a fresh look at the accident," Kaye said. "Just trying to tie up a few loose ends."

"Why? The fire department and your traffic people ruled Mr. Howell's death the result of a single-vehicle accident. I thought the matter was closed."

"Let's just say I might have some new information," Kaye said. "I'm skeptical, and, hey, it's what they pay me to do."

Anthony stared at him for a moment, then leaned forward and put his elbows on his desk.

"We're skeptical, too."

"We?" Kaye asked. "Who's 'we'?"

"All of us," Anthony replied. "The entire Ferrari family. The engineers in Maranello are beside themselves trying to figure out why there was a fire."

"So it was unusual?"

"It wasn't simply unusual," Anthony said. "It's inexplicable. Our cars are the finest designs and engineering in the world. But human beings drive them, so accidents happen. We understand that, but based on the visible damage to the car Mr. Howell should have walked away from that crash without a scratch. The car certainly should not have burned."

"You saw the car?"

"Of course. We recovered it and had it brought here for examination."

"Who examined it?"

"The company sent engineers from Italy."

"What did they find?"

"That's just it," Anthony said. "They found nothing obvious that would have caused a fire anywhere in the car, much less one that apparently started in front of the firewall."

"They concluded the fire didn't start in the engine compartment?"

"That is correct."

"Anything else?"

"One of the engineers was baffled by the damage patterns. It seems the built-in crumple zones failed to perform as designed."

"Where's the car now?" Kaye asked.

"It was crated and shipped to the factory for more analysis."

"They did that?"

"Certainly," Anthony said, nodding. "It may have gotten two column inches in the Times, Detective, but in our industry it was major news."

"Why is that?"

"Ferrari is the premier marque in the automotive world. We take great pride in our cars. When one of our owners dies in a relatively slow-speed, one vehicle crash, we want to know why so we can keep it from happening again."

"And maybe avoid a major product liability lawsuit." Kaye said.

"Certainly, there is that," Anthony said. "But that's a possibility for the legal department to deal with. Believe me when I say the engineers are taking this very personally. Someone died. They want to know if they made a mistake that caused that to happen."

"I imagine so," Kaye said. "What can you tell me about Mr. Howell?"

"Nice guy," Anthony said. "When someone waits for their car as long as he did they become a frequent, albeit sometimes impatient, visitor. Mr. Howell traveled extensively, but he came in regularly."

"How long did he have to wait?"

"About a year."

"You're kidding."

Anthony laughed.

"I'll admit it was longer than usual, but Mr. Howell's car had some special modifications to accommodate his prosthesis."

"Prosthesis?"

"Yes," Anthony said. "Mr. Howell lost his left leg while serving in Iraq. I don't know the entire story, of course, but he certainly didn't let it slow him down."

"What kind of special modifications are we talking about?" Kaye asked, thinking that might account for the unusual damage patterns Edler saw.

"Nothing very technical, really, and certainly nothing that would have contributed to the crash or the fire. There were some changes to the door hinges, the seat mounting and the rocker panel on the driver's side to make it easier for him to get in and out of the car. Our engineers have already ruled out all those things."

"Do you know what Mr. Howell did?" Kaye asked. "I mean, there probably aren't a lot of disabled vets who can afford to plunk down that kind of money for a car."

"Oh, Mr. Howell did very well. He was the CEO of his own firm, doing some kind of government contract security work. Let me pull up his owner profile and I'll give you the name and address of the company."

Anthony swiveled his chair to face his computer monitor and slid a keyboard tray from under the desktop.

"Ah, here we are," he said after a moment. "Leigh Howell" – he spelled out L-E-I-G-H for Kaye's benefit – "Chairman and CEO of Black Scimitar Corporation."

Kaye had never heard of the company, but didn't think it would be hard to track down.

"When Howell came and picked up his car, did he come by himself?" he asked.

"I assume he was dropped off for the appointment," Anthony said. "But, yes, he came in from the front, by himself."

"So he wasn't with anyone else who might have been on a motorcycle?"

"I never saw anyone else. One of our concierge staff met Mr. Howell at the front door. If you'd like to talk to her, I can certainly arrange that."

"What time did he leave the store?" Kaye asked.

"Hmm…" Anthony murmured before turning back to his computer. "His delivery appointment was at eleven a.m., and the process takes about two hours, so, say about one."

"Anything at all unusual about the delivery? Did Howell seem okay? Problems?"

"Nothing at all that I remember, except that he was very excited to finally have his car."

"Thank you for your time, Anthony," Kaye said, rising. "Is there anything else, anything at all that you think I should know?"

Anthony hesitated for a few seconds before saying, "I blame myself, really. I should have insisted that Mr. Howell complete our driving school, and I didn't. He always said he was too busy."

"Driving school?"

"Yes. A mid-engine car, especially one with that much

horsepower, is a completely different animal. If you've never driven one before, well, let's just say there is a learning curve."

"You think Howell maybe just got in over his head? Too fast, too soon?"

"I think that must be considered as a cause of the accident," Anthony said. "Why there was a fire, though, is the big unknown."

"If your engineers make a determination on that, would you let me know, please?" Kaye handed Anthony a business card.

"Of course."

Kaye left through the front door. Looking both ways he saw signals at the closest intersections. Knowing the alley behind the store was one way, he walked east to the cross street.

There were traffic cameras covering all directions.

\*\*\*

Kaye rolled into the station parking lot a little after 3:30 p.m.

He spent a few minutes bringing Captain Thompson up to date on his visit to the Ferrari dealer, getting back to his desk just in time to answer his phone.

It was Patty.

"Detective, I have a Mr. Feinmann and Mrs. Geller here to see you."

"Thanks, Patty. On my way."

Kaye guessed Feinmann to be fifty. The attorney was tall, balding on top but with shaggy black hair going to silver over his shirt collar and ears. He wore black horn-rimmed glasses and a suit Kaye guessed at three grand, minimum.

Ziva Geller's age was anybody's guess, and the estimate went up as Kaye got closer. Her clothes were conservative, her jewelry was not.

Kaye introduced himself and said, "I'm sorry for your loss, Mrs. Geller."

"I'm not," she shot back. "Saves me a lot of money and trouble."

"Ziva," Feinmann said, "we talked about this, remember?"

"Of course I remember, Howard," she said. "I'm upset, but I'm not senile."

"Let's talk in private," Kaye said. "Follow me, please."

He led them to an interview room. On the way he grabbed a more comfortable chair for Ziva Geller and rolled it into the room.

When they were all seated, Kaye led off.

"I'd like to thank you for coming in so soon, Mrs. Geller. After our conversation last evening, I didn't expect it."

"I apologize for being rude," Geller said. "I was only following Howard's instructions."

Feinmann caught Kaye's eye and the attorney rolled his and shook his head ever so slightly.

"I understand," Kaye said.

"Before we begin," Feinmann said, "I'd like to state for the record that my client is here voluntarily, and I'd also like to set some ground rules."

"Ground rules?" Kaye asked. "Look, Counselor, this isn't an interrogation. I'm just looking for background information on Mr. Geller. Things like friends, business associates, enemies, things like that. I figure if anybody knows those things, it's your client. Besides, she can always refuse to answer if she prefers not to."

"First, then," Feinmann said, "I'd like to know if Mrs. Geller is either a suspect or person of interest in Mr. Geller's murder."

"She is not," Kaye said.

"Will you be Mirandizing her?"

"No."

"Are you recording this interview?"

"No," Kaye said, "but I will be taking notes."

"I can live with that," Feinmann said before turning to Geller. "Ziva, the important thing here is that you don't have to answer any questions at all, or any questions you'd prefer not to. Do you understand?"

Kaye idly thought that for a guy who claimed to be rusty on criminal defense, Feinmann was doing a pretty good job of explaining Miranda all by himself.

"I understand," Geller said. "Go ahead, Detective Kaye."

Kaye began with the *pro forma* stuff: Name, age, address, Avi Geller's business address, etc. Then he asked how long the Gellers had been married.

"Almost thirty-four years," she replied. "Three wonderful children, all successful."

"Yet you were in the process of divorcing him?" Kaye asked.

"Yes, and no," Geller said. "Howard, would you explain?"

"Certainly," Feinmann said. "Detective, Mrs. Geller came to me several months ago and asked me to draw up divorce papers. But they've never been filed or served."

"Why not?" Kaye asked.

"I still loved him," Geller answered. "I kept hoping things would straighten out."

"What things?" Kaye asked.

"You don't have to answer that," Feinmann interjected.

"Howard, I have nothing to hide. Avi's dead. What am I gonna do, insult him?" She turned to Kaye. "You want to know? I'll tell you. At his age, after all these years together, for some reason my husband decided he didn't have to keep his zipper up when he wasn't home."

"He had a girlfriend?" Kaye said.

"Ha!" Geller blurted. "The meshugana putz didn't have a girlfriend. He had a shiksa whore, and he thought I didn't know. I could *smell* her on him when he came home. Do you know what that's like?"

Kaye ignored the question, instead asking, "Your husband was a movie producer, correct?"

"Among other things," Geller said. "He was..." She stopped and stared at Kaye for a moment, then said, "I see where this is going, but, no, Avi wasn't like that. He wasn't a casting couch kind of guy. He gave a lot of actresses – I guess they're all called actors now, such a shame -- breaks, and never took advantage."

"But he cheated on you," Kaye said.

"I'm going to stop this right here," Feinmann interrupted. "I thought this was about background, not trying to establish that Mrs. Geller had motive to kill her husband."

"Counselor, I'm trying to find out if there was anyone else, maybe a jilted lover, or a lover's husband, I need to talk to."

"It's okay, Howard," Geller said, patting her attorney on the arm before turning to Kaye. "My husband was a very successful movie and television producer. He worked hard at it, and was very, very good at it. He had more projects brought to him than he could ever handle. Directors and investors lined up to work with Avi."

"Somebody killed him, Mrs. Geller," Kaye said. "I don't think it was random target practice. Are you sure he hadn't made someone mad, maybe a deal gone bad, or financial trouble?"

"Financial trouble? Avi?" She laughed. "No, Detective. We started dirt poor. Three kids in a two-bedroom, third-floor walk-up in the Fairfax. He was always careful with money. You've seen our house. Does that look like financial trouble to you?"

"You never can tell, Mrs. Geller," Kaye said. "You know what they call the front of a house, right?"

"What's that?"

"A façade," Kaye said.

"Okay," Feinmann said. "I think we're done here."

"I have one more question," Kaye said. "If it's okay."

"Go ahead and ask," Geller said.

"You said a few minutes ago that, what, maybe six months ago, your husband started cheating on you," Kaye said. "What changed? And I'm not looking for personal specifics. I'm interested in external factors, like a problem with a project, or the company, maybe some new friends suddenly showing up, things like that."

Ziva Geller went quiet, thinking, and Kaye got the impression she was unsure about something.

"Anything at all, Mrs. Geller," he prompted. "It may have seemed trivial at the time, but it could be important now."

"There was one thing," she said at last. "But it was almost two years ago. It was the only time we ever fought about money. And it wasn't because we didn't have enough."

Kaye waited.

"Avi came to me," she went on, "to tell me he was going to diversify. That's what he called it. Diversify. He'd been approached by some people about investing in a real estate project, some kind of exclusive resort, up the coast north of Santa Barbara somewhere. I told him he was crazy."

"Why would you think that?" Kaye asked.

"Because it was crazy," Geller replied. "I've known the man since the fifth grade. The only thing Avi knew about real estate was that you have to put a sign in front of your house to sell it. Then all of a sudden he wants to give some schmuck fifty million dollars?" She shrugged. "We fought."

"Fifty million dollars?" Feinmann spoke up, dumbfounded. "Ziva, why didn't I know about this?"

She just shrugged.

"What happened after that?" Kaye asked.

"He gave them the money," she said. "He said they promised him his fifty million would be worth ten times that when the project was done."

"Was it?" Kaye asked.

"I don't know," Geller whispered. "If they ever paid him back a dime, Avi didn't put the money into our joint trust account."

"Oh, Ziva," Feinmann said, shaking his head, "I wish you'd come to me. We could have talked to Avi, straightened all this out. At least made sure the deal was on the up and up."

"I couldn't," she said, still whispering. "It wasn't about the money. We have more than we'll ever need. It was what happened after, not long after last Hanukkah, that I started noticing…things. People started mentioning…things. Avi was there, but he wasn't, if that makes sense."

"Such as?" Kaye prompted.

"Ziva, you don't have to answer that," Feinmann said.

"Thank you, Howard," she said, then looked at Kaye. "It's not important now, is it? Avi's dead."

"Who were these people?" Kaye asked. "The real estate developers?"

"I don't know," Geller said. "After we fought about it, Avi put a wall around it. He wouldn't even introduce me to them."

"I'm sure that information will be in the Gellers' financial records," Feinmann said.

"You'll turn them over?" Kaye asked, surprised.

Feinmann smiled in that way only lawyers can smile.

"Let me clarify," he said. "If you bring me a specific enough subpoena, I'll honor it as best I can."

Kaye turned to Geller.

"Mrs. Geller, there's no guarantee your husband's murder had anything to do with this real estate thing, but I'll check into it. Is there anything else I should know?"

"Not that I can think of right now," she replied.

Kaye turned to Feinmann.

"What happens to Geller's company?"

Feinmann studied him for a moment, digesting the question.

"I don't think you need to go there, Detective," he said. "It's privately held. Mrs. Geller maintains a strong equity position, and Mr. Geller had a succession plan in place."

"You don't think anybody got, shall we say, anxious to move up?" Kaye asked.

"No," Feinmann replied, shaking his head for emphasis. "Nobody in the company even knows about the plan, and they won't until the will is read after the funeral, whenever that might be."

"I think we're done," Kaye said, standing up. "I've got a couple places to start. Thanks for coming in. I'll show you out."

"We can find our way," Feinmann said, offering Kaye his hand. "And, please, if you need anything else from Mrs. Geller, work through me."

"I'll do that."

Kaye stayed in the interview room, going over his notes, looking for any hints or nuances he might have missed. Ziva Geller was a tough read. One the one hand, she said she was ready to divorce her husband, but on the other he got the impressions she was telling the truth when she said she still loved him. He knew from experience that love and murder were frequent bedfellows.

But unless he was seriously mistaken, there was no way in hell Ziva Geller was capable of putting two rounds into her husband's chest, then hitting a running, partially obscured target, at well over two hundred yards, in mere seconds.

Strange way to live, he thought idly as he got up.

Time to go home.

# DAY 4
## Thursday Week 1

Kaye rose early. It was overcast, and during his yoga session he realized the days were shortening and he'd soon have to move inside if he stuck with the early schedule.

His plan for the morning was to visit Avi Geller's offices first, since they were closer than, and on the way to, the station.

Kaye rode the Flight Red '41 Knucklehead FL, and the bike drew the usual honks, thumbs up signs, stares and comments on the ride to Century City.

AZG Productions occupied a large suite on an upper floor of one of the iconic three-sided skyscrapers.

He saw a knot of reporters and cameras on the sidewalk outside the main entrance, kept going and turned into the parking garage. He had no desire to talk to the press.

When Kaye pushed through the door his first impression was that he was in a motion picture museum. Mannequins in recognizable costumes and special effects were numerous, and the lobby walls were covered with framed posters. Most bore signatures of cast and crew members.

If these were Geller's films, Kaye knew why the guy had an estate at the top of Paloma Canyon and fifty million to toss at a real estate deal.

"How may I help you?" the young woman behind the polished mahogany desk asked, jarring Kaye from his reverie.

"Sorry," he said. He held up his badge. "Detective Kaye, LAPD."

"You're hear about Mr. Geller."

"I am."

"I'll get Mr. Baruch."

She rose and disappeared around the edge of the wall behind the desk. Less than a minute later she reappeared, trailed by a slight, casually dressed man. A black ribbon was pinned to the breast of his polo shirt.

"Les Baruch," the man introduced himself. "What can I do for you, Detective Kaye?"

"I was hoping to get a few minutes of your time."

"Sure, sure," Baruch said. He turned to the receptionist. "No calls, Denise."

Baruch led Kaye to a conference room, where Kaye counted sixteen chairs around the sculpted stainless steel and glass table. The view toward the Pacific was spectacular, with the Santa Monica pier Ferris wheel visible in the hazy distance. Baruch took the end chair closest to the door and Kaye took the chair directly to the man's right.

"Now," Baruch said, "I assume you're investigating Avi's murder. How can I be of help?"

"Your assumption is correct," Kaye said. "What I'd like to do is get a feel for Mr. Geller's business, his friends, enemies, things like that. And," Kaye smiled, "if you happen to know who shot him, you can save me a lot of time by just telling me."

A flash of panic crossed Baruch's face, then he chuckled sardonically.

"Very funny. Believe me, if I knew who killed Avi I would have already saved you the trouble of an investigation."

"So you two got along?"

"Avi was like a brother to me, Detective. I've known him and Ziva forever. I owe him everything. His death is incomprehensible to me, to all of us, really. We don't know what we're going to do without him."

"Did Mr. Geller have enemies?" Kaye asked. "People whose projects he turned down, maybe? Or competitors who weren't happy with him?"

"No," Baruch replied instantly. "People Avi turned down simply became disappointed friends, always welcome to come back and pitch the next blockbuster."

"If what I saw up front was any indication, he had quite a few of those."

"That he did," Baruch said. "In my opinion, while I admit I'm a little biased, Avi was a genius. He had an eye for great ideas and a nose for great scripts. He made a lot of people in this town a lot of money."

"What about his other business?" Kaye asked. "The real estate."

Baruch's brow furrowed and he made a face.

"Real estate? You must be mistaken, Detective. Avi made movies. He didn't do real estate."

"That's not what I heard," Kaye said. "Most recently, fifty million dollars, and my source is solid. Did you know his wife was considering divorcing him?"

"What?" Baruch said, his eyes wide. "I don't believe that. Avi and Ziva have been together forever. He loved her."

"Did you notice any changes in Mr. Geller's routines, his behavior, over, say the last six or eight months?"

Baruch looked away briefly and shifted nervously in his chair.

"Yeah," he said, staring at Kaye again. "I did. Nothing real big, but…"

"What did you notice?"

"It was nothing, really. I only noticed because we'd been friends for so long. Nobody else ever said anything. Ever."

"Okay. And?"

"This is a funny business," Baruch said. "You saw the office. But would you believe it's pretty much window dressing? The real deals aren't done here. They're done on the golf course, at the marina, maybe over dinner at a charity event. Places like that.

"Avi was a creature of habit. For years he only took office meetings on Monday and Thursday mornings, hammering out deals, signing contracts. You know, nuts and bolts stuff. The rest of the time he was out and about. Business development, he called it."

"That changed?" Kaye asked.

"Yeah," Baruch replied. "Several months ago I noticed he started to occasionally miss his Monday meetings. Then there were weeks he didn't come to the office at all. He even almost blew a major deal, which was not like him at all."

"Did he lose any projects?"

"Avi? Hell, no. Avi could schmooze anybody. He just called, made a few jokes, apologized and rescheduled. But when I asked what was going on, he told me to mind my own business. Over twenty-five years together, he never told me that. Not once. I wonder now if it was because him and Ziva were having problems."

"So, to your knowledge, Avi Geller had no enemies?"

"Not that I know of," Baruch said. "Besides, this is Hollywood. People don't get even by killing each other. They get their revenge at the box office and on HBO and Netflix."

"A young woman was with Mr. Geller when he was killed. She was killed, too. Did Mr. Geller have a girlfriend, or girlfriends, maybe?"

"Avi? Never. He wasn't like that." Baruch's brow furrowed and he asked, "Who was she?"

"I don't know," Kaye replied. "Yet."

"This is just surreal," Baruch said, collapsing back in his chair. "It's like a bad gangster movie. Life imitating art."

"We can argue Aristotle and Oscar Wilde all day, Mr. Baruch," Kaye said.

Baruch looked closely at Kaye, then said, "I'm impressed, Detective."

"Don't be. I don't have a side in the argument. It's just my job to find the killer." He rose to leave and handed Baruch a business card. "I may want to come back and talk to the staff at some point, and please call me if you think of anything in the meantime."

"Certainly," Baruch said. "Can I ask you a question?"

"Sure."

"Ever thought about being in the movies? I know a guy with a great concept and script looking for… Well, honestly, he's looking for you. You are his character. Interested?"

Kaye just laughed.

***

Kaye rolled into the station parking lot just before 11:00 a.m. There were more cars in the parking lot than he'd seen all week.

The activity level inside had gone up, too. Uniformed officers walked the hallways, and when Kaye walked into the squad room he saw two detectives, Chet Hilliard and Melody 'Mel' Lister, sitting in Lister's space studying her computer monitor.

Hilliard was a twenty-five year-plus cop, almost twenty of those as a detective. Lister had just been promoted to detective about a month before Kaye went on leave. Thompson had partnered her with Hilliard so she could learn the trade.

Lister saw Kaye, leaned back and smiled.

"Hey, Chet," she said. "Look what the cat dragged in."

"Why, as I live and breathe," Hilliard said. "Ben Kaye. Nice to see you back where you belong. What? They laying off at Harley?"

Kaye smiled.

"I've been back all week," he said. "What are you two doing back?"

"Draggin' the line," Lister said. "Making a living, even if it is the old, hard way."

"But I thought…" Kaye said.

"Yeah, well," Hilliard said, "even the idiot who hatches a bad idea figures it out eventually. They started calling people back yesterday."

"Right decision," Kaye said. "I heard it got ugly."

"Ugly doesn't begin to describe it," Lister said. "Town without pity, man. We damn near lost, Kaye. A few more days, the thin blue line would've been gone. It would've taken regular troops to restore order."

"That's what the Captain said, too," Kaye said. "Did you stay on?"

"They put me in uniform for the duration," Lister said. "Workin' in the coal mine."

"So, how was the vacation?" Hilliard asked. "Did you miss us regular folks while you were rubbing shoulders with the jet set?"

"Uneventful," was all Kaye said, staying true to his word that he wouldn't talk about the events in Aspen. "Nice place, but I don't know if I'd live there."

"So why'd you come back to loading sixteen tons every day?" Lister asked. "Hotel California, maybe? Big difference between checking out and actually leaving."

Kaye thought about it for a moment.

"Big yellow taxi."

It only took Lister about three seconds before she grinned and nodded knowingly.

"What are you talking about?" Hilliard said, exasperated and looking back and forth. "I don't get it."

"Jesus, Chet," Lister said, playfully punching her partner in the shoulder. "How do you function with such a limited knowledge base?" She turned to Kaye. "I'll explain the ironies of paradise, parking lots and tree museums to him later."

"We're glad you're back," Hilliard said before he glared at Lister and made a face.

"Likewise," Kaye said. "What are you working?"

"Thompson's letting us pick and choose from the overload," Hilliard said. "If you can believe that."

"Yeah," Lister added. "He's suddenly gone all Lovin' Spoonful on us. Pick one, leave the other behind, you know?"

Hilliard just looked at Kaye, shook his head, and said, "I give up."

Back at his desk, Kaye sat back and took stock of what he had going on.

If he hustled, he could pay a visit to Black Scimitar and start building background on Leigh Howell.

\*\*\*

The offices of Black Scimitar Corporation were a study in etched glass and stainless steel design.

The glass entry doors were each etched with an oversized scimitar, over which was superimposed a map of the world ringed by the company name.

The lobby was separated from the private spaces by six over-sized glass panels, each bearing a detailed, etched map of one of Earth's inhabited continents. The round, black enameled reception desk floated in the middle of the space in front of North America. Inside the circle, a young woman with close-cropped black hair looked up when Kaye walked through the door. He saw her reach under the desk as she smiled.

"Good morning," she greeted Kaye pleasantly, but kept one hand below the counter. "How may I help you?"

Kaye held up his open badge wallet.

"Detective Kaye, LAPD. I need to speak to the senior person on-site. Your President, CEO, whoever is in charge."

The woman relaxed and put her hands on the counter.

"May I ask what this is about?"

"I'm investigating the death of Leigh Howell."

"Oh," she said, her eyes widening. "Hold on."

She reached for the phone. On her wrist Kaye noticed a silver bracelet emblazoned in gold with the eagle, globe and anchor emblem of the U.S. Marine Corps.

He stood silently while the spoke on the phone.

"Mr. Gagnon will be out in just a moment," she said when she hung up.

"Thank you," Kaye said. "Nice bracelet. Were you in the Corps?"

"I was. Eight years."

"Me, too. But just one, well, almost one, hitch."

Movement in his peripheral vision caught Kaye's attention and he turned to see a young man round the panel etched with a map of Asia.

"Adrian Gagnon," the man introduced himself, extending his hand.

"Ben Kaye, LAPD. Thank you for seeing me."

The two shook hands. For a brief instant when their hands and eyes met, Kaye thought Gagnon was going to try and use the handshake to establish dominance, but Kaye met pressure with pressure and Gagnon resorted to a perfunctory handshake.

"How can I help you, Detective?"

"I'm investigating Leigh Howell's death and —"

"I thought that had been ruled an accident," Gagnon interrupted.

"There are some possible new developments and information," Kaye said. "If you have a few minutes I'd like to get some background information. You know, start filling in some of the blanks."

"Certainly," Gagnon said. "Follow me, please." He turned to the woman at the desk. "Elizabeth, no interruptions, please."

"Yes, sir."

Gagnon led Kaye back around the glass Asia and down a short, wide hallway. There was quite a bit of activity as other employees scurried about, some with armloads of files and folders. Gagnon greeted them all by name as they passed by, then held open an office door etched with a map of the District of Columbia.

The office was large and airy. The exterior wall was glass, affording views of downtown Los Angeles in the distance. In addition to two chairs facing what was obviously Gagnon's desk, there were two leather loveseats and a cocktail table. The decoration was mostly plants, but on one wall hung photographs of a man standing with several Presidents of the United States and others Kaye recognized as Heads of State.

"Please," Gagnon said, pointing to a chair as he stepped to the other side of the desk and sat down. "So, exactly how can I help you?"

"I'd like to find out more about Mr. Howell," Kaye said. "For example, the reports of the incident don't mention whether he was married. Things like that. First, I'd like to find out a little more about what Black Scimitar does."

"I can help with that," Gagnon said, leaning back in his chair and relaxing. "To answer your first question, no, Rod was never married except to the United States Army. He left no family behind, and his parents were already deceased. I wasn't able to trace a single relative to notify of his death."

"Rod?" Kaye asked. "I thought his first name was Leigh."

"Legally, yes, but he disliked it. In the Army he earned the nickname 'Steel Rod' Howell because of his toughness. He preferred to be called Rod."

"Got it," Kaye said. "Go on."

"As for what Black Scimitar does, we are an operational consultant and security services provider for companies doing business in places that might be, shall we say, often tenuous and rapidly changing."

"Can you give me an example?"

"Certainly," Gagnon said. "Say you're an energy company that wants to develop a major new petroleum field in a country where the government may be less than stable, or may not have a tight hold on all of its territory. You can contract with us to protect your personnel, your equipment and your supply lines, and we can also run political interference for you should the need arise."

"You said Mr. Howell was ex-military."

"Army."

"You, too?"

Gagnon laughed. "Hardly. The Sorbonne, then an MBA from the Wharton School of Business."

"Do you contract with the Department of Defense?"

"Not directly," Gagnon replied. "After working on the inside for years, Rod found their procedures onerous. But we do have the necessary security clearances to contract with service and support providers fulfilling DoD contracts they have been awarded."

"So, like sub-contractors."

"Exactly."

"Howell was driving an almost four hundred thousand dollar car," Kaye said. "You must be doing well."

"Sadly," Gagnon said, "the nature of today's world provides us with an expanding market."

"What, exactly, was Mr. Howell's role?"

"He started the company. He ran things."

"Do you have a Board of Directors?"

"We do," Gagnon said. "Rod was the Chairman. We went public a little over a year ago, and we're listed on the Big Board."

"About the time Mr. Howell ordered the Ferrari, right?" Kaye asked. "The IPO went well?"

"It did," Gagnon said with a smile that told Kaye he'd made a fortune, too.

"So, with no relatives, what happens to Mr. Howell's interest in the company?"

"Good question. With no heirs and no will, the Court will have to decide what to do with Rod's assets."

"He didn't leave a will?"

"Not that we've been able to locate. Rod was still a soldier at heart, which drove our General Counsel crazy."

"Is there an Executor of the estate?" Kaye asked.

"Obviously, Detective," Gagnon said, "you're looking for anyone who might have benefitted financially from Rod's death. We have asked the Court to name a neutral Executor. After that's settled, the first thing will be the election of a new Chairman. Rod started Black Scimitar when he left the Army, and –"

"When he lost his leg," Kaye interrupted.

"Yes," Gagnon said, staring at Kaye. "If I may continue?"

"Of course," Kaye said. "My apologies."

"This was Rod's company. His baby, if you will. Black Scimitar will continue, but without Rod's reputation and charisma, well, time will tell."

"What reputation? I've never heard of him."

"He was a ranking member of Delta Forces Command before losing his leg to an IED."

"And your role here is…?"

"I've been the Chief Financial Officer here for a couple of years. I was asked to stay on and maintain operations while all this sorts itself out."

"So Black Scimitar is still doing business?"

"Absolutely," Gagnon said. "We've exploded since going public. We have hundreds of millions of dollars in ongoing contracts and more than that in the proposal stages."

"Seriously?" Kaye asked. "From this office? Nothing personal, but I would expect a bigger footprint for that kind of money."

Gagnon laughed. "This is just our corporate suite, our nerve center if you will. Rod was sentimentally attached to it and refused to move. We now have sixteen primary operations centers and nearly forty logistics and supply locations across the globe. That's why the maps of the continents."

"That makes more sense," Kaye said. "Did Mr. Howell have any enemies?"

Gagnon laughed again. "Rod was a major player in America's counter-terrorism and special operations efforts for many years. I daresay there are thousands of other players in the world who are celebrating his death."

"But no one in particular? A business rival, maybe a pissed off husband somewhere?"

"Are you suggesting Rod was murdered?"

"I'm looking into it."

"On what basis?" Gagnon's tone was demanding.

"I can't share that right now," Kaye said. "It may turn out to be nothing more than due diligence."

"That I understand," Gagnon said, nodding. "But please understand that such an investigation, if made public, could have an adverse effect on the company."

"That's not really my concern," Kaye said. "Back to the enemies question. Anybody in particular come to mind? Maybe somebody with explosives expertise?"

"Not that I can think of," Gagnon said, studying Kaye closely. "So, you're thinking a bomb?"

"I can't say."

"Well, if there's even a suspicion of foul play, I'll instruct our Ops people to start listening for rumors, chatter, anything that might help."

"I appreciate that," Kaye said, rising. He handed Gagnon a business card. "Please, call me if you hear –"

"Adrian," a female voice interrupted and Kaye turned to see a woman stopped partway through the office door. Her hands were at shoulder level, one holding the door open and the other braced against the door frame on the opposite side as if she'd stopped herself from entering at the last second. She was tall, had medium-length, sandy blonde hair and wore black pants and a brightly colored, sleeveless silk blouse.

"Oh, I'm sorry," she said, glancing back and forth from Gagnon to Kaye. "I didn't realize you had someone in your office."

"No problem," Gagnon said, standing. "Detective Kaye, meet Tamara Goschen, my interim, and soon to be, I hope, permanent Operations Coordinator."

"Ms. Goschen," Kaye said, nodding politely.

"Detective Kaye," she said, appraising him coolly before turning to Gagnon. "The police?"

"He was just leaving," Gagnon said.

"He's all yours, Ms. Goschen," Kaye said. "I can find my way out. Thanks again for your time, Mr. Gagnon."

Goschen stepped into the office and held the door open. As he walked by Kaye took notice of a striking tattoo on her right arm and shoulder. It was a strange, anthropomorphic mix of a fierce bird and distorted, semi-human face, with what looked like a wing extending down her arm and wrapping around her elbow.

"It's my personal war dog," Goschen said when she saw Kaye

64

looking. "I'll see you around, Detective."

Another weird, ex-military spook, Kaye thought as he walked out. Using Asia as a landmark he had no trouble finding his way back to the lobby.

As he headed for the door he looked sideways to acknowledge Elizabeth, the receptionist. She saw him and held up her hand, giving him the 'come here' sign with her fingers.

"What's up?" Kaye asked, resting his hands on the counter.

"You're him, right?"

"I guess that would depend on who 'him' is."

"You know," she said, keeping her voice low and looking around. "USMC. Ben Kaye. The embassy guard that single-handedly stared down an entire mob and literally shook a bad guy to death to rescue the good guy they were about to torch. Right? I mean, I know I'm right. You're him."

"Guilty as charged," Kaye said.

"Guilty? Are you kidding me? Dude, you're a legend."

Kaye snorted.

"The brass didn't think so. I got bounced early for disobeying a direct order."

"Fuck that," Elizabeth said derisively. "Stanislav Petrov disobeyed orders and saved the entire planet."

"They teach you that in boot camp?" Kaye asked, smiling.

"Nah," she said, smiling back. "I had an intellectual Rot-Cee colonel in college. Thought we should study both sides of everything to improve our decision making skills on the battlefield. We studied your, uh, incident. You did the right thing. Just like Petrov."

"ROTC?" Kaye asked. "You were an officer?"

"Yeah, a Captain. But don't hold that against me."

"I'm confused. A Marine Corps Captain with eight years and you're the receptionist here? No offense, but…"

She laughed and said, "Today only. The regular girl called in sick, and we're thin today. I'm filling in."

"What's your regular job?"

"Anything they tell me to do, anywhere they tell me to do it."

"Anything?"

"Unless it qualifies under the Petrov-Kaye exception."

It was Kaye's turn to laugh. "Good to know."

Elizabeth looked around and lowered her voice even more.

"Watch your six, Marine."

Puzzled, Kaye looked at her.

"Friendly fire," she added, glancing toward Asia. "Shit happens."

"Thanks for the warning. Semper Fi."

"Oorah."

\*\*\*

Kaye swung by the station to do some research on Black Scimitar before going home.

He was surprised by the scope of their operations around the world and their reputation seemed solid. At least Gagnon hadn't exaggerated.

What surprised him, though, was how heavily Black Scimitar was involved in law enforcement training. They offered a full spectrum of advanced training options, and looked to be a major player in drug interdiction strategies and education.

He also dug into the company's IPO. Howell could've ordered a fleet of Ferraris had he wanted to.

Black Scimitar wasn't just a company. Howell had built an empire.

And obviously hadn't planned on dying.

# DAY 5
### Friday Week 1

One of the basic tenets of being a good investigator, at least in Kaye's mind, was that you didn't waste a lot of time running around like a headless chicken, asking a bunch of random people random questions you didn't already know the answers to. But sometimes, especially in the early stages of a case, you had no choice.

But amassing information, determining facts, then asking specific people specific questions you already knew the answers to, and listening to what they had to say, was much more efficient.

It was also absolutely the fastest way to separate the liars from the herd, and the best suspects always came from the outliers.

Kaye still felt mired in headless chicken mode. He needed information before he could determine who to seek out and what questions to ask.

He'd pick the low-hanging fruit first. He grabbed his desk phone, but before he had a chance to dial, heard someone call his name. He turned and saw one of the Police Assistants standing several feet away, a manila envelope in hand.

"What's up?" he asked.

"This came for you early this morning," the PA said. "I saw you come in, and…" He stepped closer and handed the envelope to Kaye, who tore it open, pulled out a single sheet of paper and scanned it before looking at the PA.

"Who brought this in?" he asked.

"I don't know," the PA said nervously. "I was just asked by the desk officer to deliver it to you."

"Okay," Kaye said. "Thanks."

The PA turned and left. Kaye picked up the phone and called downstairs to the desk.

"Officer Gastelo."

"Hey, Gastelo, it's Kaye. Who dropped off the envelope the PA just brought up to me?"

"A guy on a bicycle," Gastelo said. "I think he was probably a paid courier. Came in right after I took over the desk this morning. Why?"

"Just curious. Thanks," Kaye said and hung up.

He held the paper up again. It was covered in Japanese Kanji characters that he had no hope of deciphering. Grunting, he slid it to the back corner of his desk, reached for the phone again, had second thoughts about just calling, grabbed the Big Boar MC jacket and headed for the door.

Thirty minutes later Kaye rolled into the Beverly Hills Civic Center and headed for the Police Department building.

At the counter he showed his ID and asked to see Lieutenant Sarah Ross.

"Wait here," the desk sergeant said, then picked up the phone.

Five minutes later Ross, a tall redhead, opened the security door and stepped into the lobby.

"Well, as I live and breathe, Ben Kaye, right?" Ross said slowly. "I used to know an LAPD detective named Ben Kaye, but he just up and left town right after shooting somebody in one of our hotels. You know the guy?"

"Sarah, I'm really sorry," Kaye said.

"What do you want, Kaye?"

"Can we talk in private?" Kaye asked.

Ross spun on her heels and headed back into the inner sanctum. Kaye barely caught the door before it closed and followed Ross to her office.

"You've got a lot of nerve showing up here," she said after closing her office door behind Kaye, then turning and leaning against it, "and I don't suppose you're here to ask about getting together for a drink later so we can catch up, right?"

"Are you mad at me?" Kaye asked.

"Mad? Why would I be mad?" Ross said sarcastically. "You ask for my help in my city, I let you go solo, you go all cowboy on me, kill a guy with a diplomatic passport, then just disappear and leave me hanging."

"Didn't the State Department guys handle that for you?"

"With the press, yes. With my boss, not so much," Ross said. "I damn near lost my job, Kaye. If my Captain sees you in here today, he'll probably throw us both out, so make it quick and disappear again, okay?"

"I'm sorry. I had no idea," Kaye said, then explained what had happened with the Birnbaum case, the death of his father and his leave

68

of absence. "But I'm back to work," he concluded.

"And now you want something else from me, right?"

"Okay, yes. I need some traffic cam footage, if it's still available."

"Where and when?"

Kaye gave her the location and date. "I know it's been awhile, and I don't know how long you archive this stuff, but I'm interested in the time between twelve forty-five and two o'clock in the afternoon."

"What's this about?" Ross asked.

"Just trying to clear up a traffic thing that turned into a fatality, make sure all the ducks are in a row. You know how it is."

Ross, her lips tight and her head nodding slowly, stared at him.

"This is about the guy in the new Ferrari, isn't it?" she asked.

"Why do you ask?'

"Cut the bullshit, Ben. Is it, or isn't it?"

"Okay," Kaye said, "it's about the guy in the new Ferrari. You know about this?"

"Hell, yes, I know about it," Ross said. "The people at Ferrari drove me crazy trying to get me to open an investigation. They don't have local cops in Italy, just national, and it took me forever to get the concept of jurisdiction across to them. And that I had none. A concept, I might add, that even some people standing in my office right now have a hard time grasping."

"I said I was sorry. Can I make it up to you?"

"No," Ross said flatly. "Let's just move on, okay? Back to your traffic cam footage. I'm sorry, but we don't archive that far back."

"Hey, it was worth a try," Kaye said. "And, Sarah, I really am sorry I caused you grief. Call me if you ever need anything, even if it's just a drink, okay?"

She opened the door. "See ya."

He'd gone about fifteen feet when he heard Ross's voice.

"Kaye. Get back in here."

He turned and walked back into Ross's office. She closed the door behind him again.

"You get a freebie on this one because of your father," she said.

"I didn't know. I thought you just left me hanging."

"Never."

"Okay," Ross said, finally sitting down at her desk. "Let's talk about the Ferrari thing. Why are you looking at it? I thought it was a closed issue. Death caused by trauma and burns resulting from a single vehicle traffic accident."

69

Kaye ran it down for her, including his talk with Mark Edler and visit to the dealer.

"You're buying what this Edler guy is selling?" Ross asked, clearly skeptical.

"I don't know," Kaye said. "But I do know that if I don't check it out, I'll lose sleep over it."

"You're looking for a white…what did you call it? Hayabusa?"

"That was the plan, but without the video it's a dead end."

There was a brief silence before Ross spoke again.

"I have the traffic cam video."

"You do?" Kaye asked. "Where?"

"On my computer," Ross replied.

"Why?"

"Ferrari was being such a pain in the ass I got it to cover mine," Ross said. "I tracked the car all the way from the dealer to the city limits. Howell left *my* city alive, going northeast on Santa Monica Boulevard."

"I don't supposed you got the license number and registered owner's name for the white Hayabusa I think was following him?"

Ross laughed. "Ben, I know shit about motorcycles. Plus, I wasn't looking for anything but the Ferrari."

"Send me the video, will you?" Kaye asked.

"I can't," Ross said. "If my boss found out I'd be lucky to get a job working parking lot security at Dodger Stadium. But I can let you look at it here. Besides, it'll be faster. I've already gone through it and created a location and time stamp log."

While Ross brought the video file up on her computer, Kaye mentally ran through the geography. He'd ridden the Mulholland crest too many times to count. There were occasional cross streets from residential areas, and several of the 'Canyon' roads created major intersections, but he discounted most of those as being too far west.

A guy with a new Ferrari wants to be seen.

If Howell had been eastbound on Santa Monica and ended up at the crash site, where scuffs indicated he'd been westbound, there were multiple ways to get up the hill. But he most likely would have passed the intersection of Sunset and Crescent Heights. Even if he'd gone farther east, he'd have gone through Laurel Canyon and Mulholland coming back west.

He knew there had to be cameras.

"Okay, ready," Ross said.

Kaye dragged a chair around the desk and sat down next to Ross. She started the video. It wasn't more than a few seconds before she paused it.

"There's your guy," she said, pointing at the red Ferrari on the screen, "northbound on the east end of the block from the dealership." The time stamp read 13:11:53, in line with what Anthony had related to Kaye on his visit to the dealership.

Ross started the video again. Just before the light cycled, a white motorcycle, the rider in full leathers and a tinted, full-face helmet, accelerated across Wilshire and continued north, behind the Ferrari. She hit pause again.

"Is that a Hayabusa?"

"It is," Kaye said, leaning in to get a closer view. "And based on this I'd say the rider is no more than about five-seven or five-eight."

"Could it be a woman?" Ross asked.

"Could be, I guess. I have no reason to think male or female one way or the other yet. Keep going."

Ross started the video again. This time she just let it run and they watched the recorded camera intervals she'd saved for each intersection. At every one within the Beverly Hills city limits the Ferrari would appear first, then the Hayabusa. On one occasion the bike had run a red light to keep up. Several cameras captured clear images of the bike's license plate.

"Can you run the plate number?" Kaye asked.

"Stand by," Ross replied, clicking out of the video and running the plate. "Okay, that's not good. It's been in the system as stolen for over six months."

"The bike, or just the plate?"

"Just the plate," she said, peering closer at the screen. "Reported to the Santa Maria P.D."

"Thanks, Sarah," Kaye said, standing. "I really am sorry I caused you so much grief. I certainly didn't intend to."

"Like I said, free pass because of your dad. My condolences on his passing."

Kaye went back to the Road King and pondered his next move, again running the geography through his head.

His next call was to the city's Department of Transportation. He'd worked closely with them during his time as a motor officer, but that had been a few years ago.

Things had changed. After dealing with the confusing voice menu and being transferred three times only to be hung up on, he called the West Traffic Division instead. Five minutes later, armed with a name and extension number, he called LADOT back and navigated the electronic menu until he was asked to enter an extension number.

"This is Clarence."

Kaye identified himself and explained what he was looking for, and Clarence immediately told him they didn't keep footage that long.

"But hold on a minute," Clarence added. "There's something about Laurel Canyon and Mulholland from right around then that sticks in my mind."

Kaye was put on hold before he could say anything, and stayed there for two minutes.

"It's your lucky day, Detective," Clarence said when he finally came back on.

"How so?"

"There was a fatality at that intersection two days after the day you're looking for. Your traffic people were pretty sure there would be some sort of charges, so they asked us to preserve the footage. Your day might be on it, too."

"You're not sure?" Kaye asked.

"Not a hundred percent," Clarence said. "The drives are usually rotated every seven or eight days, but this one is now out of the rotation. It'll depend on the timing."

"I see," Kaye said. "What do I need to do to get the drive?"

Clarence explained that the drive, as potential evidence, was now subject to chain of custody protocols, and he wasn't responsible for that. Kaye would have to wait for the designated custodian to pull the drive, review it to see if what Kaye wanted was on it, and, if it was, make a copy for Kaye.

"How long will that take?" Kaye asked.

"If it's there, you should have it by the middle of next week, but we'll let you know either way."

"That'll work," Kaye said.

Clarence confirmed the date and time frame Kaye wanted before ending the call.

***

Back in the squad room, Kaye grabbed the phone and called the District Attorney's office. Two minutes later he was talking to ADA

Kayla Okafor, explaining the circumstances of the Geller murder and that he needed access to Geller's financials related to the possible real estate deal.

"Sorry, Detective," Okafor said when Kaye finished. "You're going to need a lot more than that to compel Feinmann to turn anything over. There's no evidence of any sort of nexus at this point. If he won't turn them over voluntarily, you're out of luck. But can I ask you a question?"

"Sure."

"Why not go to Mrs. Geller?"

"Feinmann made it clear I was supposed to work through him."

"Is Mrs. Geller a suspect?"

"No," Kaye said. "There's nothing that points to her."

"Then she has no right to presence of counsel or any other shield from the police," Okafor said. "Feinmann is over stepping by telling you not to talk to her directly. Besides, you're not looking for actual financials, right? You just want the names of the project and maybe the other parties involved."

"Right," Kaye said. "The problem is that Mrs. Geller claims to have no knowledge of this, so she doesn't even know what to look for."

"You want my advice?"

"That's why I called."

"Just be your inimitable self, Detective. Call Ziva Geller, or Feinmann, and ask them to examine the financial records and just give you the information so you can catch Avi Geller's killer. Light a fire and see which way the smoke blows."

Kaye laughed and said, "Thanks, Counselor. I'll take it under advisement."

He leaned back again, pondering what Okafor had suggested. It was good advice, but he still struggled with asking Ziva Geller for information she claimed, and he believed, she knew nothing about.

He needed to sprinkle some bread crumbs on the trail, something to give her as a starting point.

Fifty million dollars.

And that was just Avi Geller's buy in. No telling how big the project – if there was a project – really was.

Kaye snorted, leaned forward and spun to face his computer monitor.

Nobody spends that kind of money, at least legally, without

causing a splash. Find out where the ground is wet and go from there.

Ziva Geller had said 'north of Santa Barbara' when she'd mentioned the project. The problem was that most people, even most Californians, would assume that meant toward San Francisco, when the coastline between Point Concepcion and Carpinteria actually runs east-west before swinging southeast toward Ventura. 'North of Santa Barbara' was mountainous National Forest terrain.

Kaye went with the best assumption. It took him twenty minutes to compile a list of phone numbers, and he started calling.

First on the list was the Coastal Commission. He asked about any recent or pending applications for large developments, or any in progress in Ventura, Santa Barbara or San Luis Obispo Counties.

They assured him there was nothing on the scale he was describing.

Then he started with the municipalities in Ventura County. They all told him they had nothing in the pipeline that came close to his description. Ventura County was next, and that, too, was a blank.

He moved on the Santa Barbara County.

He came up dry with the City Halls.

He dialed the County and was connected to the Planning Commission offices.

A woman answered and identified herself as Alicia Valdez.

"Ms. Valdez, my name is Ben Kaye. I'm a detective with the LAPD." He gave her his badge number and a call back number for verification.

"What can I do for you?"

"I'm investigating a homicide that occurred here in Los Angeles. One of the unknowns I'm trying to track down involves a big real estate project, maybe a resort, somewhere in the central coast area. I'm trying to determine where the project is and who the principals are."

"Not much to go on," Valdez said.

"I know, and I'm sorry," Kaye said. "All I really know is that it's a large project and I'm guessing they would have submitted plans and proposals at least a couple years, maybe longer, ago."

"We haven't had anything big and new in the recent past," she said. "Most work around here lately has been rebuilding and updating after the fires and floods, and that's mostly been inside the cities."

"So there's nothing? Maybe even a little farther back?"

"Well, there was Valle delle Viti, but that application dates back almost four years. In fact, they opened for business earlier this year."

"Valle delle Viti?"

"In English it's Valley of the Vines."

"Something to do with wine?"

"Yes, it's a wine-themed resort and spa, with golf and tennis, stuff like that."

"Where is it?" Kaye asked.

"Southeast of Santa Ynez, on the north end of the Village of Chumash Oaks."

"I've never heard of Chumash Oaks."

"That's because the town is also brand, spanking new. Incorporated while the resort was under construction."

"You said the resort is open for business?"

"Yes," Valdez confirmed.

"Do you remember anything unusual about the project?"

She laughed. "Detective Kaye, this would be a lot shorter conversation if you asked me what was usual about Valle delle Viti."

"There were problems?"

"I wouldn't necessarily characterize them as problems," Valdez said. "I mean, the developers followed all the rules, but a lot of people, including me, didn't care much their methods. They got whatever they wanted, whenever they asked, and they got it fast. Somebody was obviously very well connected. Rumors swirled around the County economic development consultant, but nothing ever came of them. He was out of it, anyway, after Chumash Oaks was incorporated and their internal planning staff took control of the project."

"You didn't see it through to the end?"

"No. We surrendered jurisdiction once The Village of Chumash Oaks became a legal entity. We helped them if they called, and answered questions if they asked them, but we had no control."

"Have you visited?"

"Yes."

"And?"

"Oh, it's fabulous," Valdez said. "As an architect and planner I only wish I had the resources and opportunity to do that kind of work. The wine is already gaining an international reputation."

"I sense another 'but'," Kaye said.

"I guess it just depends on whether you think the ends always justifies the means."

"They were shady?"

"I wouldn't call them shady," Valdez replied, "and I didn't mean to give you that impression. They met every deadline, complied with all our changes and revisions requests, all the financial disclosure rules, stuff like that. Still, well, I guess the best comparison I can make is that a circus lion may do all the tricks it's told to do, but, bottom line, he's still the top of the food chain in that cage, if you know what I mean."

"Got it," Kaye said. "Who were the developers?"

"The company was called Valle delle Viti, same as the project name, but I have no idea who the principals were. I never met them. Whenever we had meetings or public hearings it was always architects and engineers that showed up. And lawyers. Always at least two lawyers, even if they just sat and listened."

"Is that normal?"

"The architects and engineers, yes," Valdez said. "The lawyers? No. I think they were just there to remind us civil servants who the lion in the room was."

"Interesting perspective," Kaye said. "Would it be okay if I called you again if I needed something else?"

"Sure," Valdez said. "I'm in the field a lot, so let me give you my cell number, too."

***

After concluding his call with Alicia Valdez, Kaye did an on-line search for Valle delle Viti.

The website was impressive, replete with photos of guests enjoying the available accommodations, restaurants and activities. He went to the reservations interface to check availability and was surprised to find the hotel completely booked through the end of the year.

If Avi Geller had put fifty million into Valle delle Viti, it might have been a wise investment.

Kaye had run many investigations rooted in fraud and bad investments, but good investments usually led to clinking glasses and bonhomie all the way around, not murder.

Unless something had gone wrong.

Then again, Avi Geller might not have a single dollar invested in Valle delle Viti. He needed more.

He called Patty Phillips.

"What's up, detective?"

"Can you track down everything you can for me on a place called

Valle delle Viti? It's a new resort not far from Santa Barbara, in a place called Village of Chumash Oaks. I specifically need as much as you can get on the legal aspects of the place; who owns it, where the money came from, contractors, stuff like that."

"Gee, sounds like it might take a visit up there on the Department expense account to gather all that."

Kaye laughed and said, "Nice try."

"Hey, if you don't ask, you don't receive, right?" she said, chuckling. "But, yeah, I can do that. The State should have those records. It might take a while, though. When do you need it?"

"Yesterday."

It was Patty's turn to laugh. "It's good to have you back, Detective."

Kaye checked the time, then punched in an outside number.

The call to Howard Feinmann's office went straight to voice mail.

Hey, he thought, I tried.

He dialed Ziva Geller's home number. She answered.

"Mrs. Geller, Detective Kaye. I wanted –"

"Howard told you not to call me," she interrupted.

"No, he didn't," Kaye said. "He asked me to work through him, and I tried. Tell him to answer his phone."

Silence.

"I'm not answering any questions," she said after a moment.

"That's fine," Kaye said. "I didn't call to ask you any questions. I called to pass along some information."

More silence.

"I think," Kaye went on, "the real estate deal your husband was involved in was probably a place called Valle delle Viti. It's past Santa Barbara up in the wine country, and it opened this past spring."

"So it was legit?" Ziva asked. "Why are you telling me this?"

"It's very successful. If your husband was an investor, maybe even a partner, well, with California being a community property state, I'm sure you can draw your own conclusions. I just thought you might appreciate a tip on what to look for in your husband's financial records."

"Thank you, Detective."

"And Mrs. Geller?"

"Yes?"

"If you find it, I'd appreciate a call."

"I'll see what I can do. Good-bye."

Kaye leaned back and smiled.

The profit motive was such a wonderful thing.

***

Kaye spent another hour brainstorming possible leads on Avi Geller's murder and Leigh Howell's fatal crash.

He was frustrated with the delays in getting information, but knew there was nothing he could do about it. It was the nature of the beast.

He was packing it in for the day when an e-mail notification pop-up on his monitor caught his eye.

It was from Arch.

> *Kaye,*
>
> *No final transcriptions or toxicology on Geller or Jane Doe until next week, but the posts are done.*
>
> *Thought you'd like to know the bullets were badly fragmented, so no chance of ballistics. But based on entry wounds and penetration depths 99% probability they were .223 or 5.56x45 like we thought. Can't tell for sure without the cartridge headstamp. As I'm sure you know, you can fire a .223 from a 5.56 chamber, but not the other way around.*
>
> *Sorry I can't nail it down any more than that.*
>
> *Arch*
>
> *P.S. Jane Doe had needle marks between her toes. Won't know what she used until tox comes back. Maybe a pro?*

The P.S. got Kaye's attention.

It lent credence to Ziva Geller's statement about her husband's sudden penchant for prostitutes.

He downloaded the crime scene photos from his phone to his computer and found the facial shot of Jane Doe.

She didn't look like a wholesome country girl, but she didn't look like a street-corner working girl, either, if one could draw such conclusions from a couple of photos of a corpse. But the high-priced call girls weren't usually addicts. There were exceptions of course, but the tracks between the toes gave him a starting point.

It took him a few minutes to compose an e-mail to the Vice and Missing Persons units, asking for their help in identifying Jane Doe. He included the few particulars he had, attached the photos, and clicked 'Send'.

He thought it was a longshot, but it was due diligence.

On the way out he grabbed the Kanji note and stuffed it in his pocket.

# DAY 6
Saturday Week 1

Kaye hadn't anticipated how tough the first weekend would be.

Going back to work had definitely cured the boredom problem, but he wasn't on the shift schedule, or on call, for Saturday or Sunday.

Hilliard, just back to duty, had drawn that assignment this week, and complained about it.

And while Kaye could work off the clock, Captain Thompson wasn't a fan of the concept.

By 10:00 a.m. he had practiced for an hour, cleaned up, fed himself and was sitting on the patio with a cup of tea while he watched the sailboats off Marina del Rey.

And chafing at his idleness.

He needed to take a ride. But, to where?

He thought about cruising out to the Rock Shop, a popular weekend destination for local bikers, but on Saturday the place would be mobbed and he wasn't in the mood to deal with crowds.

Patty's off-hand comment about visiting Valle delle Viti crossed his mind and inspiration struck. He'd take the new bike. It wouldn't exactly be working off the clock, but it might be productive. And he wouldn't put in an expense voucher. He was pretty sure he could swing it.

He drained his cup and headed inside to get ready. On the way out he grabbed the Big Boar jacket and zipped his badge and ID into the inside pocket.

***

Kaye rode Pacific Coast Highway to Oxnard, picked up the 101 North and just before one o'clock took the San Marcos Pass exit and headed into the hills on CA 154; the back way to Santa Ynez.

He was almost to the dam at Lake Cachuma when he passed a sign announcing the City Limits of the Village of Chumash Oaks, population 2,317. Twenty yards beyond that was a sign informing motorists that traffic laws were strictly enforced, and ten yards beyond that the speed limit dropped from 65 mph to 25 mph.

Kaye rolled off the throttle, stayed off the brakes and started working down through the gears to bleed off speed. It took a couple hundred yards to settle in at twenty-five.

A quarter-mile later he saw a police car, a black Dodge Charger with a push bumper and large, round driving lights in the grill, its light bar and grill lights flashing, coming up fast from behind.

"No way," he muttered under his breath as he drifted the bike to the right shoulder and stopped.

He shut down, and was in the process of removing his helmet when he heard a voice on a loudspeaker.

"Stay on the motorcycle, and keep your hands where I can see them."

Kaye complied. A shadow in his peripheral vision caught his attention and he started to turn to take a look.

"Eyes front, Mr. Big Boar MC," the cop growled. "Don't you look at me until I tell you to."

"Look, officer, I'm –"

"Shut your mouth," the cop commanded. "You speak when you're spoken to. Got it?"

Okay, Kaye thought, let's see how big an asshole you can make of yourself before I tell you I'm a cop.

"Yes, sir," was all he said.

A minute passed before Kaye saw another patrol unit coming fast from the west

It was a Ford SUV, and slowed as it went by. Kaye saw the 'K-9' sticker on the back side window. It stopped on the opposite shoulder and waited for a westbound car to pass before making a u-turn and pulling in behind the Charger.

Kaye heard a door slam and the crunch of gravel as a second officer approached.

"What've you got, Reid?" the new arrival asked.

"Flagrant exhibition of speed," the first officer replied. "Fifty-eight in a twenty-five, and illegal passing."

"I didn't pass –" Kaye started to say.

"I told you," Reid said, stepping into Kaye's field of vision. "You speak when you're spoken to."

Reid was tall and lanky, and Kaye's first impression was that the man was a bad caricature of a cop in a B-movie, complete with mirrored sunglasses and black leather gloves on a warm day.

His badge said Chumash Oaks Police. Sewn above the Department patches on both shirt sleeves was an unusually shaped rocker reading 'Special Officer'.

"I'm just trying –" Kaye said before Reid cut him off again.

"Trying what? Trying to talk your way out of jail?"

Kaye turned and stared at Reid's sunglasses.

"Oh, I'm not going to jail," he said, his voice low.

In a half-second Reid's pistol was out of its holster and pointed squarely at Kaye.

"You'll go to jail if I decide to take you to jail," the cop snarled. "Hawkins, get Titus."

Kaye again heard gravel crunch as the second officer walked away. Seconds later he heard a dog panting and whining as Hawkins returned.

"Go over the bike," Reid said.

Kaye sat quietly as Hawkins coaxed the dog, a large Shepherd breed, to sniff at the bike's saddlebags. Then the dog sat down and whined.

"Well, look at that, would you?" Reid said. "What's in the saddlebags, biker boy?"

"Nothing that should interest the dog."

"Really, now," Reid said. "Keep him going, Hawk."

Hawkins tugged the dog away from the saddlebags and in only a few seconds he sniffed Kaye's left pants pocket, sat down, and whined again.

"How much cash you got in your pocket?" Reid asked.

"None of your business," Kaye said.

"You'd like to think so, wouldn't you, biker boy," Reid said. "Hawk, search the saddlebags."

Hawkins led the dog back out of Kaye's field of vision.

"You have no probable cause to search the saddlebags," Kaye said. "If you're going to write me a speeding ticket, do it. I've got places to go and you're wasting my time."

"Oh, a jail house lawyer, are we?" Reid taunted. "We have a positive indicator from a trained and certified drug detection canine. That's all I need. So I'll ask you again, what's in the saddlebags?"

Kaye stared at Reid and just shook his head.

"They're locked," Hawkins announced.

"Are you going to open them," Reid asked Kaye, "or do I have to break them? Because right now I have enough, based on Titus there, to seize your motorcycle and all the cash on you, and that's what I'm going to do if you don't open those saddlebags. It's called civil asset forfeiture of criminal proceeds."

Kaye had had enough.

"I'm a cop, you moron. Detective Ben Kaye, Los Angeles Police Department. The only thing in my saddlebags is a change of clothes and an overnight kit. You need a new dog."

"Sure you're a cop," Reid said, his voice not quite as confident. The muzzle of his pistol dropped slightly. "You got your ID on you?"

"My badge and ID are in my inside left jacket pocket," Kaye said. "That's what I was trying to tell you while you were busy being Buford T. Justice."

"Hawk," Reid said, "check his jacket pocket." Then he asked Kaye, "Are you armed?"

"Not today."

Hawkins commanded Titus to stay, then walked to Kaye's left side.

"Keep your hands on the handlebars," he ordered Kaye.

"No problem," Kaye said. "Left side."

Seconds later, Hawkins held up Kaye's badge and ID card for Reid to see.

"Shit fire," Reid muttered, then said to Hawkins, "Keep an eye on him. I'm calling the Lieutenant."

Reid holstered his pistol and headed for his patrol car.

"What's his problem?" Kaye asked Hawkins.

"He's just doing his job."

"No, he's not. I do the job, too, but not like that."

Hawkins handed Kaye back his badge and ID and said, "Probably your jacket. We had our first homicide in the department's history last week and there was information that some bikers flying colors were involved."

"Okay," Kaye said. "That I get. But your speed trap is a joke."

Hawkins just shrugged and said, "Generates revenue."

Kaye heard gravel crunch again and turned to see Reid, his face flushed, headed toward them.

"Lieutenant says we should cut him loose," Reid said, ignoring Kaye and addressing Hawkins. "Guy's got no balls."

Kaye resisted the impulse to make a comment about the value of balls versus brains.

"How do I get to the Valle delle Viti resort?" he asked Hawkins instead.

Hawkins gave him directions. It wasn't far.

"Thanks," he said, then turned to Reid. "Find another line of work."

"Fuck you," Reid said as he turned and walked toward his patrol car.

"Keep your speed down," was all Hawkins said before he, too, walked away, Titus tight against his left knee.

Kaye waited until both cops cleared before firing up the Harley.

He had no tolerance for police officers like Reid, and briefly considered stopping at the Chumash Oaks PD to talk to the Lieutenant with brains, but no balls. But he dismissed the idea as pointless. Technically, he had been speeding, as he was sure everybody who passed the 25 mph sign was. If Reid had been professional about it and written him a ticket, he would have just written a check and mailed it in.

His mood didn't improve when, a half-mile down the road, the speed limit went back up to fifty.

***

Kaye followed Hawkins' directions, turning off the highway some two miles later onto Da Vinci Lane. The road began to trend uphill and in the distance he could see what appeared to be the upper levels of a large structure rising above the hilltops ahead.

The first sign he was in the right place was acres and acres of carefully tended grape vines. Kaye was no wine enthusiast, but to him the vines looked well-established for an operation so recent, and it crossed his mind that for a population of just over two thousand, Chumash Oaks covered a lot of square miles.

After a few miles of rolling countryside covered with vines he rounded the shoulder of a hill and found himself face-to-face with the Village of Chumash Oaks. There had been no outskirts, no ramshackle metal buildings surrounded by dead cars trying to hide in tall weeds. No abandoned, two-pump gas stations, their rusted signs touting brands long gone since the 1950s. No long-neglected, caving in shacks from the post-war era, trees now growing through their leaning chain link fences.

The Village of Chumash Oaks was suddenly just there.

And it was stunningly beautiful, instantly giving Kaye the feeling he'd ridden into a 17th Century Tuscan village.

Except the patina of fake age had been applied a little too liberally.

Da Vinci Lane was surfaced with asphalt. It snaked through the hills, the cobble-stone paved cross streets coming in when topography allowed. They also all bore Italian names, were all one-way, and all wide enough for only one car to pass through. Preference was clearly given to pedestrians. There was a total absence of traffic signs and pavement markings, forcing drivers to proceed slowly and cautiously, and twice Kaye saw small signs pointing to parking.

Many of the Da Vinci Lane crossings opened into narrow, pedestrian-only walkways, and arched stone bridges over the roadway were also plentiful. Everywhere, buildings pressed close to the streets and pathways, and flags and banners advertising many of the same retailers Kaye knew from Rodeo Drive were rampant.

The town center was a large traffic circle surrounding a decent-sized park, its center occupied by a large fountain that resembled the work of Michelangelo.

Kaye kept going, toward the large structure he'd seen from a distance, idly wondering why he'd never heard of this place.

A few minutes later Da Vinci Lane curved under the canopy of the native oak forest and climbed steeply. When Kaye emerged from the trees he found himself at another roundabout.

Across the circle, stone ramparts reminiscent of medieval times loomed over the landscape. On the left side of the road, the words Valle delle Viti were carved into the stone, and on the right was carved L'Abergo. The Hotel. Beneath and between the carvings a tunnel, blocked by a heavy metal gate operated by a keypad and monitored by video cameras, disappeared into the earth.

Kaye's eyes naturally followed the imposing stone ramparts toward the sky and he saw the hotel, designed to resemble a medieval castle, perched atop them. The only giveaways of its modern construction were lots of glass and a multitude of balconies.

He noticed discreet wooden signs; one pointing left to 'CA 154', and one pointing right that read 'Hotel Guests.'

Kaye went right. The road gradually curved away from the ramparts and went downhill, back into the oak forest.

When he again emerged from the trees he saw a stone gatehouse ahead. A single barrier wooden gate barred the way. Beyond the gate he could see another tunnel, this one obviously the entrance to an underground parking structure.

He rolled up to the gate and stopped.

"Name, please," the uniformed guard said politely.

"Ben Kaye."

The guard turned to a computer terminal and studied it momentarily.

"I'm sorry, Mr. Kaye, you're not on the list."

"The list?"

"Yes, sir," the guard said. "Only hotel guests and their accompanied visitors are allowed inside the ramparts."

"Seriously?" Kaye asked. "I can't just go in and look around?"

"No, sir. I'm sorry. Not on a Saturday."

"Pretty mysterious."

"It's not meant to be," the guard said. "The first couple of months we were open there were so many visitors that hotel guests could barely get in and out, or find a table for a meal. Access restriction became an unanticipated necessity to preserve the guest experience."

"Not to mention the exclusivity factor."

The guard smiled and said, "There is that, too."

"I tried to book a room. You were full."

"Yes, sir. We're booked solid through the grape harvest and the holidays."

"Must be nice," Kaye said. "How do I get out of here?"

"You can turn around here and go back up the hill to the traffic circle," the guard said. "If you take Da Vinci it takes you back to town, where there are plenty of things to do and places to eat. If you go straight across it'll take you around town to the west and back to the highway."

Kaye thanked the guard and turned around. At the roundabout he stopped and watched a tram packed with people emerge from the tunnel under the hotel and head into town. He opted to go straight. The road did bypass the town center, and Kaye soon saw the reason why. It was clearly the access for commercial vehicles and deliveries to the stores and restaurants in the town center, and probably the hotel. But the design was pure genius. The designers had built artificial hills between the road and the town, then built short tunnels penetrating those barriers so only smaller trucks and vans could get through. No oversized trucks could get into town.

A mile after reaching the highway and turning toward Santa Ynez, Kaye slowed for flashing emergency lights a quarter-mile ahead. Two police vehicles had a car pulled over and the car's trunk was open.

Officer Reid had the driver out of the car while Hawkins directed

Titus in a search.

Kaye shook his head, twisted the throttle and continued on.

\*\*\*

Kaye's plan was to take CA 246 west, cut through Santa Ynez and Solvang, pick up the 101 in Buellton, then head home.

But he'd eaten early, and as he rolled into Santa Ynez he started looking for a place to get some lunch.

A mile on he spotted a sign for 'Auggie's Wine'N'Diner' and decided to try it. The diner occupied the end space in a strip mall, and the parking lot was jammed with motorcycles. He found a place to park and headed for the door. Parked on the sidewalk outside was a newer, blue Harley CVO Street Glide, and he stopped for a moment to admire it.

When he stepped into Auggie's he was transported back to the 1950s. The floor was checkerboard black and white linoleum. The twenty or so booths were upholstered in red leather. The dozen or so tables and their chairs all had stainless steel legs, with the cushions upholstered to match the booths. Every booth and table in the place had a mottled Formica top, banded with ribbed stainless steel. Some were red, some green, some blue. The sound of Bobby Darin singing 'Dream Lover' filled the space.

Along the back wall Kaye saw what he thought was an old soda fountain behind a bar that matched the tables and chairs. But a closer look revealed beer taps and shelves lined with wine bottles.

And the place was packed.

"May I help you," the bright-eyed young lady stationed just inside the door asked expectantly.

"Looking for some lunch," Kaye replied as he scanned the space.

"I don't have a table right now," she said, "but I think there's one empty stool down at the far end of the bar."

"Can I eat at the bar?"

"Sure," she said. "Here's a menu."

Kaye wound his way through the crowded space. Almost everyone in the diner was wearing biker garb and a lot of them turned to check out the Big Boar jacket as he walked by.

There was one empty stool. Kaye grabbed it and pulled it around the end of the bar so he had a view of the entire restaurant, nodding politely to the leather-clad couple sitting on the next two stools.

"What can I get you?" the bartender asked. She was tall and deeply tanned, her dark hair swept haphazardly up onto her head and pinned with what looked like a knitting needle, exposing her clip- and piercing-laden ear. A black tank top showed off some impressive ink from her left shoulder down to the elbow.

"Iced tea," Kaye said, loudly to be heard over the crowd. "And do I order food from you?"

She smiled and made an exaggerated effort to look back over both shoulders before looking back at Kaye.

"See anybody else?"

Kaye smiled back and said, "I do not."

"Is that iced tea regular, or Long Island?"

"Regular, please, and a club sandwich."

"Fries, chips, or pasta salad?"

"Nothing else," Kaye said. "I'm watching my girlish figure."

She laughed and said, "Mister, you're about the least girly-looking man I've ever seen. But you got it."

She spun around, and a moment later returned with Kaye's drink.

"Auggie, we'll take our check," the man two stools down said after she'd put the iced tea down.

Kaye heard and realized the woman was the owner.

"Coming right up," Auggie said.

She delivered the check, thanked the couple for coming in and told them it was always nice to see them, then turned to Kaye.

"Your sandwich will be right out."

"No hurry."

Over the next ten minutes the place almost emptied out, and Kaye figured the bikes outside were a club ride, with Auggie's their destination.

"Here you go," Auggie said, laying a plate almost covered with a giant sandwich in front of Kaye.

"Thank you."

"My pleasure. Enjoy," she said, then pointed at Kaye's tea glass. "Refill?"

"Sure."

She returned with a pitcher and topped off Kaye's glass.

"So," she said, studying Kaye, "you looking for a slot for your club?"

"Excuse me?"

"I saw your colors. Never heard of the Big Boar MC, and you're by yourself." She paused and looked at the expression on Kaye's face. "Sorry, I think I just made a bad assumption."

"No need to apologize," Kaye said. "But I don't have a clue what you mean."

Auggie laughed heartily. "A time slot," she explained. "Like a reservation, you know, for your club to come in."

"You have a schedule?"

"Damn right," she said, leaning on the bar. "Had to. I opened about two years ago. Word got around the place was biker friendly and pretty soon we were totally mobbed on weekends. Way more people than I could handle, fights in the parking lot, shit like that.

"You know – well, maybe you don't, I don't know – most of these guys are suits during the week," she went on. "On weekends they gear up and pretend they're Marlon fucking Brando. The cops told me they were gonna shut me down, so I had to do something. I got all the club honchos together and we worked out a schedule. It rotates, so everybody gets a time slot, everybody gets a seat, everybody eats and drinks with their friends. Voila, no conflicts, no more fights, everybody's happy, and everybody makes new friends."

"And you stay busy?"

"We're pretty much slammed from about noon Friday until closing time Sunday, and steady the rest of the time," she said, nodding and drawing Kaye's attention to the front door.

Kaye looked, and saw four more bikers coming through the front door and two dozen more in the process of parking out front.

"Excuse me," Auggie said, standing up straight and turning toward the door. "Hey, Kurt, Tiffany," she shouted. "Welcome back. The usual?"

"Yep," the man yelled back. "That Ohana pinot if you've still got it."

"Coming right up," Auggie said. She grabbed a bottle from under the bar, put it on a platter with two red wine glasses and set the lot on the service bar. Then she came back to Kaye.

"You sell wine to bikers?" he asked.

"Hell, yeah," she said, grinning. "By the barrel. Technically, I guess you'd say I sell wine to the suits I was telling you about. But I only sell the really good boutique stuff, you know? You can't buy anything on our list at any liquor store in Los Angeles. A few really good restaurants, but not many. I also have a club, if you'd like to sign up."

"I'm impressed," Kaye said, and he meant it. "Mind if I hang around?"

"Not at all. I'm Auggie McMaster." She extended her hand across the bar.

Kaye took it and said, "Johnny Strabler."

"Nice try, Marlon," she said, giving Kaye the eye and holding onto his hand. "That's my favorite movie of all time."

"Ben Kaye."

"That I buy," Auggie said, letting go. "Stick around, Ben Kaye with the giant handshake. I'll be busy for a bit getting everybody what they want to drink, then it'll be less crazy…well, maybe a little…for a while, anyway."

Kaye watched Auggie's Wine'N'Diner fill almost to capacity over the next ten minutes. Only the two stools around the corner of the bar from him remained vacant. Almost all the new patrons wore the same club patches supporting Jesus on their jackets or vests.

It was frantic, but Kaye could tell it was a practiced routine and everybody was having a great time. The servers and patrons all seemed to be acquainted and he overheard conversations about families, progress at school, kids and other topics of familiarity and common friendship.

He finished his sandwich and nursed his tea, seeing that Auggie was much too busy to interrupt.

After about twenty minutes Auggie approached, pitcher in hand.

"Want a refill? Or maybe you'd like to try a glass of something? On the house."

Kaye thought for a moment before saying, "Do you have any of the Valle delle Viti wine?"

Auggie's eyes went cold and her jaw clenched as her expression hardened.

"I don't sell their wine."

Kaye caught the anger in her voice.

"I'm sorry. Did I say something wrong?"

"No, you're okay," she said, her expression softening. "It's not your problem, it's mine."

"Care to tell me about it?"

"Nope," she said curtly, then turned to walk away. She took three steps, then spun and came back.

"They stole my vines," she said. "I hate those bastards."

"You're a wine maker?"

"I am," she said, leaning over and lowering her voice. "I had forty acres of my own grapes. It was leased and had mature pinot and chardonnay vines on it. I was slowly replacing some of them with my own choices of clones and was starting to make some pretty good stuff when those assholes stole them."

"I still don't understand," Kaye said. "How does someone steal grape vines?"

"In a court room."

"Oh," Kaye said. "What happened?"

"I was about six years into a twenty year lease on my acreage, with an option for forty more acres," Auggie replied. "Valle delle Viti wanted to buy my lessor's property and all his vines, but he wouldn't sell. So you know what those fuckers did? They used eminent domain to steal that land, and those vines, for forty cents on the dollar."

"Wait a minute," Kaye said. "Eminent domain?"

"Yep. The courts can now take your property and give it to somebody else for a price they set just because the other guy claims he'll do better with it than you're doing. It's a giant economic development scam."

"I had no idea," Kaye said. "But you had a lease, right?"

"I did," Auggie said. "I fought them for almost a year. But I couldn't afford to keep fighting their army of lawyers, so I lost. They got my land, my vines, and six years of hard work."

"But they had to pay you, right?"

"Nope. Their lawyers argued that they had already paid for the land when they paid my lessor. The court agreed and told me my only recourse was to sue the lessor for abrogation of the lease terms."

"Did you?"

"I didn't have the money to pay another lawyer," Auggie said. "Plus, I just didn't have the heart."

Kaye looked at her, but didn't have to ask.

"I leased from a guy named Bud Richards. After Valle delle Viti took his life's work, Bud gave up. Took his own life. I couldn't bring myself to go after his kids. I just couldn't do it." She looked around and saw three servers waiting at the service bar. "Gotta get back to work. Nice meeting you, Ben Kaye. Bring that girlish figure back around any time."

"One quick question?" Kaye asked.

"Uh, sure."

"Who's behind Valle delle Viti?"

"I have no idea. Only people I ever saw were their fucking lawyers."

She tapped her hand on the edge of the bar twice, smiled, and turned back to business.

Kaye nursed his iced tea and watched while Auggie took orders from several customers for wine club shipments. She dealt with her employees like a benevolent Drill Sergeant, if such a thing exists, and she treated her customers like royalty. She hadn't brought him a check and he didn't want to interrupt her, so he pulled three twenties off the cash in his pocket and laid them on the bar, used a napkin to wipe the condensation off the tea glass and put it down on top of the bills.

Outside, the next group of bikers looking to be wined and dined was already starting to trickle in.

He sat on the Road King and considered what Auggie had told him. He remembered his conversation with Alicia Valdez and her comments about Valle delle Viti's lawyers.

The lions in the room.

\*\*\*

For Kaye, riding a motorcycle was almost a form of meditation. Those who practice Buddhist meditation, particularly westerners who come to the discipline later in life, know that there are good sessions and bad sessions.

The ride home from Santa Ynez was not a good session.

His mind wandered, trying to figure out how, or even if, Valle delle Viti was somehow connected to Avi Geller's murder.

People don't kill people over wine. Or do they? If Geller had put fifty million into the project, surely he – or his wife, Kaye reminded himself – would soon start to see a handsome return on the money. Which logically meant the other investors would, too, and he still clung to the belief that happy investors don't kill each other.

That Valle delle Viti might be owned by a swarm of unethical sharks was not his problem to investigate. Sure, he felt bad for Auggie, but unethical and illegal were not, unfortunately, interchangeable terms. At least not in a court of law. And with the kind of money he'd seen that morning at stake, what came out of a court of law was all that mattered.

He still wanted to know who owned Valle delle Viti, but he made the decision not to spend a lot of time digging into the operation unless and until he had a stronger connection between it and Geller's death.

To do that, he needed to know more about Avi Geller's life, and he needed to know more about Ziva Geller.

It's not always the jilted husband, wife, or lover, he told himself.

Well, yeah, it almost always was.

Getting stopped by the Chumash Oaks Police still rankled him. He'd been stopped before, not always for what he considered good probable cause, and he'd collected a few tickets over the years because he preferred to keep his profession to himself. If he thought he deserved a cite; if he'd write it if the positions were reversed; he kept his mouth shut and let the chips fall where they may.

But Reid had pissed him off. It wasn't the speed trap. Those had been around forever, with some small towns practically financing their operations with fine revenue harvested from unsuspecting travelers passing through. At least in Chumash Oaks there was little chance the cops preyed on the poor, trapping them in the endless cycle of unpaid fines that led to more fines and penalties they couldn't pay and eventually to jail, where they couldn't afford bail or a lawyer.

But that stop hadn't been traffic enforcement, good or bad. It had been a shakedown.

He'd have to look into Reid and the Chumash Oaks PD.

\*\*\*

The aroma of weed and *yomogi* filled the space behind the parking garage pillar.

But the left heel was stilled, not playing the rhythm of the rider's nerves.

This one would be easier than the Ferrari. Up close and personal, with that singular, defining moment when you could smell the fear erupting from the target's pores and see that millisecond of awareness in the eyes that they were about to die. Maybe some cleanup afterwards, assuming there was time.

Yesterday hadn't worked out. Too much workday traffic, the target emerging from the elevator in the company of several others, a couple of whom walked with the target all the way to his car.

Which made the rider wonder: Was he suspicious?

This evening was the last opportunity for this window. If the target was not alone today, the rider was prepared to take whatever steps were necessary. It was regrettable, but unavoidable. The Lord had ordered it.

Location was crucial. A preparatory survey of the garage had revealed a pattern of blind spots in the security camera coverage, allowing the rider to hang the full-face helmet on the handle bars and replace it with a baseball cap pulled low. A small, green duffel bag rested atop the bike's tank.

The rider checked the time.

Almost.

Partners in the firm seldom worked on weekends, and if they did, they didn't work late into the evening. That was left to the recent graduates, scrambling to get a foot onto the corporate ladder's rungs and willing to tromp on the toes and fingers of those already there.

Less than five minutes later the elevator bell sounded, the door opened, and the target emerged. Alone.

The joint was quickly crushed out against the pillar and went into the duffel bag.

Confidence was one thing. Carelessness was quite another.

The target walked toward his car, head down, his briefcase awkwardly clamped under his left arm while he tried to walk and send a text at the same time.

The rider, pulse and breathing escalating with anticipation, grabbed the duffel bag and walked a course calculated to intercept the target at a specific spot with no camera coverage. The weapons were double-checked and ready.

When the target was less than ten feet from the rider, he looked up, startled. His briefcase almost escaped his grasp, but a quick contortion saved the day. He continued to hold his phone in both hands.

Recognition dawned in his eyes and he stopped.

"This is a pleasant surprise," he said, smiling. "What are you doing here?"

"Hello, Clifford," the rider said, taking a few steps closer. "I stopped by to see you."

"Do we need to go back to my office?"

"No, no," the rider said. "Here will do."

"Uh, okay. What can I do for you?"

"You can die," the rider said, dropping the duffel bag and sliding forward with the speed of a striking *mamushi* while drawing the scalpel-sharp *tanto* from inside the leather jacket.

With one hand the rider grabbed the startled target's hands and cell phone and pushed upward, taking the final step in and plunging the *tanto* deep into the target's abdomen just above his belt line, over his left front pants pocket. A vicious sideways slice opened a foot-long wound in the belly.

The short dagger was so sharp it produced almost no pain. Stunned, the target looked down to see his internal organs begin to bulge through the cut. Eyes glazing with shock, he looked at the rider and managed to croak, "Why?"

The rider stared back, pushing down on the target's hands, forcing him to his knees before releasing them.

"*Anata no chinmoku*," the rider hissed. Your silence.

His cell phone was forgotten as the target desperately used both hands to try and keep his viscera from spilling onto the concrete.

The rider replaced the *tanto* and stepped quickly behind the target, reaching up with one hand to draw the *katana* from the scabbard sewn inside the back of the jacket.

In one quick motion, so as not to lose the moment and dishonor the target, the rider turned the drawing motion into a vicious, two-handed slice too fast for the eye to follow.

The corpse toppled forward as the head rolled to one side.

The rider quickly wiped the sword's blade on the dead man's jacket and returned it to its scabbard before grabbing the duffel bag. The target's wallet was taken from the inside suit coat pocket and the Rolex stripped from his wrist. The cell phone went into the duffel bag with those items.

The rider then grabbed the target's head by the hair and held it up for a moment until the blood loss slowed to a trickle. A black plastic bag, the sort suburban homeowners use to hold their lawn clippings, was pulled from the duffel and the head was lowered into it. The bundle was then zipped into the duffel bag.

Whistling now with the satisfaction of a job well done, the rider walked back to the Hayabusa and used a bungee cord to strap the duffel to the bike's pillion.

The rider swung over, pulled the bike up, made sure the transmission was in neutral and pushed out from behind the pillar into the traffic lane. From there, gravity took over and the bike slowly gained speed as it silently descended toward the street level exit.

Once off the final ramp the exit gate came into view. The rider pulled in the clutch and flicked the starter switch. The booth was unattended at this hour on a Saturday, the entrance gate down and the exit gate up.

But the rider drifted to the far left and hopped the bike onto the sidewalk separated from the two inbound traffic lanes by a six-foot pedestrian safety zone. Seconds later, now outside the garage, the engine revved and the Hayabusa disappeared into the evening traffic.

# DAY 7
## Sunday Week 1

Kaye woke very early on Sunday, feeling discomfited but unable to put a finger on exactly why.

He rose and checked the house, even padding barefoot across the patio to the garage to make sure everything was secure.

Nothing seemed amiss.

The wind was uncharacteristically onshore for the early hour and he decided he must have heard an errant traffic noise from Pacific Coast Highway.

Try as he might, he couldn't get back to sleep, finally giving up and deciding to practice. A strenuous hour later he showered, then breakfasted on the patio as he an Amy had habitually done on weekends.

His thoughts drifted back to the last time he'd dined on the patio with a woman. He'd finally let go of Amy after meeting Bebe Shahnaz on the Birnbaum case. They had hit it off, but her military career was her priority and it took her all over the globe. They both recognized there was limited potential for developing a strong relationship with someone who was almost never on the same continent.

Kaye did not long for companionship. Being alone had never bothered him. In fact, he more often wished for solitude and silence than for company and conviviality. Still, the memories tugged at him.

***

Later that morning Kaye rolled the '41 Flight Red Knucklehead through the gates of Kyokoku-Dera monastery. He wanted to ask Roshi more about *shikantaza* and the note he'd received on Friday.

In the saddlebags was a fresh cantaloupe, his traditional gift of respect for the old monk.

He stopped, as was his habit, at the crest of the graveled drive to drink in the beauty of the immaculate, beautifully landscaped grounds and the structure that looked like it had rooted and grown in this spot for a thousand years.

Roshi must have heard the distinctive sound of the '41's exhaust as it idled down the hill because he already stood on the top step when Kaye rolled up.

The flat stone for the bike's stand was in its usual spot.

Kaye fetched the cantaloupe and the two men exchanged formal greetings before Kaye mounted the steps and handed it to Roshi.

"I am in need of a walk, Benkei-bo," Roshi said. "Would you accompany me?"

"Of course, Roshi-sama."

"You come with questions," Roshi said after they had walked for a short distance.

"I do," Kaye acknowledged.

"Ask them."

Kaye explained his attempts at *shikantaza* zazen, asking for clarifications and advice. He expected Roshi, in his usual way, to simply reflect the questions back onto him as a way of guiding him to find his own answers. Instead, Roshi gave direct, succinct answers and suggestions.

"My last question is going to sound odd," Kaye said after a half-hour walking tour of the grounds.

"Only questions left unasked are odd, Benkei, because they never find the evenness of an answer."

Kaye reached into his pocket and withdrew the note. "Can you translate this?"

Roshi took the note and scanned it, then looked at Kaye with an expression Kaye had never seen before.

"Where did you get this?" Roshi said, barely whispering.

"It was delivered to me at work."

"Who brought it?"

"I don't know. The desk officer said it was a courier. What's wrong Roshi-sama? What does it say?"

Roshi looked at Kaye, then at the paper and said, "It says, 'Benkei, I have waited long for this time. Beware the power of the *onna-musha*. This time you will fall'."

"It's a threat?"

Roshi stared at Kaye and nodded.

"What's an *onna-musha*?" Kaye asked.

"*Onna-musha*," Roshi said, "were female samurai."

"I had no idea there was such a thing," Kaye said.

Cruel Vintage

"Oh, yes, Benkei. Some *onna-musha* are legendary, defeating their male opponents with ease."

Kaye considered what Roshi was telling him. It seemed far-fetched. But the note was real.

"What do you think 'this time you will fall' means?" Kaye asked. "I mean, besides I'll lose."

Roshi considered the questions for a moment before answering.

"There is a legend surrounding Benkei that is called The Standing Death," the old monk said. "Benkei was slain at the end of the Genpei Wars while defending the bridge leading to the castle where his Lord, Minamoto no Yoshitune, was committing seppuku after his final defeat. The legend is that Benkei single-handedly killed three hundred swordsmen before his adversaries rained arrows down upon him, striking him many, many times. Still, though, Benkei did not fall. It was hours before his conquerors approached and found him dead, but still standing."

"I'm not going to worry about this. Somebody's obviously just messing with me."

"Then how did they know you are Benkei?" Roshi asked. "Am I not the only one to ever call you that?"

"Yes, but you're certainly not the only one who knows about Benkei, and my name is Ben Kaye."

Roshi studied him carefully.

"I have a strange question for you, Benkei," he said at last.

"Ask, Roshi-sama."

"Have you heard voices during *shikantaza* zazen?"

"No. Should I be hearing voices?" Kaye was skeptical, but didn't want to insult his teacher.

"In theory, as your consciousness, your Self, processes the environment around you, it is not the environment that shrinks. It is your Self that expands. Legend says that Keizan Jokin could expand his consciousness to include the entire Universe. Using simple logic we may conclude that if your consciousness is everywhere, it may interact with the consciousness of others that are also present. Think of it as a collection of overlapping circles."

Kaye smiled. "Roshi, I hardly have a large circle. More like a dot at this point."

"That does not matter, Benkei. A larger circle might still overlap your growing one, and someone accomplished at *shikantaza* would sense your presence even if you do not sense theirs. You must be aware, and you must be careful. *Onna-musha* are fierce warriors."

"I'll make you a deal," Kaye said, trying hard to suppress a skeptical smile. "If anybody talks to me while I'm meditating, I'll write it down for you."

Roshi frowned and said, "Do not take this lightly, Benkei. That this note is written in Kanji means there may be danger here. Have you any other questions today?"

"No, Roshi-sama."

"Good, then I will walk back with you. I very much like your old, red motorcycle. It reminds me of my uncle's motorcycle when I was a boy, before we were sent to the camps."

Kaye was astonished. In all the time he'd known Roshi this was the first detail of the old man's life he had ever shared, and Kaye thought it might signal a watershed moment in their relationship.

After Kaye had laced his boots and swung over the '41, which Roshi gazed upon with open longing, the old monk put his hand on Kaye's shoulder.

"Be very cautious, Benkei. Write down what you hear if someone speaks to you. Even I have never experienced this, and am most curious."

"I'll do my best."

***

Kaye rode Mulholland on the way home. Kyokoku-Dera was west of where Leigh Howell had crashed his new Ferrari, but his route took him past the Fire Station, reminding him he needed to dig into Howell's life, too.

Welcome back to police work, he told himself. I'm going to need a bigger shovel.

# DAY 8

Monday Week 2

Kaye got to the squad room early on Monday. He had a long list of due diligence tasks to work through on the Geller case, even though he doubted much of anything would come of them.

At 8:05 a.m. he called the security company Megan Sullivan had told him was responsible for the listing in Paloma Canyon.

The woman who answered the phone identified herself as Marella.

"Marella, my name is Ben Kaye. I'm a detective with the LAPD." Per policy, he gave her his badge number and call back number.

"How can I help you, Detective?"

Kaye gave her the address of Sullivan's listing and asked if there had been any problems or alarms at the house over the past two weeks.

"Give me a sec," she said, and Kaye could hear the muted sound of a keyboard. "No, Detective, I don't show any recent alarms at that location."

"Nothing at all?" asked Kaye.

"Nothing, sorry."

"Was there a system downtime, a power outage, anything like that?"

"Uh, no," Marella said. "I'm not seeing any irregularities at all."

"Can you go back, say, a month?"

"Sure."

Kaye again heard the sound of the keyboard.

"I still show nothing, Detective."

Okay," Kaye said. "Thanks for checking."

His next call was to the landscaping and pool maintenance company.

"Gallegos Landscaping. This is Hernan. How may I help you?"

Kaye went through the identification process again and gave Hernan the address.

"Yes, we take care of that property for Ms. Sullivan at Classic Realty. Is there a problem?"

"Not really, just doing some background checking," Kaye said.

101

"When was the last time you were there?"

"Let me check," Hernan said, then went silent. A moment later he came back on and said, "We'll have a crew there later this morning, and we're due to be there again next Monday."

"Is it always a Monday for that location?"

"Yes, unless the weather is too bad, then we bump everybody back one day and work Saturday to catch up for the next week."

"But that hasn't happened in the last couple of weeks, right?" Kaye asked

"No," Hernan confirmed. "We've been on schedule for a while."

"Did anybody on the crew mention an open gate?"

"Did one of my guys leave the gate open?" Hernan asked, and Kaye could hear the alarm in his voice. "Did something happen? Was something stolen?"

"You have the access codes, right?" Kaye asked, ignoring the questions.

"Of course," Hernan said. "We can't get in without it. My company is bonded and insured, so if there was a problem…"

"Any chance one of your guys would cut the back gate padlock to get in, say, if they forgot the front gate code or it didn't work?"

"They'd better not!" Hernan exploded. "Jesus Christ! Classic Realty is one of my best clients."

"I don't think it was your people," Kaye said. "But it was cut, so I have to ask."

"Can you tell me what happened?"

"There was an incident on the golf course, down below the house. I'm just touching all the bases."

"That producer's murder? I heard about that," Hernan said. "No way my guys had anything to do with that."

"I don't think they did," Kaye said. "Like I said, I'm just touching all the bases."

Hernan was quiet, and Kaye could almost hear the landscaper's mind turning while he tried to put the pieces together.

"If you want to talk to the crew," Hernan said, "I can make that happen."

"That won't be necessary right now. But there is one thing you could do."

"Name it."

"Check with Ms. Sullivan. If the security company hasn't put a new lock on the back gate, she might want your guys to do it when they're out there today."

"I'll do that," Hernan said. "And, hey, I know it won't make any difference in your case, but my son is LAPD. Rampart. I'll help any way I can, Detective Kaye. Just let me know."

"Thanks, Hernan. Appreciate it."

Kaye turned back to his computer and searched up the name of the cleaning company Sullivan had given him. He linked to their website, but couldn't find an address or phone number. There was a contact form. He filled it out and submitted it, asking for a call.

Kaye's next call was to the first number on the list of names of the foursome behind Geller that Hensley had given him at the scene. Because she'd called them 'movie guys' he didn't expect any of them to actually answer.

He was right. It was a law firm.

After identifying himself to the woman that answered, and answering her questions about why he was calling, she transferred him.

He was on hold for so long he considered hanging up and calling back.

"James Calvin," a voice finally come on the line. "How may I help you, Detective?"

Kaye repeated what he'd told the woman who first answered the phone. He didn't figure it was the first time Calvin had heard the story.

"Ah, yes," Calvin said. "I've been expecting a call. I do represent Mr. Jesse and I was shocked to hear about Avi Geller. A real tragedy."

"I'd like to set up a time to interview your client," Kaye said. "Of course, you're welcome to be present."

"I'm afraid that's not possible," Calvin said. "At least not for the next eight to ten weeks. He left the country yesterday for location."

"That's a convenient coincidence."

"Look, Detective," Calvin said, "Don't read anything into it. It's been planned for months, and a couple hundred people can confirm that. I can tell you that I met with Mr. Jesse before he left, we talked about what happened, and I have a notarized written statement for you. Although I must tell you, it doesn't say much."

"What does that mean?"

"It just means my client really didn't see or hear anything. He and his friends found the bodies, and that's about it. Given the layout at Paloma Canyon, that's understandable."

"Can I get a copy of the statement?"

"I'll give you the original. If you still need to talk to Mr. Jesse when he returns, he will certainly make himself available."

"Thanks."

"Have you called anyone else about this? I mean, the other members of the foursome?"

"Not yet. You had honors."

Calvin laughed, then said, "I've spoken with counsel for the other individuals, and they've all obtained notarized written statements from their clients. I can get those for you, too, if you like. If nothing else, I can save you some time and legwork."

"I'd appreciate that, Mr. Calvin." He gave the lawyer the station's address.

"I'll have them couriered over as soon as possible," Calvin said. "Please know that if you ever need my client's testimony in court, he will be there. Avi Geller was well-liked and respected by everyone in the business. We'll miss him."

"Thank you for your time, Counselor."

Kaye leaned back in his chair and weighed the morning's progress thus far.

Not much.

One thing bothered him. If the shooter had cut the lock on the back gate to get down the hill and then climbed back up and used the gate as an escape route – which was supported by the lack of tracks below where Kaye thought the shots had come from – it meant that whoever it was had started from inside the yard.

So how'd they get into the property in the first place, and out again, without setting off the alarms?

And how did the vandalism fit into all this? Was it even connected?

Kaye reached for the phone and dialed the security company again.

"SecureLife, this is Marella," the same voice answered. "How can I help you?"

"Marella, this is Detective Kaye again. We spoke a while ago."

"Of course. What can I do for you?"

"I forgot to ask," Kaye said, mentally crossing his fingers, "if the system at the house we talked about includes front gate cameras."

"Hold on, I'll check."

Kaye leaned back again and waited. Maybe this won't be tough after all, he mused.

"Detective?"

"I'm here."

"That system does include exterior and interior front gate cameras, as well as cameras that cover the back yard."

\*\*\*

Following the directions Marella had given him, Kaye rolled into the parking lot of a small strip mall off Westwood Boulevard a few blocks south of Santa Monica Boulevard.

SecureLife Security Systems occupied a moderately-sized storefront near one end of the building. A video camera was mounted above the door, offset enough to capture the face of anyone who walked up. On the door was a sign stating 'Please Ring For Assistance'. A card scanner was mounted on the wall next to the door handle, a buzzer button above that.

Kaye pushed the button, turned to look directly into the camera and held up his open badge wallet.

"Detective Kaye?" a voice asked from a speaker Kaye couldn't see.

"Yes, I'm here to see Marella."

The door buzzed and a light on the card scanner went from red to green. Kaye grabbed the door handle and stepped into an empty room about ten feet square to face yet another secure door, this one transparent.

Seconds later, a woman appeared on the other side, held a card up to the reader and opened the door.

"Hi, Detective," she said. "Come on in. I'm Marella."

"Nice to meet you," Kaye said as he looked around.

The space was nothing more than a reception area with two desks in opposite corners angled to face the door. A young man sat at the desk to Kaye's right, absorbed enough in what he was doing that he didn't even look up.

On the far wall was yet another door. Gray metal, and it didn't have a knob.

Cameras were mounted in all four corners of the room, tucked up against the ceiling.

"That's quite the security set-up," Kaye said, glancing around.

"It's overkill, I know," Marella said. "It's real purpose is to impress potential clients. We don't just do home security. We also do tech facilities, industrial and retail, both interior and perimeter."

"From here?"

She laughed and said, "It's deceiving. That," she pointed to the knob-less door, "leads to our main operations center. We look small from the street because we want to, but we actually have about fifteen thousand square feet of the total mall and as soon as another tenant vacates we'll take that space, too."

"It's a tough world out there," Kaye said.

"Indeed it is. Now, how exactly can I help you?"

"I'm interested in any video from the front gate cameras at the house we spoke about. How they work, field of view, logs, archives, anything and everything you can show and tell me."

Marella studied Kaye for a moment before asking, "Are you working with Megan Sullivan at Classic Realty?"

"Not specifically," Kaye replied. "But I've spoken to her. Why?"

"Because Ms. Sullivan was here last Friday morning, asking for the same things. We spent a couple of hours reviewing camera captures and generating a log of traffic in and out of the front gate over the past few weeks."

"Really?" Kaye asked. "I understand there was some vandalism at the house. She must be trying to track that down. I'm working on something else. A homicide."

"Oh," Marella said, her eyes opening wide and her eyebrows lifting. "She said nothing about anything like that."

"Well, like I said, I don't think we're after the same thing. But, if I can ask, did Ms. Sullivan find anything that might help her find the vandals?"

"We thought we did," Marella said, grinning. "We saw you and your motorcycle, and we saw you jump up on the gate and peek over."

"Are you sure it was me?"

She appraised Kaye and grinned again. "I wasn't then, but I am now. You should probably call Ms. Sullivan and tell her that was you. I think she has the police looking for you."

"I'm easy to find," Kaye said. "Is there a chance I could get a copy of the file you created for Ms. Sullivan? I'm assuming everything is digital, right?"

"Of course," Marella replied, then caught herself. "I mean, yes, I created a digital file with the information and sent it to her. But I don't know about giving you a copy. I think I should check with somebody first."

"That's fine. I'll wait."

Marella went to her desk and made a call. The space was small and Kaye couldn't help overhearing her side of the conversation. After a minute or two she hung up and, wringing her hands, walk back to where Kaye stood waiting.

"I'm sorry, Detective. Apparently Ms. Sullivan has put a hold on that file. My boss says you either need to get her to tell us directly that we can release the file to you, or you should get a warrant."

"I don't need a warrant. Ms. Sullivan doesn't own the house."

"I'm sorry," Marella said nervously. "It's not up to me. I can't release it without approval."

Kaye grabbed his phone, found his call to Megan Sullivan in his call history and re-called the number.

Sullivan's voice answered, but it was an invitation to leave a voice mail, with a promise to return the call as soon as possible.

Kaye left his name and number, and requested a call back.

"Well, so much for that," he said to Marella. "Is there any chance you can at least tell me how the system is set up and how it works?"

"I'd be happy to."

She explained to Kaye that there were two cameras linked to the front gate: One that saw a short stretch of street outside and the gate approach, and one that saw the interior driveway. The exterior camera had a motion detector adjusted so the camera came on when someone entered the driveway, either in a vehicle or on foot. If the gate wasn't then activated using the keypad or a remote, the camera was programmed to go off after a preset interval.

"That's how we saw you," she said, explaining that if the gate was activated from either side using the keypads, the appropriate camera came on and stayed on until the gate closed or it timed out.

"So," Kaye interrupted, "if someone is leaving and opens the gate from the inside, the outside camera doesn't come on?"

"That is correct," Marella said. "There's a software limitation in this version that doesn't allow the simultaneous creation of two image files. Most of our clients are only interested in who's getting in, so we set the default so the external camera has priority. They can change that if they want to. But if the gate is correctly activated from the inside the interior camera gets priority."

"How long do the cameras stay on?"

"That depends on how the customer wants it programmed. If the exterior motion detector is tripped and no one activates the gate, the default is ten seconds."

The gate openings and closings, along with other system activity, were logged in the local system memory, and that file was dumped to

SecureLife every morning between 2:00 a.m. and 3:00 a.m., when the system was polled by the server in the Operations Center. The data was kept for thirty days unless there was an alarm activation that recorded an unapproved intrusion or the client made a complaint. In both cases the preservation was open ended so data could be retrieved as needed.

"Are there cameras or lights for the back of the house?" Kaye asked.

"Yes," Marella replied. "They're programmed by the client from the console inside the house, and motion activated if they are turned on. There was no video capture at all from the back of the house."

"Did you see anything out of the ordinary when you reviewed the data with Ms. Sullivan?"

"I...don't know if I should –"

"Marella, two people died. Shot to death for no apparent reason."

"Oh," she said. "I guess I could share what I saw. I mean, I wouldn't be giving you actual information, right?"

Kaye just shook his head.

"I had two impressions," she said. "The first was that Ms. Sullivan seemed happy with how many people were coming to look at the house. I guess a lot of people are interested."

"It's a nice house," Kaye said. "And the second?"

"Well, of course I could be wrong, but I almost got the impression that she was looking for something specific and didn't find it."

"What was she looking for?"

"She didn't volunteer anything, but when I asked her, she said she was looking for realtors who came and went, but didn't sign her sheet in the house."

"Was she upset about that?" Kaye asked.

"Not really, I don't think. She seemed to know them all just by their cars."

"Do you distribute the gate code to realtors when a client's house goes on the market?"

"We do not. But we can't control who Ms. Sullivan shares it with, and once one person has it, well, you know what they say about secrets."

"Indeed," Kaye said. "Marella, thank you very much for your time. I appreciate it. And if Ms. Sullivan calls me back and gives the okay, I'll call you about where you can send the file."

"You'll need Ms. Sullivan to call us directly first. No offense."

"None taken," Kaye said. "I'll have her call you."

Or, he thought as he walked to the bike, after I talk to the D.A.'s office to make sure, I'll be back with a warrant for your boss's arrest on obstruction charges.

\*\*\*

On average, there are about three hundred homicides a year in Los Angeles, which works out to roughly one murder every twenty-nine hours. Not the biggest number or the highest rate around, but enough to keep everybody busy.

Most go to Robbery-Homicide Division. But with the manpower shortage some, like Avi Geller, were being handled by Bureau detectives.

When Kaye walked into the squad there were several familiar, and a couple unfamiliar, faces gathered around Lister and Hilliard's adjoining desks.

"…and it was gone," Kaye heard Hilliard say to his audience.

Kaye heard the comments.

"You're fucking kidding."

"No way."

"That's one sick dude, man."

"Welcome to the jungle," Lister said. "Manic Monday. But not a fun day, you know?"

Hilliard groaned, a couple of the others laughed as they drifted away.

They all saw Kaye. Pleasantries and welcome backs were exchanged, introductions made. Things were getting back to normal.

"Okay, I'll bite," Kaye said to Hilliard. "What was gone?"

"The victim's head," Hilliard said. "Totally gone."

"What case?" Kaye asked.

"Not mine anymore, thank God," Hilliard replied. "Went to RHD this morning."

"You mean the victim was decapitated?" Kaye said.

"Yep," Hilliard said, making a chopping motion with his hand. "Clean as a whistle. And disemboweled. But the killer took the head. That's what I mean by 'gone'."

"You got called out?"

"Yep," Hilliard said. "Everything was quiet until about eight o'clock Saturday night. Some guy was found, well, everything but his head, in a parking garage behind a building on Wilshire. Like I said, clean as a whistle."

"Who was the guy?" Kaye asked.

"Don't know," Hilliard replied. "No ID or phone, no jewelry, pockets turned inside out. Looked like a really gruesome robbery to me. But taking the guy's head? Weird."

"A trophy," Kaye said.

"Definitely a twisted mind," Lister said.

"Any leads at all?" Kaye asked.

"Not really," Hilliard said, shaking his head. "I took plate numbers and photos of every car on that level of the garage, but, like I said, it's RHD's case now, which does not break my heart. If it was me, though, I'd have canvassed the building this morning."

"Well," Kaye said as he turned away, "let's just hope it's not the first of many."

"Amen," he heard Lister mutter.

Back at his desk Kaye checked his phone for a call back from Megan Sullivan. Missing such things was sometimes an unavoidable consequence of riding a motorcycle.

Nothing.

He debated calling her again, but decided against it. He didn't want to piss her off, and it hadn't been all that long since he'd left the message.

Next he checked his e-mail and was surprised to see replies to his inquiries from both Vice and Missing Persons.

He opened the message from Vice first.

> *Detective Kaye;*
> *I ran your Jane Doe photo through the system and showed it around. She's not on our radar. Sorry. If anybody comes up with anything, I'll let you know.*
> *Sgt. Tilley, Vice*

He printed the message to include in the file, then opened the message from Missing Persons.

> *Kaye:*
> *We may have found a match for your Jane Doe. We have an old flier from Santa Barbara County S.O. from about seven months ago on one Nicole Justine Ingram, WF DOB 08-19-*

*1995 Brn and Brn. Except for the hair color and that she's a
little rougher looking, it's a good likeness. A small facial scar
in common. The flier also noted a small scar inside her right
elbow. SBSO forwarded it to us because her permanent address
was West Hollywood. We checked the apartment at the time,
no sign of foul play. Hope this helps.*

*Ofc. Mason Westbury, Missing Persons.*

Kaye logged out and went to the Department's on-line missing
persons directory. He searched for Nicole Justine Ingram, but got no
returns because the flier was info only.

He next went to the law enforcement portal for the California on-
line missing persons directory and entered the name. Seconds later, a
picture appeared. Along with it were matching details from Westbury's
e-mail, plus the SBSO case number and contact information.

Kaye grabbed his cell phone and pulled up Jane Doe's photo from
the crime scene.

She was thinner than in the photo on-line, and the different hair
color only served to confuse the issue, but it was the same woman.
Both photos showed a very small, white scar just outside and below
the left side corner of her mouth.

"Well, shit," Kaye muttered, disappointed that this was how
Nicole Justine Ingram's story had ended.

He grabbed his desk phone and punched in the Santa Barbara
County contact number.

"Sheriff's Office, Deputy Stephenson."

"Deputy Stephenson, my name is Ben Kaye. I'm a detective at the
LAPD. I'm calling about a missing person report from your office.
Nicole Justine Ingram." He read off the case number.

"Got it," Stephenson said. "Did you find her?"

"It's not confirmed yet," Kaye said, "but, yeah, I found her. She
was the victim of a homicide here in Los Angeles last week."

"Goddamn it," Stephenson muttered. "Have you made an arrest?"

"Not yet. Until I saw your flier on-line she was a Jane Doe. Can
you give me some particulars?"

Nicole Ingram had been reported missing by her parents, Bradley
and Sylvia Ingram, seven months ago. They became concerned after
losing contact with her for almost a week, which they said was unusual.
Although she lived in West Hollywood, she had last called them from
the Santa Barbara area, which is what led them to file the report there.

Ingram's parents lived in Amarillo, Texas. Nicole had moved to Los Angeles after finishing her MFA at Texas Tech. She had disappeared from Santa Barbara while she was there to pitch a screenplay to a movie producer.

Her parents hadn't known the name of the producer.

"Do you have vehicle information?" Kaye asked.

"Her parents said she drove a silver two-thousand fourteen Jetta, Texas plates." Stephenson gave Kaye the number, then added, "We've never found the car, either."

"Seriously?"

"Yep. Still active in the system, and never even a nibble. And believe me, we scoured the countryside for that car."

"I've got a place here I can check for it," Kaye said. "I don't have a positive ID by family or friends of the girl yet, but as soon as I get one I'll call you so you can close your case."

"I'd appreciate that."

"If it's okay, I'll make the notification. I don't usually do it over the phone, but I have some questions and I think it would be better if her parents hear it from me instead of an Amarillo PD uniform at their front door that doesn't know anything about what happened."

"I'm fine with that," Stephenson said. He gave Kaye the Ingram's number and added, "Please pass along our department's condolences."

"Will do."

Kaye logged back in to his e-mail and wrote a quick reply to Westbury.

> *It's her. Nicole Ingram. Just talked to SBSO and will notify parents. Thanks again for the help.*
> *Kaye*

The next e-mail was to Arch.

> *Got a possible ID on Jane Doe from Paloma Canyon. Not confirmed yet, but almost certain it's her. Nicole Justine Ingram. West Hollywood address, originally from Amarillo, TX. Reported missing by her parents seven months ago to the Santa Barbara County SO because that was her last known location. I'll call the parents.*
> *Kaye*

He hit 'send' and leaned back in his chair.

An aspiring screenwriter, murdered along with one of Hollywood's prominent producers, goes missing seven months ago after supposedly going to Santa Barbara, where said producer has $50M invested in a real estate development not far away, to pitch a script.

He recalled Ziva Geller's outrage over her husband's infidelity and idly wondered if the Gellers owned a house in or near Santa Barbara or Montecito.

Even if they did, there was still no motive. No nexus. Why hadn't Nicole Ingram called her parents for almost seven months? The drugs? Maybe she'd been less than forthcoming about the nature of her 'business' in Santa Barbara. Who tells their parents they're hooking?

Identifying Jane Doe had done absolutely nothing to bring the case into focus. If anything, it was even blurrier now.

Kaye's reverie was interrupted by the sound of Captain Thompson's gruff voice.

"Kaye, in my office now."

Kaye followed his boss and took a chair across the desk.

"What's up?" he asked as he sat down.

Thompson put his elbows on his desk, leaned forward and stared at Kaye.

"What's going on with you and this Megan Sullivan woman?"

"Excuse me?" Kaye asked. "What kind of question is that?"

"It's a simple question, goddamn it. From your Captain. What's going on with you two?"

"Nothing's going on," Kaye replied. "I've never even met the woman, and if I hadn't seen her picture on a real estate sign, I couldn't pick her out of a crowd of two. What's this about?"

"I'll ask the questions," Thompson said. "Have you called her?"

"Yes, sir," Kaye said. "I called her the day, early evening really, of Avi Geller's murder and I called her this morning."

"How many times, total?"

"Those two times. That's it. I didn't even talk to her this morning. Left a voice mail."

"About what?"

"Information relevant to the Geller case."

"Be more specific."

"I was at the security company office this morning because I believe the shooter went through the property to get access to the golf course. The house is for sale and Sullivan has the listing. That's why I made the first call. Today I wanted gate camera footage and the system log showing in and out traffic. Sullivan had already been in last Friday asking for the same things. They wouldn't give them to me without a warrant or Sullivan's permission, so I called and left a voice mail. She hasn't called me back."

"Get a warrant," Thompson said, his expression deadpan.

"With all due respect –"

"Kaye," Thompson interrupted forcefully, "whenever you start off by saying that, I know you're about to cause me grief. Get a warrant or an okay from the DA. Do you read me?"

"Yes, sir."

"Stay away from the Sullivan woman."

"I'll ask one more time, and I deserve an answer…sir," Kaye said. "What's this about?"

Thompson sighed and leaned back in his chair.

"Okay, you should know that she officially beefed you to Internal Affairs late this morning. Claims you've been stalking her and harassing her with phone calls under the guise of police business. Told IA she was thinking about getting a restraining order."

Kaye laughed. "Let her try. As far as I know I've never been within ten miles of the woman."

"You don't get it, Kaye. She's friends with the brass. This will be on the front page of the Times tomorrow morning."

"I could not possibly care less," Kaye said, starting to rise. "Am I dismissed?"

"No, you are not. Is there any progress on finding Avi Geller's murderer?"

"I just identified the young woman with him. Nicole Ingram, from Amarillo, Texas."

"Okay, good. Stay on it. I'm getting a lot of pressure from downtown to find Geller's killer." Thompson said. "You are now dismissed. And, Kaye, stay away from Megan Sullivan."

"Yes, sir," Kaye said. "But know this. I will get the security system info, and without an unnecessary warrant, and if I find anything that helps me identify the killer, the first time I see Megan Sullivan will be to arrest her for interfering with a homicide investigation."

"It'll never stick."

"Who cares?" Kaye said mockingly. "It'll be on the front page of the Times, right?"

He went back to his desk, saw a pop-up notification of an e-mail from Arch, and opened it.

> *Kaye,*
> *That was fast. Must be why you're the detective…lol. I'll*
> *expect a call from the parents and make necessary arrangements.*
> *By the way, not that it matters, but Ms. Ingram's drug of choice*
> *was heroin. The final reports on her and Geller are attached.*
> *Arch*

Kaye skimmed the reports, looking specifically for any mention of recent sexual activity by either victim. None had been noted. There was, however, a reference to a small scar inside her right elbow. He downloaded and saved the file attachments to the case folder, grabbed the Big Boar jacket off the chair, shrugged into it and headed for the door.

On the way he glanced at the clock.

3:45 p.m.

Close enough for government work, he thought as he pushed out the door and headed for the Harley.

***

If Megan Sullivan was trying to distract Kaye from the Geller investigation, it worked.

He spent the evening doing legal research and trying to figure out why she would make a bogus complaint to the Department.

He reached two conclusions.

He'd call Kayla Okafor tomorrow to verify his opinion on the legal aspect.

And Megan Sullivan quietly slid from Kaye's mental list of Contacts to being a Person of Interest.

# DAY 9

Tuesday Week 2

It was 10:15 a.m. in Amarillo, Texas when Kaye got to the station.

He hated making these calls. It was, without doubt, the one part of his job he loathed. He knew he'd have to meditate over a beer or two later and try to reconcile how the Universe could be so supposedly interconnected, yet so random and so shitty. It just didn't work.

With a sigh, he leaned forward, grabbed the carpet with his boots, bellied up to the desk and picked up the phone.

He punched in the Amarillo area code and the number, and waited.

"Hello," a woman's voice answered.

"Hello. May I please speak to Bradley or Sylvia Ingram please."

"This is Sylvia Ingram. May I ask who's calling?"

Kaye took a deep breath.

"Mrs. Ingram, my name is Ben Kaye. I'm a detective with –"

"Oh my God! Oh my God! Did you find her? Please tell me you found Nicole."

Kaye heard the rising hysteria in her voice and swallowed hard.

Before he could speak, though, he heard a low male voice in the background.

"Give me the phone, darlin'. C'mon, Syl, give me the phone."

A moment later the man spoke to Kaye.

"Who am I speaking to?"

"Sir, my name is Ben Kaye. I'm a detective with the Los Angeles Police Department. Am I speaking with Bradley Ingram?"

"You are," Ingram replied. "Are you calling about Nicole, our daughter? Did you find her?"

"Yes, sir, I did," Kaye said as gently as he could. "I'm very sorry to tell you that Nicole is deceased."

Kaye heard Bradly Ingram take a long, slow deep breath, then a series of quick, ragged ones as he fought off a sob.

Kaye waited patiently.

"Where did you find her?" Ingram asked after a moment, his voice subdued.

"She was the victim of a homicide last week here in Los Angeles. She had no identification on her at the time, so it took me awhile."

"I think you've made a mistake, Detective Kaye. Our daughter went missing seven months ago. We reported it to the Santa Barbara authorities."

"I know, Mr. Ingram," Kaye said. "I spoke with Deputy Stephenson at the Santa Barbara Sheriff's Office yesterday afternoon."

"She's been alive all this time?" Ingram asked, obviously bewildered. "Why didn't she call us? Nicole always called us."

"I can't answer that question, Mr. Ingram. At least not yet."

"Are you sure it's her? I mean, absolutely sure?"

"I don't have a legal identification yet from somebody who knew her, which is something we need to talk about, but sir, please believe me when I say I would never call you with this kind of news if I wasn't positive it's Nicole. Your daughter had a small scar near the corner of her mouth, and one inside her right elbow, correct."

"She did," Ingram said, and Kaye could almost hear the surrender in the man's voice. "Got them both the first time she got tossed by a horse."

Kaye could hear sobbing in the background.

"How did she die?" Ingram asked.

"She was shot," Kaye replied. "It's probably small consolation, Mr. Ingram, but the medical examiner said death was almost instantaneous. She didn't suffer."

"Do you know who did it?"

"Not yet, but I will," Kaye said. "I know this is a terrible shock, Mr. Ingram, but could I ask you a few questions while I have you on the phone?"

"If it'll help you catch Nicole's killer, you ask whatever you want."

"Did your daughter like Los Angeles? Had she made friends?"

"She loved it," Ingram said. "Told us it was exciting, and the place for her to be to do what she wanted to do. Nicole never had trouble making friends, I just can't focus and recall names right now."

"That's fine," Kaye said. "Did she have a regular job somewhere?"

"Yeah, she did," Ingram said. "She worked in some big blue glass building she called the Blue Whale. Had all that design stuff in it."

"The Pacific Design Campus?"

"That's it," Ingram confirmed. "She was an event planner or

117

coordinator, something like that."

"She didn't work for one of the designers with a showroom in the building?"

"Nope, she worked directly for the people who run the place."

"Got it. The next one is tough," Kaye said, then paused a beat before asking, "Did Nicole have any history of drug use?"

There was a brief silence before Ingram answered.

"Not that I know of. I mean, except for when her doctors prescribed her something. Why would you ask me that?"

"The medical examiner found injection marks between her toes and she had heroin in her system when she died."

"Between her toes?" Ingram asked, incredulous. "Why the hell would she...?"

"I can't say for sure," Kaye said, "but in my experience users who do that don't want visible marks on their arms, usually for social reasons."

"She didn't want anybody to know she was an addict?"

"That's my guess," Kaye said. "Deputy Stephenson in Santa Barbara told me that you told him that Nicole was an aspiring screenwriter and was up there for a meeting to pitch a script. Is that right?"

"Yep," Ingram said. "She was real excited. Said it could be her first big break."

"Did she tell you who she was meeting?"

"Not that I recall, but hold on."

Kaye heard Ingram calm his wife down, then repeat the question to her. There was a brief silence before he came back on.

"Sorry, my wife doesn't know, either."

"That's okay," Kaye said. "Did you daughter ever mention the name Avi? Maybe Avi Geller, or AZG Productions?"

Ingram asked his wife again before answering.

"Not that we remember. Who is this Avi Geller guy? You think he's the one who shot Nicole?"

"No. Avi Geller was shot and killed at the same time as your daughter. They were together. Geller was a movie producer."

"You know, I heard about that. It even made our local news." Ingram stifled another sob. "Who'd've thought that unidentified woman would be my little girl."

"I'm very sorry for your loss, Mr. Ingram, and please pass my condolences, and those of the LAPD and Santa Barbara County

Sheriff's Office, along to Mrs. Ingram. That's all I have right now."

"When can I come get her?" Ingram asked instantly.

"You'll need to contact the medical examiner's office for that." Kaye gave Ingram the phone number. "Ask for Doctor Archuleta and tell him we've talked. He'll ask you to make the identification, so be prepared."

"I can do that. Can I ask you a question? There's one thing I just can't wrap my head around."

"Go right ahead. I'll answer the best I can."

"Why wouldn't Nicole have called her momma for seven months? I mean, they were close, real close. Didn't go two days without talking for two hours. Something else happened to her in the meantime, after she went missing. Maybe the drugs? I'd like to ask you to look into that, too, if you could."

"I'll do my best."

"You want to see me when I come to get my baby girl?"

"It's not necessary," Kaye replied. "But I'm certainly not going to tell you that you can't call me or come by the station." He gave Ingram the address.

"Okay, good to know. Thank you."

"One more thing?" Kaye asked.

"Sure."

"After you and Mrs. Ingram have had some time to process this, would you put your heads together and see if you can remember any names of people Nicole knew out here? You could maybe re-read letters or old e-mails or texts, if you have them, to jog your memory. Even first names would help. And let me know?"

"We'll do it," Ingram replied. "I'll let you know what we come up with."

"Thank you, Mr. Ingram. I'm very sorry to have to deliver this news to you on the phone, but sometimes that's just the way it is. Call me, anytime, and rest assured, when I get to the bottom of this, I'll be in touch"

"Thank you, Detective Kaye."

Before Bradley Ingram hung up Kaye heard Sylvia Ingram break into a long, sad wail.

He sat and regrouped for a while, going back through the conversation and trying to figure out how he could have made it easier on Nicole Ingram's parents. He remembered the agony of being told by the ER doctor that Amy had died of her crash injuries, and couldn't imagine having had to wait seven months, not knowing and somehow going about his life, to find out. He knew there was no easy way to tell a parent their child was dead, and he also knew that if it ever got easy for him, it was time to find something else to do.

The best thing he could do for the Ingrams would be to find their daughter's killer.

He roused himself and turned back to his computer, composing another e-mail to add to the thread with Arch.

> *Spoke to Bradley and Sylvia Ingram about their daughter, Nicole. You should expect a call. And he knows he has to make an ID.*
> *Kaye*

Arch must've been sitting at his computer, because his reply was immediate.

> *He's already called. He'll be here Thursday morning.*
> *Arch*
> *P.S. Thanks for making the call. I really, truly, honestly HATE having to do that.*

"You and me both, Arch," Kaye muttered. "You and me both."

*** 

Kaye's next call was to Kayla Okafor.

He'd decided not to write a warrant affidavit for the SecureLife data and make the trek downtown, since it would eat up half his day doing something he didn't think needed to be done.

Kaye hadn't finished law school, but his two years put him ahead of nearly all his colleagues and gave him a solid working relationship with several of the ADAs.

"Good morning, Counselor," he said when she picked up. "Ben Kaye. How are you?"

"I'm busy," Okafor replied. "I don't mean to be short, Detective, but what can I do for you?"

Kaye explained the situation and SecureLife's refusal to release the digital log files to him without a search warrant, then outlined his argument that neither SecureLife nor Megan Sullivan had protection under a reasonable expectation of privacy.

"This is the Geller homicide, right?" Okafor asked.

"Well, it's not technically a case for you yet," Kaye said. "Nothing's been filed, but, yeah, it's that investigation."

"Okay. My first conclusion is that you're right, at least about SecureLife. In essence, they're simply a witness with no protections against being compelled to testify, as it were.

"The Sullivan woman is a tougher call," Okafor went on. "She's acting in agency for the homeowner's, correct?"

"Her sign's hanging on the gate."

"If the agent relationship is limited to the sale of the property, you're in the clear."

"But?"

"But," Okafor said, "if she has a broader relationship with the clients, like a general Power of Attorney, you're in murky waters. She could possibly assert standing, especially since she beat you to the files."

"What difference would that make?"

"She planted her flag on that information. She made a claim of ownership, as it were."

"Seriously?"

"Seriously. I'm not saying she'd prevail, but we both know a judge is just a lawyer who calls balls and strikes. She might get the call, she might not."

"In your opinion, what should I do?" Kaye asked.

"Call Sullivan and ask her, first of all, to turn over the files to you. If she refuses, ask her if she has a notarized general Power of Attorney signed by her clients."

"I can't," Kaye said and explained about the complaint to Internal Affairs.

"You're kidding?" Okafor said, then went quiet. "Okay, serious question, Detective," she said after a moment. "Is there any basis for the complaint? Your answer is off the record."

"Absolutely not," Kaye replied. "I've spoken to the woman on the phone once, left one voice mail, and have never laid eyes on her."

"Let me think," Okafor said.

Kaye waited.

"Okay," Okafor said finally. "Here's what you do. Go to the security company and submit a written request for the files directly to their legal counsel. Give them a very tight deadline, like, say twenty-four hours."

"If they still refuse?"

"Arrest the person who conveys that refusal for obstruction of justice by withholding material information in a homicide."

"Think it would stick?" Kaye asked.

"Probably not," Okafor conceded. "But it might. In the long run, Sullivan made a mistake going to SecureLife and viewing the video clips before she told them not to give them to you. It makes her look like she's hiding something."

"My thoughts exactly."

"Then she compounded her error by filing a complaint that is, on its face, false. She's clearly trying to impede your investigation."

"I just want those files."

"You'll get them. Just do what I just told you. Oh, and Kaye?"

"Yeah?"

"If you identify a suspect from those files, bring me an arrest warrant affidavit for the Sullivan woman."

"I can do that."

Kaye bent to the task of writing a short and sweet demand letter to SecureLife. While he worked he decided to get out of the office and deliver it in person, then just stand there waiting in order to provoke a response one way or the other.

He printed the letter, spun around to grab his jacket and saw two suits heading straight for him.

"Detective Kaye?" One of them said when they got close.

"That's me," Kaye replied. "Let me guess. Internal Affairs."

"Correct," the same guy replied. "I'm Sloan, this is my partner, Detective Leale."

"Kaye," Leale said, nodding. "Been a while."

"This is about Megan Sullivan," Kaye said.

"It is," Sloan confirmed. "Mind if we grab a couple chairs and sit down, or would you rather do this in private?"

"Grab some chairs."

"So you know about the complaint?" Sloan asked after he sat down.

"Captain Thompson filled me in," Kaye replied.

Sloan and Leale exchanged glances, then Sloan advised Kaye of his rights and asked if he wanted a Rep present.

Kaye waived and declined the Rep.

"Do you acknowledge knowing and calling Megan Sullivan?"

Leale asked.

"I don't know her, and I've called her in an official capacity, yes," Kaye said. He spent five minutes running down the circumstances of how he came to call Sullivan on the night of the murders and leave her a voice mail when he called from SecureLife, and that she had never returned his call. "In fact," he added, "I talked to ADA Okafor not twenty minutes ago to figure out how to get what I need without involving Sullivan. I don't really need her any more. Did she tell you she's friends with Smithers' wife?"

"She did," Sloan said. "You're saying you've only spoken to her once, and on another occasion left her one voice mail?"

"That's correct," Kaye said. "I've never even seen the woman in person. I've only seen her photo on a for sale sign." He pulled out his phone, opened it to the home screen and handed it to Sloan. "My call history will confirm the dates and times of the calls."

"Individual calls can be deleted," Leale said condescendingly.

"I'm aware of that," Kaye said. "Make a note of my number, Sherlock, and call the provider. Then ask Sullivan for her records. I bet she refuses to give them to you."

"No reason to be antagonistic, Detective," Sloan said, glancing at Leale before asking Kaye, "Is this the only phone you have?"

"The only cell, yeah," Kaye replied, then gave them his home land line number. "Look, this is bullshit."

"So why does Sullivan have a hard-on for you, Kaye, if you've never even met her?" Leale asked.

"I have no idea," Kaye said. "But I'm going to find out. Call Okafor and ask her what she thinks."

"And you do not own or use another cell phone?" Sloan asked. "No burners, right?"

"Correct," Kaye replied. "What's she claiming, anyway? You Mirandized me, which tells me she's making a criminal allegation, right?"

"We can't tell you that," Sloan said. "One more question and we're done for now."

"Go ahead," Kaye said.

"Where were you this past weekend?"

"Saturday I rode up to Santa Barbara and Santa Ynez to do background on the Geller case. Got home about the time the sun went down. Sunday I was home most of the time except when I went to visit a friend."

"Can you verify those locations?" Leale asked.

"I can," Kaye replied. "In fact, call Officer Reid of the Village of Chumash Oaks PD. I'm sure he'll remember me. I had a late lunch at a place called Auggie's Wine'N'Diner in Santa Ynez, then hung out for a while. The owner will verify that."

"Sounds almost like you went to great lengths to establish an alibi," Leale said.

"Hardly," Kaye said. "Reid stopped me for speeding. We did not become friends."

"Did he cite you?" Sloan asked.

"No."

"Too bad," Leale smirked.

"Can it, Ernie," Sloan said to his partner, then asked Kaye, "Who's the friend you went to see on Sunday?"

"I call him Roshi," Kaye said. "He's the head monk at the Kyokoku-Dera Zen Monastery in the Hollywood Hills."

"How long were you there?" Sloan asked.

"Maybe an hour, maybe a little more," Kaye replied. "I got there about noon."

"After that?" Sloan asked.

"Home," Kaye said, shrugging. "You know, day off stuff."

Sloan studied him for a moment, then stood up.

"Okay, I think we've got the picture." He turned to Leale. "Let's go."

"See you around, Kaye," Leale said back over his shoulder as he headed after Sloan. "Real soon."

Kaye watched them leave the squad room. Before he could turn back to his desk he saw Thompson heading his way, a bundle of papers in hand.

"IA?" the Captain asked, looking after Sloan and Leale.

"Yep."

"Have you seen the Times today?"

"I have not," Kaye admitted.

Thompson handed Kaye the paper bundle. It unfolded to become the front page section of the Los Angeles Times. Below the fold was a prominent headline: LAPD Detective Accused of Stalking. Below that was the subhead: Detective Long Notorious In Department.

"Did they read you your rights and ask about a Rep?" Thompson asked.

"They did."

# Cruel Vintage

"And?"

"I waived and talked to them," Kaye said. "They can't have anything because there is nothing for them to have. Captain, the whole thing is some kind of smoke screen. I just need to figure out what's in it for Sullivan."

"You will," Thompson said. "Hey, you got anything yet on Ferrari Guy?"

"I do," Kaye said. "I've seen Beverly Hills PD traffic video showing the same kind of motorcycle Edler says he saw on Mulholland following the Ferrari from the dealership all the way out of town on Santa Monica Boulevard. I've got a request into our traffic department for any video they have from Mulholland. And get this. Turns out Howell was ex-military and big in the counter-terrorism community. The guy who's temporarily running Howell's company said there were a lot of people around the world who would've blown the guy up given half a chance."

"You think this could be a terrorism thing?" Thompson asked.

"Don't know yet," Kaye said. "But the pieces are all there."

"Let me know as soon as you find out if that bike was still dogging the Ferrari up on Mulholland," Thompson said. "If this thing has any kind of connection to Howell's history in the military, I think it should go to the FBI."

"Agreed," Kaye said. "You'll know as soon as I do."

*** 

The morning was shot, and Kaye was hungry. Rather than move the bike and try to find a parking place, he walked around the corner to a local deli. Everybody who watches TV knows about cop bars, but nobody but the cops know about cop delicatessens.

He ordered a sandwich, found an empty table, took out the notebook he jokingly referred to as his paper brains, and started planning his next moves.

Getting the names of Nicole Ingram's friends in L.A. would be a huge help. Surely Ingram would've mentioned her big break to them, maybe dropping a name to impress them. And there was her employer at The Blue Whale.

He needed to find out if Avi and Ziva Geller owned property in or near Santa Barbara. That would be simple.

It also occurred to him that Les Baruch, or someone else at AZG

125

Productions, might be able to access Avi Geller's calendar history or have a comprehensive list of the proposals the firm had received in the past year. If Nicole Ingram's name was on it, that would help connect some of the dots. If not, at least it would give him a long list of people who might have been angry with Geller. Lather, rinse, repeat until the dirt finally comes out.

He finished his sandwich and gulped down the rest of his iced tea. As he flipped the notebook closed he caught a glimpse of the page list of names and tee times he'd gotten from Lon Burridge for the day Geller had argued with the unknown guy.

A name jumped off the page.

Adrian G.

But no last name.

Adrian Gagnon, maybe?

Whoever Adrian G. was had signed in two guests by their initials: R.H. and R.M.

Kaye wondered if there had been no last name on the log sheet, or if he'd simply had too much on his mind to write it down.

The thought dictated his first stop of the afternoon.

***

Forty minutes later Kaye rolled up to the gate at Paloma Canyon Country Club, flashed his badge and rode down to the main parking lot.

It took less than five minutes to determine that Nicole Ingram's silver Jetta with Texas plates was not in the lot. He went back to the gate and asked the attendant if there was any other parking for the club.

"Yeah," the kid said. "We have overflow and employee parking. Go up the hill and take the first left. You can't miss it."

Kaye checked the overflow lot with the same results. No Jetta.

To make sure, he went back to the main lot, parked, and headed for the clubhouse. It took him only a couple minutes to locate Carol Soares.

"Detective Kaye," she greeted him. "What a surprise. What can I do for you?"

"I'm checking on something that might be relevant to Avi Geller's murder," Kaye replied. "I was wondering if you, or whoever would be responsible for it, might have had a car towed from your parking lots in, say, the last ten days."

"You mean since the shootings, right?"

"Yes, and it would have been a silver VW Jetta with Texas plates."

"Our guests sometimes get the proverbial wild hair and leave their cars here for extended periods of time, so a manager has to approve anything like that. You'd be surprised how many trips to Cabo start right here," Soares said, smiling. "We haven't towed anything in quite some time, and that was a member's car that wouldn't start."

"Does that extend to the overflow and employee lot?"

"It does. Sorry I can't help you, Detective."

"Thanks for your time, Ms. Soares," Kaye said. "It was a long shot, but I needed to check."

"Is it connected to the young woman who was with Avi?"

"Maybe, but…" Kaye replied, shrugging his shoulders. "Can you check something else for me, though?"

"Sure."

"Do you have a member with the last name of Gagnon? First name Adrian."

"Follow me," she said, then led Kaye to the Pro Shop and logged into one of the terminals there. After a moment of searching, she looked up and said, "I actually have multiple Gagnons."

"Any of them have the first name of Adrian?" Kaye asked.

"Yes," she said, looking up. "Mr. Adrian Gagnon joined us about a year ago."

***

As soon as Kaye was out of sight, Soares went outside, found a quiet, out of sight spot, and made a call.

"Kaye was just here," she said when the call was answered. "He was asking about a car and about Adrian."

She listened.

"Silver Jetta with Texas plates," she said. "Is that something we need to worry about?"

She listened again.

"You know you're going to have to do something about that guy, right?" she said.

She listened one more time.

"Okay," she said finally. "But I can't keep --"

Interrupted, she stopped and listened.

"Okay, okay, I get it," she said at last, exasperation in her voice, then hung up. "Bastard."

***

It wasn't quite 2:00 p.m. when Kaye walked into AZG Productions and asked to see Les Baruch.

Baruch emerged several minutes later, wearing a black suit and yarmulke.

"What can I do for you this time, Detective?" he asked. "I'm in a bit of a hurry."

"I won't keep you long. I have two things I was hoping you could help me with."

"Go ahead."

"Do you know if the Gellers owned any property, either a house or a condo, in the Santa Barbara area? Or had a place there they went to regularly?"

For an instant Baruch looked taken aback, then replied, "Not that I know of. Why do you ask?"

"I've identified the young woman who was killed with Mr. Geller," Kaye said. "She was an aspiring screenwriter, and my information is that she'd been to Santa Barbara several months ago to pitch a script. I'm trying to determine if that's how she knew your boss."

"What was her name?" Baruch asked.

"Nicole Ingram."

Baruch glanced nervously at his watch, then looked at Kaye and blushed. "Sorry. But I've only got a minute. Come with me."

He led Kaye to his office.

"We keep a spreadsheet of everything we receive, and from whom," he explained as he tapped away at his keyboard. He dipped his chin and looked over the top of his glasses to scan the monitor.

"Hmm," Baruch said as he glanced up at Kaye. "I've never heard of Nicole Ingram, but her name is in our log. Says here we received a screenplay from her about eight months ago, but the first follow-up note is 'copyright' with a question mark, entered about three weeks later."

"What do you think that means?" Kaye asked.

"Not sure, but I'd guess there was a question whether she had the rights to sell what she was peddling."

"You said 'first note'. Are there more?"

"Just one," Baruch replied. "About a month later it says 'UTL'."

"UTL as in Unable to Locate?"

"That's my guess."

"Who made those entries?" Kaye asked.

Baruch looked up at Kaye and said, "Avi."

"Are you sure?"

"Positive. The spreadsheet is set up so we can all scan and search the master list and cross reference it to make sure we avoid confusion and duplication. The sheet for Nicole Ingram was Avi's."

"Was it always like that?"

"Well, not always," Baruch said. "Years ago, of course, everything was paper. But we've been digital for a long time. We get too many project proposals through the door these days to keep track of them on paper. We'd have an army of clerical people instead of talent evaluators."

"So that means Avi dealt with Nicole Ingram directly?"

"Almost certainly," Baruch said, then glanced at his watch again. "I'm sorry, Detective, but I have to run. Avi's funeral is this afternoon and Ziva told us she would read the will at the burial site."

"Is that usual?" Kaye asked.

"Well, yes and no," Baruch said. "Avi and Ziva weren't what you would call Orthodox, but they were strong in their faith. I'm sure Avi left a secular will for the division of the estate and won't leave it to Halachic Law. But, knowing Avi, I'm betting he also left an ethical will that Ziva will read to the children. The fact that it's been a week and Avi still isn't buried is very upsetting to Ziva."

"I understand," Kaye said. "Please apologize to her for me about that, but under the circumstances there wasn't much else we could do. I have one more request."

"What's that?"

"Please don't tell Mrs. Geller about this conversation. I'd like to do that myself."

Baruch looked confused, but said, "Okay, I mean, if that's the way you want it."

"Thank you, Mr. Baruch."

\*\*\*

Kaye pondered what he'd learned from Baruch as he rode to SecureLife Security.

That Nicole Ingram's name was in Geller's database helped connect the dots, but the notes raised more questions. Geller's time notes pretty much matched Nicole's last contact with her family, but why the seven month gap? If nothing else, the gap between Ingram's proposal to Geller and Geller's note that he was unable to locate her helped define a possible time window for another event, one that caused her to quit calling her mother.

And if the Gellers didn't have a place in Santa Barbara, who had Ingram gone to see?

He dismissed the question as he parked the bike at SecureLife.

He went through the entry procedure again and found Marella at her desk. He told her he needed to speak to whoever had decided not to turn over the files on his previous visit, and held up the envelope containing his letter for emphasis.

"That won't be necessary, Detective," she said. "I took it upon myself to follow-up on your request for the files. Long story short, I would have called you before the end of the day. The release of the files to the LAPD has been approved. Sorry for the confusion."

"What changed?" Kaye asked.

"Well, I, uh, sort of jumped the chain of command. I mean, two people died, so I called our corporate lawyers directly. After I explained the situation, they called me back and said to give you the files. Said that Ms. Sullivan lacked... oh, what was it...?"

"Standing?" Kaye prompted.

"That's it," Marella said. "Standing, whatever that means, unless we had specific paperwork from our contracted clients, which we apparently do not have. Our lawyer said to go ahead and give you the files, and if Ms. Sullivan wants to fight you in court, that's up to her. It's not our battle. The only thing I don't have, and couldn't give you anyway, are the sign-in sheets she leaves in the house for when people enter. Those are hers."

"That's exactly what the District Attorney's office told me," Kaye said.

Marella smiled, stepped to her desk and picked up a small manila envelope.

"Here you go, Detective," she said, handing it to Kaye. "Everything is on the thumb drive." She paused for a beat, then added, "I assumed you would be more interested in what happened before the murders, so I went back several weeks and up until last Friday when she came in and asked to see them. I hope you don't mind, but I do have to ask you to sign for them."

"Not a problem. If I need any more records, can I call you?"

"Of course."

At least Kaye knew what he'd be doing in the morning.

# DAY 10
## Wednesday Week 2

Kaye opened the thumb drive and found three files. One was named Video, one was named SysLog and one was named TipSheet.

He opened and scanned each of them, then tackled the video archive first. It captured every car that went in and out, with a date and time stamp displayed on the screen. Because he didn't have Sullivan's private sign-in sheets for reference, his strategy was to write down the make, model, color and plate number of every vehicle that came through the gate. Then he ran registrations to match a name to each vehicle, did a quick on-line search to try and determine who was who and make sure they were entering legitimately, and logged everything in sequence.

Megan Sullivan was right.

Even at $18M there was a lot of interest in the house above Paloma Canyon Country Club.

It didn't take him long to start recognizing the same vehicles coming and going and identifying them as local realtors. There were six or seven of them working the house pretty hard, accounting for the lion's share of the visits. Surprisingly, Sullivan wasn't one of them, showing up infrequently during the days before the murders. He did learn that Sullivan drove a late-model, white Escalade, but the registration return didn't match, which puzzled him.

Kaye wondered why she wasn't around much until he realized that she'd collect her commission as the listing agent and was probably happy letting other realtors do the leg work.

He watched the landscaping crew coming and going on Mondays, and he watched the SecureLife mobile patrol dutifully checked the front gate every morning and every evening. He saw what he assumed was the housekeeping van enter late on the first Friday of the records and Thursday evening six days later, then at least once a week and stay for an extended time on each occasions. But the van's license plate light was burned out and it was always too dark to read the plate.

Most times a realtor came and went, it was the only vehicle on the video, leading Kaye to conclude that prospective buyers typically rode with their realtors. Occasionally, though, another car would follow the realtor through the gate. None were ever left behind, and he classified them as potential buyers, logging them separately for later research as needed.

Ninety percent of the traffic was, understandably, on the weekends, and on some weekdays no vehicles came and went at all. It was clear from the traffic that over the weekend ten days before the murders there had often been more than one realtor with potential buyers on the grounds at the same time. Sullivan arrived early and stayed most of the day. He wondered if there had been an open house, maybe a price reduction, and that had generated new interest. It would have also let people that hadn't been screened inside to see the house and its contents.

On the day of the murders he watched himself arrive at the front gate and jump up to look over the wall to confirm he was in the right place. An hour later Megan Sullivan arrived and waited ten minutes for an LAPD marked unit to show up before opening the gate. The unit left some thirty minutes later and Sullivan followed about ten minutes after that.

The days following the murders the only footage was of Sullivan meeting people several times a day and letting them in. All of the vehicles were trucks with business logos on the doors, and all of them matched the kinds of businesses Sullivan would likely call to repair vandalism damage. To Kaye, that also explained why the cleaning service van didn't visit that week. But it also reminded him that the service had never responded to his request for a call.

He hadn't really expected to get an up-close shot of the shooter, posing for the cameras and holding up his driver's license in one hand and his rifle in the other.

But it would have been nice.

After exhausting the video log, he tackled the TipSheet file.

It contained a series of instructions for decoding typical lines of data recorded in SysLog. Sample entries were displayed, then broken into bracketed segments; each segment then tagged to an explanation. The last page was a layout of the property in Paloma Canyon, complete with a floor plan, accompanied by a list of installed components and their individual locations and identifiers

He sent the file to the printer, retrieved it and opened SysLog It was line after line, without the TipSheet training wheels.

"Not as bad as I thought," he muttered to himself, then started at the top.

He'd learned from TipSheet that each line of data represented a specific system event or activity, from alarms to system activations and deactivations to component activity to system maintenance, each dated and time-stamped to the second. His task was somewhat simplified by a bold 'END OF DAY' entry and a break between lines before the next day's entries began.

Keeping TipSheet handy, he studied the file and patterns began to emerge. He soon recognized when the system was armed or disarmed at the console and when the front gate was opened or closed.

He first worked his way through the file cross-checking dates and times he'd logged from the video file against SysLog entries and checked off those that matched. There were no unsuccessful attempts to open the gate or vehicles unaccounted for, but he wished he had Sullivan's sign-in sheets to confirm identities.

Next he checked TipSheet to confirm the unauthorized access/intrusion code. He went through SysLog without finding a match, which squared with Marella's original information. He did find several instances where whoever had entered the house had fumble-fingered the disarm code at the console, but corrected it before an alert was sent to SecureLife.

On two days during the week before the murders the only entries in SysLog were system diagnostics and the system dump to the SecureLife servers.

It was laborious, time-consuming work, typical of the glamorous life of a detective.

When he matched his logged visits of Gallegos Landscaping to the SysLog data, he noticed a possible anomaly. On the Monday the week before the murders, there were no lines of activity codes between those recording the gate activation to get in and the crew's exit. But on the day before the murders, multiple lines of activity codes were noted while the landscapers were on site.

The lines showed that the front door had been opened and the system disarmed, then re-armed, and the correct door reset code entered. But there were also multiple lines indicating component activity, with no matching identifiers on the TipSheet.

He went back to the video.

The front camera clearly showed a landscape company truck entering at the matching time recorded in SysLog, then leaving later, again at a matching time. No other vehicles showed on the video.

But someone had entered the house, disarmed the system, then, according to what Kaye could decipher, manipulated components and re-armed the system twenty minutes before the landscapers showed up on video closing the front gate.

He finished going through the printout, verifying that the time stamps and action codes matched the subsequent activity shown on the videos until the log file ended, and making notes and writing questions in the margins.

He made some notes and grabbed the phone.

"SecureLife, this is Marella."

"Hi, Marella, it's Detective Kaye again. I hate to bother you, but I've been through the SysLog file and have a couple questions."

"That's fine. What do you need?"

"There are entries in the log that have the code 'GP', followed by a number, in them and there's no reference on the TipSheet you included. Thank you for that, by the way."

"Glad it helped," Marella said. "That GP code means that a group of components was turned off, the 10 identifies which component group it was. It's meant to save the client time if they want to turn off, say, an entire floor of motion sensors, things like that. They don't have to stand at the console and do it one at a time."

"If someone turns off a component, either one or a group, and then turns the system off, does the component come back on line when the system is turned back on?"

"First of all, the system is never really off unless there's a power outage that exhausts the battery backup, which is designed to last for days. As long as it has power it's in communication with our operations center. The client can arm and disarm the system at the console, but even when it's disarmed, it's on. Components can be turned off, and do not automatically reset when the system status is changed. That has to be done at the console."

"Why would people turn off components?"

"Lots of reasons, mostly cost and convenience. We charge for data storage, and sometimes you might want the system armed for perimeter security but not have inside motion detectors on, or not want to keep creating video files if a lot of your teen-ager's friends are coming and going, things like that."

"Does the system remember that for them?"

"Yes, it does. There's a display option that lists component groups and reminds clients what's on and what's off."

"Makes sense when you think about it," Kaye said. "I also noticed that when things get busy with cars going in and out of the front gate there are videos of people arriving, but not leaving. Is that because of the limitation on video files and the camera time-out we talked about before?"

"Yes. The time-out is to save disk space. For example, if the exterior gate camera is triggered by the motion detector it records for ten seconds and goes off if the keypad isn't used. If the gate is left open, there's a designated interval before the camera stops recording. It doesn't reset until the gate is closed, either from the inside or outside."

"What about the motion sensor outside the gate?"

"If the gate is open and the system times out, the motion sensor also times out."

"Seems like a hole in the system to me."

Marella laughed. "Not really. The presumption is that if clients want to restrict who's coming and going, they won't leave the gate standing open."

"Yeah," Kaye replied, "I guess that would be logical. Thanks, Marella. Appreciate the help."

"You're welcome, Detective. Call me if you need anything else."

Kaye leaned back and went over the conversation. What Marella had said about disabling components, camera priority and time-outs made him stop and think.

He grabbed his phone again.

"This is Hernan. How may I help you?"

"Hernan, Detective Kaye. Got a minute? We need to talk."

"For you, sure," Hernan said. "Is this about the movie producer?"

"Yes." Kaye gave Hernan a bare-bones run-down of the house's security system and video log, and asked, "Do your crews have the codes to get inside the houses you take care of?"

"No, we don't want them and don't even ask for them. We have no reason to go inside. Why do you ask?"

"I think your guys may have left the gate open up on Paloma Canyon Road. I think somebody else got in."

"What?" Hernan exclaimed. "Are you sure, one hundred percent?"

"Ninety-nine, yes, unless one of your people somehow got the codes and went inside."

"*Idiotas,*" Hernan said sharply and went quiet for a few seconds before continuing. "Detective, can you hold on? I'll make a call to figure this out. I'll just join him to our call, if that's all right. You'll be on speaker, okay?"

"That's fine," Kaye said.

Kaye's phone went quiet for a moment before Hernan came back on.

"Detective, I have Rigo, the head of the crew that takes care of that house, on with us. His English is pretty good, but I might have to translate some things."

"That works," Kaye said. "Hello, Rigo."

"*Hola,*" came the response, then, in English, "How can I help you?"

Kaye asked about the gate being left open on the day before the murders.

Hernan went ahead and translated. Kaye's Spanish wasn't great, but being a cop in L.A. meant you needed to pick up the basics and he thought he'd be able to tell if Hernan was sandbagging him.

Rigo answered in Spanish, and it took him a minute.

"He says," Hernan said, "that sometimes they have to leave the gate open, depending on what vehicles and equipment they have that day. He says our large trailers are easier to leave on the street instead of trying to turn them around inside when they leave and it's too dangerous to back out because the road is so winding. Because they go back and forth so much for tools and equipment, they leave the gate open. He also says that he always has somebody working in the front to watch if the gate is open."

"Ask him if he's positive the gate got closed when they left?" Hernan asked.

"*Si,*" Kaye heard Rigo say immediately. "*Absolutamente.*"

"I got that," Kaye told Hernan. "Rigo, did anybody else come to the house Monday of last week while you were there?"

"*Si. La Jefa,*" Rigo said. The boss lady.

"Who's the boss lady?" Kaye asked, not waiting for a translation.

Rigo didn't answer right away, so Hernan translated and then relayed Rigo's answer.

"He doesn't know her name, but he's pretty sure it's the lady trying to sell the house. He's seen her before, and she always gives orders."

"Pretty sure?" Kaye asked, skeptical.

Hernan questioned Rigo, who hesitated before saying something

Kaye didn't understand.

Hernan laughed and told Kaye, "He's embarrassed. He says all the blonde *gringas* look the same to him."

"Ask him if she was driving a white Cadillac Escalade."

Kaye understood as Hernan asked the question, and was surprised when Rigo instantly said 'no' and then rattled off something he couldn't follow.

"No Escalade," Hernan said, chuckling. "He knows a lot more about cars than women. He says the woman was driving a new black Explorer. Said it was really tricked out."

"He didn't happen to see a plate number, did he?"

Hernan asked, and Kaye understood when Rigo said the Explorer was so new it only had a temporary paper license plate.

"I got that, Hernan," he said. "Ask him if anybody else was with the woman."

Hernan translated, and this time there was a discussion in rapid Spanish Kaye couldn't keep up with.

"Okay," Hernan said when he came back. "He thinks there might have been somebody else in the car, but he's not sure if it was a man or a woman. He said the windows on the Explorer were tinted, and he wasn't close. He says the car came in, parked close to the front door and the woman he calls La Jefa got out and went inside. His work took him to the back yard for a problem with the pool filter for about twenty minutes, and when he came back out front the Explorer was gone. He never saw anybody else get out."

"Okay," Kaye said. "*Gracias, Rigo. Eso ayuda.*" That helped.

Hernan said something to Rigo in Spanish, then told Kaye the crew foreman was no longer on the call.

"Thanks, Hernan," Kaye said. "Don't come down on him too hard about the gate. I've been to the house, and he's right about the trailers and the street."

"We'll still have a talk. But he's a smart kid. I don't want to lose him."

Kaye immediately went to his list of vehicles that had come and gone at the house during the time covered by what he had. A black Ford Explorer showed up several times and the plate was registered to a Riley Realty.

He searched it up. On the home page was the smiling face of Lisa Riley. Forty-ish, blonde, glasses, and big realtor's smile.

\*\*\*

Kaye was gathering up to go hunt down Lisa Riley when a notification of an incoming e-mail popped up on his monitor. The header said it was from the City Transportation Department and the subject preview read 'Requested Video'.

He sat back down and opened it.

*Detective Kaye;*
*Attached is the traffic cam video from Laurel Canyon and*
*Mulholland Drive for the date and time you requested. Please*
*let me know if I need to preserve this copy. The hard drive is*
*still evidence.*
*Eric Bjornsson, Traffic Evidence Custodian*

Kaye clicked on the file attachment. Four different video frames filled his monitor screen, each showing a directional view of the intersection.

He was several minutes into it when he saw a white Hayabusa come up the hill from the south, stop at the light, and turn east on Mulholland.

No sign of the Ferrari first. Could the bike be a false alarm?

He kept watching.

Three signal cycles later he saw the Ferrari approach from the south, enter the left turn lane and stop for the light. Kaye clicked on the frame and expanded it to full screen. It wasn't a great image in terms of focus, but Kaye got his first real look at Leigh Howell and recognized him as the guy in all the photos when he'd met with Gagnon. He guessed mid-fifties, and Howell had a sun-lined face, crew cut, and broad shoulders. There was no audio, but he imagined he could hear the throaty sound of the Ferrari's exhaust at idle.

He sent the image to the squad's color printer, went back to the four-pane view, and resumed play.

The light cycled and the Ferrari turned onto westbound Mulholland. It was the only vehicle that made the turn before the light changed.

And no sign of the Hayabusa.

The light cycled again, to green for Mulholland. Kaye focused on the south-facing camera, watching for the motorcycle to come up the hill. All of the cars waiting on the east side of the intersection turned, either toward Hollywood or The Valley.

He watched patiently, not remembering the exact light sequence.

Five seconds later, the white Hayabusa went through the intersection, westbound, at a high rate of speed, swerving sharply to miss a car turning from eastbound Mulholland toward The Valley.

He backed up the video and froze it as the Hayabusa entered the intersection and enlarged the image. The rider's face was completely hidden by the full face shield. He was already sure, but toggled to the west-facing camera and found the view of the bike going through the intersection. He enlarged it enough to confirm it was the same plate number Ross had recorded.

Kaye went from camera to camera, freezing the images so he could closely study the rider. He'd ridden a Hayabusa and knew the bike's size and geometry, neither of which suited his massive size. He studied the rider's position and posture, hand and foot placement, and size relative to the bike.

Five minutes later, ninety-five percent convinced, he leaned back.

The rider was almost certainly a woman.

\*\*\*

Kaye knocked on the Captain's door and Thompson said, "Come" without looking up from the report he was reading.

"What's up?" he asked after Kaye sat down.

"I think the firefighter was right about the Ferrari."

Thompson dropped his pen and leaned back.

"No kidding?"

"Yeah. He described a motorcycle he saw twice during their response, but the timing of when and where he saw it didn't work out. I got traffic cam video from Beverly Hills PD and our people, and the same bike followed the Ferrari all the way from the dealer to Mulholland."

"You think the biker might have caused the crash?" Thompson asked.

"Edler thinks it was a bomb," Kaye confirmed. "The kid knows his stuff about the car."

"A bomb?" Thompson asked, clearly skeptical. "Is it too late to test for residue?"

"Time's not the problem. Location is. The car's in Italy."

"What?"

"Ferrari came and got it so they could try and figure out exactly what happened. They're with Edler on the fact that there should never have been a fire, and they're worried they're selling a four hundred grand disaster waiting to happen."

"Son of a bitch," Thompson muttered.

"My sentiments, exactly," Kaye said. "I'll keep chasing it and see what I can do."

"Okay. Did you ask Edler if he told the LAFD and our investigator everything he told you?"

"I did. He said he tried, but feels like they just blew him off."

"Hmm," Thompson said, then went quiet.

Kaye waited.

"Okay," the Captain said after a moment. "Open a homicide on the victim. Run it independently...keep the LAFD and Traffic out of it for now. I don't want them fucking with the investigation to cover their own asses. If you get even a whiff, and I mean anything, about a possible connection to Howell's military history, this all goes to the Feds."

"Understood."

"Anything new on the Geller case?" Thompson asked.

"As a matter of fact, yeah," Kaye replied, then gave his boss a quick run-down on the security system finding. "I've got to track down this Lisa Riley and see if she went to the house on the day of the murder, but if it wasn't her, my next stop is Megan Sullivan."

"IA's not going to like that."

"They're the least of my worries right now."

"They shouldn't be," Thompson said.

"Captain," Kaye said, "if the day comes that a Megan Sullivan can hide from us behind our own policies and procedures, we're all in trouble."

"You got that right. Just let me know ahead of time if you're going to call or go looking for Sullivan. I'll cover your ass with IA."

"That works," Kaye said, rising. "Thanks, Cap."

Back at his desk Kaye picked up the phone and called Anthony at the Ferrari store.

"Detective Kaye," the salesman said when he picked up. "What a surprise. I didn't expect to hear from you again."

"I have some news about Mr. Howell's crash. And I need a favor."

"Go ahead."

Kaye told Anthony that he'd looked into the crash and uncovered inconsistencies that convinced him to take a closer look.

"Long story short," he said in conclusion, "I'm investigating Mr. Howell's death as a possible homicide."

"Thank you," Anthony said. "Lord knows we got nowhere with the Beverly Hills police."

"Don't sell them short," Kaye said. "I talked to them. They did dig into it, they just didn't find any evidence of a crime in their jurisdiction. But it was the traffic cam video one of their people saved that got my attention."

"That makes me feel a little better," Anthony said. "You said you needed a favor?"

"I do. Would you be able to call the engineers at Ferrari and ask them to check something for me?"

"Of course. What are they looking for?"

"I'd like them to closely examine the damage in and around the passenger compartment to see if, in their opinion, it's consistent with an explosion. If they have the capability, they might want to test for explosives residue."

"Explosion? Inside the car?" Anthony asked, his tone incredulous. "That totally…" He paused for two beats and then said, "Oh, my god, you really think there was a bomb, don't you?"

"I don't know, Anthony. At this point I'm just checking everything I can think of."

"Oh, my god!" the man repeated. "Where would it have come from? You don't think we…?"

"Absolutely not, Anthony. You or your staff are not suspected of any wrong-doing."

"I'll call Maranello first thing tomorrow morning."

"You'll let me know what they find out, right?"

"Of course. Thank you, Detective. Thank you so much."

***

Kaye spent the rest of the afternoon catching up on paperwork. He opened a case on Rod Howell's death and started making a 'to do' list.

He finally wrapped the day and headed for the parking lot. He ran into Lister and Hilliard on the way out the door.

"Anything on the headless guy from the parking garage?" he asked Hilliard.

"Not yet," Hilliard replied. "I'm going to call RHD before we clear and see if they've come up anything."

"Hey, Kaye," Lister piped up. "Saw your name in the paper. Front page."

"There's nothing to it."

"Doesn't matter," Lister said. "You know how it works with those guys. Kick us whether we're up or down. Dirty laundry, Henley style."

\*\*\*

Kaye saw the piece of paper before he got to the parked Road King. It was stuffed between the windshield bag and the windshield.

It was another note written in Japanese Kanji.

Kaye folded it and put it in the Big Boar jacket pocket, then looked around. Who the hell was following him? He'd seen no hint of any sort of tail.

It was time to start paying closer attention.

# DAY 11
Thursday Week 2

Riley Realty occupied half of a former residential duplex on Bundy not far from Olympic. The other half bore a sign for a law practice. The lot next door had been turned into parking, with the obligatory signs threatening to tow away anybody who parked there without business with the lawyer or realtor.

By 7:30 a.m. Kaye was parked on the street nearby, watching and waiting.

He'd also kept a close eye on traffic during his ride in, and scanned for any familiar vehicles now looking for other nearby parking spots.

At 8:20 a.m. a black Ford Explorer came down Bundy from the north and swung into the parking lot. A tall blonde got out, walked to the realty office door, and let herself in.

Kaye fired up the Road King and less than fifteen seconds later pulled into the parking spot next to the Explorer. It had tinted windows that, back in the day, he would have considered illegal.

And it had license plates.

He recognized the number as recent issue and the expiration stickers were for ten months in the future.

He wrote down the number to check later.

He pulled on the realty office door, most of which was glass, and found it locked, so he pulled out his badge wallet and knocked.

The woman he'd seen, whom he recognized up close as the woman whose photo was on the website, came to the door.

"I'm not open," she said through the glass when she saw him.

He held up his ID.

"Ms. Riley, I'm Detective Kaye, LAPD. I need to talk to you."

Her brow furrowed, but she immediately unlocked the door and held it open.

"Come in. What's this about?"

Kaye stepped inside and she closed and locked the door behind him, but didn't ask him to sit down.

"I need to ask you some questions about the house in Paloma

Canyon listed with Megan Sullivan at Classic Realty."

Oh," Riley said. "Is this about the vandalism? I heard about that."

"Not exactly," Kaye said. "But it could be connected."

"Okay, how can I help you?"

"You've shown the house several times, right?"

"Yes, quite a few times, in fact," she said, nodding. "It's a great spot. I think the original price was a bit steep, but the new price is driving a lot of traffic. It should sell now."

"When was the last time you were there?"

"Oh, let me think," she said, and Kaye could see the wheels turning while she clicked back through the days. "Today is Thursday, so it must've been Monday afternoon, three days ago."

"Were the landscapers there when you showed the house on Monday?

"I didn't see them."

"Before that?" Kaye asked.

"That would have been the Saturday before the vandalism," Riley said. "In fact, it was the same potential buyers I took back again three days ago."

"Do you have the codes for the gate and front door?"

"I do. Megan gave them to me. I always sign the login sheet," she said. "May I ask what's going on here?"

Kaye ignored the question and asked, "How long have you had your Explorer?"

The change of subject threw her.

"Uh...I don't know," she stammered. "I guess about two months. Why?"

"When did you get your license plates?"

"They came in the mail, I think about two weeks after I bought the car. Again, why?"

"So you didn't show the house that Monday, ten days ago?"

"I did not," she replied. "I wanted to show it that day, but Megan told me it was unavailable. Some kind of security problem or something."

"Can you be more specific?"

"No. Sorry, I didn't think it was my business to ask for details."

"But you went to the house anyway, right?" Kaye asked.

"I did not. Why would you ask me that?"

"A black Explorer was seen at the house a week ago Monday," Kaye replied.

"Well, it wasn't me," she said testily.

"You're sure about that?" Kaye pressed.

"Yes, Detective, I'm sure."

"So there's no way a witness could have seen your Explorer, with you driving, go in and out of the gate on Monday morning of last week? You didn't just stop by, you know, in case? I know you'd hate to lose a sales commission on an eighteen million dollar house."

"Absolutely not! You can check the..." She stopped short, then said, "Oh, my god, that's it. The gate cameras were broken weren't they? That's why I couldn't show the house. Do you really think I had something to do with the vandalism?"

"The cameras weren't broken, Ms. Riley, and someone was careful to avoid them, then tampered with the system while they were inside. You, and your Explorer, match the description provided by a witness."

"But that's... It wasn't..." she stammered. "I swear, Detective, it wasn't me. It wasn't. I had nothing to do with vandalizing that house."

"What's your relationship with Megan Sullivan?"

"Professional, I guess is the best description," she replied. "I mean, we're not friends, but we're not enemies, either. Sometimes we work together, but mostly we're rivals. It's real estate, you know?"

"You said Sullivan gave you the security codes, right?"

"She did, but not just to me. She gave them to other agents she trusts, but we had to run our potential buyers by her first. I mean, it wasn't like she published the codes with the listing."

"Thank you for your time, Ms. Riley."

"You're not going to arrest me, are you?"

"No," Kaye replied. "There are some things I can check to verify your story. If they don't line up, we may need to talk again...at the station."

Riley gulped and went pale.

"It wasn't me," she said. She unlocked the door to let Kaye out. "It wasn't."

"One last thing," Kaye said. "Before I go, would you mind if I took your picture?"

"My picture? Why?"

"It would help me clear this up quickly, especially if you didn't go by the house," Kaye said.

"Oh, sure, why not?" Riley said, raising her hands in surrender.

Kaye took a quick photo, thanked her again, and headed for the bike. He swung over and sat there, considering Riley's story.

His gut instinct was that she was telling the truth, that it hadn't been her Explorer Rigo had seen at the house the morning before the murders.

But someone Rigo called The Boss Lady had driven a black Explorer through the open gate, gone inside, turned off the outside cameras, and left. Kaye doubted that person had just gotten lucky with the security system. They probably knew exactly when to come and go without showing up on the video.

But after talking to Lisa Riley, he was right back where he'd started. Pretty much nowhere.

***

When Kaye got back to the station he immediately went in search of Patty Phillips. He found her at her desk.

"Hey, Patty," he greeted her. "If you have some time, I'm in need of your computer expertise."

"Sure," she said. "Have a seat. What'cha need?"

Kaye sat and explained he needed to track down the details on a vehicle registration, beyond just what came up in the system when a plate was run, and gave her the plate number of Lisa Riley's Explorer.

She went to work, doing her keyboard magic.

"Okay, here we are," she said after a moment. "Two thousand twenty Ford Explorer, black, jointly registered to Lisa Riley, dba Riley Realty, and Ford Credit. So it's probably a lease."

"Can you tell me when she leased it?"

"Hang on," Patty said, clicking on a link in the screen, then studying what came up. "Just over two months ago." She pointed to the date field so Kaye could see it.

"Does DMV record when plates are issued?" he asked.

Patty laughed and said, "DMV records everything."

She clicked on another link and the screen changed.

"According to DMV, the plates were mailed eleven days, including weekends, after the dealer submitted the paperwork, and that can take a few days."

"So it could've been two weeks or more," Kaye said. "Seems like a long time."

"That's why the new paper plates are good for a month. Bureaucracy, you know."

"Who was the dealer?"

She gave him the name of a dealer in the South Bay.

Clearly, even if it had taken three weeks, Riley had received her plates weeks before Rigo saw a matching vehicle with a paper plate at the house. But Kaye knew that didn't mean the plates had been on the vehicle that day. Plates came off as easily as they went on, and if the paper plate was still valid someone trying to confuse the issue could simply put it back on. He couldn't rule Riley out yet, but she got points for being truthful.

"Thanks, Patty," he said. "Hey, can you pull up a driver's license for me?"

"Sure. Who we looking for?"

"Megan Sullivan. I don't have anything else except that her vehicle registration shows her address in the west L.A. or Malibu area, but I'll recognize her picture. I think."

Patty switched screens and went to work.

"Wow," she leaned back and said a few minutes later. "Who'd have thought there were that many Megan Sullivans in California?"

"Can you sort?"

"Sure."

"Narrow it down to dates of birth in the late seventies and early eighties."

She did, which cut the list considerably.

"Now," Kaye said, "can you look up by ZIP codes?"

"Sure."

"West side of the County, but I don't think in the Valley. Closer to me."

Patty checked a map and entered the parameters. The list narrowed to six.

"Okay," Kaye said, "Let's see what they look like."

Patty started working through the list.

"That's her," Kaye said when they came to the third name on the list. "Can you tell if it's current?"

"The license is valid," Patty said. "But if she doesn't report a move, or a change, it doesn't get updated."

"Print that for me, will you?"

Patty sent a screen print while Kaye grabbed his phone, pulled up the picture of Lisa Riley and compared it to the photo on Sullivan's license.

Rigo was off the hook. The two woman clearly weren't sisters, but without the other information on the license, including that Riley was several inches taller, they were very similar right down to the glasses.

"Run a 'vehicles registered to' on Sullivan," Kaye said.

"Nothing," Patty said a moment later.

"Nothing?" Kaye echoed. "She drives a white Escalade."

"Is she married? Own a business?" Patty asked.

"I don't know," Kaye said.

"Let me try something," Patty said, and her fingers flew over the keyboard while Kaye watched.

"Okay, got it," Patty said a moment later. "Got the white Escalade and a silver Jaguar at the address on her license, registered to a Thomas Burton. Maybe her husband and she uses her maiden name?"

"Probably," Kaye said. "But no black Explorer."

"Was that the jackpot?" Patty asked.

"Yep," Kaye said. "Would've been. Thanks, Patty. Oh, hey, I should know better than to ask, but have you heard anything back from the State on Valle delle Viti?"

"Nothing yet," she replied. "Sometimes that kind of stuff takes a while. I'll call and rattle their cage."

\*\*\*

Kaye went in search of something to eat and got a sandwich to go from the deli around the corner. When he got back to his desk, Lister and Hilliard were at their desks.

"How goes the battle?" Kaye asked.

"Runnin' down a dream," Lister said, smiling. "Chasing mysteries. The usual."

Hilliard looked at Kaye and slowly shook his head.

"Hear anything back on your headless guy?" Kaye asked him.

"Talked to RHD yesterday," Hilliard replied. "They've identified the victim."

"Who was he?" Kaye asked.

"One Dr. Clifford Collum. A consultant of some sort with an office in the building. It fits. His body was only about four spaces from where his car was parked."

"Somebody was waiting for him," Kaye said.

"That's what I think, too," Hilliard said. "But RHD's still digging on the guy to figure out why."

"Did they get anything from the security video?" Kaye asked.

"A little," Hilliard said, "and what they got was, well, weird."

"What was weird about it?"

"According to Tom Gannett, the case lead, the system was lousy to begin with, then, to make matters worse, somebody tampered with it," Hilliard said. "They got nothing of the actual murder, even though it was right out there in front of God and everybody else."

"That's too bad," Kaye said.

"Yeah," Hilliard said. "They're running down the vehicles that came and went around the estimated time of death, and there's one that has them stumped."

"Oh?"

"Yeah, a motorcycle going up and down in the right time window, but there's no footage on the gate cameras of it ever entering or leaving the garage."

"Are there residences in the building?" Kaye asked.

"Nope," Hilliard said. "Strictly a nine-to-five professional ghetto. They searched the entire place. No Hayabusa."

"Hayabusa?" Kaye asked, sitting up straight. "What color?"

"I didn't ask," Hilliard said. "Why? That mean something to you?"

"I'm looking for a white 'Busa on another homicide."

"You think it's connected?" Hilliard asked, interested now.

"Probably not," Kaye said. "But I don't believe in coincidences."

"Call Gannett," Hilliard said.

"I'll do that. But no suspect info?"

"Full leathers, full helmet," Hilliard replied. "Otherwise, nothing."

"Wanted, dead or alive," Lister sung under her breath.

"Lister, what the hell?" Hilliard asked.

"It's a song," Lister said, exasperated. "About a cowboy on a steel horse. Van Halen. Don't you listen to music?"

Hilliard just stared at her, then turned to Kaye and said, "I give up."

"Patience," Kaye said, smiling. He knew Lister was a good cop. She just needed some seasoning.

"Yeah, I listen to music," Hilliard said to Lister. "And I'm not happy to be stuck with you. At least some of the time."

Lister looked at Kaye and smiled.

"There's hope," she said.

\*\*\*

While he ate lunch Kaye made a mental list of questions for Tom Gannett, but decided not to call. It wasn't his case and there was certainly more than one Hayabusa in the greater Los Angeles area.

Instead, he went to the board and grabbed the latest crop of Dailies off the hook. The third one down, released just that morning, was a summary of the parking garage murder. It bore two photos: One a portrait of a smiling Clifford Collum, head attached, and one grainy still from the garage security video.

A white Hayabusa, its rider clad head-to-toe in black leathers and wearing a full helmet with a full, tinted visor.

He took the bulletin back to his desk, opened the traffic cam video from Mulholland and Laurel Canyon, and compared the images.

He wouldn't have testified in court that they were one and same bike and rider, but there were too many similarities, including that he thought the garage rider was also a woman, to ignore.

He changed his mind again, looked up Gannett's number and called.

"Robbery Homicide," a gruff voice answered. "Gannett."

"Tom, Ben Kaye."

"I heard you quit."

"Leave of absence. Death in the family," he said to deflect questions. "I'm back."

"Good. We need you. What's up?"

Kaye gave Gannett the two minute summary on the Ferrari case. Gannett was silent until Kaye finished, then asked several cogent questions.

"So, why are you calling me?" was the last one.

"I think we're looking for the same woman," Kaye replied.

"A woman?"

Kaye heard the skepticism in Gannett's voice.

"Yeah," he said. "Not a hundred percent sure, but you should check to see if your vic had any connection to a guy named Leigh Howell, went by the first name Rod. He's the victim in my case. Plus, I've got better video from traffic cams, and based on size, build and gear, I think it's a woman."

"Can you send me the traffic video?"

"You bet," Kaye said. "And I don't want you to think I'm trying to run your case, but I have a suggestion."

"What's that?"

"You might want to check high end dojos with a kendo sensei."

"Why would I do that?"

"Your victim was killed in a staged seppuku, a ritual Japanese suicide," Kaye said. "Whoever did it has a knowledge base and the skill to go along with it. They had to learn it somewhere."

"Sounds reasonable," Gannett said.

"I don't know if all the garage video was as grainy as the photo on the Daily –"

"It is," Gannett interrupted. "Shitty system, shitty coverage."

"You might want to take the best side shot, with the most contrast, you have and have Tech try to enhance it."

"What would I be looking for?" Gannett asked, and Kaye caught the first hint of offense in the RHD detective's voice.

"The hilt of a katana, a –"

"I know what a katana is," Gannett interrupted again. "Why would I look for one?"

"Chet Hilliard used the word 'surgical' when he described the decapitation cut to me. That would require a very sharp, long-bladed sword like a katana. If the rider is the killer, she had to be carrying it somewhere. Look behind her head and see if the hilt is sticking out of her jacket. If it is, at least you have a solid suspect."

There was a protracted silence, and Kaye knew Gannett was deciding whether to consider the suggestion or tell him to fuck off.

"I'll check it out," Gannett said at last. "Hey, you sure you don't want to come downtown and work? We've got a slot. Hell, we've got more than one."

"I'm happy where I am, but thanks."

"Think about it."

"I'll do that," Kaye said, "and if you find anything, let me know."

"Sure," Gannett said. "Thanks, Kaye, and welcome back."

Kaye forwarded the traffic cam video to Gannett and checked the time.

He needed to talk to Ziva Geller about Nicole Ingram, and should probably have Howard Feinmann there, too.

He grabbed the phone and called the lawyer's office. Five minutes later he had a meeting for the following Monday set up and was headed out when his desk phone rang.

The caller ID read 'desk', so he answered it.

"Detective, this is Hudson at the front desk. There's a Bradley Ingram here to see you."

"Tell him I'll be right down."

Kaye shrugged out of the Big Boar jacket, grabbed his paper brains and headed for the lobby.

Bradley Ingram looked like he came straight off a western movie set. Tall and lanky, bushy mustache, too-long denim pants puddled atop cowboy boots with a riding heel, silver belt buckle and a western-cut sport coat over a white shirt with pearl button snaps. A bolo tie with silver aglets and a silver and turquoise clasp finished the look.

The only thing missing, Kaye thought, was a Stetson.

"Mr. Ingram," he said as he approached and extended his hand, "I'm Detective Kaye. We spoke on the phone. I'm very sorry for your loss, sir."

"I appreciate that, Detective," Ingram said as he shook Kaye's hand. "I don't mean to bother you, but I wanted to pass on some information that might help."

"You are not bothering me, Mr. Ingram. Let's go someplace we can talk." He led Ingram through the security door and found a vacant interview room in the Patrol area.

"Have you talked with Doctor Archuleta yet?" Kaye asked as they sat down.

"This morning," Ingram replied. "I also made the identification, if that helps."

"It does," Kaye said. "Thank you. I know it's not easy."

"You got that right," Ingram said. "I don't know if I was more worried about making sure it was her or coming all this way after all this time and finding out it wasn't, then having to call and tell her momma we still don't know."

"I wouldn't have called you and put you through this if I wasn't sure," Kaye said. "But I can't make a legal identification. I hope you understand."

"I do, and I appreciate how you handled it."

"How's Mrs. Ingram?"

"Crushed," Ingram said, then paused for a beat before adding, "like me."

Kaye saw tears in the man's eyes.

"Did you get everything arranged with Dr. Archuleta?" he asked.

"I did," Ingram said, nodding. "I guess I should say 'we', because without Dr. Archuleta's help I wouldn't have known what to do. Not exactly something you study up on and practice ahead of time." He stopped for another beat and added, "I take my girl home tomorrow."

Kaye sat quietly and watched Bradley Ingram sag under the weight of his sorrow.

"You said you had some information for me?" he asked after a bit.

"Oh, yeah," Ingram said as though he'd forgotten, then reached under the sport coat into his shirt pocket and came out with a piece of paper. "I've got a couple names for you. We think they were friends of Nicole's."

He handed the paper to Kaye, who unfolded it and looked at the names.

Rachel Turner.

Storm Chase.

Ruthie.

"Who were these people to Nicole?" he asked.

"Rachel Turner was Nicole's roommate when Nicole first moved to Los Angeles, but she moved on after a while. I think the two of them had some sort of falling out."

"And Storm Chase?"

"We're not real sure," Ingram said. "Syl – my wife – found the name in a text she got from Nicole a few months before... Before Nicole went missing. Being from tornado country, Nicole kind of made fun of the name, to tell you the truth, but she mentioned it several times after that."

"Could be a stage name," Kaye said. "But you never know. I'll track it down. Any idea if Storm is a male or female?"

"Nope," Ingram said, shaking his head. "Syl was worried it was a stripper's name and the influence it might have on Nicole. Sorry, but those are the only two last names we found. Lots of first names, like Ruthie, but..."

"But you put Ruthie on the list. Who was she?"

"We think she was one of Nicole's neighbors. Syl doesn't remember Nicole ever telling her Ruthie's last name, but Nicole talked about her a lot."

"Was Rachel Turner your daughter's roommate at the address on the missing person report?" Kaye asked. "Or someplace else?"

"That address was the only place Nicole lived while she was out here. She loved her apartment," Ingram said. "In fact, that's my next stop. I had them put Nicole's stuff in storage after she'd been missing long enough to miss a month's rent. I need to go settle up and go through it. There are a few things her momma wants. The rest will go to charity."

"I don't know if you know, or not," Kaye said, "but our Missing

154

Persons detectives went through the apartment. They found no sign of foul play."

"Yes," Ingram said. "We knew that. The Santa Barbara deputy called us."

"I almost hate to ask you this, Mr. Ingram, but do you have a photograph of Nicole I could get from you? What she looked like at the time she went missing?" He almost said 'not what she looked like when she was shot', but caught himself in time.

"You bet," Ingram said, reaching into his coat for his wallet. He opened it and fished out a wallet-sized photo and handed it to Kaye.

It was a much better picture than the one on the missing persons flier. Nicole Ingram had been a real beauty before the heroin.

"Thank you," Kaye said. "I'll get this back to you."

"Don't worry about it. Just catch the son of a bitch that did this."

"I plan to," Kaye said.

Kaye walked the grieving father to the door.

"I'll be in touch," he said as he shook Ingram's hand again.

\*\*\*

Back at his desk, Kaye composed and sent an e-mail to Deputy Stephenson in Santa Barbara, letting him know that Nicole Ingram had been officially identified by next of kin, and the body released. Stephenson could close his case.

Next, he bent to the task of finding out who Storm Chase was.

It didn't take long.

Storm Chase was the professional name of one Dennis Bettencourt, an actor in, and producer of, a multitude of porn films.

Kaye leaned back, tented his fingers, and stared at the monitor.

Good girl from the Southwest comes to Hollywood to make it big, meets and falls in with the wrong people, life takes multiple turns for the worse, and she ends up addicted to heroin and dead on a golf course cart path.

In a sad way, it all made sense. Heroin-addicted porn actresses didn't usually call their momma to catch up.

But how the hell did she end up on a golf course with Avi Geller? Was Geller paying for her company?

He was glad he hadn't known about Storm Chase before talking to Bradley Ingram. Telling a father that one of his daughter's friends was a porn star wasn't high on his list. One thing, though, was certain:

He was going to make sure he and Dennis Bettencourt got better acquainted in the very near future.

No sooner had he done a print screen and closed his browser when a pop-up notified him he had an e-mail from Patty.

> *Detective Kaye:*
> *Figures... Because I called the State about the Valle delle Viti information it came today. The company's Disclosure Form is attached. I hope you have better luck figuring it out than I did.*
> *Patty Phillips P.A.*

The attachment was a copy of a California Form LLC-S; Application to Register a Foreign Limited Liability Company.

According to the form, Valle delle Viti, LLC was a private company held by Valle delle Viti SRL of Reggio Calabria, Italy. The California offices were in the Village of Chumash Oaks. The only other information on the form's front page was that the Registered Agent for Valle delle Viti LLC was one Jeffrey E. King. No separate address was listed.

The second page was a Statement of Authority from the Italian government certifying that Valle delle Viti SRL was legally authorized to do business in that country.

It told Kaye absolutely nothing. He knew that most LLCs appointed an in-house attorney as their Registered Agent, or went with a firm providing those services, but Registered Agents were not required by law to be members of the bar. And there must be thousands of Jeff Kings in California.

He wasn't chasing that shadow. Not yet, anyway.

Frustrated, he worried about how he was going to unravel Valle delle Viti enough to figure out what was going on.

He sighed and decided he'd worry about it tomorrow.

# DAY 12
### Friday Week 2

It was obvious why it was nicknamed The Blue Whale.

Huge, it dwarfed everything around it, and the blue glass exterior was dazzling. Officially, it was now the Blue Center on West Hollywood's renowned Pacific Design Center campus. The original giant, blue building had been joined over the years by equally stunning, but smaller scale, red, green and yellow structures.

After finding a parking spot for the '61 Duo Glide, it took Kaye nearly a half-hour just to find Human Resources, only to find the door locked and hours posted showing they didn't open until 10:00 a.m.

He found a sidewalk coffee shop and waited.

When he walked in at 10:01 a.m. the young man behind the counter, his spiked hair tinted, appropriately enough, blue and the sleeves of his taupe linen sport coat rolled up to his elbows, looked up and froze in horror.

"It's okay," Kaye said, suppressing a smile and holding up his badge wallet. "I'm a cop, not the Grim Reaper."

"Oh, thank GOD!" the staffer said, clutching a hand to his chest. "I thought…Oh, well, the worst!"

"Well, you can relax. I'm Detective Kaye, LAPD, and I'm here on business."

"I'm Aubrey. How can I help you?"

"I'm looking for anything you might still have on a young lady named Nicole Ingram. I understand she used to work here."

"I remember Nicole!" Aubrey exclaimed. "I really liked her, and her Texas accent was SO cute."

"You were friends?" Kaye asked.

"At work, for sure," Aubrey said. "We got along great. But we didn't move in the same social circles, if that's what you mean."

"Did you know any of her friends?"

"Not really, I'm afraid," Aubrey replied. "I mean, I met a few people she knew, but… Wait, why are you looking for Nicole?"

"I'm not looking for Nicole," Kaye said. "I'm looking for whoever killed her."

"Killed…Oh, my Lord," Aubrey croaked, going deathly pale. "I wondered what happened to her."

"What do you mean?"

"Well, she was very good at her job," Aubrey said, "and really liked it. At least, I thought she did. I mean, I know she wanted to be a screenwriter, but one day she just didn't show up for work. We never saw her again."

"Did you try to find her?"

"Me? Why would I try…?"

"Not you personally," Kaye said. "Did anyone here try to locate her and find out why she didn't show up? Try to call? Stop by her apartment?"

"Oh," Aubrey said. "I know my boss tried her emergency contacts, but we didn't really try to search for her, if that's what you mean. I know it's hard to believe, but people in West Hollywood tend to be, um, flaky sometimes, if you know what I mean. We all just thought something happened and she decided to go home to, uh, I think it was Armadillo. In Texas?"

"Amarillo."

Aubrey laughed. "Like there's a difference?"

"Can I take a look at her personnel file?"

"My boss isn't in yet," Aubrey said, then hesitated and added, "Oh, sure, I don't see why not. I mean, who's going to complain, right? Wait one sec."

Aubrey disappeared into a side office and returned carrying a gray file folder.

"Here you are," he said, handing it to Kaye. "Gray means we wouldn't rehire her. Unreliable."

Kaye gave him a look and Aubrey blushed.

"Oh…yeah, right," he stuttered. "She's, uh, dead."

The file was pretty thin, but he still took out his notebook.

Nicole Ingram had worked at the Blue Whale for less than a year. She'd been hired on as a marketing assistant-slash-event coordinator at a thoroughly inadequate wage for living in West Hollywood, which to Kaye explained Rachel Turner.

Nicole had done well on her 90-day evaluation, with her boss specifically calling out her writing skills. They gave her a half-decent raise and she had two letters of commendation for doing an outstanding job under difficult circumstances.

Kaye wrote down the names of Nicole's boss and the signatories of the letters of commendation, just in case.

There was also a paper-clipped bundle of computer printouts showing biweekly payroll records.

The last item in the file was Nicole's handwritten job application. It showed the same address that was on the Santa Barbara County missing person's report.

In the space for local references, Nicole had written 'I just moved here and don't have local references'.

At least she was honest, Kaye thought.

Rachel Turner was listed as Nicole's emergency contact and had the same address. Kaye made note of the contact phone number. Nicole's parents weren't listed, which made him wonder.

"This is all you've got?" Kaye asked, handing the file back to Aubrey.

"I'm afraid so."

"Did you know Rachel Turner? Nicole's roommate?"

"I think I met her a couple times," Aubrey said. "She was nice, but not as nice as Nicole."

"Does the name Storm Chase mean anything to you?" Kaye asked. "Or Dennis Bettencourt?"

Aubrey instantly blushed a deep crimson.

"What?" Kaye asked.

"You seriously don't know who Storm Chase is?"

"Why don't you tell me?" Kaye said, deciding to hear Aubrey's version.

"Storm Chase," Aubrey said, "is…let's see, how do I put this delicately to an obviously straight officer of the law? Okay. He's the biggest, uh, thing," Aubrey stopped, made air quotes and winked, "to hit gay porn in years."

Kaye stayed quiet and waited.

"But that's not all," Aubrey continued. "He's way past just doing it for the money. He has his own YouTube channel and does podcasts, too. He has over two million subscribers. The dude is going to be richer than God by the time he's thirty-five."

"He does porn on YouTube?"

"Of course not," Aubrey said, rolling his eyes. "He does, like, this gossip show about Hollywood and the West Valley – that's where most porn is made, you know – and he's famous for outing current Hollywood actors that used to do porn."

"Really?" Kaye said. "That must make him some friends."

"Hey, you'd be surprised," Aubrey said.

"I probably would be."

"So, anyway, Storm made his rep in the porn biz, but he's really smart and really funny in a calm kind of way, and he's branched out. Started his own production company and wants to go legit. I mean, not that porn isn't legit, but... You know what I mean."

"Have any idea why Nicole's parents would know his name?" Kaye asked.

"Sure do," Aubrey said, smiling. "He is, or at least he was, Nicole's roommate's boyfriend. I've even met him."

"I thought you said he did gay porn."

"Hello!" Aubrey said. "In case you hadn't noticed, Detective, it's a tough world out there. A lot of people do things they'd never do for free if the paycheck's big enough. And, I will admit, I'm a fan of his work." He blushed again.

"Can you describe Chase, or Dennis, to me?" Kaye asked.

"You know you can look him up on-line, right? He's all over the internet."

"I did that," Kaye said. "Hard to believe, I know, but sometimes the internet is wrong."

"Well, he's tall, dark and handsome," Aubrey said. "And, of course, well, you know..."

"I got that," Kaye said without looking up from his notebook. "Can you be more specific? Height, weight, general build, eyes, things I might notice if he had pants on?"

Aubrey stifled a giggle and said, "Let's see. Tall, and I mean tall, like six foot six, at least. Built like a basketball player, so, maybe two hundred, two ten? Dark hair and eyes. Honestly, probably the best description I can give you is that Storm looks just like a young Robert Mitchum, even has the whole chin dimple thing going on. Has the voice, too, which is probably why his podcasts are so hot."

"You said he was trying to go legit. You mean more mainstream Hollywood?"

"That's what I hear."

"Any idea where he might live?"

"None whatsoever. If people knew that, they'd be camped out with the paparazzi."

"How about Rachel Turner? Know where she lives?"

Aubrey just shook his head.

"Okay, I think that's all I need," Kaye said, tucking his paper brains back into his pocket. "Hey, Aubrey, thanks for the cooperation and help. I appreciate it."

"You're very welcome. I hope you find whoever hurt Nicole."

***

Kaye walked back to the Duo Glide and saw the piece of paper, again tucked between the windshield bag and the windshield, from fifty feet away.

"You gotta be kidding me," he muttered under his breath as he looked around. He'd been attentive since finding the last note left on the bike, but had seen no sign he was being followed. Whoever was leaving the notes was, if nothing else, very good at being stealthy.

He unfolded the note, knowing already that he'd find a page of Kanji characters. He at first crumpled the paper into a tight ball and looked for someplace to throw it away, but decided to keep it and let Roshi see it.

He swung over and sat on the Duo-Glide outside the Blue Whale, making notes of his conversation with Aubrey, which, all things considered, hadn't given him much he didn't already know except how Dennis Bettencourt, a.k.a. Storm Chase, had been added to the mix.

He still wanted to talk to Rachel Turner, and definitely needed to find and talk to Dennis Bettencourt.

He grabbed his cell phone and punched in the number for Rachel Turner he'd copied from Ingram's file. It was a Valley area code.

"Hello," a woman's voice answered tentatively.

"May I speak to Rachel Turner, please?"

"This is Rachel. Who is this?"

"Ms. Turner, my name is Ben Kaye. I'm a detective with the LAPD. I was wondering if you had a few minutes today that I might sit down and talk with you about a case I'm working."

"I don't live in L.A. anymore," Turner said. "I moved home about three months ago."

"Where's home?" Kaye asked.

"Tulsa, Oklahoma," she replied. "I kept this number because I couldn't afford a new phone."

"They're not cheap," Kaye said. "Obviously I can't come to Tulsa today. Would you mind if I asked you a few questions while I've got you?"

"I guess not. What's this about?"

"Nicole Ingram."

"Did she report me?"

"Why would she report you?"

"She accused me of stealing from her, which I did not, when we lived together," Turner said. "It broke up our friendship. But that was a long time ago. Why would she call the police now?"

"She didn't call us, Ms. Turner," Kaye said. "I'm investigating Nicole's murder, and your name came up as a friend."

"Nicole was murdered?" Turner said, her voice cracking. "Oh my God. What happened?"

"She and another individual were shot and killed last week."

"In L.A.?"

"Yes."

"That doesn't make sense," Turner said. "Months ago, like six or seven months, maybe, her boss at Pacific Design Center called me because Nicole hadn't shown up for work for a week."

"Had you talked to Nicole?" Kaye asked.

"No," Turner replied. "I told the woman that called that I didn't know, or care, where Nicole was."

"Really?" Kaye asked. "Her parents gave me your name. They said you two were good friends."

"Not after she accused me of stealing from her and I moved out."

"What did she think you took?"

"Some stupid pages out of something she was writing," Turner said.

"A screenplay?" Kaye asked.

"I guess," Turner said. "Anyway, it turned out to be her mistake and a big misunderstanding, but it ruined our friendship, so I moved."

"How was it her mistake?"

"She found the pages in the trunk of her Jetta," Turner said. "She must've forgotten where she put them. But she never apologized."

"I see," Kaye said. "Things happen. Too bad it cost you a friendship."

"No joke."

"I'm also trying to track down a guy named Dennis Bettencourt, goes by the stage name Storm Chase," Kaye said. "Did you know him?"

For a moment Kaye thought Turner had hung up on him.

"Ms. Turner?"

162

"I'm here," she said. "You know about Dennis? All I can tell you is that's a part of my life I'd like to forget."

"You were his girlfriend for a while, right?"

"Yes. Not for long, though. I don't stay with anyone who plays that rough."

"I don't need the details," Kaye said. "If you can tell me where he lives or where I might find him, that would help me out."

"Last I heard, and it's been since before I left L.A., he had a place in Venice. I don't know the address, though."

"Thank you," Kaye said. "One more question?"

"Sure."

"Who's Ruthie?"

"Ruthie was one of our neighbors," Turner said. "Lived on our floor. Kind of became like our grandma, you know, somebody we could go to, who sort of looked out for us."

"Do you remember her last name?" Kaye asked.

"Williams, I think. Maybe Williamson. Something like that."

"Thank you, Rachel," Kaye said. "I appreciate you taking the time to talk to me."

"Sorry I can't help you more. Nicole was good people. I thought she'd make it there." Turner's voice was wistful. "And, Detective?"

"Yes?"

"Be careful around Dennis. He's, uh, really kind of scary sometimes."

***

Kaye had no sooner put his phone away and was going through his start-up routine when the phone rang.

It was Captain Thompson.

"Kaye, where are you?"

"I'm out detecting, Captain. It's my job."

"Good," Thompson said. "Don't come back to the station."

"Did you say 'don't come back'?"

"That's what I said," Thompson confirmed. "Sloan and Leale are here waiting for you. They want your phone."

"My phone?" Kaye asked. "They can have it if they want it. I'll get a new one."

"Getting a new one might be a good idea," Thompson said. "Seems the Sullivan woman visited them this morning and showed them the call and text history on her phone. Leale couldn't help but spill to me that there were over thirty hang-up calls, a couple of voice-mails, and quite a few crude texts from your number."

"Bullshit. Somebody else is calling her and spoofing my number."

"That's what I said. Sloan seemed to consider it, but Leale just laughed," Thompson said. "And get this. Leale also let it slip that Sullivan has a court appearance scheduled for three this afternoon to request a temporary restraining order against you. I think IA wants your phone to help her case."

"Okay," Kaye said. "Thanks for the heads up. Anything else?"

"Here's what I want you to do," Thompson said. "First, get a new phone, forthwith. Call me with the new number, but do not, repeat do not, use it to call anyone even remotely connected to the Geller case. Before you go home today I want the phone you're on now in my possession. I'll wait here as long as I need to for you to bring it in."

"You sound like you're building me a defense."

"Hell, yes, I'm building you a defense!" Thompson exclaimed. "This is serious shit. If Sullivan gets her order you're out of a job on a firearms restriction and those two turds will be down at the DA's office asking for a warrant for your arrest."

"Okay, I'll get a new phone."

"Good choice, Detective. I'll be here."

Kaye thought for a moment, then punched in another number.

"District Attorney's office, Kayla Okafor."

"Counselor, Detective Kaye. How's it going?"

"It's going busy," she said. "I can give you three minutes before I'm due in court."

"I'll talk fast."

He recounted his conversation with Thompson, their plan for him to swap phones and what the Captain had heard about Sullivan going to court.

"Okay," Okafor said, "so what do you want from me?"

"Who's assigned to Orders today?"

"Judge Gardner, I think," she said. "Why?"

"If you have time, could you visit with Gardner before three o'clock and get her to put a hold on this?"

"Then do what?" Okafor asked, her skepticism obvious. "Ask her to quash Sullivan's request just because you're a nice guy? You know I can't do that."

"I don't want Gardner to quash it," Kaye said. "I just want you to tell Gardner I need time to respond to this before something that's total bullshit costs me my job. I have new information, too complex to explain right now, but I want to give Sullivan every possible chance to dig herself a deep, deep hole before she can stop my investigation."

"You sure about this?"

"I am. In fact, tell Gardner I know what's going on, and why, and just ask her to take it under advisement instead of just granting it on Sullivan's say so. If she issues an order I'm suspended, if not fired, and I believe that's why Sullivan's doing this."

"Kaye, you're –"

"Trust me, Counselor. Please."

"Okay," Okafor said. "I'll see what I can do."

Kaye spent the next hour buying a new phone.

Because he was getting an entirely new phone with a new number, and not trading in the phone he had, they refused to transfer any data. It led to a heated argument with the store manager, which Kaye lost even after he slammed a one hundred dollar bill down on the counter.

"Sorry, dude" the young man told him. "Not our job to duplicate your stuff on two phones."

He left the store with a newfound appreciation of why Rachel Turner still had her Los Angeles phone number, and powered down the old phone on the way to the bike.

He called Thompson, gave him the new number and recounted his conversation with Okafor. Thompson told him that Sloan and Leale had given up waiting for him, but he still thought Kaye should wait until after three to show his face at the station.

"I wouldn't put anything past those two weasels," Thompson said. "Especially Leale. What did you do to that guy, anyway?"

"He was in my Academy class," Kaye said. "I must've done something to piss him off, but I don't remember what."

"Well, have a nice afternoon and, please, keep detecting. It's your job. For now, anyway."

Kaye's next stop was lunch. While he ate, he went through his paper brains again, looking for anything he might be missing.

Two things bothered him the most.

One was how much time and effort Megan Sullivan was devoting to cause him trouble and block his investigation. Surely she realized it was a giant red flag. Why? Why would she be involved in Avi Geller's murder? Was there a connection he'd missed, or hadn't found yet? What could she possibly gain?

The second was the dearth of available information on the financial interests behind the Valle delle Viti development. It looked to Kaye to be almost a purposely constructed shield. He realized it could be for any one of various legitimate reasons, such as a liability defense or a tax strategy, but he had neither the information nor the financial acumen to figure it out.

But he knew somebody who did.

Thirty minutes later he walked into the FBI field office in the Federal Building at Wilshire and Veteran.

"Agent Iwamura, please," he said to the receptionist, holding up his badge wallet.

She called back to see if Iwamura was available, then told him to wait.

Special Agent Kai Iwamura had helped Kaye and Kaye's then-partner Greg Senske unravel the financial miasma at the bottom of the Birnbaum murder case just months ago. Iwamura had gotten himself in hot water for helping.

The door to the secure area opened and Iwamura stepped out.

"Ben, great to see you! Come on back. To what do I owe the pleasure?"

"I need your expertise, Kai," Kaye said as he walked around Iwamura and through the door. "That is, if after listening you decide you can help."

"Uh-oh," Iwamura said, then laughed as they headed for his office.

"Not this time," Kaye said after they both sat down. "I'm working a local homicide, but this time there are no spies or diplomats involved," he paused, then added, "at least not yet. I just need to pick your business brain for a minute."

"Ask away."

Kaye gave Iwamura the basic background on the Geller case, how he'd come across Geller's investment in Valle delle Viti, and that there was just something about it that bothered him.

He related his efforts to track down the resort's backers to make sure Geller wasn't the victim of a massive fraud, then murdered to keep him quiet, but that he'd run into a dead end with the Italian SRL company and didn't know how to get around it.

"I'll be glad to help," Iwamura said. "I don't have legal reach in Europe, but I have a friend there who might be able to help. I'll call and ask her to look into it. I might not be able to reach her until Monday, if that's okay."

"Not a problem," Kaye said. "I really appreciate it, Kai."

"Anything else?"

"Have you heard anything about the guy who burned up in his new Ferrari up on Mulholland?"

"Only what I read in the paper," Iwamura said. "Why?"

"I'm looking into it, and I think it might not have been an accident. I also found out the driver was ex-Delta Forces Command made good."

"Good enough to buy a Ferrari?"

"Apparently so," Kaye said. "Anyway, the people I talked to at his company said there were probably a lot of terrorists celebrating the guy's death. I told my Captain that and he said he was going to make some calls. I was curious if you'd heard anything."

"I have not," Iwamura said. "But he might have called my boss. Given the guy's background, it might be something we want to look at. Who are we talking about?"

"His name was Leigh Howell. Went by Rod. He was the head of an outfit called Black Scimitar."

"I've heard of them," Iwamura said. "Real up-and-comers, but there have been some rumors lately."

"Hadn't heard that," Kaye said. "Anyway, if it wasn't a terrorist hit, and I was you, I'd probably start by looking into their stock IPO last year. Made a lot of people rich."

"Rich enough to buy Ferraris, apparently. You think there might have been a financial motive?"

"Worth looking at, I think."

"Okay," Iwamura said. "I'll make some inquiries and pass the word. What's the best way to reach you?"

"Just call my cell."

\*\*\*

Banished from the Station until the odds of running into Sloan and Leale diminished, Kaye had to concentrate on things he could do over the phone.

His next call was to Patty. He gave her his new number and asked her to run Dennis Bettencourt through the system.

"Okay," she said after a moment. "I've got a Dennis R. Bettencourt," she read off the particulars. "Last known address in the Venice area. Two priors for misdemeanor assault and one for domestic battery. Most recent, the domestic battery, was about three years ago. Found guilty on the domestic battery, paid the fine, got probation and cleared it, and hasn't been heard from since. At least by us. Sounds like the kid finally grew up."

"Does the record list the domestic battery victim's name?"

"Not on this page, but stand by."

Kaye again heard the magic sounds of Patty's fingers on a keyboard and waited.

"Got it," she said. "According to the arrest report the victim was his wife, Caroline Bettencourt. Oh, and it says here she didn't want to press charges, but had visible injuries so the officers hooked Dennis anyway. But that's probably why he got probation."

"What's the address on the report?" Kaye asked. "Is it the Venice address?"

"Uh, no," Patty said. "Santa Monica."

"Probably means he and Caroline split after the arrest, right?"

"That'd be my guess, too, Detective."

"Can you pull up his license and see if it has a Venice address?" Kaye asked.

She read off the last known in Venice a few seconds later.

"Can you do one more thing for me?"

Patty laughed. "Detective, that's my job. What do you need?"

"I need a photo line-up that has Megan Sullivan and a woman named Lisa Riley in it, along with four other comparators. You know how this works. I'll send you a picture of Riley."

"I can do that," Patty said. "How soon do you need it?"

"Whenever you can get to it is fine."

"I'll try to have it on your desk by Tuesday morning."

"Thanks, Patty," Kaye said. "Now, can you transfer me to the Watch Commander?"

"Sure. Have a great weekend."

Ten seconds later he was talking to Lieutenant Crenshaw.

"What's up, Kaye?"

"Lieutenant, can you go into the system and look at the call log for Tuesday, ten days ago, and find a vandalism call in Paloma Canyon? Should be around eighteen hundred hours, give or take. RP's name will be Megan Sullivan. I need to know who handled the call."

"Sure," Crenshaw said, and Kaye could hear him working his keyboard, a lot slower than Patty. "This about the Geller case and the bimbo he was with?"

168

"It is."

"All right," Crenshaw said. "That call was handled by Officer Devon."

"No partner?"

"Not that night. We were thin."

"When does Devon work next?" Kaye asked.

"Actually, it's your lucky day," Crenshaw said, "He's on duty now, and I think I just saw him walk by."

"I need to talk to him," Kaye said. "Can you page him for me?"

"Hang on."

Kaye heard Crenshaw page Devon to his office on the overhead P.A. system and a moment later he heard the Lieutenant say, "It's Kaye. He wants to talk to you about a call. Take it over there."

There were two louds clicks before Kaye heard, "This is Officer Devon. What can I do for you, Detective Kaye?"

"You took a vandalism call in Paloma Canyon last week, Tuesday, early evening?"

"I did," Devon confirmed.

"What can you tell me about it?"

"Uh, let's see," Devon said slowly, and Kaye visualized Devon grabbing his own set of paper brains. "Okay, RP's name was Sullivan, first name Megan. The house was furnished but nobody living in it. She's the listing realtor."

"How much damage was there?" Kaye asked.

"Some of the walls were spray painted, books pulled off bookcases, a few broken items, a couple of lamps, but not that bad. Kids, probably. She insisted there was thirty grand in damages, but, honestly, I didn't see it."

"Must've been expensive lamps." Kaye said. "Tiffany's maybe."

"No shit." Devon laughed.

"Did you take pictures?"

"I did. They're in the system," Devon said, then gave Kaye the report number.

"Did she show up with anybody else?" Kaye asked.

"Can't say for sure. She got there first, and it looked like she had waited outside, but I don't know that for sure, either."

"So you didn't see anyone else?"

"No, sir," Devon replied. "But I didn't go upstairs."

"Why not?"

"Sullivan told me she'd checked the house and the vandalism was limited to the main living spaces on the ground floor."

"Did she say anything about the security system being tampered with?"

"No."

"Any sign of forced entry?"

"No," Devon said, then paused momentarily before adding, "I did find an unsecured gate in the back yard, but I have to admit I have no clue how the little shits got into that house. It was like they had keys and the codes."

"Did you ask Sullivan about that?"

"I did. She gave me a bullshit answer about one of the realtors that showed the house forgetting to turn the security system back on. In my opinion, Detective, she was less than forthcoming. I think the call was just to cover her ass with the insurance company. I doubt she even notified the owners."

"Did she happen to mention that she'd talked to me on the phone about an hour before you got the call?" Kaye asked.

"She did not," Devon replied.

"Okay, thanks Officer Devon," Kaye said and ended the call.

He checked the time. If Sloan and Leale had wanted his phone to bolster Sullivan's application for a restraining order today, they'd long missed their time window.

He suddenly remembered he needed to send Riley's picture to Patty and went to the Photos folder on his phone. It was empty.

"Well, crap," he muttered, reaching into his pocket for his old phone. A minute later he'd sent the photo.

***

Kaye walked into the Squad room and headed directly for Thompson's office.

The door was open. Thompson saw him coming and waved him in.

"Did you bring your old phone?" the Captain asked.

"I did." Kaye reached into this pocket and extracted the old phone.

Thompson instantly scooped it up.

"Thank you," he said. "I told the judge I would keep this."

"The judge?"

"ADA Okafor and Judge Gardner called me from chambers

before Sullivan's hearing. Gardner wanted to make sure I knew about what was going on and you weren't just bullshitting Okafor."

"Is she convinced?"

"The judge, you mean? Not totally. She said she'd hold Sullivan's order, but only temporarily, and said she'd pay close attention to what happens."

"Good to know," Kaye said.

"Just stay away from the Sullivan woman until she steps in it, okay?"

"I'll try, but no promises."

"Then at least notify me before you attempt or make any kind of contact at all with her so I can cover your ass," Thompson said. "Got anything for me on the Ferrari case?"

"I met with Kai Iwamura a while ago. I mentioned it to him."

"I haven't called over there yet. I guess I should. You stay on the Geller case for now."

"I can do that," Kaye said. "I'm making progress." He got up to leave.

"Oh, and Kaye?"

"Sir?"

"You do know that if your new number shows up on Sullivan's call history on Monday, you're history, right?"

Kaye stared at his boss.

"Gee, Captain, thanks for the vote of confidence."

\*\*\*

Kaye practiced for an hour out on the patio, doing some especially brutal strength and balance moves to take his mind off Thompson's well-intentioned but insulting warning about Megan Sullivan and his new phone number.

He had no doubt that Sullivan was hiding something, and was obviously willing to go to great lengths to deflect his investigation.

But why?

He had nothing that connected her to Avi Geller or Nicole Ingram, and, at least that he knew of yet, she had nothing to gain from the death of either one.

Maybe there was something going on in her life she didn't want the police to know about? Even if it had nothing to do with the murders. His gut told him he needed to know a lot more about Megan Sullivan.

He also needed to find and talk to Dennis Bettencourt and Ruthie, Nicole's neighbor.

He finished exercising, grabbed a bottle of water and sat on the patio gazing out to sea, wondering if he needed to work Saturday.

Or if he needed to ask Thompson for a partner. He chuckled. That would probably create a Captaincy promotional opportunity due to heart attack. But the details were adding up and they all needed to be checked out.

He laughed out loud. Partner? Seriously?

After cooling off he decided to meditate before grabbing dinner. After all, as Roshi often reminded him, exactly zero percent of those who do not actively seek enlightenment ever achieve it.

The evening was mild, so he decided to sit outside.

For Kaye, meditation had always been an 'either/or' experience. He knew when he was having a second-rate session while he was having it, but he didn't know he was having a first-rate session until it was over. There was, for him, no point of recognition or anticipation ahead of time and no sense of time passing.

He moved a cushion to the ground, assumed his posture, focused on Roshi's instructions for *shikantaza* and slowly surrendered his mind to his surroundings.

At one point he had a stray thought that the session was going well, which he knew meant it wasn't, really.

He gathered himself, focused, and felt a gentle wave of calm wash over him.

It didn't last long.

He suddenly heard a woman's voice, as if she was standing right behind him, say, "Beware the beauty of the falling sun."

Startled, Kaye spun and looked behind him. He was alone on the patio.

He realized he was sweating profusely. What the hell?

He knew that hearing voices was a symptom of psychosis. He'd seen it a lot in suspects over the years.

But he'd never shared the experience. Until now.

He moved to the edge of a chair and tried to rationalize what had just happened. Were the notes getting to him? He didn't even know yet what the two he'd found on the bike this week said.

The only conclusion he came up with was that Roshi's question had somehow subconsciously affected him, making him vulnerable to the power of suggestion.

It was time to go see Roshi again, and get the recent notes translated.

That, or call a psychiatrist.

# DAY 13

### Saturday Week 2

Unnerved by the experience of hearing the voice, Kaye slept fitfully, worried that if he fell hard asleep the voice would come to him in his dreams. Or nightmares. It was late before he forced himself to get out of bed and go about his day.

He didn't practice, but after breakfast he took his new phone out to the patio.

"Hello."

"Hi. Mom," Kaye said.

"Benjamin?"

"It's me," Kaye said. "I called to give you my new number."

"No wonder your name wasn't on the Caller ID."

"Yeah, sorry about that, but I just got it yesterday afternoon," he said.

"Did your old phone break?" she asked. "You know you can keep the old number with a new phone, right? They just change out that little card thing."

"It wasn't about a new phone, Mom. It was about a new number."

There was a moment of silence.

"What's going on?"

"I'm back to work."

"At the police department?" she said. "I thought you decided to give that up."

"Well," he said, "turns out it wasn't as easy as that."

She laughed and said, "I'm not surprised. If ever I knew anybody who was doing the job God intended for them, it's you."

"Thanks, Mom."

"So, tell me why you needed a new phone number."

He gave her a quick summary of recent happenings, didn't mention murders, and focused on the fact that the woman making the complaint was wrong.

"Are you sure you're okay, son?" she asked. "Honestly, you sound a little...off. You're not sick, are you?"

174

"No, just tired. Didn't sleep well last night." He changed the subject. "So, how do you like the new place?"

She had planned on selling the family home after the death of Kaye's father, but after taking some time to think about it, she had deeded the house over to Kaye's sister and her family and moved into a condo not far away.

"I like it," she said. "Not nearly as much upkeep, which is nice, and I'm still close to everyone."

"Everybody's okay?"

"Oh, yeah. Just busy. You know how it is."

"I do," he said. "Well, I won't keep you. I've got some errands to run, so I'll let you go. I just wanted to make sure you had the right phone number."

"Thank you, Benjamin," she said. "I'll edit your Contact form." She laughed, then said, "Listen to me! I'm becoming quite the tech expert!"

"Tell everyone I said hello."

"Will do. And Benjamin?"

"Yeah?"

"If you don't feel good, you go to the doctor, okay? I know you're practically Superman, at least on the outside, but please take care of yourself."

"Will do, Mom. Love you."

"Love you, too."

Kaye looked at his phone. How do they always know?

With a sigh he rose and got organized.

His first stop was the grocery store, which meant the pickup instead of a bike, where he bought enough provisions to feed a platoon for the next month. While waiting at the check stand he picked up the latest free motorcycles for sale newsprint magazine.

After he got home and put things away he stood at the kitchen counter and thumbed through the listings.

On page sixteen he spied a small classified.

1951 HD Hydra Glide Panhead

Total basket case, but should be all here.

Serious inquiries only

The ad had no price, only a phone number in the 818 area code.

What the hell? He had a '41 and a '61. Might as well fill the inside straight.

He called the number.

"This is Damion Spencer," a voice answered.

"Hi," Kaye said. "I'm calling about your '51 Panhead. What can you tell me?"

"Pretty much all I can tell you is that it's just what the ad said, a total basket case. Except in this case boxes might be more accurate. Almost all the parts are in cardboard boxes."

"Your ad said that it should all be there. What does that mean?"

"Look," Spencer said, "I'm not really a motorcycle guy. I was told it was all there, but I can't guarantee anything. You need to come look at it."

"I hope you don't mind my asking," Kaye said, "but if you're not a bike guy, how'd you end up with a 1951 Harley in boxes?"

"I got it from my brother," Spencer replied.

"How long ago?" Kaye asked.

"About six years ago."

"Did he decide not to tackle it?"

There was a brief silence before Spencer said, "Mister, you ask a lot of questions."

"I'm just trying to find out about the bike," Kaye said. "I'm not trying to offend you, and I apologize if I did."

Another, longer silence.

"Okay, here's the story," Spencer said finally. "I got if from my brother. He bought it before he joined up and planned on restoring it when he got out. It's still in boxes because when my brother came home, he was in a box. That cover it for you?"

Kaye was embarrassed and speechless.

"So," Spencer asked, breaking the silence, "you want to come look at it or not?"

"Yes, I would like to come look at it," Kaye said. "I'm sorry about your brother. Truly sorry."

"No worries. Are you coming out today?"

"Where are you?"

"Chatsworth," Spencer replied, then gave Kaye a street address.

"I'm on the way," Kaye said. "Give me an hour."

"I'll be here."

"You want my name?"

"Nah. You're the only guy that's called."

A little less than an hour later, Kaye, riding the '41 Knucklehead, rolled up in front of the address Spencer had given him.

It was a well-kept two-story that looked like a crane had been used to plop the mismatched second floor down atop the original house in a desperate bid for more square footage. A boxwood hedge surrounded the front yard. In front of the closed, two-car garage door were an newer, black, full-sized SUV and an older, dark blue Jeep CJ with a canvas top.

Seconds after he rang the bell the door opened and Kaye looked down at a tow-headed little girl, maybe five years old.

She took one look at him, yelled, "Daddy, the motorcycle man is here! He's a giant!" and turned and ran.

She stopped where the entry way became the living room and turned around, eyes wide and fingers in her mouth, and stared at him.

A man rounded the corner, saw Kaye, and knelt down next to the little girl. Kaye heard him whisper, "It's okay. He's big, but he's not a giant. And what have I told you about answering the door by yourself? Now, go find your mom."

She was off like a flash.

"Hi, Damion Spencer," he said. "You called about the bike?"

"That was me. Ben Kaye. I'm sorry if I was rude on the phone."

"That's okay," Spencer said. "I guess I'm a little touchy about the bike. It's taken me a long time to be able to let it go."

"I understand," Kaye said, remembering how he'd agonized over letting go of Amy's beloved '67 Corvette until he met Behar Shahnaz and she saved his life.

"So, let's go take a look at it," Spencer said. "If you want to wait outside the garage, I'll open the door."

Basket case was an apt description. The bare frame stood up against one wall, surrounded by some of the larger pieces. Six good-sized boxes, obviously the worse for wear, were stacked against the wall. The gas tank and fenders protruded from the top layer of boxes, too full to close, and a box tucked under the frame was filled with a tangled mass of wires and cables, across the top of which rested the handlebars.

"Don't say I didn't warn you," Spencer said, smiling. "Basket case, right?"

"That it is," Kaye said, walking slowly around the pile. He lifted the red pearl and black gas tank to check it, and was surprised to see that it was undented and the paint wasn't all that bad. He put it back and looked around.

"Do you have the front forks and tree?"

"Oh, yeah, sorry," Spencer said, spinning on his heels and walking to the opposite back corner of the garage. He came back with the necessary pieces. "Too big for a box. The pipes are there, too."

"The rest is in the boxes?"

"As far as I know," Spencer said. "But, like I said, no guarantees. It's strictly as-is, cash and carry."

"Do you have paperwork? A title, old registration?"

"Yep. It's still in my brother's name, but he gave me Power of Attorney before he deployed."

"How much are you asking?" Kaye asked.

"Daddy," a small voice said from behind Kaye. He turned and saw the little girl who'd answered the door.

"What, Punkin'?"

"Is the giant taking Uncle Alex's motorcycle away?"

"Maybe," Spencer said. "But it's time for Uncle Alex's motorcycle to find a new home with somebody who can fix it up and ride it and love it. Uncle Alex would've wanted that, right?"

"But I love Uncle Alex's motorcycle, too," she said. Her eyes fill with tears and her chin trembled as she slowly turned and walked, head down, back into the house.

"How old is she?" Kaye asked.

"Four," Spencer said. "She wasn't even born when my brother was killed in action, but…she hears us talk and sees his picture."

"When was he killed?"

"April the fifth, two thousand and thirteen, Helmand Province, Afghanistan."

"I'm really sorry for your loss," Kaye said. "As an ex-Marine, I thank you for his service and his sacrifice."

"Thank you. I –"

"Damion, what did you tell Ellie?" another voice interrupted, and Kaye turned to see a very pregnant woman, one hand held under her belly, standing in the open door to the house. She nodded at him and he acknowledged her.

"I told her it was time for Uncle Alex's motorcycle to find a new home."

"Oh, okay," the woman said. "I'll talk to her." She turned and disappeared.

"My wife," Spencer said. "Casey."

"I gathered that," Kaye said, smiling. "I don't mean to be rude again, but when's she due?"

"Any time now, and trust me, we are both very ready. It's the big reason we're selling the bike."

"Do you know if it's a boy or girl?" Kaye asked.

"Boy," Spencer said. "His name will be Alexander."

"So," Kaye said, steering the talk back to business, "what's your asking price?"

"I've kind of settled on five hundred," Spencer said, avoiding eye contact.

"Five hundred?" Kaye said. "I can't in good conscience give you five hundred dollars for this."

"I think that's pretty fair," Spencer said.

Kaye laughed. "Not to you, it's not. This may be a pile of boxes filled with old motorcycle parts, but inside those boxes is a very desirable bike, even if there are a few things missing."

"What do you think it's worth?"

Kaye did the math.

"A fully-restored 1951 FL sold at auction not long ago for a hundred times what you just told me you'd take for it. Even if everything is here, it's going to cost a bit to put it all back together and make it road worthy. And whatever isn't here isn't going to come cheap."

"How about you make me an offer?" Spencer said, trepidation in his voice.

Kaye looked at the dusty frame, which he could tell was straight, and the pile of parts and boxes, and thought about the very pregnant wife and the brother killed in action.

"How about fifteen?" Kaye asked.

"Fifteen hundred dollars? For this?" Spencer said, astounded.

"No," Kaye said. "Not fifteen hundred. Fifteen thousand. If that's not good, I'd go seventeen five."

Damion Spencer's mouth hung open and he stared at Kaye.

"Seventeen thousand five hundred?" he managed to say.

"Sold!" Kaye said, holding out his hand.

Spencer grabbed it with both of his and pumped it up and down.

"Thank you. I don't know what to say." Tears welled up in Spencer's eyes.

"Don't thank me," Kaye said. "I'm still coming out ahead, and I think I got lucky being the first guy here." He reached into his pocket and pulled out his cash. "Obviously, I don't ride around with that kind of cash on me, and, also obviously, I can't take it with me today," he hooked his thumb toward the Knucklehead, "but if you're willing to take a thousand as good faith money and confirm the sale in writing for me, I'll come back in my truck, with cash, tomorrow and we can do the paperwork."

"I… I guess we could do that," Spencer stammered. "Are you sure?"

"I'm sure," Kaye confirmed.

"I've got a Bill of Sale form inside," Spencer said. "Will that do?"

"Works for me."

Spencer headed inside, and Kaye could hear him shouting excitedly.

"Casey! Casey!"

Thirty minutes later they'd worked out the details of Kaye picking up the bike, and a Bill of Sale listing the terms, which Kaye would hold onto until the next day, had been signed.

Just as Kaye was about to head out to the '41, the door from the house opened and Casey, holding Ellie's hand, stepped into the garage.

"Go ahead," Casey urged the little girl.

She took two tentative steps toward Kaye and looked up.

"Are you taking Uncle Alex's motorcycle away?"

Kaye knelt on one knee to look her in the eye.

"Yes," he said. "But not until tomorrow. I'll make sure it has a good home."

"You promise?"

"I promise," Kaye said, crossing his heart. "When I get it all fixed up and shiny I'll bring it back and show it to you. Shake on it." He held out his hand.

She looked at Kaye's hand and her eyes got big. Slowly, she reached out, managed to grab his index finger, and started to shake it.

She looked up at her father, her eyes still wide, and whispered, "See, Daddy, I told you he's a giant!"

*** 

Kaye was elated on the ride home. He knew he'd uncovered a diamond in the rough, and while he'd paid handsomely for it, he was confident it would be worth considerably more when it was back on the road.

It would also provide a much needed distraction.

He found himself wishing he had someone to share his good fortune with, and, to his surprise, Auggie McMaster was the first person that came to mind. He thought about it for a minute, then dismissed it and went back to mentally planning the restoration of the '51 Panhead.

After going to the bank the bulk of the afternoon was spent preparing the garage to receive the Pan-in-a-Box, as Kaye had already dubbed it. It didn't take much. Had the Corvette still occupied one end of the garage it might have been tight, but now he had plenty of room.

As the afternoon wore on he realized he was doing busy work and decided to call it. He'd do a short practice, clean up, and ride to the café at Paradise Cove to treat himself to a celebratory dinner.

About an hour later he idled the new Road King down the driveway and headed for Coast Highway.

When he approached Paradise Cove Road the light was red and traffic was stacked in the left turn lane. He slowed and started working down through the gears. When he hit third, the northbound lights turned green. He hit the throttle, shifted up, stayed in the through lane and kept going.

He wondered, why not? It's a nice evening for a ride.

Two hours later, almost fully dark outside, Kaye rolled into the Auggie's Wine'N'Diner parking lot.

The lot was packed, at least a hundred bikes lined up in rows that basically conformed to the lines painted on the asphalt. Oddly enough, no riders hung out outside.

The tricked-out Street Glide was again parked on the sidewalk not far from the front door.

Auggie's was jammed, the noise and activity level twice what it had been at lunch a week ago. The space seemed much larger, and Kaye realized a portable wall had been opened to make room for many more tables. They were all covered with white linen tablecloths and every chair was occupied.

He stood at the unattended hostess's podium for several minutes, scanning the room for Auggie, but not seeing her. The bartender was a man Kaye didn't recognize.

Maybe this was a bad idea, he thought.

He turned to leave and almost ran into a woman, elegantly dressed in a black, mid-calf length skirt and a white, ruffle-front blouse with an elaborately embroidered collar and lower sleeves. Her black hair was done up, held in place with a wide, diamond-studded clip that matched her diamond earrings.

"Welcome back, Mr. Strabler," she said, smiling as she leaned in close to his ear to be heard over the din.

Kaye suddenly tumbled to the fact that he was face-to-face with Auggie McMaster.

Almost.

In her heels she was three inches taller than he was.

"Glad to be back," he said loudly. "I almost didn't recognize you."

She laughed. "I noticed."

"Well, you look…" He stumbled for the right word.

"Different?" She helped him out. "Yeah, we're having a special event tonight. A tasting. I'm in my finest Master Sommelier get-up, including," she reached up and touched an elaborate silver necklace that competed for space with a string of pearls, "my tastevin."

"Your what?"

"My tastevin." She held it up, opened it, and Kaye realized he was looking at a small cup. "They're mostly ceremonial these days, but they're coming back. Plus, they're part of the whole wine schtick, so I wore it."

"Looks like it's going well," Kaye said.

"Very," Auggie said. "We're jammed."

"I see that. Maybe I should come back another time."

She frowned. "If you'd like to stay, Ben Kaye, I'll make a place for you." She smiled again. "After all, I do own the joint."

"I'd like that," Kaye said. "I'll be fine at the end of the bar, out of everybody's way, if there's room."

Her smile expanded. She put her hand on his shoulder and leaned in close to his ear.

"Follow me." She led him through the main part of the restaurant toward the bar.

To Kaye, the whole place was a visual contradiction. Tables set with elegant dinnerware, candles, a variety of stemware glasses and a single red rose in a crystal vase, all atop snow white tablecloths, were surrounded by diners who looked more suited for a South Dakota saloon in August.

But the concept clearly worked, and by the number of people obviously enjoying themselves immensely, it worked very well.

Auggie led him to the same end-of-the-bar spot he'd occupied on his first visit, held up a finger in a 'wait a sec' gesture, disappeared through the door behind the bar and reappeared carrying a bar stool.

"Here you go, officer," she said as she put the stool down.

Kaye stared at her.

"Oh, please," she said over the din. "My Dad was on the job for

182

thirty years. I can spot a cop a mile away, and your preference for the gunfighter seat just confirms it."

Kaye smiled and said, "You got me. LAPD."

"Oh, the big time," she teased. "Dad was SLO – she pronounced it 'slow' – County Sheriff's Department. Retired as the head of the Patrol Division. What's your grind?"

"Detective. And what's 'slow'?"

"That's how the locals shorten San Luis Obispo," Auggie replied. "Let me welcome you, Detective Kaye, and your definitely un-girlish figure, back to my establishment. As you may have noticed, we're big on local wines here, so feel free to imbibe those of your choice, on the house. I trust you'll use extra caution if you're riding."

"I always ride," Kaye said, stopped, and added, "Almost."

"Me, too," she said, then signaled the bartender. He came over, they put their heads together in a conversation Kaye couldn't hear, and then she turned back to him. "Please stick around?"

He nodded, and she headed off to mingle, throwing a smile back over her shoulder.

The bartender brought him the menu for the evening. It was hardly the bar food selection he'd seen on his first visit. Instead, there were a half-dozen exotic sounding selections with French and Italian names. Listed below each one were several suggested wine pairings, and flights were available.

Kaye chose the one he could translate; steak; and ordered a glass of one of the suggested wines. He also made it clear to the bartender he was not in a hurry.

It was after 10:00 p.m. when the last of the diners straggled out the door, many carrying bagged wine club orders to stash in the saddlebags on the ride home, and all of them wanting one last good-bye from Auggie.

After seeing off the last of them, Auggie walked over and sat down on the barstool across the corner of the bar from Kaye.

"I'm glad that's over," she said.

"You don't do this every Saturday night, do you?" Kaye asked.

"Oh, God no. Tasting dinners are only twice a year. One in the spring when the newly-pruned vines start to leaf out and one, this one, around harvest time. It's kind of an appeal to the wine gods for a good vintage."

"Does it work?" Kaye asked, grinning.

"Only time will tell. Sometimes the vines can be cruel," she replied.

She reached out and laid a hand on Kaye's forearm. "Hey, I've got about thirty minutes of stuff I absolutely have to do tonight, but the rest can wait until tomorrow. If you have the patience, what say a girl buys you a beer after that?"

Kaye looked around, then back at Auggie and said, "Do I know her?"

She looked at him murderously for about three seconds, then burst out laughing. "Oh, the detective has a sense of humor! Good thing for him he's so big, or I'd toss him out."

"I'll wait," was all Kaye said.

Just under a half-hour later, after all the employees had gone, Auggie came back. She had changed clothes and now wore jeans, a t-shirt and black boots. Her hair was down and captured by a bright red bandana, and a motorcycle helmet hung by its strap from her fingers.

"Okay, so how about that beer?" she asked.

"What've you got?" Kaye asked

"Not here, silly. I know this place in Solvang that has too many beers to count. If you can't find something there that you like, you're not trying."

"I'm in," Kaye said. "Lead the way."

Auggie set the security system and led Kaye out the front door. She walked directly to the Street Glide and started putting on her helmet.

"That's yours?" Kaye asked.

"Yep. Got it last year. Pretty much retired my car and van except when I need to carry stuff, or it's foggy."

Kaye shook his head and smiled. She was describing him.

"What?" Auggie asked.

"Nothing," Kaye said. "What's the name of this place and where is it, in case we get separated."

She gave him directions and told him she'd meet him there, that she had to make a stop first but it would only take about two minutes.

"I'll be there," Kaye said.

Fifteen minutes later Kaye had parked and was waiting on the sidewalk outside a noisy Biergarten that occupied about half of a large, timbered structure off Solvang's main drag.

"Hi."

He heard Auggie's voice from behind him and spun around.

"Hope you haven't been waiting long," she said, grimacing slightly.

"Just got here. Where's your bike?"

"Home. That was my stop," she said. "I only live a couple blocks that way." She pointed. "It's an easy walk, so now I can have more than two beers if I want to." She laughed.

"Good plan." Kaye pulled the door open. "Shall we?"

The place was hopping. Thanks to Kaye's massive size, he was able to shoulder through the crowd surrounding the fifty-foot long bar and find a small table in a relatively quiet corner.

Over ninety minutes and two pitchers of very good Belgian microbrews, Auggie McMaster and Ben Kaye got acquainted and swapped stories.

He told her about growing up in Wisconsin and joining the Marines to escape a strained relationship with his father, his time in the Marines, how he'd landed in Southern California after his early discharge, how he'd met Amy at Harley Charlie's bike shop, about her writing, and her death in a motorcycle crash.

"Oh, my God," she said. "Ben, I'm so sorry. I'm almost embarrassed to admit I've never read her books, but I know who she was. I have seen the movies. What happened to the other driver?"

Kaye looked at her and said, "I got him."

She told him she'd been married once, too young, that it hadn't lasted and she was relieved there had been no children. She warned him it had made her a bit of a cynic when it came to men.

She told him she was the third generation of her family to be born in the Central Coast area. In 1933 her great-grandfather had given up and abandoned his farm in Harper County, Oklahoma, after his infant daughter choked to death inside the house during a night time dust storm. He'd loaded up his family and, like many others, headed for California.

"They were honest-to-God Okies," she said. "Grapes of Wrath is my second-favorite movie, after The Wild One, and I always imagine that Henry Fonda's Tom Joad is my great-grandpa, except he was never in prison." She paused, then added hastily, "At least as far as I know."

She told him that her grandfather had also been a farmer, passing the family land along to one of her uncles. Lettuce and strawberries had never done anything for her, but she'd been fascinated by grape vines and grapes, and subsequently wine, since she was old enough to be aware of them, and that her only goal in life had always been to make great wines.

"Until Valle delle Viti came along, I was doing great," she said.

"They slowed me down, but I'm not giving up."

He told her about his uncertainty about being a cop since Amy's death, but that he'd finally accepted that it was what he was supposed to be doing.

He told her about buying the '51 Panhead Pan-in-a-Box that morning, how excited he was to have a project bike, and gave her the quick history of the '41 and '61.

"Wow," she said. "I wish I had that kind of skill set."

"I'll teach you, if you teach me how to make wine," Kaye said. "I'm assuming you still want to make wine again, right?"

"I never stopped making wine," she said. "They took my vines, but I still have all my equipment. I'm just using grapes I buy instead of grapes I grow, and, really, a lot of vineyards operate that way."

"But you want to grow your own."

"I do," she said, and went on to tell Kaye about a sixty acre plot she had her eye on. It was still native vegetation, probably because it was a little steeper than many larger growers liked. "I snuck in at night and took soil samples. They were outstanding, and I figure I can eventually terrace the steeper slopes if I have to, without spending a ton of money. I have an option on it now, with about three months before my right of first refusal runs out."

"Think you'll make it?" Kaye asked, idly wondering if she'd consider taking on a silent partner.

"Yeah, absolutely," she replied. "In fact, I don't want to jinx it, but I'm really close. The restaurant has turned out to be a terrific investment. I'm way ahead of projections."

"Can I ask you a really personal question?"

He caught her in the middle of raising her mug, and she stopped short of her mouth.

"Sure," she said. "I guess." Then she took a big drink.

"How'd you get the name Auggie? Honestly, you look more like a Giselle or Cindy or Naomi to me."

She snorted, choked on her beer, started to cough and grabbed a napkin.

But she came up laughing.

"I'm sorry," Kaye said. "I didn't mean…"

"No, no, it's okay," she said breathlessly, wiping tears from her eyes. "I'm used to it, really."

She told Kaye her father, who had died less than a year before, had dreamed as a boy of being a history professor, but lacked the family resources to go to graduate school. So he became a cop. But he never lost his fascination with history and was especially interested in the Roman Empire.

"I have two brothers and two sisters," she said, counting them off on her fingers as she named them. "Marcus, Julius, Octavia and Livia. And I'm Augustina."

"So, why not Tina?"

"I think that was actually Dad's plan, because that's what he always called me. It worked until the third grade. There was already a Tina in my class, and it confused the issue. Then the boys figured out that Auggie rhymes with doggie, the teacher heard them, and I've been Auggie ever since."

Kaye suddenly felt compelled to tell Auggie about Roshi and the Zen monk's belief that Kaye was the reincarnation of legendary 12th Century warrior-monk Benkei.

That led to a discussion of Buddhism versus other religions. Kaye told her he meditated and practiced yoga, but didn't really consider himself a Buddhist, that he was too western for that.

"You do yoga?" Auggie asked, amazed. "At your size? Really?"

"Yep," Kaye said, and told her the story about discovering it after getting hurt in the Corps, and that it had led him to what he now considered to be his Path.

"I'm impressed," she said. "I've never even tried to figure all that stuff out."

"Not a church-goer?"

She laughed and said, "I'd probably get struck by lightning if I tried to walk into a church. I am, after all, the namesake of a Roman Emperor. You know, the guys who crucified Jesus."

Kaye bit his tongue. After his recent experience in Aspen, he wasn't about to start that discussion.

Instead, he said, "Yeah, but Tiberius, not Augustus, was Caesar then."

"I'm impressed," Auggie said, grinning. "You know, Ben Kaye, I'm sure glad you walked into my little grape juice joint. What was up with that, anyway?"

"Good fortune," he replied. "I'm working a case that might have a financial connection to Valle delle Viti. I visited, I got hungry, and voila, there you were. Great sandwich, by the way."

"A case connected to them?" Auggie asked, leaning forward. "Did you find anything?"

"No," Kaye said. "It's a homicide case, and the victim was an investor. But after seeing how well the resort is doing, all I can say is that people who make money together are usually friends, not enemies, so I doubt there's a connection. But I did have a run-in with the Chumash Oaks police."

"Please don't call them the police," she groaned. "That's an insult to you and my Dad. Those people are thugs. Absolute thugs."

"I got that impression."

"Talk around the aging barrels," she smiled, "is that they make a lot of sketchy, oh, what did Dad call it? You know, when they confiscate your property for being related to crimes?"

"Civil asset forfeiture," Kaye said, remembering Reid's threats to confiscate his bike and cash.

"That's it. My memory is going, which means it must be getting late."

It was. Kaye looked around and saw fewer than ten other people still in the place.

"Yeah, I'd better get going," he said. "Two hours home."

"You could stay at my place."

Kaye looked across at Auggie.

She looked back, and a second later he saw her eyes open wide.

"Whoa," she said, and Kaye saw a blush creep up her neck above the t-shirt. "Pump the brakes, turbo. I know we talked about families, religion and kids' names, but I meant you could sleep at my house and ride home in the daylight. Separate quarters."

"Are you sure? About the invitation, I mean." He felt himself blush.

"I'm sure. I like you, Benkei," she smiled and winked. "I just thought it would be better if you didn't have to ride home in the dark after drinking beer." Kaye saw the blush mount again.

"I appreciate the invitation, Auggie, and normally I'd take you up on it. But first thing in the morning I have to pick up that old Harley I bought today. I have to get home, get my pickup and be back to Chatsworth pretty early. If I stay the night, I'll never make it."

"Oh, okay," she said, and Kaye could tell she thought he was blowing her off.

"But can you send me a text real quick?"

"Why —" she stopped and Kaye again saw her blush. "Oh, duh."

Kaye recited his new number and a second later he had hers.

"I'm going to call you, you know," he said.

"You'd better, Strabler, or I'll have Lee Marvin... all...over...your ass."

\*\*\*

As he rode through Santa Barbara and Montecito on US 101 he couldn't help but look up at the lights spread across the hills and wondered if any of them shone from the place where Nicole Ingram's life had taken an unexpected, and ultimately fatal, detour.

The ride home didn't take any longer than usual, it just seemed like it to Kaye. He interpreted that as meaning he would rather have stayed in Solvang, and that surprised him. It had been a while since he'd felt that way.

# DAY 14
## Sunday Week 2

Dog tired, Kaye still managed to keep his appointment to finish his transaction with Damion Spencer and pick up the Pan-in-a-Box. After unloading the big parts and boxes and stacking them in the garage, he went inside to get some lunch, and, after eating, promptly fell asleep on the couch.

He dreamed.

A fierce warrior, wielding two swords and dressed in odd armor, was after him. The warrior wore a helmet with large horns, but Kaye could see the face beneath and it looked, like the tattoo he'd seen on the woman at Black Scimitar, to be an odd mix of animal and human.

He knew the warrior was samurai.

No matter where he turned or how fast he ran, the samurai was always in front of him, waiting. It was then that he saw himself dressed in the same unusual armor, carrying swords.

Realizing he could not escape, he decided to stand and fight. His father appeared and stood beside him.

"Run, Ben. You've met your match. You can't defeat this one," Matthew Kaye said, then disappeared.

The samurai came at him, the sword so fast Kaye could barely see it, and before the warrior delivered the killing blow said, "You will die, Benkei. My Lord will be avenged."

The voice was female..

*Onna-musha.*

Her sword whistled through the air and Kaye was suddenly looking up at his own headless body as it crumpled to the ground.

He awoke with a start, drenched in sweat as he'd been when he'd heard the voice on Friday.

The dream had been startlingly vivid and it took Kaye a moment to gather his wits.

He had never dreamt his own death before, at least that he could remember, and wondered what it meant. He also wondered if he'd fallen asleep during his last *shikantaxi* session and the voice had been nothing more than a dream fragment.

He got up and headed for the kitchen to get some water, then stopped short.

A piece of paper was taped to the French doors that opened to the patio.

With the light behind it, he could clearly see Kanji characters.

\*\*\*

Two hours later Kaye passed through the gate of Kyokoku-Dera Monastery.

This time he was blind to the view that opened before him and idled the Road King down the slope to the main building.

Roshi must have heard him coming, because when Kaye had finished parking and got off the bike, the old monk stood on the top step, smiling.

"I like your old, red motorcycle better, Benkei," he said.

"I will ride it next time, Roshi-sama, " Kaye said, bowing slightly. "Forgive me, but I come to your home today without a gift."

"Your presence is gift enough, Benkei-bo," Roshi said, returning the bow. "Come, we will walk."

The two walked slowly toward the pond. Kaye tried to figure a way to ask Roshi about the notes, the voice and the dream, but the master beat the pupil to the punch.

"You are troubled, Benkei. Tell me, why have you come today?"

They stopped. Kaye reached into his pocket and withdrew the three notes he'd received since his last visit to Kyokoku-Dera and handed them to Roshi.

The old man read them silently, then looked at Kaye, perplexed.

"You do not see the person who gives you these?"

"No, two were left on my motorcycle, and that one," he pointed, "was taped to my back door today. While I was home, but asleep. What do they say?"

"Which is the first you received?" Roshi asked.

"That one," Kaye replied, tapping the paper.

"It says, 'Your presence is strong, Benkei. I sense you during zazen. Yoshitune is not here to protect you and the beauty of the falling sun will take your head'."

Roshi went to the next note and read, "Do not look for me, Benkei. I am a ghost. You will not see me until I decide it is time."

191

"And the one I got a little while ago?"

"We meet soon, Benkei. Destiny. This time you will fall," Roshi said, then glanced at the notes again. "It is also interesting that each note, while not bearing the name of the writer, carries the same hanko."

"What's that?"

"You would call it a seal, or a stamp of identification."

"Do you know whose hanko it is?"

"No," Roshi replied. "But I will see if I can find out."

Kaye was silent, considering the contents of the notes, then asked, "What does the beauty of the falling sun mean?"

"I do not know," Roshi said, "and I will not speculate. Why do you ask?"

"Because I had a strange dream while I was napping. In it, a samurai used that phrase, and until just now I had no idea it was in the note," Kaye replied. "I heard a woman's voice threaten me during a *shikantazi* session when there was nobody near. Or maybe I fell asleep and dreamed that, too."

"Remember our talk of circles on your last visit?"

"Yes, of course, but…"

"But you do not believe."

"I'm sorry, Roshi," Kaye said. "I don't mean to insult you."

Roshi looked up at him and Kaye saw sadness in the old man's eyes.

"You do not insult me, Benkei. You insult yourself." He started walking back toward the main temple.

They walked without talking. Kaye felt he'd hurt the old monk, whom he loved like a grandfather, but didn't know how, or even if, he could repair the damage. He thought about the notes, the voice and the dream, and came to the inescapable conclusion that Roshi was right. He didn't truly believe. It was all a little too supernatural for him to buy into.

They had reached the Road King when Roshi turned to Kaye.

"I believe I rushed you, Benkei. You were not ready for *shikantaza*. You should return to koan meditation."

"Whatever you think is best, Roshi. What is my first lesson?"

Roshi nodded curtly and said, "If a man follows a path he does not trust, does he walk forward or backward?"

With that the monk turned, went up the steps and disappeared into the temple.

# DAY 15
## Monday Week 3

It was still dark when Kaye backed the pickup out of the garage. The change in mode of transport was necessary because of his plan for the day, and he wore slacks and a polo shirt instead of the usual biker garb. A sport coat lay on the front seat, with three different colors of baseball caps and a small set of binoculars atop it.

Traffic was light and he reached his destination well ahead of time. The surroundings weren't great, but driving around the block a couple of times identified the best available spot: Not obvious, but accessible, with a great view of the Classic Realty office.

Kaye called Thompson's office, knowing his Captain wouldn't be in yet, and left a voice mail about what he was doing, then settled in to wait.

At 8:40 a.m. the white Escalade pulled into the parking lot, parked in a designated handicapped space, and Megan Sullivan went to work.

Kaye knew the surveillance was a big risk. If Sullivan saw and recognized him, his LAPD career was likely over despite the message for Thompson. Based on his interactions thus far with Sloan and Leale he'd probably face a criminal complaint.

But he was more and more convinced that Sullivan had knowledge of Avi Geller's murder, and he needed to know how.

At 9:15 a.m. Sullivan came out of the office, a Classic Realty lawn sign hanging from one hand, loaded it into the back of the Escalade and took off.

Single vehicle surveillance is tough compared to a team effort, and Kaye hung back as much as possible without creating too much risk of losing contact at a traffic signal. He was relying on Sullivan not being concerned about being followed and not spending half her time checking her mirrors.

Which is what Kaye did because of the Kanji notes.

Twenty minutes later Sullivan parked in front of a beautiful, well-landscaped Tudor-style house in the neighborhood north of Wilshire between UCLA and Beverly Glen.

Kaye immediately turned into an intersecting side street to avoid driving past her, drove past a half dozen driveways, then made a u-turn and went back to park where he could see the Escalade.

He decided not to call in his surveillance location, thus avoiding an official record of his whereabouts, and settled in to wait again.

It was nearly an hour before Sullivan came out of the house, accompanied by a man and woman with their arms intertwined. Sullivan went to the Escalade, grabbed the sign out of the back and, with a ceremonial flair, planted it in the front yard while the couple clapped.

Hugs and handshakes were exchanged all around before Sullivan took her leave.

Her next stop was a showing, meeting a young couple with two small children and spending thirty minutes giving them the grand tour of a nice bungalow on the north side of Santa Monica.

While Kaye watched and waited, his phone buzzed.

"Kaye, are you out of your mind?" Thompson practically roared when Kaye answered.

"Not at all, Captain," Kaye said. "I drove the truck today. She's not going to make me and I need to do this. It's a hundred percent legit and related to the case."

"It damn well better be," Thompson said. "Sloan and Leale have already been here looking for you."

"What did they want?"

"They wouldn't say, but they asked me to call them if you showed up, which I have no plans to do."

"With any luck," Kaye said, "they were looking for me because Sullivan reported that I violated the order over the weekend by calling her. You still have my old phone, right?"

"Yes, I do," Thompson replied. "It stayed turned off and in my possession all weekend. If Sullivan reports that you called or texted her from that number, we've got her by the shorts."

"Thanks, Cap."

"How long you going to sit on her?"

"I can't do this all day. I've got other things to chase down this afternoon."

"And tomorrow?"

"Maybe. But I meet with Ziva Geller and her lawyer tomorrow."

"Okay, just keep me informed."

"Yes, sir," Kaye said. "Hey, I need to go. She's on the move."

Sullivan's next stop was a drug store. Then she got her Escalade washed.

From the car wash she headed into Santa Monica. The midday traffic and the number of traffic lights forced Kaye to stay closer than he wanted to be, but the sheer volume of vehicles provided some extra cover. He grunted when he remembered it worked the same way for anyone who was following him.

As Sullivan crossed Lincoln, Kaye knew he had a problem.

She was going to the Promenade, the portion of 3rd Street restricted to pedestrians, and, based on the time, probably meeting somebody for lunch.

Sure enough, Sullivan turned on 4th Street and then swung into the first valet parking garage she came to.

Kaye drove past. There was zero chance of following her into the garage and there wasn't really a good option for tailing her into the mall.

It suddenly dawned on him that Megan Sullivan had never actually seen him up close and in person. Her only glimpse had been when he jumped up on the gate at the house and she'd seen the video without knowing it was him. His size was an almost dead giveaway, but from a distance he would likely be okay.

He swung into the next available parking lot, grabbed a hat and the binoculars, and left the truck for the valet. There was a pedestrian pass-through to 3rd just to his south and he hustled through it, stopping and looking north before entering the Promenade proper.

Sullivan was almost a full block away, walking north. He set off after her, but not so quickly he'd close the gap by much.

She turned and cut diagonally across the space and Kaye could tell she was headed for one of the more popular eateries with outdoor tables. As she got close, a woman already seated at a table inside the railing stood to greet her.

The two women hugged across the railing, but by the time Kaye got the binoculars up Sullivan was blocking his view of the other woman's face. After a moment, though, Sullivan stepped away and headed for the restaurant entrance.

Kaye looked through the binoculars again, then lowered them and muttered, "I'll be damned."

He recognized Sullivan's lunch date.

Ziva Geller.

Kaye went back to his truck. He would've loved to hear the

conversation between the two women.

He'd gotten what he needed just by seeing them together.

Plus, he had someone else he needed to find.

\*\*\*

It's not far from Santa Monica to Venice.

Kaye found the address and was surprised to find it was one of the high-end places that back onto one of the area's eponymous canals.

It definitely wasn't cheap real estate, if there was such a thing in Los Angeles anymore, and Kaye recalled Aubrey's comment about Dennis Bettencourt being on his way to being 'richer than God'.

Like all the houses in the neighborhood it was built to take advantage of the canal, not the streets, which were really little more than alleyways. All Kaye could see was a two-story stucco façade, the first floor of which was almost entirely garage door. Two small windows showed on the top floor.

The driveway, too short to park perpendicular to the garage door, was empty.

On the east side of the garage a walkway passed under an arbor covered in blossoming trumpet vines and led into the narrow space between houses and toward the canal. As Kaye followed it he considered how to deal with Bettencourt, if he found him. Knowing Bettencourt had priors he decided not to dance around with him, but just go at him a little and see what happened.

He rang the bell and waited.

No answer. He knocked loudly, waited a bit, then knocked harder.

Almost a minute went by before the door opened wide.

Kaye's first thought was that six foot six might be a little conservative. The guy was tall, and stared at Kaye with hard eyes. Kaye's second thought was that Aubrey had been right. The resemblance to a young Robert Mitchum was startling.

"Storm Chase?" Kaye asked, shifting his gaze to look inside.

"Look," the guy said irritably, "how many times do I have to tell you assholes not to come to my house? I'm not looking for new talent at the moment, okay?"

"That's good," Kaye said, holding up his badge wallet, "because I already have a job. Again, are you Dennis Bettencourt, also known as Storm Chase?"

"I am," the guy said, his voice softer but his eyes still hard. "What's this about?"

"Nicole Ingram."

"Who's that?"

"You know Rachel Turner?"

"Yeah, I know Rachel. So what?" Bettencourt said, and Kaye saw the look in the man's eyes change. "Oh, yeah, you mean Rachel's old roommate, right?"

"I do," Kaye said. "Any chance I can come in?"

"Actually, no. Not unless you have a warrant."

"No warrant. Just looking for some background information."

"About Nicole?" Bettencourt asked. "Why? I heard she went home to Texas months ago."

"Where'd you hear that?" Kaye asked.

"Uh..." Bettencourt stammered. "I don't know. Around, I guess."

"She didn't go home. She was murdered about two weeks ago," Kaye said.

"That concerns me how?" Bettencourt asked.

"That's what I'm here to find out."

"Look, I hardly knew Nicole. I dated Rachel for a while, that's all. You should talk to her."

"Already have. We had a very interesting chat about guys who play rough."

Bettencourt's eyes narrowed slightly before he said, "Then there's probably nothing else I can tell you."

"Did you know that Nicole and Rachel parted on bad terms?" Kaye asked.

"Yeah," Bettencourt said, nodding slightly. "Some phony bullshit about Rachel stealing something from Nicole."

"A screenplay, or at least part of one," Kaye said. "Rachel told me it turned up in the trunk of Nicole's car."

"I wouldn't know about that."

"Did you rough Rachel up while you were dating?" Kaye asked.

"Why would you ask me that?"

"You've got priors, Dennis. Seems like you like to hit people, especially women."

"Hey, I never laid a hand on Rachel she didn't like."

"I hear you're in the movie business," Kaye said, looking past Bettencourt into the house. "Must be doing well."

"I'm into a lot of stuff," Bettencourt said glibly, noticing Kaye's look and pulling the door closed until the view was blocked.

"Yeah, I hear that, too," Kaye said, winking and grinning.

"Okay, yeah, I do porn. So what? Besides, it's a means to an end, that's all."

"Not judging," Kaye said. "So there's nothing you can tell me about Nicole Ingram's murder?"

"No."

"Okay then. Thanks for the semi-cooperation. Oh, and Megan said to tell you hello."

Bettencourt blinked and looked surprised.

"Megan?"

"Yeah, Megan Sullivan. She says hi."

"I don't know who you're talking about."

"Sorry," Kaye said. "My mistake, I guess."

"Go away," Bettencourt said sharply. "Don't come back without a warrant. Otherwise, talk to my lawyer."

Young, tall Bob Mitchum slammed the door in Kaye's face.

That went well, he thought as he headed back to the truck.

***

The address Kaye had for Nicole Ingram was in what City Planners would call a 'multi-transitional' neighborhood in West Hollywood. Originally platted back when that part of the Los Angeles basin was developing into the Mecca of the motion picture industry, it had been a quiet collection of modest single-family bungalows, many with a stucco and tile Spanish motif.

In the 50s and 60s, as Los Angeles grew exponentially, modest two- and three-story apartment buildings began to supplant the bungalows, but retained the Spanish influence. Thirty years after that, all pretense of design went out the window as cheaper, boxier apartments began to spring up, replacing most, but not quite all, of the original houses and apartments. Stucco, mullions and red tile had been replaced with vinyl siding, aluminum sliders and flat, tarred roofs.

The building turned out to be one of the last remaining multi-unit buildings from the Golden Age days. An ornately carved set of doors opened into a wide, hardwood-floored entryway and hallway. An elaborate carpet runner led from just inside the door down the hallway to the first-floor apartment doors, and off to one side was an old-fashioned bank of slotted mailboxes. To Kaye's left was a set of stairs, with elaborate newel posts and turned railing.

His plan was to knock on the door of Nicole Ingram's former apartment and ask the current occupant if they knew a Ruthie who lived in the building.

It turned out to be easier. Every mailbox had a name tag affixed. On Number 6 was R. Williams.

The apartment was on the second floor.

Kaye knocked and waited.

"Who is it?" a woman's voice asked from behind the door.

"Police, ma'am," Kaye replied. "LAPD." He held his badge wallet up to the peephole. "I'm looking for Ruthie Williams."

Kaye wasn't sure who he'd expected Ruthie Williams to be after Rachel Turner had described her as 'grandma', but it certainly wasn't who answered the door.

Probably at least in her eighties, Ruthie Williams' silver hair was carefully coiffed, her dress and make-up were flawless and her eyes bright and fierce.

"Land sakes," she said, eyeing Kaye. "You're a big one, aren't you?"

"A blessing and a curse, ma'am. Are you Ruthie Williams?"

"The one and only," she said, smiling.

"I was wondering if I could get a few minutes of your time."

"Certainly, certainly," she said, stepping back and holding the door wide open. "Please, come in. May I offer you some refreshment? Coffee, perhaps? Or tea?"

"No, thank you," Kaye said as he stepped inside. "I'm Detective Kaye."

He stopped short and looked around. It was a time capsule from the post-WWII era. Hardwood floors strewn with elaborate rugs mirrored the planked and coffered ceiling. A stacked stone fireplace dominated one end of the living room and the furniture was all mid-Century modern. Vibrant abstract paintings were everywhere.

"Nice place," Kaye said.

"Thank you, but I know it's old fashioned." Ruthie said. "I've just lived here for many, many years and I can't bear to think of changing it."

"I've been here ten seconds," Kaye said. "I wouldn't change it, either."

"You're very kind. Please, sit down," Ruthie said, gesturing toward a sofa. "Now, what can I possibly do for the police?"

"I'm here about a former neighbor. Nicole Ingram."

Ruthie's face took on a look of alarm.

"Please tell me she's not in trouble."

"Worse than that, Ms. Williams," Kaye said. "I'm afraid Nicole was killed."

The words visibly stunned the old woman. Alarm was replaced with shock as a tear slid down her cheek.

"I know who did it," she finally managed to whisper. "As God is my witness, I know who did it."

"Who would that be, ma'am?" Kaye asked.

"That tall boy who looked just like Robert Mitchum, the one Nicole's roommate liked. Oh, what a horrible person! I always thought he was responsible for Nicole's disappearance. Now he's murdered her."

"His name is Dennis," Kaye said. "Can you tell me if he was still around after Rachel Turner moved out? I spoke to Ms. Turner and got the impression she and Dennis broke up before she moved."

"First of all," Ruthie said, "Rachel did not move out. Nicole threw her out. For stealing. I'm sure that horrible young man put her up to it. Just thinking of him makes my skin crawl."

"When you say stealing, are you talking about some pages of Nicole's writing that went missing? I thought they turned up in the trunk of Nicole's car."

"Well, yes, they did," Ruthie said. "But Nicole was convinced that Rachel took them first."

"But she got them back, right?"

"You don't understand, Detective Kaye. Ideas are currency in this town. I know. I was a contract studio writer for many years and writers guard their words like treasure because that's what they are to them."

"Nicole's screenplay was treasure?" Kaye asked.

"It was brilliant," Ruthie said. "She asked me to read it because she was very, very nervous about pitching it. I told her not to change a thing."

"Did you know she took it to Avi Geller?"

"I told her to. She said he…" She stopped short and the shock returned to her face. "Oh, no, please tell me Nicole wasn't the young woman who was shot with Avi."

"She was."

Ruthie didn't say anything for several seconds.

"But that doesn't make sense," she said at last. "That was only, what, two weeks ago? Nicole disappeared months and months ago.

Where did she go?"

"That's one of the things I'm trying to sort out," Kaye said. "Her parents told me that the last time they talked to Nicole she was excited about going to Santa Barbara to meet with a producer about the screenplay. Do you know who she went to meet?"

"No, I'm sorry. She didn't even tell me about that."

"Why did you tell her to take it to Avi Geller?" Kaye asked.

"I've been around this town for a long, long time," Ruthie said. "I keep up on what's happening, and I don't mean by watching the gossip shows on television. I've known the Gellers for many years, from when Avi first started. I couldn't think of anyone better for Nicole to get into business with."

"So, you don't know of anyone who would have a motive to kill Mr. Geller?"

"Heaven's no," Ruthie said emphatically. "Avi was a wonderful man. Kind, generous, and fair."

"Still, somebody shot him," Kaye pointed out. "I think whoever killed Geller also killed Nicole just because she was there."

She shrugged and said, "I think you're wrong, Detective. It's about the treasure. The words."

"Is there anything else you can think of that might help me find who killed Nicole and Avi Geller? Anything at all?"

"Find that tall boy. He did it. His aura was pure evil."

"I'll do that," Kaye said. "Oh, one more thing. Did Nicole tell you what Geller thought about her screenplay?"

"She said he was very interested and would get back to her very soon."

"Thank you for your time, Ms. Williams," Kaye said, rising. He took out the obligatory business card and handed it to her. "If you think of anything else, please call me."

Kaye was halfway to the stairs when he heard Ruthie call to him. "Detective Kaye, wait!"

He turned to see her standing in her open doorway, a brown paper-wrapped bundle in her hands.

"I almost forgot I had this," she said when he walked back. "She gave it to me for safe keeping. If you know how to reach her parents, I think they should have it."

"What is it?" he asked, hefting it.

"Nicole's treasure," the old woman said as a tear slid down her cheek. "Guard it with your life."

\*\*\*

Kaye walked to the truck. From twenty feet away he saw the piece of paper pinned down by the driver's side windshield wiper and swore softly as he looked around.

It was another note written in Kanji.

He got in the truck, looked at it again, crumpled it up and tossed it over his shoulder into the back seat.

Somebody's just messing with you, he told himself. Don't let them get to you.

Somebody who was very, very good at covert surveillance.

He sat in the truck thinking about his conversation with Ruthie Williams. He hadn't even considered, until now, anyway, that Avi Geller, and not Nicole Ingram, may have been the collateral damage. He doubted it, but it now had to be in the mix, just in case.

\*\*\*

Kaye got back to the squad just before 5:00 p.m., hoping Captain Thompson was still in his office.

He was, working his way through the never-ending stack of reports.

"Captain, can I interrupt you for a minute?"

"Come on in," Thompson said, dropping his pen and rubbing his eyes.

Kaye sat down. "Do you still have my old phone? Here, I mean."

"I do. Why?"

"I need to get some of my contacts off it. It's not an emergency, but it is a royal pain in the butt.

Thompson studied him closely before saying, "Okay, I guess we can do that." He opened his top desk drawer, extracted the phone, powered it on, waited for it to find service and download what it had missed, then handed it to Kaye.

Five minutes later Kaye powered it off and handed it back to Thompson, who put it back in the drawer.

"Thanks, Cap."

# DAY 16
## Tuesday Week 3

The photo lineup he'd asked Patty to put together was on his desk when Kaye got to the Squad. As usual, she'd done a great job. Almost too good, in fact. Kaye had to look carefully to pick out Megan Sullivan.

His first call was to Hernan to find out where Rigo's crew was working. Luckily, they were at another house in Paloma Canyon and not halfway to Palos Verdes.

He rode past his house of interest on the way and was surprised to see a 'Sold' sign attached to the sign bearing Sullivan's photo.

"Well, shit," he muttered. The sale, especially if it was a cash deal with a short closing time, could compromise his investigation. He idly thought about calling Sullivan to congratulate her on the sale, but knew it would be a foolish thing to do.

Five minutes later he rolled up to the address Hernan had given him. Men were working in the yard and two maroon pickups bearing the Gallegos Landscaping logo, one with a trailer for landscaping equipment hitched to the back, were parked on the street. He parked, retrieved the lineup folder from the saddlebags and went in search of Rigo.

"Rigo?" he asked the first man he encountered.

"Out back," the man paused long enough to say and point.

Kaye walked around the house and stopped. After watching the dynamic of the crew for only a few seconds he was able to tell which man was Rigo.

"Rigo, right?" he said. "I'm Detective Kaye. We spoke on the phone with Hernan."

"I remember," the young man said, apprehension in his eyes as the other workers stopped to watch.

"Relax, Rigo, nobody's in trouble. I'm here because I need your help."

The apprehension disappeared and Rigo asked, "What can I do for you, Senor?"

"When we talked, you said you saw a woman you called La Jefa come to the house, driving a new black Explorer. Remember?"

"Si," Rigo said, nodding. "I remember."

"I'd like to show you some pictures and see if you can pick out the woman you saw that day. Can you do that for me?"

"Sure."

Kaye went through the standard photo line-up spiel, then handed the folder to Rigo.

The man studied the photos for less than ten seconds before turning it around toward Kaye and pointing at one of the pictures.

"That's the woman I saw. La Jefa."

"You're sure?"

"Yes," Rigo said.

He was pointing at Megan Sullivan.

"Why do you call her La Jefa?" Kaye asked, causing one of the other workers standing close by to snicker.

Rigo shot the man a hard look, then turned to Kaye and said, "She orders us around like we work for her, not Senor Gallegos. So we call her boss. La Jefa. In this case it is not a sign of respect."

"You also said you thought someone else might have been in the car with her."

"I think so, but I'm not positive, and if there was I didn't really see them. Sorry."

"Did anybody else see?" Kaye asked.

"Not that I know of," Rigo said. "But my crew has changed since then. I'll ask around if you want me to."

"I'd appreciate that," Kaye said. "And, hey, did you notice if the back gate, the one that leads out to the hill, was locked that day?"

"Si, it was when I checked it," Rigo said.

"One more question."

"Go ahead."

"Why did he," Kaye looked at the other nearby worker, "laugh when I asked why you call the woman La Jefa?"

"The crew has another name for her," Rigo said, looking down.

"What's that? It's okay, I won't tell anyone."

Rigo looked back up at Kaye.

"Bruja," he said softly. Witch. "She's very, how you say, critical?"

"Yeah," Kaye said. "I can relate to that."

By the time Kaye got back to the Harley the crew had finished and were loading up their tools and equipment.

He idly wondered if Hernan and Rigo knew anything about taking care of grape vines.

\*\*\*

The meeting with Ziva Geller and Howard Feinmann was set for 11:00 a.m. It was 11:05 a.m. when Kaye pulled into the parking lot, parked, and hurried for the door.

Kaye had figured Howard Feinmann for a solo, maybe a small, practice. Boutique law, at boutique prices.

That wasn't what he walked into.

The building was an old, three-story warehouse converted to office space and the firm's name was the only one listed on the main entry doors. Feinmann was the third of four partner names, and Kaye assumed they were the firm's founders. When he pushed through the doors into the lobby and saw the full directory, he stopped and did a double-take. There were at least forty additional names listed.

Don't underestimate this guy, he told himself.

The reception desk, staffed with three people, was straight ahead and he told one of them why he was there.

"Mr. Feinmann is expecting you," she said. "Ten minutes ago."

Kaye smiled his best and said, "I invoke Los Angeles Standard Excuse Number One."

She looked at him askance.

"Traffic," he said, knocking his knuckles on top of the desk.

She laughed, then directed him to Feinmann's office.

"Sorry I'm late," he said when he walked in.

Feinmann was seated at a conference table on one side of his spacious office. Ziva Geller sat beside him.

Kaye took a seat across from Feinmann.

"Okay." Feinmann got right to it. "You asked for this meeting."

"I did," Kaye acknowledged, looking at Ziva Geller. "I have some information I think your client will find interesting."

"And that would be…?" Feinmann said.

Kaye reached into his inside pocket and pulled out the photo of Nicole Ingram her father had given him. He leaned across the desk and laid it in front of Ziva Geller.

"Do you recognize her?" he asked.

She glanced at the photo, then looked at Kaye.

"I do not."

"Her name is Nicole Ingram," Kaye said.

"This affects my client how?" Feinmann asked brusquely.

"She's the young woman who was shot with your husband, Mrs.

Geller," Kaye said in reply.

"Then she's a whore," Ziva blurted.

"No, she wasn't," Kaye said. "At least not when she first met your husband about eight months ago. She was a screenwriter, or maybe I should say aspiring screenwriter. From Amarillo, Texas."

Ziva picked up the photo and studied it.

"Oh, my God. I think Avi might have mentioned this girl," she barely whispered.

"Ziva, you don't –" Feinmann started to say.

"Yes, Howard, I do." She turned to Kaye. "About that time, Avi told me a young lady he'd never heard of just walked into his office and asked to see somebody, anybody about a screenplay. He was standing at the front desk and had a minute, so…

"She had a concept and a script," Ziva went on. "Avi said it was brilliant, like nothing he'd ever seen. I remember him saying 'even Shakespeare didn't think of this one'."

"Did he option it?" Feinmann asked. "Because if he did, you own it now, Ziva."

"He didn't," Kaye said.

"That's right," Ziva said. "Avi said it was so good, too good, that he wanted to do some checking around. He could never find her again."

"Nicole Ingram went missing a short time after meeting with your husband," Kaye said. "Even her parents didn't hear from her for seven months before her death. They reported her missing to the Santa Barbara authorities."

"Did she live there?" Ziva asked.

"No," Kaye replied. "But the last time she talked to her mother, Nicole told her she was in Santa Barbara to meet a producer about the script."

"You think it was Avi?" Feinmann asked.

"No," Kaye said. "I don't know who it was. It might not even have anything to do with her disappearance or murder. All I know is what she told her mother, and nobody she knew ever saw or heard from her again after she went up there."

"How did she end up with Avi on the golf course?" Ziva asked.

"I don't know," Kaye said. "Not yet, anyway. She certainly wasn't a member at Paloma Canyon, and on the starter's list she was down as Jane Smith. She didn't drive there, because I looked for the car she was driving when she disappeared."

"Jane Smith?" Ziva asked.

"That's how she was signed in," Kaye confirmed.

"By Avi?" Ziva asked. "Why would he do that if he knew her name?"

"I can only speculate," Kaye said. "She may have been hiding from someone. The last months of her life were not kind to her."

"What does that mean?" Feinmann asked.

"She had heroin in her system when she died," Kaye replied.

"Perhaps she simply succumbed to the temptations of Hollywood," Feinmann offered. "She wouldn't be the first."

"True," Kaye said. "But from talking to her family and friends, I doubt that's the case."

Feinmann studied Kaye for a moment, slightly and slowly nodding his head.

"Okay," the lawyer said at last. "I understand your concerns about Ms. Ingram, but those concerns are, frankly, not ours. Ours center around Avi's death and you, and by extension the LAPD, finding whoever killed him."

"That's my objective, Counselor."

"So why the sad tale of Nicole Ingram?" Feinmann asked.

"Because," Kaye replied, looking at Ziva Geller, "I think there's a possibility that Nicole Ingram, not your husband, was the real target."

"That's absurd!" Feinmann exploded. "Why would somebody orchestrate an elaborate scheme to kill a, what, twenty-four year old junkie, and probably a prostitute, and then shoot a major, well-respected Hollywood producer? Just for fun? I don't think so."

Kaye shrugged. He wasn't about to share his theories on the case with Howard Feinmann, especially when he still lacked a lot of the pieces.

Feinmann glared at Kaye and said, "Will there be anything else, Detective?"

"Actually, yes." Kaye looked at Ziva again. "Mrs. Geller, did you find any record of the real estate transaction we discussed previously?"

Ziva glanced at Feinmann, who gave a slight nod.

"I did," she said. "I found two withdrawals from our trust accounts, each for twenty-five million dollars. One was about two years ago, not long after Avi and I fought about this, the other was not long after the first of this year."

"Were they payable to a company called Valle delle Viti?" Kaye asked.

"Yes," Ziva replied. "Just like you said."

"Has any money come back in?" Kaye asked.

"Not that I could find," Ziva said.

"One more," Kaye said. "Mrs. Geller, do you know a Megan Sullivan?"

"Yes, I know Megan," Ziva replied without hesitation. "In fact, we had lunch together yesterday."

"How'd you meet her?"

"She sold Avi and me our house in Paloma Canyon a few years back. She's a little younger, but we hit it off and became friends. Why do you ask?"

"Just curious," Kaye said. "I came across her name, that's all."

"She's a nice girl," Ziva said. "We occasionally go to the club together."

"The club?" Kaye asked.

"Paloma Canyon."

"Ms. Sullivan is a member?" Kaye asked, surprised.

"Of course not," Ziva said. "She goes as my guest."

"I hate to interrupt," Feinmann said. "But if we're just chit-chatting, I do have another meeting. Sorry, Ziva."

"No need to apologize, Howard. With what you bill me per hour, fifteen minutes saves me enough to buy a nice pair of Italian shoes." She laughed.

Kaye saw Feinmann start to turn red and said, "I'm done, Counselor. I appreciate your time, and yours, Mrs. Geller."

"I'll walk out with Detective Kaye," Ziva said. "That is, if you don't mind, Howard."

"As long as you don't mind I don't walk you out, that's fine."

Good-byes were exchanged and Kaye walked with Ziva Geller toward the front doors.

"Thank you," she said to Kaye.

"For?"

"For letting me know that Avi wasn't out on the golf course with some shiksa bimbo, that he knew her from his business. I owe you a favor."

"You're welcome," Kaye said. "Honestly, Mrs. Geller, I just can't find, yet anyway, anything or anybody that might have led to a motive for your husband's murder."

"I'm not surprised, Detective. Everybody loved Avi, even the people he turned down."

"That's what Les Baruch told me."

"It's true."

"Can I ask for that favor, Mrs. Geller?"

"You can ask."

"Don't tell Megan Sullivan I asked about her today," Kaye said.

Ziva stopped just inside the doors and looked at him.

"May I ask why?"

"I'd rather you didn't," Kaye said. "At least not right now."

"Okay, I can do that. Tit for tat. We're even."

She turned and headed out the doors, leaving Kaye staring at the 'K' section of the firm's directory. He immediately wondered how long Howard Feinmann had been of counsel to Ziva Geller.

She was waiting for him outside the front doors.

"I was just thinking," she said. "It might be a good idea if you owed me a favor."

"You can always ask, too," he said, smiling.

"Something occurred to me during our meeting that I think you might find useful."

"What would I owe you in return?"

"Too soon to tell," she said. "In fact, how about this? You decide what the favor is worth, and when the time comes, you pay me back. If I think you're short-changing me, I'll let you know."

"Fair enough."

"You said the young lady screenwriter went to Santa Barbara to meet a producer, right?"

"I did," Kaye replied.

"Well, there was a big surprise at Avi's funeral when the will was read."

"Really? What kind of surprise?"

"Turned out Avi didn't give the company to Les," she said, referring to Baruch. "He gave it to our oldest son, Schmuel."

"I bet Baruch was upset."

"Upset doesn't begin to cover it," she said. "I think 'pissed off beyond belief' is the phrase you want. Les was late to the service, and was already very upset when he arrived. Howard seemed really upset after that, too, although I don't know why."

"Baruch told me he and Avi were like brothers."

"That's what I thought, too. I checked, and it turns out Avi changed his will about six months ago."

"Any idea why"

209

Ziva shook her head.

"So, what's Baruch going to do?" Kaye asked. "Stay on and teach your son the ropes?"

"No, he decided to retire. He moved out of Los Angeles."

"To?"

Ziva stopped again and turned to Kaye.

"His condo," she said, then paused before adding, "In Santa Barbara."

"Got an address?" Kaye asked instantly.

She said nothing, but resumed walking to the parking lot. Then she looked back over her shoulder and said, "That would be another favor, Detective. You already owe me one."

Kaye sat on the Road King, thinking about how the information he'd gleaned over the last hour fit in with what he already had.

That Les Baruch had a place in Santa Barbara could be significant, but might mean nothing.

Lots of people had condos in Santa Barbara. Les Baruch also just happened to work for a major motion picture production company.

Visiting Baruch had just moved up his priority list.

He was about to start the bike when his phone buzzed. He recognized Thompson's number.

"What's up, Captain?"

"Kaye, where the hell are you?"

"Outside Ziva Geller's lawyer's office. Why?"

"I just got off the phone with Kai Iwamura over at the FBI," Thompson said. "He's been trying to call you since this morning. Wants to talk to you ASAP."

"Really?" Kaye said. "My phone…"

He stopped short, realizing Iwamura had the wrong number.

"Okay," he told Thompson. "I'll call him. Thanks, Captain."

He ended the call and called Iwamura.

"Ben, where the hell have you been?"

"In Stupidville," Kaye said. "I got a new phone and didn't give you the number. Sorry."

"But you're okay?"

"I'm fine. What do you need?"

"I went ahead and called my contact in Europe over the weekend," Iwamura said. "She didn't even have to dig. I've got information for you on Valle delle Viti. I'll tell you all about when you get here."

"You want me to come there?"

"I don't want to do this over the phone," Iwamura said. "Hope that's okay."

"Give me thirty minutes."

\*\*\*

A little less than a half-hour later Kaye was riding the elevator to the FBI's main floor in the federal building at Wilshire and Veteran. When he stepped out, Kai Iwamura, in the typical FBI gray suit, was waiting.

"Wow," Kaye said. "This must be important."

"It is. Follow me."

After sitting down Iwamura grabbed a file folder packed with pages and put it on his desk.

"Okay," he said. "I talked to my contact about Valle delle Viti, and you're not going to believe what I found out."

"Try me."

"It's strongly tied to organized crime."

"You were right," Kaye said, smiling. "I don't believe you."

"Then listen to this," Iwamura said. He pulled several stapled pages from the folder and started running it down for Kaye.

"In Italy, SRL means the same thing LLC does here. There are two individuals listed as the owners of Valle delle Viti, SRL, and the company address is in Reggio, Calabria. The Italian version of Valle delle Viti was formed about six years ago, one year before registering as an approved foreign entity in California. The declared nature of the business in Italy is real estate development and construction, but since being formed Valle delle Viti, SRL, has not acquired any property or applied to any Italian jurisdiction to build so much as a dog house."

"Sounds like a front to me," Kaye observed.

"You have no idea," Iwamura said. "Ever heard of Lorenzo Maisano?"

"Doesn't ring a bell."

"Maisano runs a company that translates into English as Cargo Expediters Unlimited, headquartered at the Port of Gioia Tauro, just north of Reggio. Gioia Tauro is Italy's largest port and Maisano's company handles ninety-five percent of cargo in and out, mostly containers."

"I assume you're telling me this because Maisano is who formed Valle delle Viti here."

"Correct," Iwamura said. "But what's most interesting is that

Interpol, Europol and the Italian Guardia di Finanza all believe Maisano heads an organized crime syndicate based in Calabria. They reputedly control nearly all the illegal drug traffic into and out of the European Union. What better way to do that than control the port?"

"You think the Italian mob is investing ill-gotten gains in Santa Barbara County?" Kaye asked. "I don't know. I've been up to Valle delle Viti, and it's a pretty impressive place."

"I think Valle delle Viti resort might be legit," Iwamura said. "But building a place like that is also the perfect way to launder money. Cost overruns, change orders, import duties, legal fees, service contractors, all kinds of things come to mind if there's an international border involved. Hell, you could hide a fortune just in currency exchange rate fluctuations."

"Does anybody know if Maisano is in the U.S.?"

"They know where Maisano is every single minute of every single day, and, no, the guy hardly ever leaves home except to go to his office."

"Is the Bureau going to open a case on this?" Kaye asked.

"That's not up to me," Iwamura replied. "I'll need more before I can take this to the boss."

"What do you need to know?"

"I guess mostly why you asked me to look into Valle delle Viti."

Kaye spent the next twenty minutes filling Iwamura in on, and answering questions about, the Geller case, from the crime scene to Avi Geller's possible investment in Valle delle Viti to Megan Sullivan all the way to that morning's meeting with Howard Feinmann and Ziva Geller. He trusted Iwamura implicitly and held nothing back.

"So," Kaye said in closing, "I'm starting to put the connections together, but I'm no closer to tagging the actual shooter than I was on the day of the murder. I do have one question."

"Sure."

"Who's the other principal in Valle delle Viti, SRL?"

"Oh, yeah," Iwamura said, grabbing the folder and shuffling through it momentarily before coming up with a single sheet.

"His name…is…Adrian Gagnon. No other information given. I ran him and got nothing."

"Adrian Gagnon? Are you sure?"

"That's what it says." Iwamura turned the form around so Kaye could see it. "Why? You know this guy?"

"Remember we talked about the guy in the exploding Ferrari?"

"Yeah, and that it might have been a revenge terror attack."

"I think we can forget that angle.," Kaye said.

"I'm not following," Iwamura said.

"Howell, the guy who died in the Ferrari, ran Black Scimitar."

"Yeah, I remember you telling me that."

"The guy who now runs the company," Kaye said, "Howell's right hand man for the last two years, is named Adrian Gagnon, and he went to school in Europe."

"Shit," Iwamura said. "If it's the same guy, that means Black Scimitar, which does a lot of work for defense contractors, could be tied to organized crime. We need to track that IPO."

The odd-shaped patch on Officer Reid's uniform suddenly made sense to Kaye.

"Gagnon is not a common name," he said.

"No, it's not," Iwamura said.

Kaye pondered what Iwamura was telling him. If the people behind Valle delle Viti resort were either directly involved or fronted by organized crime, it helped explain some of the hardball legal tactics Alicia Valdez had described.

Kaye nodded, then said, "He's connected to Valle delle Viti. What better way to keep a tight hold on things than build your own town, all nice and legal, then hire your own people to control it?"

"They built their own town?" Iwamura asked. "You mean like employee housing and stuff?"

"No, I mean they literally built their own town and incorporated it. The Village of Chumash Oaks," Kaye said. "They got Santa Barbara County to use eminent domain to condemn some of the property they wanted so they could get their hands on it. I didn't know they could do that."

"They can," Iwamura said. "Back, oh, almost fifteen years ago the Supreme Court ruled that government entities' use of eminent domain to transfer property from one private owner to another for economic development was constitutional. They just have to convince the local courts and pay the owner fair market value."

"Sounds shaky to me," Kaye said. "I know of at least one instance where a guy's vineyard was taken from him, and it's still a vineyard, but now it's owned by Valle delle Viti."

"I'd have to see all the paperwork, Ben, and read the decisions."

"Don't get me wrong," Kaye said. "I'm just saying that we both know that money influences both processes and opinions."

"That is true," Iwamura said. "The irony of the particular eminent domain case that set the precedent is that the developer's financing fell through after the original owners all lost their homes, and the pharmaceutical company that built a production facility and hired a bunch of people laid everybody off and left town as soon as their tax breaks ran out. The entire site is now a landfill."

"Doesn't sound like a higher use to me," Kaye said. "Oh, and I also hear that the local cops are making a lot of civil asset seizures."

"Maybe so," Iwamura said. "But it's not that easy in California anymore. The State changed their rules recently."

"But it still goes on, right?" Kaye asked.

"Oh, yeah," Iwamura said. "I'm not saying it's right or foolproof, but it is legal."

"Seems like there should be a connection there somewhere."

Iwamura laughed and said, "Geez, Ben, did you just get off the bus?"

\*\*\*

When Kaye got back to the Squad he headed directly for his Captain's office. The door was closed, but the blinds were open, and two guys Kaye didn't recognize, both wearing suits, occupied the chairs across the desk from Thompson.

He went to his desk instead and found the message light on his desk phone on.

The first message was from the DA's office.

"Kaye, this is Kayla Okafor. I just checked with Judge Gardner's office and thought you should know there's been no activity on the restraining order front. No further requests or allegations of any kind, nothing like that. Whatever you're doing, keep doing it, and keep your Captain in the loop."

No news is good news, he thought, then punched the delete button.

The next message made him sit up and listen.

"Kaye, this is Stephenson, Santa Barbara County. Just had a report cross my desk that I thought you'd find interesting. It came to me from San Luis Obispo PD. Several weeks ago they were contacted by the Vancouver, Washington PD about a missing person. It was a young woman, reported by her parents. She was on her way back to L.A. for school, last known whereabouts a Best Western just off the one-oh-one, from where she called her parents. She let them know she was okay and would call them when she got to school. She hasn't been seen or heard from since. She was driving a blue Honda with Washington plates, which has not been located. Sounds familiar, right? Call me if you want more information. Thanks."

Kaye kept that message.

He leaned back and thought about it.

Could there be a serial kidnapper working the Central Coast region? If so, it was not his problem, right? Out of his jurisdiction, right?

Right.

But…

He searched his desk drawers and finally found the contact information for law enforcement support at NamUs, the national database for missing and unidentified persons.

Five minutes later he was talking to Farida, giving her the gist of the similarities between Nicole Ingram's disappearance and the case he'd just heard about.

"Is there a way to search the database for a particular geographic area where people went missing?" he asked. "Not where they lived, but where they disappeared from?"

"I follow," Farida said. "You want to know if there have been more possible abductions in that area?"

"Correct."

"I'm sure there must be," she said. "Can I put you on hold for a moment?"

"I'll be here."

He waited almost five minutes.

"Sorry for taking so long, Detective Kaye," Farida said. "Here's what we can do. The bad news is that the standard search algorithm doesn't do that. The good news is that our database administrator says she can write a custom query that will get you what you're after."

"That's great," Kaye said. "What do you need from me?"

"She asked for some basic parameters, like last known whereabouts, place of residence, race, sex, age range, stuff like that. The more specific you can be the better. It'll refine the search results and you won't get flooded with returns."

Kaye had to think about that for a moment.

"Okay," he said at last, "let's narrow it down. Got a pencil?"

"Ready when you are."

He gave her his list: Females between eighteen and thirty, no race or ethnic restrictions. Last known whereabouts the coastal counties from Ventura to Monterey and the contiguous inland counties. Vehicle descriptions and the State of registration. Time frame of the last twenty-four months.

"Can you do that?" he asked.

"She's very good. She'll figure it out."

"How long will this take?"

"That I can't tell you," Farida said. "If you give me your e-mail we'll send you the results as soon as we have them."

Kaye gave it to her. "Thanks, Farida, you've been a big help."

"That's what we're here for, Detective."

Kaye checked the Captain's office and saw that Thompson was still in conference. He decided to wait a while.

He found his notes from his conversation with Officer Devon, logged in, and pulled up the vandalism photos tagged to Megan Sullivan's report.

Devon had taken a lot of pictures, getting each spray paint tag from multiple angles and carefully documenting the few broken items.

Kaye's first thought was that Devon was doing a good job of making sure the department's ass was covered in case there was a damages dispute with the insurance company.

His second was that, in his opinion, anyway, the damages were almost superficial. The pictures clearly showed a target-rich environment if the perpetrators were interested in wreaking major havoc. Yet the vandals had passed over many easily accessible items, almost as if they were afraid to break anything of real value. Which he knew could mean kids.

Though he'd never been in the house, several pictures of the living room tickled his memory. He had the feeling he'd seen the fireplace, the elaborate ormolu clock on the mantel and the painting hanging above that somewhere before. Even some of the furniture, which was mostly upended, looked enticingly familiar.

While he dredged his memory, his desk phone buzzed.

"Kaye."

"Detective, this is Bates at the front desk. Just got a call from some guy named Hernan who says he needs to talk to you, but hasn't been able to reach you."

"Thanks, Bates. I'll call him."

Kaye used his desk phone to make the call.

"Hernan, Detective Kaye. Just heard you were looking for me."

"Yes, I tried to call."

"It's a long story. What do you need?"

"Rigo told me you talked to him this morning."

"I did," Kaye said. "He's not in trouble and he was very cooperative. Tell him I appreciate it."

"Good to know," Hernan said. "But he also told me something he thinks you should know."

"What's that?"

"He said he asked around if anybody else saw anything at the house on the day you asked him about, and one of the guys who used to be on his crew did see something."

"Go on," Kaye said.

"The guy, Miguel, told Rigo he saw the man who came to the house with La Jefa that day. He said the man got out of the car after La Jefa went inside, and he was carrying a large black bag. He also told Rigo that the man didn't leave when La Jefa did."

"Did Rigo give you a description?" Kaye asked.

"All his guy told him was that the man had dark hair, was wearing sunglasses, and was tall," Hernan said. "In fact, Rigo said his guy said the man was 'really tall'."

"Where can I find Miguel?"

"That's the thing," Hernan said. "He won't talk to you."

"Why not?"

Hernan laughed. "Because you're la policia. Plus, Miguel quit after he talked to Rigo."

"Hernan, I don't care about Miguel's status. But if he can help me solve two murders, I really need to talk to him."

"I understand," Hernan said. "I'll tell Rigo and have him put the word out. We'll see if we can find him."

"Thanks, Hernan," Kaye said. "Hey, how's your boy doing? Staying safe?"

"He's doing good. Loves his job. I'm very proud of him."

"You should be. Thanks again."

When he hung up, Captain Thompson's office was dark and empty.

# DAY 17
### Wednesday Week 3

By 6:00 a.m., again driving the pickup to try and stay under the radar, Kaye was parked in the Venice canal neighborhood in a spot that gave him a view of Dennis Bettencourt's garage doors.

Because the houses fronted the canals, finding a vantage point hadn't been easy, and because the houses were so close together it was difficult to park the pickup without blocking someone's driveway.

Having no idea what kind of schedule porn producers worked, when he'd finally settled in he'd called the Pacific Division station to let them know he was in the area doing surveillance so they could avoid him.

It turned into a long morning. Traffic was thin and sporadic, with no mass exodus of early morning commuters. People whose money worked for them, not people who worked for their money, lived on the canals.

At 9:15 a.m. he called Marella at SecureLife and asked her to send him a system log for the house dating back to the day the contact information had changed from the homeowners to Megan Sullivan.

"I can try," she said. "I know that account was frozen the day Ms. Sullivan was here, because I did it myself. I can get you from that day back to the last purge. Do you need videos?"

"Not this time," Kaye replied. "Just the log. I think I've got that figured out."

She promised to have it to him by the end of the day.

By 11:00 a.m. Kaye was starting to think he was sitting on a dry hole, but his talk with Hernan the night before convinced him to sit tight.

Fifteen minutes later he saw the garage door go up, and a few seconds later Bettencourt emerged, carrying a full white plastic garbage bag that he dumped into the outside container before disappearing back into the garage.

With the description from Rigo's crew member bolstering his theory, Kaye made the snap decision to change tactics. His original plan had been to see if Bettencourt had a black Explorer tucked into the garage, and maybe tail the man for a bit.

Instead, he decided it was time to apply a little pressure and see what happened.

Kaye rolled down the alley and stopped directly in front of the open garage.

Two vehicles were parked inside. One was a new red Corvette convertible and the other an off-white van. Kaye grabbed his phone and took photos of both license plates.

Bettencourt was nowhere in sight, so Kaye waited.

A minute later Bettencourt came out of the house, a small gym bag in one hand. He glanced in Kaye's direction but showed no sign of recognition. He dropped the gym bag into the Corvette, then headed around toward the driver's seat.

When he saw the truck still blocking the driveway he changed direction and came outside.

"Hey," he said, "I need to get…"

He recognized Kaye and stopped short.

"What the fuck are you doing here?" Bettencourt demanded. "What do you want now?"

"Just passing by," Kaye said, smiling. "Saw the door up and stopped to say hello. Nice car. How long have you had it?"

"None of your business."

"I can look it up. I am the cops, you know."

"You do that," Bettencourt said. "Now, get out of the way. I need to get out."

"Going to work?" Kaye asked, looking at his watch. "Must be nice. I started at six this morning."

Bettencourt scowled, but stayed quiet.

"Hours are good, I guess," Kaye went on. "But I bet the work is tough. Or should I say hard?" He smiled. "Better be, at least, or you're out of business, right?"

"Fuck you," Bettencourt growled and took a step toward the truck.

"I guess I'd better get out of your way," Kaye said, dropping the truck into gear. "Nice seeing you, Dennis. We'll talk again soon. Real soon, I think."

Bettencourt, fists clenched, watched Kaye drive away.

Kaye looked in the rear view mirror and half-smiled.

*\*\*\**

On his way out of the canal district Kaye called Patty and asked her to check the State firearms registry on the off chance Dennis Bettencourt was the proud owner of either a .223 or 5.56 caliber assault rifle. He didn't expect her to find anything, but he needed to check it off the list.

After stopping for a quick lunch, Kaye headed to AZG Productions.

The first thing he noticed when he walked in were multiple blank spots on the walls where hit movie posters had been on his previous visits.

The receptionist recognized him.

"Hello, Detective," she said. "If you're looking for Mr. Baruch again, I'm afraid I can't help you. He's no longer with the company."

"I heard," Kaye said. "I was hoping to get a few minutes with the new Mr. Geller."

"He's here," she said, reaching for her phone. "Let me see if he's available."

Kaye waited while she called and announced his presence.

"He'll be right out," she said as she hung up.

A moment later a young man Kaye guessed as still in his twenties came around the corner into the lobby. The striking resemblance left no doubt he was Avi Geller's son.

"Detective Kaye, isn't it? I'm Sam Geller," he said, shaking Kaye's hand.

"Nice to meet you, Sam," Kaye said. "Sorry it had to be under these circumstances."

"Me, too. What can I do for you?"

"Is there someplace private we can talk?"

"Sure. Follow me."

Sam led Kaye to a large, corner office. Both outside walls were floor to ceiling glass and offered spectacular views. Several of the posters that had been on the lobby wall now hung in the office. The furnishings were minimalist, serving to accentuate the movie and television industry awards statuettes lined up on the black marble fireplace mantel.

"This was Dad's office," Sam said, gesturing for Kaye to take a chair in front of the desk. "I'm still getting used to it being mine."

"I can only imagine," Kaye said. "Based on what your mother told me, I take it this all came as quite a surprise."

"That's putting it mildly," Sam said. "I guess we all figured Uncle Les would take over if anything ever happened to Dad. That's why I went to law school after film school."

"I didn't know Les Baruch was your uncle."

"Well, technically he's not. But that's what I've called him since I learned to talk."

"I bet he was crushed when your dad left him out of the will."

Sam studied Kaye closely for a moment, then said, "He was. But, honestly, I think he kind of expected it."

"Do you think something happened between them?"

"Yeah, I do," Sam replied. "But I have no idea what. Even Mom doesn't know. It must've been pretty recent."

"I know this is a tough question," Kaye said, "but do you think whatever happened could be tied to your dad's murder?"

Sam hesitated again for just a few seconds.

"An event?" he said. "Sure. I mean, there's no logical way to disqualify the possibility. But there's no way I can believe that Uncle Les had anything to do with killing my Dad."

"Have you ever heard of Nicole Ingram?"

"I saw her name in the paper. I know who she is, or was, but nothing else about her."

"Did you know she pitched your dad a screenplay earlier this year?"

"I did not," Sam said. "How do you know that?"

"Your Uncle Les found her name in your dad's notes. On the computer."

"Oh, right. I scanned that database, but haven't really had time yet to get up to speed on it."

"Could you look something up for me?" Kaye asked. "A name?"

"Sure," Sam said, spinning his chair to face the computer on his desk. "What's the name?"

"Dennis Bettencourt," Kaye said, then spelled it out.

Sam typed it in and clicked the search button.

"Sorry," he said almost instantly. "No returns."

"Did your Uncle Les have a spreadsheet like the one your dad kept?"

"He should have," Sam said. "But that's going to be a problem."

"How so?"

"He deleted all his files before he left."

"Do you, and by that I mean AZG Productions, back up your

files?" Kaye asked.

"We do," Sam said. "In fact, my little brother and I set up the system back when all the studios were getting hacked."

"Did your uncle have access to the backups to delete them, too?"

"No," Sam said. "That's not how it works."

"Can you check a backup archive from, say, a week or two before your Dad's death?"

"Good idea," Sam said. "Yes, I can, but not from here. We store all our backups off-site so they're not accessible from our network. I'll have to go to the storage company and check from their server console."

"You don't use the cloud, or whatever they call it these days?"

Sam laughed. "Detective, all that cloud and hazy nebula storage stuff is nothing but marketing. You have to have media to store data. It's all just a giant server farm somewhere. Whoever owns the hard drives has access to your intellectual property anytime they want it. And because it's all connected to the internet, it can be hacked."

"So you guard it like treasure," Kaye said, remembering his conversation with Ruthie Williams.

"Indeed we do," Sam said. "Because to us, that's what it is. We encrypt our data and store it offsite twice a week with a bonded disaster recovery service."

"I get it," Kaye said. "You need to either go to the media or have it brought to you."

"Correct," Sam said.

"If you could do that sometime soon I'd appreciate it."

"Our service is scheduled to pick up at end of business today," Sam said. "I'll call and have them bring what I need. You're looking for this," he glanced at his note, "Dennis Bettencourt guy, right?"

"Right," Kaye said. He gave Sam his number and stood to leave. "Oh, one more thing. Do you have your Uncle Les's address in Santa Barbara?"

Sam grabbed his cell phone, tapped the screen a couple of times and read the address off to Kaye, who felt a little sheepish as he wrote it down in his paper brains.

"Thanks, Sam. Please call me about Bettencourt, whether you find him or not."

"Will do," Sam said. "And please catch the guy who killed my Dad."

"I'm planning on it, Sam. I'm planning on it."

\*\*\*

The parking lot at Paloma Canyon Country Club was jammed. Kaye finally found a space big enough along a curb bordering a planter to put the pickup.

Lon Burridge was hard at work under the starter's desk umbrella, with a knot of people competing for shade and Burridge's attention clustered around.

From what Kaye could hear as he approached, some of the people were not happy. The more he heard, the more obvious it became that there were more people who wanted to play golf than Burridge could get onto the 1st tee, and the starter was trying to accommodate some and assuage those he couldn't.

Burridge looked up, saw Kaye, and held up two fingers while he mouthed 'two minutes'.

Kaye waited longer than two minutes, but almost everybody went away happy.

"Sorry about that," Burridge said when Kaye finally walked over. "I take a few days off and come back to a total shit show. But I'm here now, so what can I do for you, Detective?"

"I'd like to take another look at the start time log from the day you overheard Avi Geller arguing with the guy we can't identify, if that's okay."

"Sure," Burridge said, leaning down to reach under the desk. He came up with the book in hand, laid it on the counter, opened it to the right day, and spun it around so Kaye could read it.

"If you tell me what you're looking for, maybe I can help," Burridge said.

"A couple of things, really," Kaye said, scanning the page until he found what he wanted. "Number one, this Adrian G. is listed with a start time thirty minutes after Geller's group. I found out his last name is Gagnon, and like the log shows, he had two guests that day. All that's written down are initials."

"Yeah," Burridge said. "Sometimes the members let the guests do that. Believe it or not, the press is always snooping around looking to see who's talking to who. Like I told you last time, though, I don't question it. If the member is standing right there, they're good to go."

"I understand," Kaye said. "Do you remember if the guy who

223

argued with Avi Geller was R.H. or R.M.?"

Burridge's brow furrowed and Kaye could almost see the man's wheels turning.

"I think that would have been the R.M. guy," Burridge said at last.

"You think?"

"Yeah, well, I'm pretty sure," Burridge said. "Now that I think of it, the other guest, the R.H. guy, was different."

"Different how?" Kaye asked.

"Okay, look," Burridge said, "I don't want to stereotype anybody, and everybody is welcome here, but the guy caused a bit of a problem for me."

Kaye looked at Burridge and waited for him to go on.

"Yeah, I remember now," Burridge continued. "The group behind Mr. Geller was upset that I put those three guys with Mr. Geller because they thought this R.H. guy would slow them down."

"Why would he slow down the group behind them?"

"The guy had an artificial leg. I mean, you couldn't even tell except he had shorts on, and he was a beast. He was probably close to Mr. Geller's age, but he not only didn't slow anybody down, he walked the whole freakin' course and carried his own clubs."

Kaye instantly knew that R.H. had to be Rod Howell.

"Have you ever seen R.H. again?"

"Nope, and if I had, I'd remember."

Kaye looked again at the date on the log. It was one week before Rod Howell was killed in the car crash.

"You said Gleason didn't show that day, right?" Kaye asked.

"Right."

"Who is he?"

"Mr. Gleason's been around forever. He and Mr. Geller played together a lot."

"Do you know what Gleason does?"

"I'm pretty sure he's retired," Burridge said. "Word is he made a fortune in the telecommunications business."

"How old is he?" Kaye asked.

"I'd guess sixty-five, plus or minus."

Kaye looked at the page again.

Who was R.M.? And what deal had he and Avi Geller argued about? Valle delle Viti, maybe? But the resort had already opened by then, so it couldn't have been a construction or timeline issue. Operational? Why would Geller be worried about that?

It still didn't make sense to Kaye.

"Looked like quite a mess when I got here," Kaye said.

"Like I said, a real shit show. Too many people booked start times for the available spots."

"Does that happen often?"

"Not when I'm here," Burridge said, smiling.

"That's the second thing I need to ask about," Kaye said. "How does this all work? I mean, the process. It looks like you're still on paper. No computers?"

Burridge smiled again, reached under the counter and came up with a tablet computer.

"The members love the old way, you know. Makes them feel like they're back in the glory days or something, or at least out of the crazy fuckin' world we live in now. I keep the ledgers front and center when they sign in, but I manage the slots using this." He laid his hand on the tablet.

"Would there be guest names in there?"

"No, sorry," Burridge replied. "What I do is use the scheduling program to book using the member's number and how many will be in the group. Then, every afternoon I post printouts for the next three days, going forward one day each day, that show the remaining available slots. People can sign up for the next day until the course closes. I put them in the system first thing in the morning, print the sheets, post them, and then use the printout as reference. That's how I avoid the mess you saw a while ago. My substitute didn't keep up on cycling the sign- up sheets, and people assumed they could show up and play."

"When you post the advance sheet, does it show member's names?"

"Yeah, the system matches the number to a name for the printout, but only displays the name of whoever booked the time and how many are in the group."

"Can you put in standing tee times?"

"Yep, the app takes care of all that."

"Did Avi Geller have a standing tee time?"

"He did," Burridge said. "He missed a few weeks, like everybody else, when the town went crazy, but I left him in the system. He always booked a foursome. He said he never knew who he was going to have to schmooze next week. That day of the argument, when Mr. Gleason couldn't make it, he agreed to let the other guys play with him. I mean, it was obvious he knew them."

"What about the day Geller was shot?" Kaye asked. "Was Gleason supposed to play with him?"

"Not that day. Mr. Gleason cancelled several days before that. Mr. Geller asked me to leave his foursome open because he might have a guest, then showed up with the young woman for his regular time and asked me not to put anybody else with them. The schedule was pretty light, and the group behind him was already four, so it was okay with me."

"She was a screenwriter, by the way," Kaye said. "Nicole Ingram. I think she was trying to schmooze him."

"That I can understand," Burridge said. "But why sign her in as Jane Smith?"

"I don't know yet," Kaye said. "So, you normally post the upcoming Tuesday tee time schedule on Saturday, and it would already show standing times, like Geller, booked on Tuesday?"

"Correct."

"Who else has access to the scheduling system?"

"Let's see," Burridge said, thinking again. He started holding up fingers as he named people. "Me, of course, both club professionals so they can schedule lesson rounds, the pro shop manager and his assistant, the head groundskeeper, and the GM and his assistants. Nine. I think that's it. But anybody who walks by the posted sheets sees who's playing, and when."

Kaye mulled over what Burridge had told him.

"Okay, that's all I needed," he said. "Thanks, Lon."

"Glad to help. Are you getting closer to finding who shot Mr. Geller and that girl?"

"Getting closer every day."

Back in the pickup Kaye tried to meld Burridge's information into his developing theory about Geller and Ingram's murders. He'd been stuck on how the shooter could have known Geller would be on the course on that day at that time. Now he knew.

The problem was that so did everyone else who had access to the system or read the posted sheets for days ahead. Throw in every member who knew Avi Geller and the number soared well into the hundreds.

The real question now was how anyone would know that Nicole Ingram would be there. Ingram apparently hadn't driven to the club and had used a lame alias to sign in. Had she arrived with Geller?

It created a major hole in Kaye's growing belief that Ingram had been the real target.

Could Geller have been the target all along? And aspiring screenwriter-turned-junkie Nicole Ingram was just in the wrong place at the wrong time?

At least he could now place Avi Geller and Rod Howell together not long before Howell was blown up, and only weeks before Geller was shot.

Pretty long odds.

His mood improved when he got back to the truck and there wasn't a Kanji note on the windshield.

He got in, sat for a minute, sighed, and started the truck.

Maybe he wasn't as close as he thought.

\*\*\*

Carol Soares saw Kaye walk across the parking lot and get into his truck, then watched him drive away.

She immediately found a quiet corner and made a call.

"Kaye was just here again," she said into the phone. "He talked to the starter for a long time."

She listened.

"If that's what you want to do," she said after a moment. "He wasn't riding a bike, he was in the truck."

She listened again.

"I'll keep my word," she said. "But if you even touch her I'm going to the cops."

She closed the call.

\*\*\*

Kaye got back to the Squad and immediately gathered his things to head home. It had been a very long day and he wanted to practice.

He'd think about meditation after that.

His phone buzzed as he stood up. He looked at the screen and saw the preview of a text from Marella at SecureLife. Sighing, he sat down and opened it.

She apologized for texting, but wanted to let him know that she had run into a snag with the system log trying to get more days, but had just sent it, and to please call her if he needed anything else. He replied with a 'thank you.'

Before he could get to his feet, his phone buzzed again. He was tempted to ignore it, but the persistent buzz told him it was a call, not a text.

He grabbed the phone out of his pocket again, looked at the screen, and smiled.

"Hi," he said, the smile carrying over to his voice.

"Hi," Auggie McMaster said. "Where are you?"

"Just leaving the station," he replied. "Why? Where are you?"

"Santa Monica. Chez Angelique. I'm in town today making deliveries."

"Deliveries?"

"Yeah," she said. "I have restaurants that buy from my boutique list, including my label, and every other Wednesday is the day I stock them up."

"Sounds like work to me," Kaye said, smiling again.

She laughed and said, "Hey, beats a real job all to hell."

"Are you done?" Kaye asked, then hastily added, "With the deliveries I mean."

"Yes, I'm done, and that's why I'm calling. Care to join me here? I've got an extra bottle with your name on it. Well, actually my name, but what the hell. It's yours if you want it."

"I'd love to," Kaye said instantly, his fatigue forgotten. "Give me half an hour?"

"I'll be here," Auggie said, "anxiously listening for the sound of rumbling exhaust."

"Sorry to disappoint you, but I drove the pickup today. Needed it for work."

She laughed again. "Phew, I'm off the hook. I needed my truck today, too. Bet mine's bigger than yours."

"Not taking that bet," Kaye said. "Where, exactly is this place?"

Twenty-five minutes later Kaye pulled into the nearly-full parking lot of Chez Angelique. In the parking spot farthest from the entrance was a white cargo van. On the side a half-circle of stylized script arched above a graphic depicting grapes on the vine.

La Vigna di Augustina.

Kaye walked in and was immediately greeted by a smiling woman.

"You're here to meet Auggie," she said, and it wasn't a question. "I mean, you've got to be Ben, right?"

"I am."

"She's at the bar."

Even from thirty feet away Kaye picked her out easily. She wore a black t-shirt with the same La Vigna di Augustina logo printed inside a large, white circle on the back. Wisps of her hair had escaped the loose bun atop her head and trailed halfway down her back. She wore black shorts and tennis shoes, and even from bar stool height one long, bare leg easily reached the floor.

She held a glass of red in one hand as she chatted with one of the women behind the bar, and another full glass sat in front of the empty stool next to her.

"Is this seat taken?" Kaye asked when he walked up behind her.

Auggie spun at the sound of his voice and grinned.

"It is now," she said, putting her glass down and her hand on his shoulder. "Sit down, take a load off."

"Don't mind if I do," Kaye said, sliding onto the stool.

"Ben," Auggie said, turning to the woman standing across the bar, "this is Angela. Angela, Ben. Be nice to her, she owns the joint."

"Nice to meet you, Ben," Angela said. "Auggie's told me all about you."

"Nice to meet you, too, Angela. And don't believe everything you hear."

Angela laughed, then said, "Time for me to head for the kitchen. Auggie, don't leave without saying good-bye, okay?"

"Never," Auggie said.

"How long have you known her?" Kaye asked once Angela was out of earshot.

"She was my very first wholesale customer," Auggie said. "A little over a year ago she came to me and asked if she could copy my basic concept here in town. I told her she was good to go as long as she bought her wine from me."

"It's going well?"

"It's going gangbusters," Auggie said. "What she's got over me is that she's an absolute genius in a kitchen. In thirty minutes this place will be too crowded to walk through."

"Good for her," Kaye said before taking a sip of his wine. "Wow, this is good. Is this yours?"

"My finest yet," Auggie said, beaming. "The vintage is already sold out, and Angela bought almost all of it."

"I'm no businessman," Kaye said, "but have you thought about

229

franchising?"

"I have," Auggie said, making a face. "But, honestly, there's just not that much great wine to go around. Lots of wine is made everywhere, but outside of where I am on the Central Coast, there's Napa, maybe the Willamette Valley in Oregon and the Columbia River Valley in Washington. Other than that, pickings are pretty slim for really, really good wine unless you go offshore. Besides, I want to make wine, not run a restaurant chain. I want to crush grapes, not the competition."

"Good for you," Kaye said. "Stay true to yourself."

"That's the plan. I learned early on from my grandfather not to worry about what I was going to do with my life. Focus on who I wanted to be and do what I had to do to become that person."

"He sounds like Roshi."

"I'm glad you think so," she said, raising her glass to touch to Kaye's. "So, how was your day, Detective Kaye?"

"Long," he said. "Started surveillance at six this morning. That's why I drove the truck. Too hard for me to hide on a motorcycle."

She laughed, then took a drink of wine. "You are rather distinctive looking, you know."

"I get that a lot."

"In fact," she said, smiling, "I'd go so far as to call you quite the specimen."

"Coming from you, I take that as a real compliment."

He saw the telltale blush creep into her neck as she looked down into her glass.

She looked up and asked, "Was the surveillance connected to the Valle delle Viti case?"

The question momentarily stumped Kaye. In his mind, he didn't have a Valle delle Viti case.

"I don't know," he admitted. "It was related to the same case I went up there to look at the place for. But a direct connection?" He shrugged his shoulders.

She took another sip of wine and looked over the rim of the glass at him. "Can you tell me about it? As a cop's daughter, I'm really interested, you know."

Before Kaye could answer, a hostess came and showed them to their table.

"We're eating?" Kaye asked.

"Of course, silly. I give her a discount, she feeds us. Quid pro quo."

When they were seated at a quiet corner table, Auggie prodded him again.

"So, tell me about your case."

"Shouldn't we decide on dinner first?"

"Angela and I already took care of it," Auggie said. She saw the look of skepticism on Kaye's face and laughed. "Relax, it'll be fabulous. Now, spill about the case before I decide to get really demanding, and trust me, you don't want that."

Kaye started with responding to Paloma Canyon County Club and worked forward. There were, of course, things he couldn't and didn't tell her, but he gave her the gist and enough details to keep her spellbound. When he mentioned the Kanji notes her eyes got very wide. He didn't mention the voice.

"Seriously?" she asked. "That is totally freaky. Who would do that?"

"I have no idea," he replied. "Roshi says they're threats, but we, uh, had a bit of a disagreement about what I should do."

"Oh, no," she said. "I'm sure you'll work it out. I know he's important to you."

Their food came. While they ate, he also told her about the mysterious exploding Ferrari case.

"Are they connected?" she asked.

"I think it's possible. There's some overlap and some commonalities. No direct link yet, but I don't believe in coincidences, either."

"Suspect?" she asked. A cop's daughter.

"Let's just say a strong person of interest, at least on the golf course case. But I can't prove anything yet. I've got no witnesses, no ballistics, no DNA or trace, nothing. At this point it's all circumstantial, and I'm not even totally sure who the real target was and why somebody wanted either, or both, of them dead. On the Ferrari thing, I'm absolutely nowhere, but I think the FBI is going to start looking into it."

"But you have a theory about the golf course case, right?"

"I do," Kaye replied. "But my variables keep changing. Besides, theories don't fly in court."

"You'll come up with something," she said.

The conversation changed from murder to more conventional topics for the remainder of their dinner.

"Well," Kaye said after coffee and dessert, "you were right. That's the best meal, and best wine, I've had in a long, long time. My compliments to Angela and the outstanding winemaker."

"Glad you enjoyed it," Auggie said, blushing again. "I'll go pass that along. I do have to say good-bye to her."

Five minutes later, Auggie's arm looped through Kaye's, they crossed the parking lot to her van.

"You win," Kaye said. "Yours is bigger."

She laughed and squeezed his arm.

"You know," he went on. "I don't live far from here. If you don't want to drive back in the dark, I'll extend the same offer you made me, and your choice of quarters."

"Oh, Ben, I'd love to," she said, stepping around to face him and taking his hand in both of hers.

"I sense a 'but'," he said.

"Yeah," she said. "I can't. I have a meeting I cannot miss early tomorrow morning."

"I understand. Another time maybe?"

"Count on it," she said as she stepped in close, put her hands on his shoulders and kissed him.

It wasn't symbolic. She kissed him hard, and he wrapped his long arms around her as she slid hers around his neck.

"Phew," she said a long moment later. "If I don't stop now we might end up in jail."

Kaye's arms were still around her waist and he pulled her tight against him.

"The offer's still open."

"Oh, Ben, I would if I could," she whispered. "But I can't. I'm presenting an offer on that ground I told you about. I have to be there."

"I understand," he said again.

"Are you sure?" she asked.

"Absolutely. Hey, last weekend it was me. How could I be upset with you?"

"Thank you," she said, laying her head on his shoulder for a moment before pulling back. "What are you doing this weekend?"

He smiled and said, "As a matter of fact, I was planning a trip to Santa Barbara tomorrow or Friday. There are a couple people I need to talk to. I thought I'd see if I could find a good reason to swing up to Santa Ynez after that."

"A good reason?" she asked mockingly.

Kaye just shrugged his shoulders.

"When were you planning on telling me this?"

"I just told you," Kaye said, grinning broadly.

"Is it okay if I save you your favorite seat at the end of the bar?"

"I'd like that. Have a preference on which day?"

"Uh, Friday," she said, then leaned in and kissed him again, this time leaving her hands against his chest. "Maybe you can stay the weekend?"

"Good night, Auggie," Kaye said, slowly dropping his arms from around her waist. "Thank you very much for the great surprise. Made my week."

"My pleasure. See you Friday?"

"That's the plan."

He stood in the parking lot and watched her drive away, then headed for the pickup.

\*\*\*

The driver of a dark colored Toyota sedan also watched.

After Kaye drove away the driver made a phone call.

"It's me. I have a prospect for you. She's leaving Santa Monica right now, probably headed for Santa Ynez. At least that's what it says on the side of the van she's driving." The driver gave the other side of the conversation a description of Auggie and the van, then listened.

"Look," the driver said. "I know, but this relates to Kaye. Make the stop, then use your discretion."

The driver ended the call, then took one last hit off the *yomogi*-laced joint, causing its tip to glow brightly before dropping what was left out the window and starting the car.

"You have done well," The Lord said.

"Thank you," the driver said, smiling shyly. "It is my goal to please you."

"And, as always, you have. Now, though, you must finish the job."

"I will bring our enemy to us, my Lord, and I will present you with his head."

The thought caused the driver to smile. Killing cops was risky business, but it was *Gi*.

Justice.

# DAY 18
### Thursday Week 3

Rain.

Mudslide rain. The kind that roars in off the Pacific to remind the hill dwellers, who have already endured the devastation of Lucifer's fiery breath, that things could get even worse.

Ah, beautiful California.

Berating himself for getting old and soft, Kaye decided to drive the truck again. As a consolation, he opted to wear the Big Boar colors anyway.

The entire Department must have planned on working inside to avoid the rain, because Kaye ended up parking on the street a half-block away.

When he stomped into the Squad, Mel Lister was at her desk poring over several tall stacks of field interview cards.

She looked up and saw Kaye, wet from his walk.

"Nice day outside, eh,?" she said, eying him up and down. "Of course, I'd lie for you, and that's the truth."

"It's really coming down," Kaye said, looking around. "Where's Chet? Haven't seen him all week."

"Didn't you hear? He's got a secret. Well, had a secret I guess. Chet's leaving on a jet plane."

"What?" Kaye asked. "In English, please."

"Chet retired," Lister said. "Monday was his last day, and the jerk didn't even tell me until end of watch."

"I didn't even know he was thinking about retiring," Kaye said. "Thought he loved the job."

"Love is a battlefield, Kaye, and sometimes it's tainted," Lister said. "The Chief pissed him off with the whole 'don't deserve to wear the badge' thing after he gave so many years to the Department."

"What's he going to do?"

"Sing Tiny Bubbles with Don Ho," Lister said. "Took a job as head of security at some resort in Hawaii. I guess he'd applied a while ago, interviewed, then never heard anything. But they got in touch right before we got called back and offered him the job. It was take it or lose it, I guess."

"That's too bad. I mean, good for him, bad for us."

"The Shirelles had it right," Lister said. "Mama said, man. Mama said. But all we can do is roll with it." She paused for two beats and then asked, "Hey, you think the Captain will put us together? I mean, we both need partners now, right?"

"I have no idea," Kaye said. "But you should know that people I partner with usually don't fare well."

Lister laughed. "That's not exactly your dirty little secret."

"Let's not worry about it unless and until Thompson brings it up."

"I'm good with that," Lister said, spinning back to her desk and waving at the stacks of FI cards. "Better get back to the dirty work."

"What are you working?"

"We've got a Billy Joe and Bobby Sue team scamming jewelry stores on this side of town. They stay away from the high-end stores, but they're pretty sophisticated and making quite the haul."

"Scamming how?" Kaye asked, curious.

"They come in separately, the guy first. He engages the sales person, then she comes in and distracts them while he pockets one or two decent pieces and leaves fakes. They also leave separately. Sometimes the stores don't even know they've been hit until someone else wants to see the same items or they pull the inventory at the end of the day."

"Weapons?"

"Nobody has seen one yet."

"Video?"

"That's actually why I think I'm working the same team," Lister replied. "They've used some pretty damn good disguises, so the descriptions are always a little different. But in every instance the wireless security cameras have been jammed."

"Pretty sophisticated for low-end thieves."

"I think they're rehearsing. They obviously case the places first, pick out some nice pieces and make sure the cameras are wireless so they can jam them."

"How much take are we talking about so far?"

"Just over a hundred grand in the last ten days."

"Wow," Kaye said. "Quantity counts."

"Yeah, and I've got zip. Eyewitness descriptions that don't match, no video, no vehicle, nothing. Bob Seger, man. Mysteries with no clues.

But not those kind of mysteries, if you know what I mean."

"You're down to FI cards?"

"Every rose has its thorn," she said. "But, hey, you never know. I can't just let these two take the money and run, right?"

"Well, good luck," Kaye said. "If Thompson says anything to me about partnering, you'll be the first to know."

She gave him a thumbs-up sign and bent back to the FI cards.

Kaye sat at his desk, thinking about where to start. There were a lot of loose ends to tie up, but others had to deliver the string first.

He did have one knot that he could work on untangling, though, thanks to Marella at SecureLife.

She'd done well. The new security system log file was nearly six weeks' worth of raw data dating back to not long after Sullivan became the contact. Thankfully, he'd already learned how to decipher it fairly easily and started with the oldest date.

When he'd first started analyzing the front gate video and SysLog file, Kaye had focused on the daylight hours because the murders had happened in the middle of the day.

But now he wanted around-the-clock details.

If what he was looking for was there, he figured it would be within a pretty consistent, narrow time frame, so he ignored about eighteen hours of every day and focused on the other six.

It turned out to be relatively easy to spot once he got a sense for the cadences and layout of the data and in less than ninety minutes he had what he needed.

Starting two weeks after Megan Sullivan became the SecureLife contact the cleaning service van was at the property at least once a week, never arriving before 10:00 p.m. and never leaving before 5:00 a.m. During that seven hours or so, the entire system was disarmed at the main console in the house.

Which made sense. But seven hours to straighten and vacuum? With what Kaye thought he knew now, the extended visits made sense. Now he just needed to figure out how to use the information to his advantage.

He printed the pages he needed and put them in the case file.

"Detective?"

Kaye spun in his chair.

"Hey, Patty. What's up?"

"I wanted to talk to you about the gun registry."

Kaye slid his chair across the floor, grabbed another from an empty work spot and offered it to the P.A.

"What did you come up with?" he asked.

"I didn't find anything connected to Dennis Bettencourt."

"That's kind of what I expected," Kaye said, then paused a moment before asking, "How about we widen the net a bit?"

"That's what I was thinking. What am I fishing for?"

"You remember the 'vehicles registered to' search we did on Megan Sullivan?"

"Sure. We wanted the black Explorer."

"Right," Kaye said. "See what you can dig up on Sullivan. Her husband, siblings, friends, stuff like that, and search the gun registry for them."

Patty's eyes widened.

"You think she's involved in the murders?"

"It's looking more and more like she might be," Kaye said, "but I've got no proof yet. I know it'll take some digging, but see what you can come up with."

"Digging?" Patty said and laughed. "The woman's a real estate agent, right? She'll have profiles on every social media platform out there. By the end of the day I'll have the names and birthdates of everyone she's ever known, their spouses and those people's kids, right down to high school classmates. Give me until tomorrow morning."

"Sounds like a plan. Thanks, Patty. Oh, hey, have you thought any more about the Academy?"

She sighed heavily and said, "With the call-back and all, I think that window's probably closed. Plus, I don't want to disappoint you and I appreciate your confidence in me, but to be perfectly honest I like what I do now. I like the hours, and most of all I like that I don't have to deal with fools with guns."

"I get that," Kaye said. "Plus, I don't know what I'd do without you."

Her eyes lit up and she said, "Thank you, Detective. I appreciate that. I'll have something for you tomorrow, okay?"

"Sounds good. Stay dry."

She looked back over her shoulder and smiled. "Another advantage of my job. A roof."

Kaye leaned back in his chair and tried to think of where to take the case next. He decided to go through the file from beginning to end again, looking for things that might mean something now that his knowledge base had expanded.

The positions of the bodies now perplexed him.

If Nicole Ingram had been the primary target, why had Avi Geller been shot first? Had Geller been shot first? It seemed logical based on entry wounds and the fact that Ingram had two exit wounds, attributed by Arch to bullet fragments, but no damage to the seat she'd been in. To Kaye that seemed to say Ingram had a chance to stand up before she was shot, which meant she must have seen Geller get hit. Did that make Geller the target? Or was the shooter just that good?

He plowed through the file and his notes. Some things now seemed to make more sense, but others now seemed to make less.

It didn't faze him. In his experience, when a big case came together it usually did so in a hurry. It just needed a trigger, a tipping point. It might be a major breakthrough or it might be something small and trivial that blossomed and became the key for the entire case. It would happen if he just kept after it.

He grabbed the desk phone and called the LAFD Station up on Mulholland, identified himself and asked for Edler.

"Detective Kaye, I honestly didn't expect to ever hear back from you."

"Sorry," Kaye said. "I've been pretty busy, but I do have some news."

Kaye ran it down for the kid, from his belief it had likely been a bomb, that Ferrari had fetched the car back to Italy to investigate the possibility, and that he had a possible culprit but no identity to go along with it."

"The guy on the Hayabusa, right?" Edler asked.

"I think it was a woman on the Hayabusa," Kaye said. "But the plate on the bike was stolen, so…"

"A woman?" Edler asked. "Wow. Are you still looking?"

"Not personally, no," Kaye said. He quickly explained who the victim had been in the grand scheme of things and that his boss was considering turning the case over to the FBI as a possible terrorist attack.

"Holy shit," Edler said softly. "Hey, thanks for letting me know."

"Thank you for raising your hand and being persistent."

"Will you let me know what happens?"

"If I find out, you find out," Kaye assured Edler.

Kaye took a breather and went to look out the break room window. The rain seemed to be slackening a bit, but from inside a second floor window it was hard to tell for sure. But there was no way he was walking around the corner to get a sandwich. Instead he picked out two of the least unhealthy snack items and a water from the vending machines and headed back to his desk.

Captain Thompson's office was still closed and dark.

Must be downtown, Kaye thought. Or home working on an Ark.

He sat down just in time for his phone to ring. He recognized the Robbery-Homicide number.

"Kaye."

"Ben, it's Tom Gannett. How's it hangin'?"

"Can't complain. What's up?"

"I called, first of all," Gannett said, "to thank you for the tip on the traffic cam images on the phony hari-kiri murder suspect." Gannett pronounced it 'Harry Carey' like the famous baseball announcer. "I had them blown up and enhanced. You were right. There was something sticking out of the rider's jacket, angled just enough not to interfere with head movement, and it could be the grip of a sword."

"Yeah, a longer blade is consistent with the decapitation."

"What about the abdominal cut? I did some research and the guy who's offing himself is supposed to do that himself, right? But this wasn't a suicide."

"Agreed," Kaye said. "If this guy was looking to kill himself, he'd have likely done the deed in his office instead of the middle of the parking garage. Maybe gone off the roof. A lot easier and a lot less painful."

"Plus," Gannett said, "there's no hint he was depressed and his business was thriving."

"What did he do?"

"He was a Ph.D. economics professor," Gannett replied. "And a consultant with an extensive list of loyal clients. I'm slogging through them, just in case. Can I ask you another question about this ritual suicide thing?"

"Sure."

"Okay, so, if I've got this right, the person who wants to kill himself sits or kneels down, uses a short blade to slice his belly open, then a twisted friend cuts off his, or her, head to end the pain, right?"

"Basically, yeah," Kaye said.

"So, assuming Collum didn't open himself up to begin with, do you think one person could've done this? Or am I looking at two perps?"

"It could've been two, I guess. I think one person with the right skills and speed could do it, but…"

"But what?" Gannett asked.

"If one person did this, they would've had to get pretty close to start with."

"Which means Collum probably knew whoever it was."

"Probably."

"Okay, good. That's what I was thinking, too. Thanks."

"No problem," Kaye said. "Don't forget to check the dojos."

"I got help on that. Nothing yet."

"Good luck," Kaye said and disconnected.

While he ate, Kaye browsed the Times website to try and catch up with what was going on in the world. To him it seemed like the names changed, but the problems didn't. Nothing was ever really solved, but the arguments kept the news outlets scrambling.

Near the middle of the home page, though, was a link to an article headlined 'LAPD Internal Investigation Continues'. He clicked on it and learned that he was still being investigated by Internal Affairs for stalking and harassment, with the revelation that the alleged victim, who was not named to protect her privacy, was rumored to have applied for a restraining order.

The story went on to quote Detective Leale of Internal Affairs, who said, "We continue to look at this very closely and are still gathering evidence for possible criminal charges. But we all know Detective Kaye's history. We should have this wrapped up soon."

Kaye closed the website. Next time he saw Leale he'd have to resist the temptation to separate the man's head from his shoulders. No sword involved.

His desk phone rang again. This time he didn't recognize the number.

"LAPD. Detective Kaye."

"Detective Kaye, my name is Glynis Mitchell. I'm the database administrator at the National Missing and Unidentified Persons System. How are you today?"

"I'm well, Ms. Mitchell," Kaye replied. "Is this about my request for information?"

"It is."

"I was expecting an e-mail."

"I wanted to talk to you directly about my findings."

"You found something?" Kaye asked.

"Oh, yes, I found something very interesting, and quite troubling,"

Mitchell said. She proceeded to give Kaye an outline of her process and the tailoring of his search parameters into a workable query. She had added a couple additional data points, like credit card usage and mileage, to help refine the results.

"When I first ran it, I honestly thought I had a bug in my query," she said. "But I didn't. Detective, I got returns on thirteen additional missing women in the last eighteen months. For all of them, their last known whereabouts were in your search area. Santa Barbara, San Luis Obispo and Kern Counties seem to be the hub."

Kaye was stunned.

"I thought we might get a couple hits, but thirteen? And I take it Nicole Ingram is not included in that number."

"She is not," Mitchell said. "In fact, she's not even the most recent."

Kaye thought for a moment before asking, "Ms. Mitchell, could you make me a list with particulars?"

"I already have. I'm sending it to you right now."

Seconds later the e-mail and attached file dropped into Kaye's inbox.

"Got it," he said.

"Interestingly enough," Mitchell said, "almost all of these young women were only reported to the local authorities where they lived, and not directly to the jurisdiction where they went missing."

"I know Nicole Ingram was reported to the Santa Barbara Sheriff's Office by her parents in Texas," Kaye said. "I was able to identify her after their people sent a bulletin to us because she had a West Hollywood address on her driver's license."

"Unfortunately, not all agencies are that thorough," Mitchell said. "I will be sending this list to the counties involved and expanding the search to more of the surrounding counties. I hope that's okay with you."

"Absolutely," Kaye said. "Thank you, Ms. Mitchell. I appreciate how fast you got on this."

"I had to, Detective. It became pretty obvious, pretty fast, what's going on."

"What's that?" Kaye asked.

"Someone, possibly a serial killer or human trafficker, is harvesting young women in the central California area."

Kaye spent an hour combing through the summary report Mitchell had sent.

There was no particular type, no set of shared characteristics or appearance among the missing women. Ages and race varied. They had lived all over the country.

Kaye could find no pattern, rhyme or reason at all other than at some point they had all passed through his search area and disappeared.

The only commonality was that all were young and pretty and, except for Nicole Ingram, gone without a trace.

***

Outside, the rain was still coming down, but it wasn't the downpour it had been earlier. Kaye again thumbed through the Geller case file, more anxious than before he'd spoken with Glynis Mitchell, looking for something, anything, he might have missed. Some rational explanation of how Nicole Ingram, reported missing seven months before, had ended up on the Paloma Canyon Country Club golf course with Avi Geller.

It just didn't compute.

And he was still troubled by the fact that Rod Howell and Avi Geller, both with either personal or business connections to Valle delle Viti, had been murdered within a relatively short time. Especially after what Kai Iwamura had uncovered about Valle delle Viti.

He was missing something, something key.

***

After his unexpected dinner date with Auggie the previous evening, the thought of going home to a big, dark house and scrounging up something to eat put Kaye in a funk as he walked through the rain to the truck.

He thought again about selling the house, then beat himself up all over again for not being able to make a decision about it.

Even in the rain he saw the piece of paper, tucked under the windshield wiper, from thirty feet away.

"Are you kidding me?" he muttered.

The rain had left the note so saturated that it tore in half on the wiper blade and hung limply in his hand when he grabbed it. When he managed to peel it open he could tell it was a note in Kanji, but the rain had so obliterated it that the characters were unreadable.

He turned it into a tight round ball, tossed it into the footwell and began the long drive home.

His mood went even more sour only a block later when he heard the ding of a system message from the truck and looked down to see the amber-colored gas pump light and a 'low fuel' message. He'd driven the pickup more in the last week than he'd driven it in the last three months, and hadn't paid attention.

While he mentally berated himself, the rain picked up again.

"Well isn't that just wonderful?" he asked the windshield.

He decided that gas would be the first order of business, then food, and started looking for a gas station.

He pulled into the first one he saw and was confronted with yet another dilemma. The only open pump was on the end. If he chose not to wait, there was just enough wind from just the right direction that he'd end up getting wet if the wind gusted while he gassed up.

He stopped, sighed deeply, then took the open spot.

"It's only water," he told himself as he pushed the door open.

The next spot over was occupied by a blue SUV, and the woman putting gas in it smiled weakly at Kaye when they made eye contact, as if to say 'yeah, me, too' and share the misery.

Kaye slid a finger under the edge of the gas cap cover to pry it open. About a third of the way, it stuck.

"Are you kidding me?" he muttered.

Enough was enough. He hooked a second finger under the edge and, because right now the thought of breaking something appealed to him, gave the cover a hard yank.

It hung for a split second, then popped open. A wire clipped to the inside support of the cap snaked down the filler tube into the tank.

Kaye froze for a fraction of a second before turning and sprinting away from the truck just as a muffled thud came from under the bed.

Moving as fast as he could, he made the few feet to the end of the pump island just as the woman who'd smiled at him was reaching for her SUV's door handle. Without thinking, he took a sideways step, hooked one giant arm around her waist, lifted her from the ground and kept running, shouting, "Get down! Everybody down!"

The now-screaming and struggling woman didn't slow him. In another split second he rounded the front of the SUV and headed into the open parking lot, pulling the woman around in front of himself to protect her as much as possible.

He'd cleared the SUV by less than five feet when his truck

exploded into a huge fireball.

The pump island and the SUV helped lessen the shock wave, but it still pummeled Kaye, pushing him forward and causing him to lose his balance. He staggered and started to go down, doing his best to shelter the woman from both the blast and his weight before hitting the pavement.

He glanced back over his shoulder. His pickup was a blazing inferno, fully engulfed in flames. The pump island's overhead canopy was still intact, but tilted and twisted at a crazy angle. The back half of the blue SUV was ablaze. He could feel the heat, but thanks to the rain there was no immediate danger.

He pushed himself from his elbows to his knees. The woman was curled in a fetal position, her arms wrapped around her head as she whimpered and trembled uncontrollably.

Kaye laid a comforting hand on her shoulder.

"It's okay," he said, sounding to himself like he was talking in the bottom of a barrel. He used the other hand to check his ears for bleeding. It came away dry.

"It's okay," he repeated. "We're okay. We made it."

Her arms slowly unwrapped from her head. She twisted to look up at Kaye, her eyes huge.

"It's okay," he said again, gently squeezing her shoulder. "You're okay."

She dissolved into hysterical sobs.

Kaye stayed down with her, pulling off his Big Boar jacket and grabbing his cell phone from the pocket before draping the jacket over her shoulders and head to give her some shelter from the rain.

He dialed 9-1-1.

"This is Detective Kaye," he said in response to the operator's 'what is your emergency' question, giving her his badge number and location. "I need a full response at this location. Explosion and active fire, possible injuries."

The dispatcher acknowledged and told him units were in route.

He turned his attention back to the woman.

Her sobs had quieted to occasional hiccups and ragged breathing.

"Are you okay?" he asked. "Do you hurt anywhere?"

"I…I think I'm okay," she said. "I can't…think… What happened?"

"My truck exploded."

"What? How…?"

"I don't know," Kaye said. "Help is on the way. Let's get you out of this rain. Can you stand up?"

"I think so."

"What's your name?"

"Emmary."

"Okay, Emmary, let me help." He went to one knee and offered his hands. "Take it slow. If it hurts, tell me and we'll stop. On three, just roll over and sit up."

He counted slowly. On three she grabbed his hand and he helped her roll to a sitting position. She put her heels on the ground and tried to hug her knees. He made sure the jacket stayed on her shoulders.

"Good," he said. "You doing okay?"

She nodded.

"Okay, on three again. I've got you."

With his strength helping, she stood up, wobbly but up.

"Oh, my God," she said, eyes huge as she looked past Kaye at her burning vehicle.

Kaye's truck was already burning out as the fire units arrived and set a perimeter.

Two LAPD units, followed closely by two medic units, rolled into the parking lot, all lights blazing. Officers and paramedics immediately fanned out and started assessing the scene. Kaye saw one of the officers talk into his lapel microphone and then head his way while the other three spread out and started establishing crowd control.

"Detective Kaye!" the approaching officer shouted just as Kaye recognized him as Devon. "Are you okay?"

"I'll live," Kaye said. "But this lady needs to be checked out."

Devon turned, caught the attention of one of the medics and waved her over.

"Emmary, I'm going to turn you over to more capable hands," Kaye said. "They'll take good care of you."

She nodded and looked at him, and he saw her notice the badge and holstered Kimber on his hip.

"You're a cop," she whispered.

"I am."

She stared at him for a long second, then flung herself forward, wrapped her arms around him and buried her face in his chest as she again began to sob.

"Thank you," she said, gasping. "Thank you."

"We've got her, Detective," one of the medics said as he reached out for Emmary's shoulders. Then he held out the jacket and said, "This must be yours."

Kaye took it and his heart sank.

The Big Boar patch showed how hot and powerful the blast had been. In places the thread was badly scorched. In others it had been burned away altogether, leaving only tiny bits of frayed thread sticking out of the backing.

He felt the back of his pant legs. The fabric was still there, but the texture had changed. Unconsciously he reached for his head. His hair felt...different and he felt some of it break off under his fingers.

He realized how close a call he'd just had, then looked up and let the rain pepper his face.

He didn't care.

It had just saved his life.

***

It took nearly two hours for the scene to clear.

After Kaye had surrendered Emmary to the medics, he'd found Devon and made sure the patrolman took pictures of the crowd.

The bomb squad investigators interviewed Kaye. They'd been skeptical at first, ready to attribute the explosion to a fuel leak and some sort of electrical problem, or to Kaye unwittingly causing some sort of static discharge and igniting the fuel tank vapors. But after Kaye described the chain of events they slowly came around and started taking it seriously.

The delay between Kaye yanking what they thought was a trigger device and the actual explosion was, they concluded, either purposeful or the device had used a slow, deflagrating explosive compound rather than an almost instantaneous detonating compound.

"It's just a theory, but it explains why you had those extra few seconds," one said. "Had it been a detonating device, you'd have been blown to bits. It's almost like somebody was sending you a warning instead of trying to kill you."

"Pretty sophisticated, though, to fit down the filler tube," the other said. "We'll take a closer look at things when it all cools off and see if we can find pieces of the device and detonator. Most bombers have a signature. If we get lucky, we'll figure out who did this."

"Okay, thanks guys," Kaye said. "Let me know."

Devon and his partner were cleared to drive Kaye home, where he finally cobbled together some dinner.

While he ate, his phone buzzed. He recognized Thompson's cell number.

"Are you okay?" the Captain asked.

"A little singed," Kaye replied, "but not hurt."

"I talked to the bomb squad guys. Any idea who did this? Think it's the same guy who blew up the Ferrari?"

"I don't believe in coincidences."

"You need a day off?" Thompson asked.

"No," Kaye said. "I'm okay. Just need a new truck."

"You know where to find me if you need me," Thompson said. "I'm glad you're okay."

Kaye had no doubt that the attempt on his life was connected to his investigations. He also had no doubt that whoever had been following him and planting Kanji notes was either responsible, or knew who was.

Twice during the night he was awakened by random, unfamiliar noises and got up, pistol in hand, to check the house. He found nothing amiss, which led to self-rebuke, self-doubt, and more fitful sleep.

Kaye had never feared anyone. His size and preternatural strength imbued him with tremendous self-assurance. He knew where he ranked on the physicality charts, and also knew that the odds of him ever encountering someone who ranked higher were virtually non-existent. It wasn't braggadocio, it was simply quiet confidence, and he'd always remembered a sage piece of advice his father had offered after Kaye had gotten into trouble for beating a particular high school tormenter to a bloody pulp.

"Ben, if people even think a dog will bite, that dog never has to bite anybody."

Since the Kanji notes, though, things had changed and the close shave at the gas station forced him to acknowledge it.

He was not invincible, physically or psychologically.

His final, fleeting thought before falling asleep was that maybe it was time to call Dr. Dellamartre, who had helped him get through the worst of it after he lost Amy. He would tell her about Aspen, and perhaps she could simply explain to him that Father Francis Healey had made him seriously consider, perhaps for the very first time, his own mortality.

# DAY 19

### Friday Week 3

Californians are wont to brag about their weather. After Thursday's deluge, Friday was working on being a day of redemption. The cool morning air had yet to soak up all the moisture from the pavement on the less-traveled streets, but the cloudless sky and climbing sun promised a day to write about to the folks back home in less hospitable climes.

Now truckless, Kaye guided the Road King through uncharacteristically light mid-morning traffic, which seemed to part for him, as the Red Sea had for Moses, in payback for the tough day yesterday.

Patty Phillips, file folder in hand, was waiting when Kaye entered the squad room.

"I wasn't sure you were coming in today," she said. "I heard what happened. Are you okay?"

"A little sore," Kaye admitted. "But overall, I think I got very lucky."

"Did you see the paper this morning?"

"No."

"You're on the front page again. In a good way this time." She smiled. "Mostly, anyway."

Lister's comment about dirty laundry flashed across Kaye's memory.

"From zero to hero and back again in four or five tight paragraphs," he said. "Sells papers. But, really, I'm fine."

"That's good news," Patty said, then smiled again. "You'll be finer when you hear the juicy stuff I found on social media."

"Really? Already? That was fast."

"Really. And thank you. I try."

"Well then, step into what passes for my office and tell me all about it."

When they were settled, Kaye said, "Okay, show me what you've got."

"Like I figured," Patty began, resting the folder on her lap, "Sullivan has social media accounts on pretty much every platform out there, probably because of the business she's in. I didn't really have to dig any deeper than the big three to find what we needed."

"Did you find anything specific to tie her to what we already know?"

"I did." She pulled a page from the folder and handed it to Kaye. It was a post featuring a picture of a smiling, dark-haired woman standing proudly next to a shiny black Explorer. "That's Brianna Carson showing off her new car, purchased exactly one week before the murders."

"I take it she's friends with Sullivan."

"More than that. They're cousins. Carson is the daughter of Sullivan's mother's brother. They grew up together and worked together in real estate for years. They're tight."

"Tight enough that Carson would loan Sullivan her brand new car?"

Patty reached into the folder, pulled out another page and handed it to Kaye. It was a screen print of an exchange of tweets between @BCarson87 and @RealSalesMegan, with @RealSalesMegan thanking Carson for letting her borrow the new ride and that the repairs to the Caddy hadn't cost as much as she thought they would. At the bottom of the post was #ThickerThanWater. The post was dated two days after the murders.

"You're certain that account is our Megan Sullivan?" Kaye asked.

"Absolutely," Patty said, then retrieved another page and held it out to Kaye. "Meet Thad Carson, Brianna's husband."

Kaye took the page and stared at it.

Thad Carson was a hunter. His profile picture showed him dressed in camouflage, kneeling behind the carcass of a coyote and smiling as he held the dead animal's head up to face the camera. In his other hand Carson grasped a rifle with a scope and a long, curved magazine. Kaye recognized it immediately.

"Right caliber," he said. "It would do the job."

"I checked the registry," Patty said. "I didn't find anything registered to Carson."

"He doesn't have to register that gun," Kaye said. "No pistol grip and no flash suppressor. But we now have links between Sullivan, a matching vehicle, and access to a possible weapon. Thank you."

"I'm not done yet," Patty said, grinning broadly.

"What else did you find?"

She grabbed more sheets from the folder, but this time she held them face down on her lap.

"Sullivan has a lot of friends and followers, so I was lucky to find this," she said, then handed the top page to Kaye.

It was Dennis Bettencourt's profile page, or at least what Patty had been able to capture with a screen print. A smiling Bettencourt was sitting in the driver's seat of his red Corvette.

"Sullivan and Bettencourt are friends on social media," Patty said. "On Sullivan's profile page it says she's married, but on Bettencourt's page it says he's in a relationship with a 'Megan', no last name."

"I also found this," Patty said, handing Kaye another page.

It was another shot of a home page, but this one was for Storm Chase.

Kaye kept staring at the profile picture and muttered, "I'll be damned." It was definitely Dennis Bettencourt, but what Kaye saw was the cover photo.

It was the same living room shown in Officer Devon's photos accompanying the vandalism report taken from Sullivan on the evening of the murders, minus the damage. The photo instantly triggered Kaye's memory on where he'd seen the living room before: On a poster promoting Bettencourt's porn production company hanging on the wall of Bettencourt's house before the tall man had pulled the door closed.

"The first one is on his personal page," Patty replied. "That's where I found out he was friends with Sullivan. But I got curious and found that one," she pointed at the second page. "Notice he updated to those photos just after Sullivan listed the house in Paloma Canyon. I printed it because the date was so close. I also found this." She handed him a third page.

It was another screen print of Storm Chase's home page, but with different cover and profile pictures.

"Why this one?" Kaye asked.

"That's what's been on the page since the day before the murders. I thought the timing was suspicious, so I printed them. Did I do good?"

"Better than good, Patty," Kaye said. "You did great."

\*\*\*

The loss of the truck was more nuisance than real problem. Nothing irreplaceable had been consumed in the fire, and Kaye had the resources to replace the truck without waiting for the insurance company to decide what, if anything, they would cover under the circumstances.

He called the dealership where he'd bought the burned truck about a year ago, talked to the Sales Manager about what he wanted and confirmed they had a match in stock. After some haggling, they arrived at a price Kaye thought was fair. He then called his bank and arranged payment. On the second call to the dealer he was promised that the new truck would be parked in his driveway before the end of the day on Saturday.

\*\*\*

Kaye was thinking of going around the corner for a sandwich when he heard Captain Thompson's voice as his boss came through the doors into the squad.

"Let's hope he's here."

"If he's not, we need to find him."

Kaye recognized the second voice, too. ADA Kayla Okafor.

The two rounded the corner, saw Kaye, and stopped.

"In my office, please," Thompson said, then turned and headed that way.

"Close the door," Thompson said when Kaye followed them in.

Thompson sank into his chair. Okafor perched on the edge of a filing cabinet and Kaye took his usual chair across from his Captain.

"What's up?" he asked.

It was Okafor who answered.

"We just spent an hour in chambers with Judge Gardner. Megan Sullivan filed a motion this morning asking Gardner to lift the hearing delay and allow her to present her request for a restraining order." She handed Kaye a sheaf of papers. "That's a copy of the affidavit. She's asking that you be removed from the LAPD and face criminal stalking charges."

"Let her," Kaye said. "She can't show cause, because there's no cause to show."

"You're positive?" Thompson asked.

Kaye glared at his boss. "Yes, sir, I am positive."

"I've got to tell you, Detective," Thompson said, leaning forward, "Sloan and Leale are backing her. Leale's been bragging for two days how he's going to put the famous Ben Kaye in jail."

"I'm famous?" Kaye said, smiling. "I had no idea."

"Detective," Okafor said, "you need to take this more seriously."

"Why?" Kaye asked. "There is absolutely nothing, repeat nothing, to this. I saw Megan Sullivan in person for the very first time just the other day when I followed –"

"You did what?" Okafor interrupted.

"Surveillance, Counselor," Kaye said. "One hundred percent legitimate and discreet. He," Kaye pointed at Thompson, "knew all about it. He has also had the cell phone she claims the calls and texts are coming from for a week."

"He told the Judge that," Okafor acknowledged. "You're positive the surveillance was case related?"

"Yes," Kaye said. "One thing I was able to establish is that Megan Sullivan and Ziva Geller have a longstanding friendship. They had lunch together in Santa Monica the day I followed Sullivan."

"Really?" Okafor asked.

"Really," Kaye said. "And I can connect Sullivan to the person I believe shot Avi Geller and Nicole Ingram. If I get what I think I'm going to get over the next couple of days, I was planning on bringing her in for questioning on Monday." He looked hard at Okafor. "With your permission, of course."

"You can connect Sullivan to the murders?" Thompson asked.

"Indirectly, but yes, I can," Kaye said, "but it's still pretty much circumstantial. I either need time to track down and interview a couple more people or I need the okay to pick up Megan Sullivan and question her. Did Gardner schedule the hearing?"

"Yes, she did," Okafor said. "Monday morning at 10:00 a.m. That Captain Thompson has had your phone for a week convinced her to let me file a written response before five o'clock today. She said she'd take it under advisement. But, I've got to tell you, with Sloan and Leale pushing, I think the odds are against you. For your sake, Detective, I hope you've got some strong evidence against Sullivan, or Howard Feinmann will have you by the throat."

"Howard Feinmann is Sullivan's attorney?" Kaye asked, surprised.

"He is," Okafor said. "Why?"

"He represents Ziva Geller and some other people I'm looking into. He also knew how old Nicole Ingram was."

"Is that pertinent?" Okafor asked.

"I never released Ingram's age to Media Relations," Kaye said.

Okafor and Thompson exchanged looks. "Well, well, well," Okafor said, smiling. "What an interesting development. I'll make sure Judge Gardner knows that, too. Can you at least give me a bare bones summary of what you've got by mid-afternoon so I can review it and pass it along to Gardner?"

"I can do that," Kaye said, rising to leave. "If nothing else, on Monday I get to be in the same room as Megan Sullivan without the threat of going to jail." He looked at Okafor. "Might be a good time to ask the lady some questions, right?"

\*\*\*

Kaye immediately went to work on the summary for Okafor. He was careful not to exaggerate, and if he was still waiting for confirmation on something, he said so and didn't speculate. His primary purpose wasn't to defend himself against the claims Sullivan was making against him, but to include information he felt would help explain her motivation for making them.

About ten minutes into it, he realized it was becoming the catalyst for his thoughts on the case, and the deeper he got into it, the more it all fit together.

Kaye was tired when he finished, despite having spent the entire day in the Squad. He went to the break room and got a bottle of tea out of the vending machine.

When he got back to his desk his phone was ringing yet again. He thought about just letting it go to voice mail, but instead said, "What now?" out loud and picked up.

"Kaye."

"Detective Kaye, this is Sam Geller."

"How are you, Sam."

"Fine, thank you," Geller said. "I just finished going through that system backup we talked about."

"Did you find anything?" Kaye asked.

There was a slight hesitation before Geller said, "As a matter of fact, I did. I found a copy of Uncle Les's spreadsheet from before my Dad was killed. The name Dennis Bettencourt shows up twice."

"When?"

Geller gave him the dates. Baruch's first meeting with Bettencourt was almost three weeks before Nicole Ingram walked into AZG Productions and the second was a few weeks after Ingram's sit down with Avi Geller.

"Are there any notes?" Kaye asked.

"Some," Geller replied. "After the first meeting, Uncle Les wrote 'wow' in capital letters, then 'get a completed script to Avi before somebody else grabs it'. It must've been good."

"What about the second meeting?"

"There's a note, and it's odd. Uncle Les wrote 'put together with a ghost. Got to have this'."

"What does that mean?" Kaye asked.

"I think it means that the script either wasn't finished, which the first note supports, or needed polishing. Uncle Les was going to have a more experienced writer help this Bettencourt guy."

"That's a big change from the first note," Kaye said. "The wow factor is gone."

"Yeah, I noticed that, too. And there was something else."

"What's that?"

"I got curious about Uncle Les deleting his files. I figured he was mad because Dad left him out of the will. He deleted them on the day Dad was buried, but the time stamp was before the funeral, not after."

"Do you think he knew about the will ahead of time?" Kaye asked.

"Could have, I guess. I mean, why else would he do that?"

Kaye had an idea, but kept it to himself. Instead he said, "Thanks for checking the files, Sam. That's what I needed. Can you hold on to those backups in case I need them later?"

"I can do that," Geller said. "Would you do something for me, Detective? I mean, if you talk to Uncle Les? He won't take my calls. I'd like you to deliver a message for me."

"I can try."

"Tell him I really miss him," Geller said, "and I'd like him to come back. I need his help. Partners, fifty-fifty."

"Sam, if I see him I'll tell him."

After the call ended, Kaye leaned back and regrouped. Knowing Bettencourt had visited Les Baruch at least partly confirmed what he believed was going on.

Tomorrow he was going to Santa Barbara to talk to Les Baruch.

*** 

By 4:00 p.m. he had a basic outline of what he believed he knew about the murders of Avi Geller and Nicole Ingram, who he thought was involved, and why. He copied it into an e-mail and sent it to ADA Okafor with an apology for taking so long.

Then he grabbed his cell phone and faced the crappiest task of the day.

He dialed and it went to voice mail.

"Hi, Auggie. It's Ben. Hey, my schedule got totally turned upside down and there's no way I'll be in Santa Ynez tonight. But I am going to Santa Barbara on the Geller case tomorrow, come hell or high water, and want to make sure it's okay if I come up after that. Call me when you get this, and, again, I'm really sorry. I'll explain when I see you."

\*\*\*

He hadn't been off the cell phone for five minutes before his desk phone rang. It was the District Attorney's office, and he figured it was probably Okafor.

"That was fast, Counselor," he said when he answered.

"I'm a fast reader," Okafor said.

"So what can I do for you now?" Kaye asked.

"First, let me say that if you had brought me this information in an arrest warrant affidavit for Megan Sullivan, I'd have taken it to a judge in a heartbeat. In fact, I forwarded it to Judge Gardner already."

"You said 'first'. So, what's second?" Kaye asked.

Okafor laughed. "Kaye, you think just like me. Second, though, because of the overall situation, that can't happen. The arrest warrant, I mean. But you gave me an idea."

"I'm listening."

Okafor spent five minutes laying it out.

When she finished, Kaye smiled as he hung up.

Monday morning was going to be very interesting.

# DAY 20
### Saturday, Week 3

He decided to take the '61 Duo Glide and show it to Auggie.

The Big Boar jacket was replaced with an old-style, oblique zipper jacket with a waist belt, the kind worn before sprung rear suspension became the norm and rigid frames were tough on the kidneys. Plus, it was very similar to what Brando wore in The Wild One, which Auggie would like.

Kaye took his normal route. On the way he mentally constructed how he would approach Les Baruch and what, exactly, he wanted to get from the man.

He didn't know for certain what he'd expected, but when he found the address Sam Geller had given him, it didn't come close to preconceptions.

Because Baruch had toiled for Avi Geller for all those years, then quit when he found out he wasn't going to head the company and reap the reward, Kaye had formed the impression that Baruch had been Bob Cratchit to Geller's Ebenezer Scrooge.

Hardly.

The address was only blocks from Stearns Wharf and the harbor. The brilliant white structure, adorned with outdoor spaces and arches and topped with the ubiquitous red tile roof, was a beautiful piece of architecture already half-covered in climbing green ivy.

He was unable to access the secure underground lot, but found an adequate spot about a half-block away. There were only eight units in the building, and Kaye had no trouble finding Baruch's.

Kaye's immediate impression was that the place had probably set Baruch back at least a million five.

Les Baruch answered the door and, clearly taken aback, stared at Kaye.

Kaye stared back.

"Well, this is certainly unexpected," Baruch said after an uncomfortable silence. "What brings you to my door, Detective Kaye?"

"I'd like a few minutes of your time, Mr. Baruch, if it's not too much trouble." Kaye paused, then added. "I was going to be in town today anyway, and thought this would be a lot easier for you than making you come all the way to the police station in Los Angeles."

Baruch obviously got the message, and Kaye saw a fleeting glimpse of doubt cross the man's eyes.

"May I come in?" Kaye asked.

"Oh, sure, sure," Baruch said, stepping back and holding the door open wide. "Welcome, welcome."

The place was spacious and airy, and lavishly decorated in the old California Mission and Craftsman style.

"Nice place," Kaye said, looking around before fixing his gaze on Baruch. "A little strange that you didn't mention it when we talked about Nicole Ingram and I asked if the Gellers owned a place up here."

Baruch started to say something, stopped, then said, "I guess I just didn't think about it. We didn't expect to be living here full time just yet, but it's working out."

"We?"

"My wife, Estelle."

"Got it," Kaye said. "Is she here?"

"Not right now," Baruch said. "She went up to Goleta to see her sister and go shopping."

"If I can be nosy," Kaye said, "what did this place set you back?"

"One point seven five," Baruch said. "And a bargain at that. We bought it when it was just a set of plans before they tore down the old building that was here. It's already worth a lot more than we paid."

"Good investment. I guess you know more about real estate than Avi did," Kaye said. "I heard about Avi's will. Must have been a real shock for you. I know it surprised Sam Geller."

"You've talked to Sam?"

"He gave me your address. He also asked me to deliver a message."

"He did?" Baruch seemed surprised. "What is it? Go to hell?"

"Hardly," Kaye replied. "He asked me to tell you that he misses you, he needs your help, and he'd love to have you back. As an equal partner."

"That's what he said?" Baruch asked.

"That's what he said," Kaye confirmed.

Baruch was silent for a moment, then said, "But I'm sure you didn't drive all the way up here to tell me that."

"I didn't drive," Kaye said. "I rode. A motorcycle. Somebody blew up my truck Thursday night trying to kill me."

Baruch turned white as a sheet and swallowed hard.

"Why would you come to talk to me about that?"

"That's not why I'm here. I'm here about Avi," he paused for a second before adding, "and Nicole Ingram."

The slowly returning color in Baruch's face vanished again at the mention of Ingram.

"Do I need a lawyer?" Baruch barely whispered.

"You're entitled to counsel, Mr. Baruch, if that's what you want or think you need."

"Am I a suspect?" Still barely a whisper.

Kaye stuck with the plan.

"No, you are not a suspect. But I think you know a lot more about what happened, and what brought this about, than you've told me. In fact, I think you probably know more than you realize."

Baruch broke eye contact and looked down at his shoes.

"I need your help, Les," Kaye went on. "I think I know who, and why, but there are things that don't fit together. Help me connect the dots here so I can make sure everybody responsible is brought to justice. Regardless of what happened between you and Avi, you owe him that."

Kaye waited. It was Baruch's decision now. If he asked for a lawyer or declined to discuss the murders, Kaye was dead in the water.

"You want some coffee or something while we talk?" Baruch asked, and Kaye heard the surrender in the man's voice.

"I'm fine," Kaye said, "but get yourself something if you want."

Baruch nodded and headed to the kitchen. Kaye heard the sound of a coffee maker and Baruch was back shortly carrying a cup that said 'Santa Barbara' and had the image of a sailboat on it.

"What would you like to know," Baruch asked as he sat down.

"I'll start by asking you what you know about a man named Dennis Bettencourt, and why you deleted your files the day of Avi's funeral, before you found out Avi left you out of the will."

Les Baruch deflated, his shoulders sagging as he looked at Kaye with final defeat in his eyes.

The two talked for over an hour. Baruch told Kaye what had happened between him and Avi Geller that had broken their trust and friendship, and it fit with Kaye's conclusions.

When Kaye prompted Baruch with details he knew that the producer didn't, Baruch often offered more information that he hadn't considered relevant before.

Other things Baruch told him surprised Kaye and filled in a lot of the gaps in his timeline.

But what really surprised Kaye was the scope of events swirling around Avi Geller and Nicole Ingram before the murders.

"Avi was scared," Baruch said. "I could tell. He didn't know what they would do when they realized he knew. Then, when they were murdered..."

"Why didn't you tell me this before, when I first came to you?" Kaye asked.

"Because I'm scared, too," Baruch said. "You don't know these people."

"They'll know me before I'm done with them," Kaye said grimly. "Les, would you be willing to write this all down for me?"

"Like a statement?"

"Exactly."

"Will I have to appear in court?"

"I can't answer that for sure yet," Kaye said. "But I'd say, eventually, yes."

"Okay, I'll write it out," Baruch said after a brief hesitation. "When do you want it?"

"As soon as possible. I have at least one, maybe two, more stops in town. How about I come back by later this afternoon?"

"I'll have it done."

"Thank you," Kaye said, shaking Baruch's hand. "And call Sam, okay?"

"I will," Baruch said, then looked at Kaye. "You know, I can still hook you up with a guy if you're interested in being in the movies."

***

Back at the '61 Kaye made a call.

"Hello," a woman answered.

"Could I speak to Alicia Valdez, please? This is Detective Kaye from the LAPD. We spoke on the phone about Valle delle Viti, oh, a few weeks ago. You gave me this number."

"I remember," Valdez said. "What can I do for you, Detective Kaye?"

"I'm sorry to call you on a Saturday, but as it happens I'm in Santa Barbara," Kaye said. "I was hoping you might have a few minutes to talk, in person, a little more about Valle delle Viti."

Valdez hesitated for a moment, then asked, "Is there a problem?"

"On your end, no," Kaye assured her. "On my end, yeah, maybe. I'd just like to verify some things I've heard from other sources, if that would be okay. I certainly don't expect you to disclose private or proprietary information, at least without proper authorization from the court."

Kaye figured Valdez was smart enough to understand he'd just told her he'd get a subpoena if necessary.

"Uh, sure, I guess that would be okay. Where are you now?"

"I'm near Stearns Wharf."

"How about I meet you at the Starbucks downtown in, say, an hour?"

"I'll find it," Kaye said. "Thank you, Ms. Valdez."

It only took Kaye a few minutes to find the coffee shop, and he picked up a legal pad at the drugstore next door. While he waited, he filled nearly ten pages with his own recollections and impressions from his talk with Les Baruch. If Valdez could verify just a couple details to back up Baruch's story, he knew he might have uncovered a real viper's nest.

An hour and fifteen minutes later there was still no sign of Valdez.

Kaye was about to call her again when she came through the door, saw him, and walked over.

"Sorry I'm late. I almost didn't come."

"Thanks for taking time on a Saturday to see me," Kaye said as she settled into the opposite chair. "I had planned to be in town yesterday, but my schedule got totally blown up."

"No problem," she said. "You said you wanted to ask me about Valle delle Viti?"

"I do," Kaye said. "I guess my first question is more of a procedural thing. I talked to a friend about how eminent domain works. I honestly had no idea a local government could take private property from one person and give it to someone else, just based on the second person's promises. I always thought it was for things like roads, bridges, dams, public buildings, stuff like that."

"It used to be," Valdez said. "But that changed in our business with what's called a Kelo Taking. Let me assure you, we strictly adhered to the law in every eminent domain proceeding we initiated during the Valle delle Viti process. It was all legal and above board."

"Just not very popular with the people who lost their property."

"I think that's to be expected. But the court decides on reasonable compensation."

"My friend explained all that to me," Kaye said. "I'm not questioning the process."

"Then what's your question?"

"Does your office use eminent domain routinely?" Kaye asked.

Valdez stared at Kaye intently before answering.

"Not routinely, no. We have used it a few times during my time here for things such as you mentioned a moment ago, plus, especially here, projects like wildlife and marine habitat preservation. But only as a last resort. We try very hard to reach a satisfactory agreement with property owners, including easements and such, before entering into good faith negotiations to buy their property at fair market value."

"What happened when those negotiations didn't lead to a mutual understanding?"

"We accept the court's ruling, whatever it is," Valdez said. "But we almost always reached amicable settlements before Valle delle Viti came along."

"Really?" Kaye said, genuinely surprised. "How many Kelo actions were court-ordered during the Valle delle Viti project?"

"I think it was seventeen total," Valdez said. "Somewhere right in there, anyway. But those were not all ours, not even close. After the Village of Chumash Oaks was incorporated the actions were initiated by their legal staff, and the number climbed dramatically."

"Wow," Kaye said, "that seems like a lot. Do you know how many sellers reached agreements with the developers and sold voluntarily?"

"Four."

Kaye was stunned.

"What was your professional take on that?" he asked.

"My input was not solicited."

"We're not in court, Ms. Valdez," Kaye said. "I'm not taking notes, and I'm not recording this. I'm not writing this up in a report or going to the press. We're just two people talking about a project that's already completed and how it might be connected to the murders of at least two people in Los Angeles. I'm just asking what you think."

She looked around to see who was sitting within earshot. The place was busy, but everyone looked absorbed in their own conversations or screens.

"I thought it sucked," she said, leaning forward and keeping her voice low. "I think Valle delle Viti was low-balling people, possibly falsifying appraisals, then using the courts to get what they wanted."

"Whose idea was that? Your boss's? Because obviously your County Executive and Supervisors endorsed it."

"The Valle delle Viti lawyers pitched it to the Board early on, when it became obvious people up there didn't want to sell. They presented some very optimistic revenue projections."

"And the Board bought them."

"No," Valdez said. "The weasels punted and brought in a hired gun."

"Hired gun?" Kaye asked. "You need to explain. I don't think that means the same thing in your business that it does in mine."

"Probably not," Valdez said, smirking. "What I mean is that the Board didn't vote directly on the project. They voted to outsource the decision and hired an economic development consultant to provide guidance."

"Why would they do that?"

"Politics," Valdez said. "They all have to run for re-election at some point. If the whole thing went to hell, they had somebody to point the finger at."

"Funny how that works."

"Unless you get the short, brown end of the stick, like the people in northwest County who lost their homes and land."

"The consultant gave it the thumbs up, right," Kaye asked.

"Yes," Valdez said. "Dr. Collum's firm evaluated the project proposal and endorsed it unconditionally."

Kaye hesitated, then asked, "Dr. Collum? Clifford Collum?"

"Yes, that's him. Do you know him?" she asked. "He's a very well respected economist and economic development consultant. The firm's offices are in Los Angeles."

Kaye said nothing about the parking garage murder, but it had to be the same guy.

"Did Collum work for Valle delle Viti or the County?" Kaye asked.

"Both, actually," Valdez replied. "The County and developers agreed to split the fee and signed a binding agreement ahead of time to proceed according to Dr. Collum's recommendations."

"And he recommended the project move forward."

"He did."

"Who got what they wanted?"

"Valle delle Viti," Valdez said instantly. "It's just my opinion, but I think we gave away the building to buy the inventory, if you know what I mean."

"How so?"

"The deal had so many tax breaks and deferments, job creation incentives and other freebies for what became the Village of Chumash Oaks that it's costing the County and other municipalities more than a billion dollars in potential revenue over the next twenty years."

"A billion?" Kaye asked.

Valdez nodded, raised her eyebrows and said, "With a 'B'."

"Wow," Kaye said. "What a perfect scam."

Valdez remained silent this time, her expression neutral.

"I remember you making some comments about their lawyers," Kaye went on, "and I loved the whole 'lion in the room' thing. Do you by chance remember their names? Or the firm's name?"

"Not off the top of my head," Valdez replied. "My interactions with them were really pretty limited. They dealt mostly with the County Attorney. But I can find out, if you like."

"I would," Kaye said.

Valdez picked up the phone and punched in a number. When the call was answered she identified herself, asked the question, then wrote on a napkin while she listened.

"Thanks, Danny," she said, then hung up and handed the napkin across to Kaye.

He almost wasn't surprised. Just like on the door.

Armstrong, Nobile, Feinmann and Jenkins.

\*\*\*

Kaye walked back to the bike and shook his head. Somebody was putting in as many miles as he was, because another note was stuck between the windshield and windshield bag. He didn't even look at it, just folded it one more time and stuffed it into his jacket pocket.

He rode back to Baruch's house, trying on the way to figure out just how deep Howard Feinmann was into Valle delle Viti, or vice versa, and how that might connect to Avi Geller's murder.

He rang the doorbell and waited. Thirty seconds later he pushed the button again and, on the off chance a million seven five doorbell had failed in the last three or four hours, knocked loudly.

No answer.

Kaye peered through the beveled glass panes that bracketed the door and saw no signs of activity.

"Well, crap," he muttered, immediately thinking Baruch had lost his nerve and run. He thought about calling the Santa Barbara PD and asking for a broadcast, then realized he had no clue what Baruch drove. What would he tell them, anyway? That he had a faint-hearted potential witness?

He turned from the door and stepped across to the street-facing side of the porch, grabbing his cell phone.

He'd started to call Patty when he heard the sound of a high-revving motorcycle approaching. Turning, he saw a white Hayabusa coming fast from the west. The rider wore full black leathers and full-face helmet with a darkly tinted visor. A small, green duffel was strapped to the back of the seat.

The bike slowed quickly as the rider stepped down through the gears to stop at the intersection.

As the bike came even with Kaye, the rider brought the 'Busa to an abrupt stop short of the stop sign and started directly at him.

Kaye stared back, unable to see anything behind the face shield, but where he stood was close enough that he could tell the rider was a woman.

Twice the rider revved the bike's engine to an ear-shattering shriek while continuing to stare at Kaye, then dropped the clutch and accelerated hard, running the stop sign and disappearing around the corner.

Kaye listened to the sound fade with distance, then, with a sense of dread, turned back to the door. He tried the knob. It was locked. He pounded on the door again and shouted, "Baruch! Les Baruch! It's Ben Kaye! Open the door!"

Nothing.

"C'mon," he muttered, fighting the urge to break down the door. Should he call Baruch's number? What if the house was empty and nobody was home? It took less than five seconds for him to decide.

The white Hayabusa had been too much of a coincidence.

He grabbed the knob and launched his shoulder against the door. The latch and deadbolt splintered from the frame and the door swung inward.

"Les Baruch!" he shouted as he drew the Kimber, "Ben Kaye, LAPD! I'm coming in!"

Les and Estelle Baruch were both in the living room.

Estelle sat on the couch, her bloody hands in her lap and her head slumped forward. Still-red blood soaked the front of her blouse. Kaye wasn't about to touch the body, but guessed her throat had been cut.

Les was on the floor. He had been disemboweled and decapitated. His head was nowhere to be seen.

"Damn it, damn it, damn it," Kaye said softly. He grabbed his phone again and called 9-1-1, identified himself to the dispatcher and told her what he'd found.

"Please stay at the scene, Detective Kaye," she said.

"I'm not going anywhere."

He headed for the front porch to wait outside, but as he passed the dining room he caught sight of a yellow legal pad on the table, a pen next to it.

It was obvious that multiple pages had been torn off the pad, but he could only guess as to when. The top sheet was blank, but when Kaye looked closely he could see residual impressions from what had been written on the now-gone page.

He wanted that page.

He heard sirens approaching from multiple directions. If he was going to tamper with the crime scene, he needed to do it quickly.

He used his phone to take a picture, then anchored the pad with his elbow and, careful not to touch anything else, peeled back the first four sheets and ripped them from the pad.

He carefully rolled the pages, top sheet in, and headed for the kitchen. He tore several paper towels off a roll hanging beneath a cabinet and wrapped them around the legal pad pages. In the second drawer he opened, he found the plastic bags, put the bundle inside one and carefully slid the package into the over-sized zippered pocket inside his riding jacket.

It was a fifty-fifty shot, at best, but it was all he had time for.

He put the pen and pad in the drawer with the plastic bags just as the first responding unit slid to a stop outside.

\*\*\*

He was at Baruch's for the next two hours, mostly staying out of the way, but keeping himself available to the Santa Barbara PD detectives investigating the murders.

When they finally sat down to talk to him, he held nothing back – except the bundle of papers in his pocket.

Estelle Baruch had put up a fight. She had multiple defensive wounds on her hands and forearms.

Les Baruch had no defensive wounds, leading the locals to assume that Baruch may have known his attacker. They also agreed that Les had probably been killed first, and that Estelle had likely walked in on the killer while he, or she as Kaye pointed out, was busy removing Les's head.

When the Deputy Coroner moved Estelle's body, it turned out that her throat had not been cut. She had been stabbed once with a fairly wide, double-edged blade.

Why Estelle had been posed was anybody's guess.

When Kaye related the circumstances of Clifford Collum's murder and the white Hayabusa with a woman rider, the SBPD guys became skeptical. Taking the head was surely the act of a serial killer collecting a trophy, and women just didn't do that.

Kaye didn't argue the point. He gave them the LAPD Robbery-Homicide number and told them to ask for Detective Gannett.

"Are we done?" Kaye finally asked.

"Yeah," one of the locals replied. "We're done. We'll call you if we need you and we'll call," he glanced down at his notes, "Gannett on Monday. Thanks for your help."

Kaye smiled inwardly. He had a different opinion about who was helping whom here. Not unusual, he decided, for a department that had, maybe, a murder a month. They asked the right questions and seemed competent, but he guessed they'd never clear the case, which reaffirmed his decision to take the pages from the legal pad.

He walked back to the '61. He was anxious to get the pages to the forensics techs, but it was late on a Saturday and he didn't want to forgo Santa Ynez and the chance to see Auggie.

Les and Estelle Baruch weren't going to get any deader before Monday.

***

About an hour later he passed the 'Welcome to the Village of Chumash Oaks' sign at a sedate twenty-five miles an hour.

A quarter-mile later, a black Charger, lights flashing, was behind him.

He pulled over and waited, watching in the rearview mirror as he unstrapped his helmet.

Sure enough, it was Reid.

The cop walked up, stopped just behind Kaye's shoulder and said, "Driver's license, registration and insurance, biker boy," just as Kaye pulled off his helmet.

"Good evening, Officer Reid," Kaye said. "Care to explain your probable cause for this stop?"

"Well, well, well," Reid said, hooking his thumbs in the front of his gun belt. "If it ain't mister hotshot LAPD."

"That's me. Probable cause?"

"You were speeding again."

"Bullshit," Kaye snorted. "I'm a fast learner. Try again."

"I don't need to explain anything to you," Reid said.

"Then you'd better be able to explain it to a judge," Kaye retorted.

"Nice bike," Reid said, changing the subject. "What's this beauty worth?"

"Why?" Kaye asked. "You checking the vehicle seizure value threshold? I hear your department picks up a lot of stuff."

"All perfectly legal," Reid said drolly, "within the laws of the State of California and the United States of America."

"I bet."

Reid glanced at Kaye, but kept his mouth shut.

"Either cite me or let me go," Kaye said sharply. "I have someplace I need to be."

"On your way to see your bitch?" Reid sneered. "Good luck with that, you freak."

"Excuse me?" Kaye asked and started to stand up.

"Ain't that what you biker boys call your women?" Reid said, taking a step back. "Bitches? I mean, Saturday night and all, there's gotta be a bitch in your plans somewhere, right?"

"You know, Reid, it would almost be worth it to turn you into a wet spot on the side of the road."

"Go ahead and try," Reid taunted, taking another step back and snatching his pistol from its holster. "I'll put sixteen rounds in your ass before you can get off that motorcycle."

Kaye stood still, straddling the bike.

Reid laughed. "You have a nice night." He turned to leave, holstering his pistol.

Kaye again saw the Special Officer rocker above the Chumash Oaks PD patch. This time, though, the odd shape made sense.

Reid worked for Black Scimitar.

"Hey, Reid," he called out, "say hello to your boss for me."

The cop's pace faltered for a half-step, but he didn't stop and turn around. "Fuck you," he shouted back, holding up one hand, middle finger extended.

\*\*\*

It didn't take long for Kaye to make it to Auggie's Wine'N'Diner. Befitting a Saturday night, the parking lot was jammed with motorcycles.

He parked in the far corner of the lot, next to the van Auggie had been driving on Wednesday. When he walked to the door, he stopped and looked around.

No custom blue Glide.

He looked around, trying to pick Auggie's bike out of the sea of gleaming paint and chrome, but couldn't see it.

Well, he thought, she's got to have a car she drives sometimes.

He pushed through the door into the crowded, noisy restaurant. Looking around, he couldn't see Auggie and figured she was in the back.

"Well, hi there," the same hostess said when he walked up. Today she wore a name tag. Cheri. "You're becoming a regular."

"I am. I'm supposed to meet Auggie."

"Tonight?" she asked, a puzzled look on her face. "You're sure?"

"Yeah, I'm sure," Kaye replied. "I saw her Wednesday in L.A."

"Yeah, that's when she goes to town to make deliveries," Cheri said. "But Auggie's not here."

"Not here?" Kaye echoed.

"Yeah," Cheri said. "I haven't seen her since Wednesday. We had our regular meeting and laid out everything for the week before she left to make deliveries. The van was back here Thursday morning and her bike was gone, so I know she made it back, but I haven't seen or heard from her."

"Is that unusual?" Kaye asked. "I mean, does she sometimes just take off?"

He thought about the Thursday morning meeting Auggie had told him about to present an offer on the plot of land she hoped to plant. Maybe it hadn't gone well.

"Well, it's not usual," Cheri said.

"You've tried to call her, right?"

"Of course. All I got was voice mail. I've left, like, five messages."

"Okay," Kaye said. "You know, maybe we got our wires crossed and I screwed up."

"Could be," Cheri said, "Since you're here, you're welcome to hang around and see if she comes in."

"Thanks," Kaye said. "I think I will, for a while."

The stool around the end of the bar was open. Kaye sat, nursing a glass of wine and looking up expectantly every time the front door opened, running all kinds of nightmare scenarios in his mind. That the van was parked outside and Auggie's Glide was gone flummoxed him. Obviously, nothing had happened while she was in transit back from Santa Monica and she'd made it home. But she hadn't seemed to him to be someone who would stand him up.

Maybe she was angry he hadn't come yesterday, and decided to avoid him. After all, she hadn't called him back.

He'd been sitting, sipping his wine and watching the comings and goings for about twenty minutes when he noticed two men threading their way through the tables, heading his way. One was average size, the second was a big guy. They both wore the biker gear that seemed standard at Auggie's and Kaye could see some generic patches on their vests, but none that identified a club.

Two tables from Kaye, they split up. The larger man disappeared from Kaye's field of vision over his left shoulder and the other approached the bar, used his hip to push the last stool sideways to make some room and leaned forward, elbows on the bar and hands clasped.

He glanced at Kaye. "How's it going?"

"Can't complain," Kaye replied. "You?"

"Nothing I can't handle. Got a question, though."

"For me, or just in general?"

The guy's jaw clenched and his eyes narrowed. "For you, wise ass."

Kaye said nothing and took a sip of his wine.

"Where's you colors?" the guy asked finally. "We've seen you here a couple times lately, always by yourself, like some sort of scout or something. Big Boar MC. Suddenly, you're plain wrap. What's up with that?"

Kaye half-smiled. "Had a little accident. Had to go to a back-up jacket."

"Too bad," the guy said, and Kaye knew he didn't mean it. "We also noticed that things suddenly changed after you started showing up."

"Changed?"

"That's what I said."

"How so?"

"You're here, and Auggie's not."

269

Kaye looked at the guy, glanced over his shoulder and saw the big guy leaning against the wall about five feet behind him. He spun on his stool enough to keep an eye on both of them.

"You think those two things are connected?"

"We heard you might have seen her in L.A. on Wednesday, and she missed a meeting on Thursday morning that was very important to her."

"Who told you that?" Kaye asked.

"Some mutual friends," the guy answered, half-smirking.

"All I can tell you is that you're making a bad assumption."

"So you don't know where she is?" asked the big guy leaning against the wall.

"That's what I'm telling you."

"Why were you meeting her tonight?" asked the guy at the bar.

Kaye glanced at him, took another sip of wine, and said, "I don't think that's any of your business."

The guy stood up straight, reached inside his jacket and came out with a wallet. He laid it on the bar and flipped it open. "I'm making it my business."

Kaye looked down to see a gold star that identified the guy as a Deputy Sheriff for San Luis Obispo County. "Why is the SLO County Sheriff looking for Auggie?"

"I don't think that's any of your business," the deputy replied mockingly.

Kaye looked at the deputy for several seconds, trying to read him. "You're worried about Auggie, aren't you?"

Both men just stared at him.

"That's good," Kaye said, "because I'm worried about her, too."

"What?" the Deputy asked.

"I was supposed to meet her here. I did see her in L.A. on Wednesday, but I haven't been able to reach her since, either."

"Can you back that story up?" the big guy asked.

Kaye looked at the Deputy at the bar. "I'm going to reach into my pocket. Don't get excited."

He reached inside his jacket and came out with his badge wallet, laid it on the bar next to the Deputy's and flipped it open.

The Deputy looked down, looked up at Kaye, and said, "Are you kidding me?"

Kaye shook his head.

"Brett, he's a cop. LAPD," the Deputy said to his friend. Then he held out his hand. "Joey Stangland. My friend, Deputy Brett Adams."

"Ben Kaye."

They shook hands all around.

"You were supposed to meet Auggie here?" Stangland asked.

Kaye told them about his dinner with Auggie on Wednesday, that he'd planned to be in Santa Ynez yesterday, but got hung up and hadn't been able to reach her.

"I thought maybe she was just mad at me," he said, "and since I was in Santa Barbara today I came up to ask forgiveness."

"How do you know Auggie?" Adams asked.

"I stumbled onto this place a couple weeks ago, just riding through, and came in for lunch. Auggie was bartending, and we sort of hit it off. Last Saturday I came –"

"The tasting dinner," Stangland interrupted. "I saw you."

"Why are you guys looking for her?" Kaye asked.

"Technically, we're not," Stangland replied.

"We're just worried about her," Adams added. "She hasn't been here all week, and she didn't tell anybody where she was going. That's not like her."

"She's one of us," Stangland said. "Not officially, but we watch out for her."

"Because of her dad," Kaye said.

"Yeah," Adams said. "Since he passed, we, uh, well, we're all kind of like adopted big brothers. Mess with Auggie, you answer to us."

"I get it," Kaye said. "Still, why me?"

"Your colors," Stangland said. "We looked up the Big Boar MC and came up empty, like you guys make a special effort to stay under the radar. That worried us."

Kaye filled in the blank. "You thought she might be trying to avoid me."

"Right," Stangland said. "Then you show up tonight, no colors, and hang out to wait. And here we are."

"And still no Auggie," Kaye said.

"And still no Auggie," Stangland echoed. "We're worried. She's important to us."

"She's important to me, too," Kaye said and saw the two SLO deputies exchange a quick glance. "Think it might be time to call somebody? Make a report?"

"Might be," Adams said. "Let's put it this way: We won't stop you."

"But you haven't reported her missing, right?"

"No," Stangland replied. "We wanted to talk to you first, maybe straighten the whole thing out. Plus, this isn't our jurisdiction. There'd be some messy politics involved."

"Why does that not surprise me?" Kaye said, picking up his wallet. "Thank you, gentlemen."

The three exchanged handshakes again and Kaye headed for the Harley.

*** 

The Solvang office of the Santa Barbara County Sheriff's Office was little more than a store front and a patrol unit parking lot. The hour was late enough that Kaye had to push the button outside the front door, announce himself, and wait for a Deputy.

There was no desk officer. The Watch Commander, a Lieutenant Barker, let him in. Kaye introduced himself and said he was concerned about a possibly missing friend.

"Her name is Auggie McMaster," Kaye said. "Nobody's seen her since Wednesday night."

"Doesn't ring a bell," Barker said. "But this is my Monday. Let me check the system, just in case."

Kaye waited in the lobby while Barker went into the back. A few minutes later, he was back, a piece of paper in hand.

"Auggie McMaster is a friend of yours?" the Lieutenant asked, and Kaye detected a change in the man's tone.

"She is."

"You have some interesting friends."

"What does that mean?" Kaye asked.

Barker looked at the paper. "One Augustina McMaster, white female, thirty-four, was arrested early Thursday morning on charges of Driving Under the Influence and Possession of Narcotics with Intent to Distribute by the Chumash Oaks Police Department. Transferred to the main County jail in Santa Barbara on Friday morning after failing to make bond in Chumash Oaks within twenty-four hours. Bond was posted late yesterday afternoon and she walked, next court appearance in five weeks."

"What?" Kaye asked, incredulous. "That doesn't sound like the woman I know."

Barker shrugged. "I'm only telling you what shows up in our system."

Kaye was speechless and skeptical. The Chumash Oaks PD was,

he was certain, corrupt.

"Who was the arresting officer?" he asked.

Barker referenced the note again.

"D. Hawkins."

Kaye recognized the name as the K-9 officer from when Reid had stopped him the first time.

"May I see that?" Kaye asked.

Barker handed the paper to Kaye.

"No booking photo," Kaye pointed out as he scanned the sheet.

"She never came through our door," Barker said. "You can get it at the jail in Santa Barbara on Monday."

"What was the bond, and who posted it?" Kaye asked.

"Uh, looks like fifty thousand, and it says here she posted it, cash."

"Really?" Kaye asked, surprised. "Who brought her the cash?"

"I don't have that information," the Lieutenant replied. "You'd have to check with the court in Santa Barbara on Monday."

As soon as Kaye went outside he tried Auggie's number again. All he got was a recording that the voice mail box was full.

He fired up the bike and rode back to Auggie's restaurant to tell Stangland and Adams what he'd found out, but they were gone.

He tried Auggie's number one more time, just in case.

Mail box still full.

$$***$$

It was late when Kaye rolled into the driveway and had to stop because of the new truck parked alongside the house. He spent all of five minutes looking it over, moved it into the garage, put the bike away and headed for bed.

# DAY 21
## Sunday Week 3

Sleep had been nearly impossible, a series of short catnaps between long periods of anxious wakefulness, staring at the ceiling or out the window at the dark Pacific below, wondering where Auggie was.

At one point he dreamed of the Paloma Canyon Country Club murder scene. It was strikingly vivid until he went to check the dead woman sprawled next to Avi Geller's golf cart.

It wasn't Nicole Ingram. It was Auggie McMaster. He rolled her over, and as she died she looked deep into his eyes and said, "Oh, Ben, we shouldn't have crucified Jesus."

He recoiled to find that Avi Geller had been replaced by a grinning Father Francis Healey, Order of the Perpetual Guardians.

In his dream, he said, "It's okay, Father. They're not like you. I'm going to nail every damn one of them to a cross."

He jolted awake, and didn't go back to sleep again.

*** 

Kaye caught up on household chores and spent a grueling ninety minutes practicing. He purposely avoided meditation, then found himself wondering about his conversation with Roshi and if he would ever meditate again.

That thought disturbed him deeply.

He had a slew of people and things he needed to deal with, and the one that called loudest for his attention, the one he heard over the official background noise, was the one he didn't have the time for.

Trying to pass the time, he immersed himself in the Pan-in-a-Box, putting the frame on the stand and slowly but surely beginning to mock up the bike to see what was there and what wasn't.

Twice he tried Auggie's number. No luck.

He ate a light dinner and decided to take a ride to Paradise Cove. The end of the pier there was a spot where he often went to reflect and sort out problems.

The sun was about to disappear under the horizon when he arrived, and as he walked to the end of the pier he couldn't help but consider the irony that the beauty of the falling sun might be something, someone, ominous.

He stood, staring out to sea and listening to the surf behind him sigh with contentment after finally reaching its destination.

There were quite a few people on the pier. Some, forever hopeful, fished. Others sat, hunched against the deepening chill as the warmth of the day disappeared with the sun, and stared out at the necklace of brightening light that curved from Santa Monica all the way to the first cliffs of Palos Verdes. One family of four made a game of being the first to spot outbound traffic from LAX, then speculating on where the plane might be headed.

Kaye lingered, captivated as always by the overwhelming presence of the place, as others gave way to the darkness and made their way toward shore and warmth.

He, too, finally decided to call it a day. He had to be downtown early, and hoped Okafor's plan would work.

He headed in. On the way he saw a young couple, hand in hand, headed in his direction as they passed through the circle of light under one of the standards mounted to the pier railings.

As the gap narrowed, Kaye could hear that they were engaged in a good-natured debate about something. When they were close enough to make out in the darkness, he saw them go from holding hands at arm's length to close together and in step, the banter and laughing non-stop.

When they were about fifteen feet away from Kaye he heard them both laugh heartily and the man exclaimed, "You bitch!"

The woman laughed as well, pulled on the man's arm to get closer, wrapped her arms around his waist and matched him step for step.

"But I'll always be your bitch," she said serenely as they walked past Kaye.

Kaye took two more steps and pulled up short, Reid's words echoing in his mind.

*On your way to see your bitch?*

Kaye stood, rooted in place, stunned.

Could it be?

His conversation with Glynis Mitchell and what Les Baruch had told him about Avi Geller's relationship with Nicole Ingram rushed through his memory in a millisecond.

Someone is harvesting young women in the Central California area.

*On your way to see your bitch?*

But Auggie didn't fit the profile, such as it was. She was beautiful, sure, but she was several years older than the oldest victim on Mitchell's list. She was local and well-known. She drove not one, but two, very distinctive vehicles. Her cop friends were looking for her already.

*On your way to see your bitch?*

Kaye suddenly got it.

They knew.

Whoever had planted the bomb in his truck had been following him, and seen him with Auggie.

This wasn't about Auggie. It was about him.

Reid's words rang again.

*On your way to see your bitch? Good luck with that, you freak.*

Kaye now knew what Reid hadn't said.

Because we've got her now.

# DAY 22

Monday Week 4

At 8:05 a.m. Kaye walked through the front door of the Forensics Science and Technical Investigations Division and headed straight for the Questioned Documents Unit.

He opened the door and saw a familiar face behind the counter.

"Hi, Della," he said.

"Why, hello there, Detective Kaye," Della Robinson, Unit Supervisor, greeted him. "Nice to see you. Last I heard you pulled the pin."

"Vicious rumor," Kaye said, smiling.

"No doubt started and spread by Internal Affairs," Della said seriously, then laughed. "What brings you to my cave on this fine Monday morning?"

Kaye held up the plastic bag containing the pages from Baruch's house.

"Oh," Della said, "a new evidence collection technique. Nobody told us. Whatever's in there, I hope you didn't get too much discharge."

"It was an emergency and I had almost no time. This is all I could come up with."

She used a set of large surgical tweezers to take the bag from Kaye's hand.

"I don't see any tags," she said, glancing at Kaye. "Or a case number. Is this official?"

"It is," Kaye assured her. "The Geller murder. I haven't been back to the station to log it or generate labels yet. If I can use one of your terminals, I'll do that right now."

"First, if you want to cut in line, you need to tell me what it is."

Kaye trusted Della and gave her the complete rundown on the events at Les Baruch's house the day before. Her eyes grew wide as she listened.

"Without Baruch's testimony, or even a partial statement," he said in conclusion, "I've got nothing but my notes of his conversation, which are inadmissible without corroboration. I need you to get whatever you can off the legal pad pages in there so I can see if it ties in to what he told me."

"Do you have a known source comparator for me?" Della asked.

"I can get one if we need one," Kaye said, "but I'm not to that point yet. Right now I just need to know what, if anything, is on those pages."

"Okay, I can do that," Della said. "But I have to log a case number into the system for every examination, so come on around and use that terminal," she pointed, "to get me some labels and tags."

Kaye sat down and e-mailed the pictures he'd taken at Baruch's from his phone to his department e-mail. Then he logged in, waited briefly for them to show up and downloaded them to the Geller file. He logged the details of discovery, collection and chain of custody since then, let the system assign the proper evidentiary item sequence numbers and printed the labels, which he signed.

He knew there were gaps a good defense lawyer could probably drive a golf cart through, but he'd just have to deal with it when and if the time came.

Della walked up behind him and asked, "Labels?"

"Here you go," Kaye said, handing them to her. "I've got to be in court in a little while. Any idea how long it will take? Can I wait?"

"I'm good, Detective, but I'm no miracle worker. I don't know how long this will take. Might not even be today. How 'bout I call you when I'm done?"

"It takes a long as it takes, I guess," Kaye said. "Thanks, Della."

Kaye didn't pretend to understand the science of questioned documents examination. There were conflicting theories of density versus residual static electricity and it was far from settled science.

He only cared that it worked, and that Della Robinson was the Grand Mistress of finding things that had been written down by someone that didn't want anyone else to see them.

\*\*\*

At 9:40 a.m. Kaye found Kayla Okafor waiting in the hallway outside Judge Gardner's courtroom.

The look of astonishment on her face when she saw him was hard to mistake.

"What?" Kaye asked. "You didn't think I'd show? Maybe be on

the way to Mexico?"

"I knew you'd be here," she said. "I've just never seen you in a suit before."

"Court is court. Appearance counts."

"That it does. Is Captain Thompson with you?"

"No, but I saw him drive in. He should be here in a minute."

As if on cue, Thompson stepped off the elevator and headed their way.

"Good morning," the Captain said. "Wow, Detective, nice suit. Didn't know you owned clothes like that."

"Thanks," Kaye said, not rising to the bait.

"Do you have the phone?" Okafor asked Thompson.

He patted the outside of his suit jacket as he asked, "Are Sloan and Leale going to be here?"

"I don't know," she said. "They're not my witnesses, so I didn't call them. Feinmann might have, but I don't know. There's no disclosure in these situations. Let's go in and talk strategy for a minute, and then I need to get five minutes with the judge before we start."

The three entered the empty courtroom and Okafor headed for the Respondents table.

To Kaye the courtroom looked like a chapel, the altar replaced by the judge's bench and the rose window replaced by a large County seal. Rows of wooden benches that could have been pews filled the back of the room and a wooden railing divided the space in half. The illusion simply replaced a black-cassocked priest with a black-robed judge.

"Okay," Okafor said after sitting down. "Detective, I forwarded the outline you sent me to Judge Gardner on Friday so she could review it over the weekend. My plan is this: Captain, I'll call you first to testify about your possession of Kaye's phone for the last ten days." She turned to Kaye. "Then I'll put you on the stand, Detective. You know the drill. Just answer my questions honestly and hope Gardner doesn't shut us down."

Kaye nodded.

"I'll be right back," Okafor said, then stood and headed for the door.

The courtroom gradually filled up with spectators, several of whom Kaye recognized as local print and broadcast media reporters. Okafor returned just before Megan Sullivan and Howard Feinmann entered the courtroom and took seats at the Petitioners table. Behind them were Detectives Sloan and Leale, who sat behind them on the other side of the railing.

At exactly 10:00 a.m. the bailiff entered and intoned, "All rise," and announced that court was in session, the Honorable Kathleen Gardner presiding. Gardner entered and told everybody to sit down.

Kaye had been before Gardner on other occasions and knew her to be an astute, but pragmatic, jurist.

"Good morning," Gardner began. "We're here this morning on the matter of Megan Sullivan versus Benjamin Kaye on a request by the Petitioner for the issuance of a Restraining Order against the Respondent based on allegations of stalking and harassment." Gardner looked up. "Is Detective Kaye present?"

The question was purely rhetorical, for the record. Gardner knew Kaye by sight.

"He is, Your Honor,' Okafor said as she stood up. "Deputy District Attorney Okafor of counsel for Detective Kaye."

"Thank you, Ms. Okafor." Gardner turned her gaze to the other table. "And I see that Ms. Sullivan is also present, with counsel. Good morning, Mr. Feinmann."

Feinmann stood and straightened his tie before saying, "Good morning, Your Honor. And let me say how unfavorably impressed, and chagrined, I am that the District Attorney's Office is now providing defense services to LAPD officers in civil matters." He sat back down.

Gardner surveyed the room, then looked down at the bench momentarily before looking up. "Mr. Feinmann, your client's allegations against Detective Kaye and the purported supporting evidence are well summed up in your motion and amended request for this hearing, which I have reviewed carefully. I have also reviewed Respondent's written response, and I believe the reason for Ms. Okafor's presence will become clear as we proceed. Additionally, Ms. Okafor has waived her right to cross examine your client, so unless you have new information that was not in your hearing request I'm going to excuse Ms. Sullivan from taking the stand and going over everything again, and go straight to the Respondent. I trust that meets with your approval."

Feinmann stood again and said, "No objections, Your Honor. Ms. Sullivan's petition speaks for itself." When he sat back down, Kaye saw him smile at Sullivan as if he'd just scored some kind of victory.

"Ms. Okafor, call your first witness, please," Gardner said.

"I have a motion first, Your Honor, if I may."

"Make your motion, Counselor."

"I move that Detectives Sloan and Leale," she pointed, "be sequestered if they intend to testify."

"Your Honor," Feinmann said as he stood up. "I do not plan on calling either of them. They are here of their own volition." He smiled. "Probably to arrest Mr. Kaye at the conclusion of this hearing."

Gardner glared at Feinmann, then looked at Okafor. "Motion denied, Ms. Okafor."

"Thank you, Your Honor," Okafor said, then called Captain Thompson, who went forward and was sworn in.

The Captain's testimony was basic and straightforward. He confirmed that he had been in sole possession of Kaye's old phone, the one Sullivan claimed was the originating number for the harassing and inappropriate calls and texts, for over a week and that the phone had remained powered off.

"Do you have that cellular telephone on your person now, Captain?" Okafor asked.

"I do," Thompson replied, reaching into his inside suit pocket and retrieving it.

"Is it turned on?" Okafor asked.

"It is not."

"Turn it on, please, and let the court know when it has service."

Thompson powered on the phone and watched the screen. A moment later he said, "Four bars, Counselor."

Thompson had barely finished speaking when the phone in his hand began to ding and chime rapidly.

"What's all the noise, Captain?" Okafor asked.

"It looks like there are a lot of missed calls and texts coming in," Thompson replied.

"You mean like the phone has been turned off for a long time?" Okafor asked.

"Yes, ma'am."

Okafor advanced, took the phone from Thompson and stepped in front of the bench.

"Your Honor, we can probably save some time by having you look at this." She held the phone out to Gardner. "If you check the call and text histories you will see that there are only two outgoing communications to Ms. Sullivan during the time she is alleging that my client was stalking and harassing her, and all the unread texts and missed calls are from the time Captain Thompson testified that the phone was turned off."

Gardner spent a moment studying the phone, then looked at Feinmann.

"Counselor, would you like to see this?"

Feinmann was on his feet in a split second. "Not necessary, Your Honor. But I do have some questions for the Captain."

"Ms. Okafor, have you any more questions for Captain Thompson?"

"Not at this time, Your Honor."

"He's all yours, Mr. Feinmann," Gardner said.

Feinmann smoothed his tie and approached the playing field in front of the witness stand and the bench. "Captain," he led off, "how long have you known Detective Kaye?"

"Five, almost six, years."

"Would you, as his commanding officer, say he's a good cop?"

"Maybe the best detective I've ever met," Thompson replied.

"Then why do you write him up so much?" Feinmann asked.

Thompson was taken aback by the question and it took him a moment to formulate an answer.

"Kaye is a great detective," Thompson said. "Sometimes his methods are, shall we say, a bit unorthodox is all."

"Unorthodox," Feinmann repeated. "Are they unorthodox enough that you've had occasion, several occasions, in fact, to suspend Detective Kaye?"

"Yes, sir," Thompson said. "But –"

"Your Honor," Feinmann interrupted, "please instruct Captain Thompson to simply answer the question. We're not interested in his 'but'."

Grunts and stifled laughter came from the spectators and Gardner glared at them before turning to Thompson. "You heard the man. Just answer the question."

Thompson nodded. "Yes, I have suspended Detective Kaye on more than one occasion."

"Are you and Detective Kaye friends?" Feinmann asked.

"No."

"But you're both LAPD, right?"

"Yes."

"So you've got each other's backs, right?" Feinmann asked. "You know, brother officer and all that boys in blue stuff?"

"We take care of our own," Thompson said.

"Good to know," Feinmann said. "Captain, are you aware that text conversations and outgoing calls can be deleted from a phone's histories?"

"Yes," Thompson replied.

"And that there is no real way to track a phone or know when that phone is turned off and on except through provider records?"

"Yes," Thompson said.

Feinmann turned and went back to his table and grabbed a sheet of paper out of his briefcase. With a smirk toward Okafor he approached the bench and held it up toward Gardner.

"Since we're apparently all about saving time here today, Your Honor, I would offer this telephone service provider record for your examination. You can see that it is for the number assigned to Detective Kaye's allegedly former phone. Please take note of the highlighted lines, which indicate that the phone registered with a tower well after Captain Thompson testified he had possession of the phone and that it was always turned off. The phone was turned on for several minutes, during which time someone, anyone, could have scrubbed the histories of that phone." He handed the paper to Gardner, who studied it intently for a moment.

Feinmann turned back to Thompson. "Captain, do you know what a SIM card is?"

"It's what makes a phone a phone," Thompson replied.

"They're unique, right?"

"I would imagine they'd have to be."

"But did you know they can be removed from one phone and put into another one? Like a car engine can be swapped?"

"I've seen it done, yes," Thompson said.

"You've seen it done?" Feinmann said incredulously. "Maybe with Detective Kaye's phone?"

Before Thompson could answer Okafor was on her feet. "Objection!"

"Withdrawn," Feinmann said, then looked at Okafor. "I have no further questions for this witness."

Gardner examined the sheet of provider data and held them out toward Okafor.

"You might want to take a look at these, Counselor."

Okafor advanced, took the sheet and scanned it.

"Redirect, Your Honor?" she asked.

"I think that would be a good idea, Ms. Okafor," Gardner said.

"Thank you." She turned to Thompson.

"Captain, did you turn the phone on when it was in your custody? Specifically at," she glanced at the pages and read off the date and time.

"I didn't," Thompson said sheepishly. "But Detective Kaye did. It was in my office. I was present, and he needed to retrieve some of his contact information. That's all. I had forgotten about that."

"Did you at any time remove the SIM card from that phone while it was in your possession?"

"No, ma'am."

"Thank you, Captain."

"Re-cross, Mr. Feinmann?" Gardner asked.

"No, Your Honor."

"Call your next witness, Ms. Okafor."

"I call Detective Kaye to the stand."

***

Kaye went forward and was sworn in before taking his seat in the witness box.

Okafor's first few questions were procedural: Name, occupation, how long he'd been at the LAPD, and basic groundwork. Then she got down to business.

"Detective Kaye, did you make the phone calls and send the texts, some of which, I must admit, are quite salacious, to Ms. Sullivan as she alleges in her petition?"

"I did not," Kaye replied.

"Then how do you explain the volumes of records Ms. Sullivan submitted to this court in support of her petition, which shows both calls and texts originating from your number?"

"I can't," Kaye said. "All I can say is that I get calls all the time that don't really come from the number that shows up on my caller ID. Usually it's people trying to sell me something or a scam of some sort."

"Are you referring to 'spoofing'?" Okafor asked.

"I believe that's what it's called."

"Have you ever met Megan Sullivan?"

"Not formally, no."

"Have you ever called or texted Megan Sullivan?"

"I've never texted her," Kaye replied. "I have called her phone twice, spoken to her once, and the second time left her a voice mail.

She did not return my call."

"Why did you call her?" Okafor asked.

Kaye explained the circumstances on the day of Avi Geller and Nicole Ingram's murders and why he'd called Sullivan.

"So, your call was official business?" Okafor asked, turning around and glancing at Sullivan.

"Yes. I wanted access to the property and house, and hoped Ms. Sullivan could let me in."

"Did she?"

"No."

"Why not?"

"She was an hour away, and I couldn't wait."

"Did you enter the premises without her?"

"I did not," Kaye said. "I didn't have a warrant, and didn't believe a valid exception existed."

"What was Ms. Sullivan's reaction when you called her?" Okafor asked.

"She was concerned about the house," Kaye answered, "and wanted me to wait in case she needed to make a police report."

"Why didn't you wait, Detective?"

"I needed to talk to the wife of one of the homicide victims as soon as possible."

"Did you tell her that?"

"Not specifically, no," Kaye replied. "I told her to check the house, and if there was a problem, call it in and an officer would respond."

"Did she?" Okafor asked. "File a report, I mean."

"She did," Kaye said, then explained that Patrol Officer Devon had responded to take a vandalism report.

"Tell the court what happened the next morning, insofar as it relates to Ms. Sullivan."

Kaye told the story about being called in to Captain Thompson's office because Sullivan had called a friend, whose husband was a high-ranking LAPD officer, and complained about him. The husband had called Thompson's boss, and Thompson had come to him. "You know what they say about the effluent flowing downhill," he concluded.

"Did Captain Thompson take disciplinary action against you?" Okafor asked.

"No. I explained the situation and he agreed with how I handled it under the circumstances."

"If I may," Howard Feinmann said, again smoothing his tie as he stood up. "Your Honor, this is all well and good, but I fail to see the relevance of this testimony in the matter before the court and ask that Ms. Okafor be directed to stick to the question at hand."

"Your Honor," Okafor spoke up first, "Ms. Sullivan is claiming improper, indeed illegal, acts by Detective Kaye vis-à-vis their interactions. I'm simply establishing some context as to how and why, out of four million residents of Los Angeles, their paths crossed in the first place."

Gardner thought for a moment, then said, "Sit down, Howard," then turned to Okafor and said, "You may continue."

"Thank you, Your Honor," Okafor said, then turned to Kaye. "Detective, would you explain to the court the circumstances of your second call to Ms. Sullivan?"

Kaye went through it, from his first visit to SecureLife and their initial refusal to surrender any data from the relevant security logs, why, and how he ended up obtaining it.

"Why would Ms. Sullivan do that?" Okafor asked when he was finished.

"I can only speculate," Kaye said. "But it did make me wonder."

"Isn't it true that it was right about then that you found out Ms. Sullivan had filed a formal complaint against you with the LAPD?"

"Yes."

"But isn't today the only time you've ever laid eyes on Megan Sullivan, other than her photograph on the For Sale sign in front of the house in question?"

"No," Kaye replied. "I conducted surveillance on her at one point, with prior notification to Captain Thompson and with his approval, in relation to the Geller investigation."

"So, one other time before today. Is that correct?"

"Yes, ma'am."

"On official business?'

"Yes, ma'am."

"Did you learn anything about Ms. Sullivan?" Okafor asked, turning to look at Feinmann and his client.

"Objection!" Feinmann shouted as he leapt to his feet, oblivious to the fact that his tie hung outside his suit coat. "Your Honor, this line of questioning is absurd. We're here on a matter involving Detective Kaye's conduct, not that of my client. Frankly, this is starting to sound like a witch hunt, with Ms. Sullivan as the target. She is not suspected of committing a crime. Detective Kaye is."

Gardner again listened patiently, then looked at Okafor. "Rebuttal, Counselor?"

"I think I can clear this up, Your Honor," Okafor replied

Gardner nodded.

Okafor turned back to Kaye.

"Detective Kaye, is Megan Sullivan a suspect in any crimes that you are aware of?"

"She is," Kaye replied deliberately, staring at Sullivan, who visibly tensed as her eyes went wide.

"In what matter, Detective?" Okafor asked.

"In the deaths of Aviram Geller and Nicole Ingram."

Gasps and exclamations erupted from the crowd behind the railing, filling the courtroom.

"Order!" Gardner shouted above the din as she pounded her gavel repeatedly. "Order, or I will clear this court!"

Kaye looked at Sloan and Leale. Sloan looked bemused and was nodding ever-so-slightly. Leale was bright red as he stared back at Kaye, then got up and stalked out of the courtroom.

***

When order had been restored, Howard Feinmann was standing.

"Do you want to say something, Counselor?" Gardner asked.

"Your Honor, I would request a thirty minute recess." Feinmann unconsciously smoothed his tie with one hand.

"Not on your life, Counselor," Gardner said immediately, then looked out over the spectators. "I know you will all be disappointed, but I'm moving this proceeding *in camera* and off the record." She then looked at Okafor and Feinmann and added, "Ms. Okafor, you may dismiss Captain Thompson, but everybody else, in my chambers, now."

It only took three minutes for Gardner to reconvene the proceedings in chambers.

Megan Sullivan looked like the proverbial deer in the headlights as Feinmann tried to soothe her nerves.

"I must say," the Judge began, "this is not what I expected today to be like when I got out of bed this morning." She turned to Kaye and asked, "Detective, do you have any real evidence connecting Ms. Sullivan to those murders?"

"You can't ask him that in front of my client!" Feinmann

exploded. "She has not been charged with anything, much less homicide. In fact, Detective Kaye hasn't even interviewed her. Or advised her of her rights."

"Detective Kaye," Okafor spoke up, "was respecting the Order requested by your client, though no such Order has, in fact, been officially issued."

"Nice try, Counselor," Gardner said, smiling. "But I'm familiar with the Detective's reputation and I don't believe that for one second."

"Your Honor, if I may," Kaye said, "I haven't interviewed Ms. Sullivan because the case is still developing rapidly. I have two more people to interview and search warrants to prepare after we conclude our business here. If I get the results I expect, I'll be seeking warrants for Ms. Sullivan's, and one other suspect's, arrest."

Feinmann turned and looked at Sullivan, who looked back defiantly as if to say, 'Do something!'

"Well, I have an idea," Gardner said. "That is, if Mr. Feinmann is okay with it."

"I won't know until I hear it," Feinmann said.

"Howard," Gardner continued, "would you be amenable to allowing Detective Kaye to interview your client here, now with you present?"

"I don't think I like that idea," Feinmann said after a brief pause. "I've had no opportunity to even consult with Ms. Sullivan on anything remotely connected to a capital murder charge, and my advice to her," he turned and looked at Sullivan, "is to assert her Fifth Amendment rights and not to answer any questions."

There was silence.

"How about this," Kaye said, looking at Feinmann. "I won't ask her any questions. I'll just lay out what I've got, for her and for you, Counselor, then you can consult with her on what you think is best for her."

"What's the catch?" Feinmann asked instantly.

"No catch," Kaye said. "I'll show you my cards. That's all. Then you decide."

"May I consult with my client privately?" Feinmann asked Gardner.

"Of course," the judge replied. "Use the jury room."

Feinmann and Sullivan got up and went through the door to the jury room.

Gardner turned to her bailiff and said, "Make sure they don't leave," and he went to watch the jury room's other exit.

"I've got to ask, Detective," Gardner said as soon as the bailiff exited chambers. "Why are you willing to reveal your case like this?"

"I believe Megan Sullivan is complicit in the murders," Kaye said. "But I don't think she pulled the trigger, and maybe didn't even fully realize what she was involved in. I want the shooter."

"And you hope Ms. Sullivan gives you that shooter." Gardner grasped it immediately.

"Yes, Your Honor," Okafor answered for Kaye. "I know this is irregular —"

"Irregular?" Gardner interrupted. "That doesn't even begin to cover it, Counselor. I could be looking at a Judicial Commission inquiry here."

"I get it," Kaye said. "But Judge, I believe there's a much larger conspiracy going on behind these murders, and lives are at stake, including Sullivan's, if I let her walk out of here. All I ask is a chance to tell her what I've found out and let her make her own decision."

Gardner leaned back in her chair and looked at Kaye.

"How about this," she said after a minute. "If Howard says you can talk to her, you can talk to her, but not in my chambers. I'll suspend this hearing without a ruling and find you a room, but I cannot be present and what happens after you leave here happens independently of this court. I will not put my imprimatur, even unofficially, on your opinions in this case. Also, Detective, do not, I repeat, do not, bring any arrest warrant affidavits in this case to me. Understood?"

"Yes, your honor," Kaye said.

At that moment the door to the jury room opened and the bailiff led Megan Sullivan back into the room.

"Where's Mr. Feinmann?" Gardner asked the bailiff.

"I fired him," Sullivan said. "He's no longer my attorney." She turned to Kaye and said, "I'll listen."

Sullivan's attitude and demeanor were subdued, but Kaye's first thought was that he might have just been had.

\*\*\*

With Feinmann gone, Judge Gardner insisted on, and agreed to witness, Kaye's advisement of Sullivan of her rights under Miranda. Once that was completed, and Sullivan had signed the form and the waiver of counsel, the bailiff led Okafor, Kaye and Sullivan to a small conference room with a window looking out at downtown. A pitcher of water and four upside-down plastic glasses sat on a tray in the middle of the square, faux wood table surrounded by four brown, molded plastic chairs.

Okafor sat and Sullivan took the chair opposite her. Kaye ended up in the middle.

"Ready?" Okafor asked.

Sullivan nodded, then asked, "Can I ask questions?"

"Of course," Okafor said. "In fact, I'd encourage it, and I expect Detective Kaye," she looked at him, "to give you forthcoming answers. Detective, you have the floor."

Kaye leaned forward, put his elbows on the table, knitted his fingers together and looked Sullivan squarely in the eyes.

"It was the back gate lock, really. It was the big inconsistency and didn't fit with the vandalism report. If he'd have just picked it up, who knows, you might have gotten away with it. But you couldn't ask for a key ahead of time, either. Somebody would have remembered.

"You still might have gotten away with it, even after calling Smithers' wife and complaining about me, if you hadn't called Internal Affairs. That, and that you tried to keep me from getting my hands on the surveillance images and system logs from the house.

"But you made me curious, so I dug deeper. Let me tell you what I came up with.

"First, I know you've been providing Chase Storm, real name Dennis Bettencourt, unauthorized access to your vacant, high-end listings as locations for his porn shoots and that his van, which you told me belongs to the cleaning service I can never reach, matches the one on the security videos.

"I know that you lied to other realtors about the availability of the house for showings on the day before, and the day of, the murders.

"I know you usually drive a white Escalade, but I have a witness who identified you as the driver of a black Explorer that entered the already open gate of the house on the morning before the murders. I know you know that the cameras and motion sensors time out if the gate is left open – in this case by the landscape maintenance crew – and there would be no record of your visit.

"I know you didn't come alone. My witness perfectly described Dennis Bettencourt as getting out of the Explorer, carrying a large duffel bag.

"I know that once you got inside you disabled the security system, including interior motion sensors and the back yard cameras, and you didn't reactivate them when you re-armed the system and left. My witness also says you left alone.

"I know you made the vandalism report on the evening of the shootings. I know you told Office Devon there was no need to check upstairs because you'd already checked, and everything was okay.

"That all combines to tell me that you left Bettencourt at the house overnight on Monday. At some point he cuts the lock, shoots Avi Geller and Nicole Ingram, then returns to the house. He stages the vandalism and hides upstairs when Officer Devon comes to take the report, then leaves with you on Tuesday evening after Devon clears. After all, what better witness at the scene than a police officer? And you fully reactivated the outside cameras and interior motion sensors when you left.

"I know where you got the Explorer, and I think I know where you got the gun. I'll be bringing in your cousin and your brother-in-law for questioning as soon as I can.

"By this afternoon I'll have search warrants for Dennis Bettencourt's DNA and the house in Paloma Canyon and we'll turn your listing, sold or not, upside down and inside out. He was there for almost thirty-six hours. We'll find something.

"I know why Bettencourt shot Nicole Ingram, and when I talk to him I'll find out why he shot Avi Geller."

Kaye stared at Sullivan, who looked down and stayed quiet.

"I didn't know Dennis was going to kill Avi Geller," Sullivan said finally. "I swear."

"That can help you," Kaye said, looking at Okafor, who nodded.

"Why are you telling me all this?" Sullivan asked, her voice subdued.

"Because," Kaye said, "I want to hear your side of the story, how you got swept up in all this. You don't fit, Megan. You are a very square peg jammed into a very round hole, and, honestly, I don't get it. How does a successful woman like you get sucked into something like this?"

"This is your only chance to grab the brass ring, Megan," Okafor said. "Cooperate. Tell us what you know. There's a lot more going on here than I think you know about. Right now you're looking at two counts of conspiracy to commit and accessory to murder, obstruction of justice, and perjury. That adds up to hard time, for a long time."

Sullivan sat quietly for almost two minutes.

Kaye and Okafor waited.

Finally she looked up and said, "I'll tell you, but I want a deal first. In writing."

Okafor studied her for a moment, then said, "Let me see what I can do," before leaving the room.

Sullivan reached for the pitcher and a glass, poured herself some water and gulped it down.

"Let me tell you something about deals," Kaye said. "If you're interested, that is."

Sullivan looked at him and nodded.

"Make sure that the deal the DA offers is on the charges and not on the sentence."

"Why?"

"A judge doesn't have to accept a plea deal or a sentencing recommendation, but they seldom turn down the plea deal because it saves them from presiding over a trial. They can only sentence you for the charges you plead to. But they could, and sometimes do, ignore a sentencing recommendation and throw you into a deep, dark hole for as long as they want to."

"You're telling me this because...?"

Kaye shrugged. "You ever been in jail?"

"No."

"I didn't think so. You cannot imagine what it's like. You won't do well, Megan."

"Are you trying to scare me?" she asked, studying him closely.

"If you're not already scared, I've badly misjudged you. Just telling you the truth."

The conversation stopped and the two sat silently across from each other for almost fifteen minutes before Okafor opened the door and came back in.

"Okay," Okafor said as she sat down and slid a piece of paper and a pen across to Sullivan. "I did the best I could. If what you tell us pans out, we'll drop all the charges except one count of conspiracy in exchange for your testimony against Dennis Bettencourt and anyone else charged in the murders of Avi Geller and Nicole Ingram."

"How much time could I get?" Sullivan asked.

"Actually," Okafor replied, "you could be sentenced to the same time as if you committed the murders, but we'll make a sentencing recommendation that recognizes your cooperation and hope the judge agrees. But I can't promise you that."

Sullivan looked at Kaye, but didn't say anything as she reached out and grabbed the paper and pen, signed, and slid it back across to Okafor.

Okafor scanned the document, then took a small recorder out of her purse, dictated her name and office, and the date and time, then laid it on the table. "She's all yours, Detective. I'm just going to sit here and listen."

"Okay, what do you want to know?" Sullivan asked.

"I guess my first question," Kaye said, "is how you got involved with Dennis Bettencourt?"

"Howard Feinmann introduced me to Dennis and his ex-wife, Carol, at the Spring Fest dinner at Paloma Canyon Country Club," Sullivan replied. "I went with the Gellers."

"Carol?" Kaye asked.

"Yes," Sullivan said, nodding. "She's an assistant manager there. She went back to her maiden name after they got divorced. They have a daughter, and they share custody. They keep it civil for the little girl's sake."

"So it was Carol Soares who tipped Dennis off about Avi Geller's tee time?"

"I don't know. I do know she called him pretty often."

"But it was Dennis who decided he needed to be in the house on Tuesday."

"Yes."

"Do you know how Howard Feinmann knows Dennis?"

"Howard was Dennis's lawyer when Dennis got arrested for getting drunk and hitting Carol. But that was a long time ago. And, by the way, Carol didn't want to press charges, but the police made her."

"Right," Kaye said, trying to keep the sarcasm out of his voice. "So Feinmann introduced you to Dennis. Did Avi and Ziva know Dennis already?"

"I don't think so," Sullivan replied, "but I'm not sure."

"Who recommended Howard Feinmann to you as your lawyer?" Kaye asked. "Ziva Geller?"

"No, it was Dennis who referred me to Howard after I started getting all those calls and texts. I really thought for a while they were coming from you."

"For a while?" Kaye asked. "You don't still believe it?"

"No," Sullivan said. "At first I did, but then Dennis said something that made me wonder."

"What did he say?" Kaye asked.

"That he had a tech friend who was working on making you look bad, and we wouldn't have to worry about you much longer."

"Why did you call your friend about me the night I told you I couldn't wait for you?"

"Dennis told me to."

"The same with making the formal complaint to the department?"

"Yes," Sullivan said, looking down. "The whole restraining order was his idea, too. He said it would get you fired."

"Megan," Kaye said softly, "did you know Dennis was going to kill Nicole Ingram?"

She nodded without looking up.

"Ms. Ingram," Okafor spoke up, "I'll need a verbal response to the question."

"Oh, yeah," Sullivan said. "Yes, I did know Dennis intended to shoot her, but at the time I didn't know her last name."

"Do you know why?" Kaye asked.

"Dennis told me Nicole was one of his regular, uh, performers, I guess you'd call them, you know, in his movies. He told me she had something written down that he wanted, and if she gave it to anybody else he would be ruined. He said he wasn't going to let her do that. But I swear I didn't know he was going to shoot Avi, too."

"Do you know why he did that?" Kaye asked.

"At first I thought it was my fault." Sullivan replied. "Ziva told me several months ago she thought Avi was messing around, and when I told Dennis that, he told me that Avi was screwing one of his stars."

"Was that before or after he told you about Nicole Ingram having something that could ruin him?"

"It must've been before, because when he told me about the Nicole that could ruin him, I didn't put it together that it was the same woman. I guess in my mind I couldn't picture Avi Geller having an affair with a two-bit porn actress. After Dennis…you know…shot them…we had a big fight about it. He told me somebody else told him to, and he didn't have a choice."

"Who told him that?"

"I don't know. He wouldn't tell me. But he told me I'd better keep my mouth shut."

"Tell me about the gun."

"It belonged to Dennis," Sullivan said. "He said he bought it from a guy in another state and never registered it, so we'd be in the clear."

"You didn't get the gun from your brother-in-law?"

She looked at Kaye questioningly. "No. Why would you think that?"

"But you did borrow your cousin's Explorer."

"Yeah, but please don't drag her into this. She doesn't know anything."

"I can't promise that," Kaye said. "I'll probably have to talk to her just to confirm what you're telling us. Back to my original question. How'd you get tangled up with Bettencourt?"

"When I met him at the club dinner that night, I thought he was very handsome and charming," Sullivan said. "Then, over the next month or so we just seemed to keep bumping into each other. I know it'll sound like an excuse, but my husband travels a lot, and, well, it just... happened."

"You were having an affair with Dennis Bettencourt?" Kaye asked.

"Yes," Sullivan said, barely whispering. "I couldn't believe he was interested in me. Then I found out he was recording us when we..." Her voice trailed off again.

"And he blackmailed you," Kaye said.

"Not directly, but it was implied. Besides, at the time I didn't care. I was infatuated. I just couldn't stop. My marriage, such as it was, just fell apart, and I hardly cared. Dennis even talked me into being in one of his movies. He owned me after that." She looked up at Kaye and he saw tears in her eyes. "Sometimes you find out things about yourself you were better off not knowing." She sat quietly for a moment, then asked, "So, what happens now?"

"Detective Kaye will place you under arrest," Okafor replied. "You'll be transported to jail and booked in. And I must warn you, if you have any communication with Dennis Bettencourt your deal is off the table."

"I won't call him," Sullivan said. "If he finds out I talked to you, he'll kill me if he gets the chance."

"We don't want that," Okafor said, then turned to Kaye. "If you're okay with it, I'll go get started on warrant affidavits and requests on Bettencourt. Since I was here and heard the whole thing, it should be a slam dunk."

"That's fine," Kaye said.

Okafor packed up her things and headed out.

"Megan," Kaye said, "before we go, I need the names and contact information for the owners of the house. I'll need to notify them when I execute the search warrant."

Sullivan gave him the information.

"Now I'd like to run some names by you. Tell me if you know them. It's off the record, okay?"

"Sure, why not," Sullivan said, shrugging her shoulders.

"Jeffrey King?"

"Yeah, I've met Jeff, but I wouldn't say I know him," she said. "Short, a little pudgy, glasses. Works for Howard, kind of his right hand man from what I gathered."

"Leigh Howell?" Kaye asked. "You might know him as Rod."

"Doesn't ring a bell."

"Clifford Collum."

"No."

"Adrian Gagnon."

"Him, I know," Sullivan said. "He's friends with Dennis. I think maybe they went to school together, or have a mutual friend or something."

"Really?" Kaye asked. "Where'd you meet Gagnon?"

"Dennis took me to a resort up by Santa Barbara. We ran into Adrian there."

"Valle delle Viti? The hotel and winery that looks like an old Italian village?"

"That's the place."

"How many times did you go?"

"Dennis took me a couple of times."

"Did you meet anyone else there? Maybe through Adrian Gagnon?"

She thought about it for a moment, then said, "Both times we had dinner with Adrian, and once this other guy came," Sullivan said. "They were all friends, but I think he runs the place, or manages it, or something. I could tell he was a bigshot."

"What was his name?"

"Lorenzo," she said. "But he told me to call him Renzo. Sorry, I don't remember his last name, but I know it was Italian."

"How old is Renzo?"

"Late twenties, maybe early thirties. In the same ballpark as Dennis and Adrian, anyway."

Kaye knew that Renzo Maisano had to be the R.M. that argued with Avi Geller at Paloma Canyon Country Club.

"Just a couple more," Kaye said. "How about Les Baruch?"

"I've never met him, but I know he worked for Avi Geller. Ziva talked about him a lot, almost like a family member."

"Okay," Kaye said. "Last name. Tamara Goschen."

"I think I've heard Adrian mention that name. Maybe she came to work for him or something? But I've never met her."

"You said that the Nicole who could ruin Dennis was one of his stable of performers. Do you know how that came about?"

"I'm not positive," Sullivan said slowly, clearly dredging her memory, "but I think maybe that Renzo guy put them together."

\*\*\*

Kaye called a uniformed unit to transport Sullivan, and an hour later he had turned her over to the Custody Services Division.

Before he left the building he tried Auggie's number again.

Same result: Voice mail box full.

It was still relatively early, and Okafor was working on warrant affidavits. He really wanted the warrant for Bettencourt's DNA in hand before he went hunting for the guy because it was a solid, defensible reason for picking him up.

He wasn't sure that was the real reason, or if he was just trying to buy some time to look for Auggie before he had to hunt down Bettencourt.

Before he headed out, he tried Auggie's number. No answer and mail box still full.

\*\*\*

Thirty minutes later Kaye rolled into the station parking lot and headed inside.

Patty Phillips saw him come in and waved for him to come see her.

"How'd it go?" she asked.

"Great," Kaye said. "We got her, and she gave up Dennis Bettencourt."

"Outstanding." Patty exclaimed, holding up a hand for a high five. "I knew you'd figure it out."

"I appreciate the confidence, Patty."

"And I wanted to tell you," she said, "you had a visitor looking for you first thing this morning."

"Really? Who?"

"A very old Japanese man in an orange robe," Patty said. "If I understood him correctly, he said he was your Roshi? Or maybe that was his name, I'm not sure."

Kaye was surprised. He'd known Roshi for years and had never known the old monk to leave the grounds of Kyokoku-Dera Monastery.

"Did he say what he needed?"

"Only that he wanted to see you," she replied. "I told him you had court this morning and didn't know when you'd be here."

"Okay, thanks Patty. I'll go by and see him."

Captain Thompson saw him push through the Squad doors and met him at his desk.

"Well, what happened?"

"She fired Feinmann, asked for a deal, then rolled when Okafor offered her one," Kaye replied. "Dennis Bettencourt is the shooter, and Nicole Ingram, not Avi Geller, was the original target."

"No shit?" Thompson said, amazed.

"Yeah, but it's deeper than that," Kaye said. "Turns out Bettencourt is also connected to people at Black Scimitar and Valle delle Viti. I also think Howard Feinmann, the lawyer, is in this up to his eyeballs, way beyond attorney-client privilege. Valle delle Viti's registered agent works for him and Feinmann's firm did all their legal dirty work during development."

"You're kidding?" Thompson asked, aghast.

"I wish I was."

"So, what's next? You going hunting for Bettencourt?"

"Not yet," Kaye replied, and saw the skepticism on Thompson's face. "Okafor's drafting warrant affidavits. I want them in hand before I snag the guy. She said she'd let me know, and Gardner recused herself from the case, so she has to find another judge."

"Gardner what? I don't even pretend to understand that."

"Covering her ass, I guess," Kaye said. "She may have strayed off the reservation by letting me question Sullivan this morning."

"Okay," Thompson said, nodding, "Outstanding work, Detective. Again, keep me in the loop, please."

"Appreciate it, Captain, but hold that thought until I have all these people in cuffs."

Kaye went back to his desk and started getting his next moves organized.

Despite the time difference, his first call was to the homeowners in Italy.

At first, the man he spoke with was upset about the late call, but Kaye managed to calm him down and explain the situation.

"Our realtor can let you in," the man said after Kaye told him about the warrant.

"I'm afraid Ms. Sullivan isn't available," Kaye said. "Is it okay if I deal directly with the security company?"

"Sure."

It turned into a very fruitful conversation. Kaye learned that Sullivan had never notified them of the vandalism report and that they had never received a Notice of Claim from their insurance company about the damages. To Kaye, that meant Sullivan, or maybe Bettencourt, paid out of pocket to avoid disclosing the incident. He also learned that the house had, indeed, sold, but the closing wasn't set for another two weeks.

His next call was to Marella at SecureLife to tell her he would be entering the house in Paloma Canyon, probably the following morning, to execute a search warrant, that he would call first, and not to send the cavalry if the alarms went off.

He spent most of the rest of the day making paper on the day's events and developments.

Just as he was wrapping it up and thinking about going home, his desk phone rang.

"I've got your warrants, Detective," Okafor said. "Search warrants for the house in Paloma Canyon, Bettencourt's house and his DNA, and an arrest warrant for him. I called Forensics and gave them a heads up. Just call them in the morning. Do you want to come get the warrants tonight or should I put them in the interdepartmental packet?"

"The packet will work. I'll look for them in the morning." Kaye hesitated for a second, then said, "I do have a question."

"Go ahead."

"Do you think we should have told Sullivan how deep Feinmann was wrapped up in the whole thing? At the very least, I'd think there was a conflict of interest."

Okafor went silent for a moment, then replied, "I don't think we were obligated to do that. I did tell Gardner, and if she thought it was something that should have been disclosed, she would have ordered us to do so. Or she would have done so herself. Besides, Sullivan fired him."

"Yeah, I know. That bothers me, too. I got the feeling the whole firing thing may be some kind of strategy by Feinmann. If it's not, it just kind of bothers me she doesn't know about Feinmann's involvement."

"Don't lose any sleep over it, Detective. Megan Sullivan is right where she belongs, and I'll be in court in the morning arguing against bail."

"Okay. Good work today, Counselor."

"Thank you. Now, just catch Dennis Bettencourt."

"That's the plan."

Before heading home he tried Auggie's number one more time. Nothing.

# DAY 23
### Tuesday Week 4

When Kaye got to the Squad an envelope with copies of the warrants was already on his desk.

He was reviewing them and mentally allocating his time and resources when Lister, whistling a happy tune, walked in.

"Good morning," Kaye greeted her. "You're in a good mood."

"Walkin' on sunshine," she said with a smile as she shucked off her jacket and hung it on her chair.

"What's the happy occasion?"

"Hooked up Billy Joe and Bobbi Sue late yesterday afternoon. Except they weren't Billy Joe and Bobby Sue, young lovers wanted in El Paso for robbing a gas station. Richard and Jeanine. Dick and Jenny, two meth head losers from Fresno."

"You sound almost disappointed."

"Oh, no," Lister said. "Not at all. A closed case is a good thing."

"How'd you break it?"

"Stroke of luck," she replied. "Ironically, from the garbage."

"What?"

Lister rolled her eyes and said, "Hey, that's okay. Probably not what you're into. Anyway, a sharp-eyed citizen saw somebody dump something into a dumpster and take off, so he checked it out. Disguises. He called it in."

"Did he see a vehicle?"

"He did, but no plate number. I checked the business security and ATM cameras in the area and came up with a good image. From there I just went all Sparks and pretended I was Sherlock Holmes."

"You got them?"

"Isn't that what I just said?"

"I didn't understand a lot of what you just said."

"Yeah, Kaye, I got them," she said. "Recovered a shitload of swag, too."

Kaye just shook his head and asked, "What are you working on now, this morning?"

"I'm waiting for the Captain to tell me."

"I could use you."

"Like partners?" Lister asked, grinning. "I'm in!"

Kaye told her about the hearing, Sullivan's subsequent arrest, that she had given up Dennis Bettencourt as the shooter, and laid out the morning plan. First up was meeting a forensics team at the house in Paloma Canyon and executing that search warrant.

"Are we waiting around?" Lister asked.

"No. Once the techs are inside we go look for Bettencourt. He lives in the canal neighborhood in Venice."

"I'm ready when you are." She smiled, winked and added, "Partner."

"You're driving."

On the way to Paloma Canyon Kaye called Forensics and asked for a response to the scene. Then he called Marella at SecureLife, explained that he had a search warrant for the house and asked her to have a mobile response guard meet him there to receive service and provide access. He made it clear that whoever responded was welcome to remain on-scene during the search, as long as they stayed out of the way and secured the premises afterwards.

When Lister rolled up to the house there was a SecureLife vehicle already there. Kaye was surprised to see Marella leaning against the front fender.

"Good morning, Detective Kaye," she said as he and Lister approached.

"Good morning to you," Kaye responded. "This is Detective Lister."

"His partner," Lister chimed in, drawing a look from Kaye.

"I didn't expect you to show up personally," Kaye continued, "but thanks for coming."

"Due diligence, Detective," Marella said. "I assume you've spoken to the owners?"

"I have. Last night." He handed her a copy of the warrant. "Are you staying?"

"I'd like to," Marella said. "I find it fascinating. Are you staying?"

"No," Kaye replied. "We're off to find someone else. The forensics team supervisor will have command and will answer any questions you have."

"Do you plan to take anything from the house?"

"The only things we're looking for are prints and trace evidence that might connect a known suspect to the scene. The team will vacuum, open drains, and dust whatever they think might yield some results, things like that. They might take any open food containers or dirty dishes they find, if there are any, but nothing that can be considered personal property is specified in the warrant. If they do take anything at all, you'll get a receipt."

"I'm looking forward to watching," Marella said, then hastily added, "without getting in the way, of course."

The forensics team showed up less than five minutes later. Kaye introduced Marella to the Supervisor, spent five minutes explaining exactly what he was looking for and wanted done, then he and Lister excused themselves and headed for Venice.

On the way Kaye called and arranged for a uniformed, two-man beat car as back-up.

They met a half-mile from Bettencourt's house. Kaye briefed them and Lister on the general geography and layout, then outlined his plan.

"Watch this guy," he cautioned the officers. "He's big, and he's already killed two people, so he's got nothing to lose."

"But we're not kicking the door?" one of the officers asked.

"No," Kaye said. "If he's not there now I don't want to leave his place in the condition that shouts 'the cops were here'. He'll run for sure. I'd rather wait on him a bit."

It turned out, to Lister's dismay, to be a fruitless effort.

The house was closed up tight, all the blinds closed and drapes drawn, and Kaye's pounding on the front door failed to raise a response.

They tried the garage door to check for vehicles, but it, too, was locked.

Kaye cut the patrol officers loose. He and Lister stood in front of Bettencourt's garage door.

"That sucks," she said. "I really wanted to help you get this douche bag."

"We'll get him. He's in the system."

"You're giving up?"

"For today," Kaye said. "I have someone else I need to go see on another matter."

"I'll come with."

"Not on this one, Mel. Sorry."

"Kaye, you're bad company. You'll leave me abandoned and alone?"

"I can't leave you. You're driving, remember? Besides, it's personal."

"Why didn't you just say so?" Lister said, smiling. "That I can live with."

They turned to head for Lister's unit just in time to see the garage door on the opposite side of the alley open. The first thing they saw was a set of pale, spindly legs and knobby knees way too skinny to fill the legs of the plaid shorts that came next. When the door topped out they saw an old man, his shoulders like a hanger for his red polo shirt, staring at them.

"I think Bob's gone," the old man said.

"Bob?" Kaye said. "We're not looking for anyone named Bob."

"Ah, that's just what I call the guy," the old man said. "Don't know his real name, but I'll be damned if he ain't a dead ringer for Bob Mitchum in the Story of G.I. Joe."

"That's what I hear," Kaye said.

"Yep," the old man said. "And from what I've seen, he's got Mitchum's touch with the ladies, too."

"What makes you think he left?" Lister asked.

"Saw him loading a bunch of stuff, oh, yesterday about dinner time, then he high-tailed it out of here. Don't think Bob's coming back."

"Did he take the van or the Corvette?" Kaye asked.

"Yep."

"Excuse me?" Lister asked. "What does that mean? How…?"

"Means he had a woman with him," the old man said. "Bob drove the Vette and she drove the van."

"What did she look like?" Kaye asked, expecting the old guy to describe Carol Soares. He didn't.

"Kind of hard to tell, really. That Bob is so damned tall, you know. But she wasn't short, if you know what I mean, and had a pretty good figure from what I could tell." He looked at Lister and hastily added, "Not that I was looking all that hard, ma'am. You know what I mean."

"Indeed I do," Lister said. "What about hair color, stuff like that?"

"Couldn't tell for sure," the old man replied. "Had her hair all up under a baseball cap and she was wearing big sunglasses. But if was guessing, I'd say her complexion was more of a blonde than a brunette. Oh, and she had a hell of a tattoo on one shoulder."

"Okay," Kaye said. "Thanks for the information."

"What'd Bob do?" the old man asked.

"We just need to talk to him," Lister replied.

"Yeah, right," the old man said, his voice dripping with sarcasm.

"Good luck selling that one." He reached up, grabbed the door handle and pulled. The door came down slowly at first, like the curtain at the end of a play, reversing the old man's unveiling, until with a final rush it settled into place.

"What do we do now?" Lister asked.

"We'll start looking for him in the morning," Kaye said. "Vehicles, associates, credit cards, see if we can ping his phone, the usual stuff."

"Any idea who the woman might have been?"

"I think I know who it was. But if they left here at six or seven last night, they could be long gone by now."

"Six or seven?"

"Yeah. You heard the guy. Dinner time."

Lister laughed. "Are you kidding? Did you see that guy? I guarantee he hits the closest senior discount all-you-can-eat buffet, every day of the week, before the roast beef is gone. Dinner at four o'clock, tops."

Kaye laughed, too. "Funny," he said. "But what's not funny is that Bettencourt knows we're looking for him."

\*\*\*

They stopped for a quick sandwich on the way back to the Squad and Kaye found himself enjoying Lister's company. He asked her about her fixation with music.

"Growing up, all my mom ever wanted was for me to be a singer," she said. "I mean, with the name Melody, what else was I supposed to do, right? My mother was one of those Stage Moms and just kept pushing me out there. But I never got anywhere. So I made it my mission to learn every song I could, especially the old ones. I figured that if it came down to it, and nobody else knew the lyrics, they'd have to let me sing because I did. Took me a long time to realize I had zero talent. To this day I cannot carry a tune with a forklift."

"How many songs did you get to sing?"

"Exactly zero."

"Really?"

"Really. You'd have to hear me to understand. Can we change the subject now?"

They talked about work, and Kaye slowly decided that if Thompson was going to require him to have a partner, he could do worse than Mel Lister. Chet Hilliard immediately came to mind as the counterpoint.

*** 

Kaye idled the Road King down the gravel drive leading to the main temple of Kyokuku-Dera Monastery. He didn't notice the striking beauty and tranquility of this small spot of Earth.

After his last visit, he was anxious about seeing Roshi again, but his anxiety lost out to his curiosity and concern.

The flat stone for the kickstand was still in its usual spot near the bottom of the main steps, which helped.

He retrieved the cantaloupe from the saddlebag and started up the stairs.

When he glanced up, Roshi was there, waiting.

At the top, Kaye bowed slightly and offered a formal greeting and the cantaloupe. Roshi did not smile, but accepted the melon and offered a formal reply.

"Come with me, please," Roshi then said, going around Kaye and down the steps.

Roshi led Kaye around the side of the temple and down a short, winding path to a beautiful moon gate dripping with a variety of colorful blossoms. Through the gate Kaye could see a large, black stone Buddha head, water slowly overflowing from its crown into a bed of black stones of various sizes, carefully arranged into a complex mandala.

It was a part of the monastery grounds he'd never seen.

A sharply curved teak bench faced the Buddha fountain, and Roshi atypically invited Kaye to sit first before taking a seat himself.

"Thank you for coming, Benkei-bo," Roshi said.

"I was worried, Roshi-sama, when I heard you came to the police station to find me."

"My first time outside Kyokuku-Dera in many years. The automobiles have changed. The people have not."

"Why did you come?" Kaye asked.

Roshi was silent for a full minute before answering.

"To apologize."

"I don't understand."

"Benkei, I value our friendship more than I could ever explain," Roshi said. "But I erred in my duties."

Kaye was lost. All he could do was stay silent and wait.

"It is not my duty," Roshi continued, "to tell you which path to follow, whether you walk forward or backward." He managed a weak smile. "Your path is yours to discover and follow. I can only offer lessons I hope will help you to make wise choices. But those choices are yours, Benkei, not mine to make for you. Nor is it my place to tell you your choices are wrong. If they are your choices, they are right for you. For doing so, I offer my most humble apologies."

Kaye was overwhelmed.

"I would have come back, Roshi-sama," he said at last. "As soon as I had an answer to your koan I thought worthy of presenting. I also treasure your friendship."

"I could not wait. I believe I have also discovered who has been leaving you the Kanji notes."

"Who?" Kaye asked instantly.

"An *onna-musha* named Tomoe Gozen," Roshi replied.

"Who is Tomoe Gozen?"

"She was a fierce samurai who lived during the same time as Benkei," Roshi said. He saw the instant skepticism in Kaye's eyes and added, "I do not think you are dealing with an eight hundred year old woman, Benkei. I believe you are dealing with someone who believes she is Tomoe Gozen, but you must understand why that delusion makes her so dangerous."

"I'm listening," Kaye said.

"The Genpei Wars of Benkei and Gozen's time resulted in the first Shogun, a man named Minamoto no Yoritomo.

"But there were also other members of the Minamoto clan who wanted to be Shogun. One was Yoshitune, the only swordsman ever to defeat Benkei and to whom Benkei swore fealty."

"You've told me about Minamoto no Yoshitune," Kaye said.

Roshi nodded and continued. "Yoritomo, who became Shogun, and Yoshitune were half-brothers. Another contender was Yoshinaka, cousin to Yoritomo. Yoshitune and Yoritomo allied to defeat Yoshinaka. Yoritomo then turned on Yoshitune and dealt him a crushing defeat at the battle of Koronogama Castle. That is where Benkei died the legendary Standing Death, about which we have already spoken."

"That's why the notes say I will fall this time?"

"I believe so," Roshi said. "There is more. Gozen's beauty was legendary. It was said to eclipse the beauty of the falling sun, which is also a phrase used in the notes. I also found that the hanko is that of Yoshinaka, who became known as Lord Kiso."

"But how does this Tomoe Gozen fit into this right now, with me?"

"Tomoe Gozen was the wife of Lord Kiso. The woman leaving the notes may well blame you for her supposed-husband not becoming Shogun."

Kaye's head was spinning. What Roshi was telling him put a lot of the pieces in the right places. But...

"Is there anything else you can tell me that will help me find this woman?" Kaye asked. "I believe she's killed at least four people, staging two of the victims to look like they committed seppuku. And she takes the heads."

"It is difficult to separate the legend of Tomoe Gozen from reality," Roshi said. "As with any legend, much is considered true simply because people choose to believe it. But her skills as a samurai were unsurpassed, even though she used a katana weighted for a strong man rather than a woman. The katana itself became legendary as the Hayabusa, the fastest creature on earth."

"Roshi, what does Hayabusa mean in English?"

"Peregrine Falcon. It is said she adopted it as her *tengu*."

"What's a *tengu*?" Kaye asked.

"A *tengu* is a supernatural being that some Japanese adopt as spirits, much like you would think of a guardian angel, but not so benign. Were it written in Kanji, like your notes, it would be the character for 'dog' and 'heavenly'. But a samurai would use the Kanji for 'dog' and 'war', since many believed war to be a divine state."

"A war dog?" Kaye asked, stunned as the pieces fell into place. Tamara Goschen.

"She left me another note," Kaye said, remembering the page in his jacket pocket. He extracted it and handed it to Roshi.

"It says 'Benkei, the time is near. You will soon come to me to die'." Roshi stared at Kaye and said solemnly, "Be very careful, Benkei. *Tengu* are very powerful and very dangerous, especially if they guide a psychotic."

*** 

Kaye spent another hour with Roshi. It was late when he got back to the Squad. Lister was already gone.

He immediately called Tom Gannett at Robbery-Homicide, but the call went to voice mail.

"Hey, Tom, it's Ben Kaye. Don't ask me to explain how I found this out, because I'm not sure I understand it, either, but I think the woman you're looking for on the parking garage homicide is one Tamara Goschen. I don't know where to find her, but I think she's connected to an outfit called Black Scimitar and may work for a guy name Adrian Gagnon. He might be able to point you to her. And be careful with Gagnon. His hands might be dirty on this, too. Thanks."

# DAY 24

Kaye got to the Squad early and started working on a strategy to track down Dennis Bettencourt. He knew that few, if any, of the tools he'd mentioned to Lister the day before were likely to yield results. The guy's phone had been his biggest hope for a quick catch, but if Bettencourt knew somebody with the technical savvy to spoof Kaye's cell number and have it show up on Sullivan's phone, he probably wasn't stupid enough to keep carrying the same phone around.

He was brainstorming when his desk phone rang.

"Kaye."

"Detective, this is Della at Questioned Documents. How are you today?"

"Good, Della," he replied. "How about you?"

"I'm just dandy," she said, and Kaye could hear the smile through the phone. "I just e-mailed you about three and a half pages of Mr. Baruch's statement that I was able to recover. I think we got most of it, and we hit the jackpot. We got Baruch's signature and he references you by name."

"That's great, Della," Kaye said. "Thank you very, very much. You're a wizard."

"Well, don't tell anybody else. It'll spoil my image." She laughed. "As usual, the actual pages now belong to me in chain of custody, but I took pictures and sent you those images. If you'll get me a comparator, we're in business."

"Della, did you read it?"

"I did," she said, and the humor disappeared from her voice. "Nail those bastards, Kaye, and make them pay dearly."

"I'll do my best. And thanks again. I owe you one."

"I drink scotch, Detective, and any time."

Kaye immediately opened his e-mail. The message from Della Robinson was right at the top of the queue. He downloaded the attachment, opened it, and began to read.

*...when Howard Feinmann talked Avi into investing in VdV. I tried my best to talk him out of it because, like I told you already, Avi didn't know shit about real estate. He got really mad at me because I not only questioned him, I wouldn't go in on the deal with him. He kept saying, 'Les, we're partners' and I kept having to remind him, 'No, Avi, we're not partners. I work for you' and after all these years that became a sore point between us. I finally gave in and invested some symbolic money, but not even close to what Avi put in because I didn't have it, hoping to save our friendship. But Avi just couldn't seem to get past it.*

*Then, one day early this year – I don't remember exactly and I deleted my files – a guy named Dennis Bettencourt walks in unannounced and asks if somebody can take a look at a screenplay. I wasn't busy, and the kid looked just like a young, tall Robert Mitchum, so I thought, 'hey, if he can't write worth a shit, maybe he can learn to act', so I looked at it. The premise and the writing were unbelievably good, but it wasn't finished. Because of how things were between Avi and me, I told the kid to finish it and come back, and decided to keep it under my hat, just in case.*

*A few weeks later Avi comes to me and tells me about this script some girl named Nicole pitched to him. It sounded exactly like the same idea Bettencourt had pitched to me and I told Avi I'd already seen it from somebody else. That made him doubt the girl, and me, and he could never find her again to see what was going on. It was like she disappeared. Then Bettencourt comes back with a finished script, only it's not half as good as what he showed me before. I decided not to tell Avi, see if I could get it polished up, and maybe use it to go out on my own if things kept getting worse between us.*

*Then VdV had their grand opening and all the investors were invited to a private party, kind of a soft opening. About two hours after we get to this giant shindig at the hotel, Avi comes to me madder than hell and tells me the girl with the script, Nicole, is there, but she's high as a kite and didn't even recognize him. He also tells me that Renzo Maisano offered her to him as a 'party favor' to use however he wanted, and that if Nicole didn't appeal to him, he could take his pick of some others. Avi was so pissed he confronted Maisano and offered to buy Nicole out. Maisano laughed in Avi's face and I had to drag Avi out because I thought he was going to kill Maisano right then and there. If Maisano's girlfriend hadn't been there and stepped in, I don't know what might have happened.*

*Avi was mad, so we left, and on the way back to L.A. Avi swore to me that he was going to rescue Nicole. Said she was too big a talent to end up like that. I begged him to just go to the police and let them handle it, but he had so much money into VdV that if Maisano went down he'd probably lose it all, and he didn't want to do that to Ziva. Over the last few months, Avi went to VdV at least once a week, asked for Nicole, and stayed overnight to make it look good. He was there the night before he was killed. I don't know for sure, but I think Nicole was with him that day because he was finally going to get her out of the whole VdV mess and away from Maisano. But I'm thinking Maisano must've somehow figured out what Avi was trying to do and had them killed.*

*I swear, Detective Kaye, that what I told you earlier today and what I have written here is the whole truth as I know it, and I'm very sorry I didn't just tell you all this the first time we met. I will testify to it in court if necessary.*

Baruch had signed and dated the statement at the bottom.

Kaye leaned back and considered Baruch's partial statement. What was written would likely not stand up court as a dying declaration, given that Baruch hadn't known he was about to be murdered when he wrote it. But it validated his notes from their conversation.

It also made him worry even more about Auggie McMaster.

He grabbed the phone and called Kai Iwamura.

"Hey, Ben," Iwamura answered, "you must have ESP. I was just picking up the phone to call you."

"About?"

"Black Scimitar. I looked into that IPO and the SEC filings. A company controlled by Lorenzo Maisano bought a huge chunk of shares on opening day, and has continued to acquire stock steadily since then. It's possible that Maisano has been pulling the strings there for a while. You know, activist investor tactics, and maybe even had something to do with Rod Howell's death."

"I'm not surprised," Kaye said. "But that's not why I'm calling. I need your help."

"With what?" Iwamura asked, and Kaye heard the skepticism in the agent's voice.

Kaye told him he'd made an arrest in the Geller case, that the woman had rolled on the shooter, and that he'd learned the shooter had connections to both Black Scimitar and Valle delle Viti. He also told Iwamura that he was certain he knew who had killed Rod Howell and several other people, and she was connected to Black Scimitar. Last, he told Iwamura about Auggie and his belief that Renzo Maisano had taken her to put pressure on him, and that Maisano might kill her as soon as word of the arrest got out.

"I need help getting her out," Kaye said in closing. "I was hoping your people in Santa Maria could help."

"But you don't know for sure if she's even there, right?"

"Ninety-nine percent. I'm not risking her life on that one percent."

Iwamura was silent for several seconds and then said, "Sorry, Ben. I don't think we have any assets available on such short notice."

"You don't think?" Kaye said, trying to keep the anger out of his voice.

"Those agents don't work for me, and I won't ask if you have a valid warrant, or even probable cause."

"Really, Kai? That's what you're giving me? Bureau bullshit? Thanks, Agent Iwamura. See you around."

As Kaye reached out to hang up the phone, he heard Iwamura say, "Ben, wait!"

"What?"

"Look," Iwamura said, his voice much quieter than before. "All I can tell you is that after we talked about Valle delle Viti I took it to the boss. Turns out we're already up on it, and have been for a while."

"That doesn't help me, or Auggie McMaster."

"I understand that. But believe me when I tell you there's no way the Bureau will move on Maisano now. Our entire investigation would be blown and lives would be at risk."

"Lives are already at risk, Kai."

Iwamura was silent again for two beats, then said, "Bureau lives, Ben."

"You've got somebody on the inside."

"You know I can't tell you that."

It was Kaye's turn to go quiet. This time, Iwamura didn't try to keep him from hanging up.

Kaye stewed about his conversation with Iwamura for almost fifteen minutes, trying to figure out what to do. There was zero chance he could get on his bike, ride to Valle delle Viti and simply knock and ask for Auggie McMaster.

He needed to somehow get inside, get to Renzo Maisano.

An inspiration struck, and he smiled as he got up and headed for Thompson's office.

He knew how he could get inside.

After all, he'd already all but been invited.

Thompson, who was on the phone, saw him coming and waved him in. Kaye sat and waited.

"Okay, Detective," the Captain said when he hung up, "what can I do for you?"

"I need to go back to Santa Barbara on the Geller case, and I need some help."

"Help? How so?"

"Lister."

Thompson was immediately skeptical. "You're asking for a partner? Okay, what's really going on?"

Kaye laid it all out. That he'd connected Avi Geller and Nicole Ingram's murders to both Black Scimitar and a possible organized crime and racketeering operation being run out of the Valle delle Viti resort.

"So how is someplace in another county our problem? Why not just call the locals?"

Kaye hesitated. He didn't want to make his problems the LAPD's problems, but he knew his chances of rescuing Auggie were slim to none if he didn't have help.

"A friend of mine up there has been missing for almost a week," Kaye said. "I think the Black Scimitar people took her to get to me. I need help finding and getting her back, and the local PD is literally owned by the bad guys. They'll kill her as soon as the phone rings."

"Hmm," Thompson said. "I see your point. But why Lister?"

"These people know me. I've had two run-ins with them already. They don't know Lister."

"How long?" Thompson asked.

"She should be on her way home later tonight."

"With you and your friend, right?"

"Let's hope so."

The Captain leaned back and tented his fingers under his chin, weighing Kaye's request against all the things he knew could go wrong with it.

"Detective, I'm sorry, but I need more than your gut feeling to involve another department detective in this, especially since there's an official record of your friend's arrest. If something goes south and you or Lister get hurt, or have to hurt somebody else, we're all in the crapper. I can't risk that."

"But, Captain, I'm telling –"

"I know what you're telling me, Detective. I need more before I can put Lister at risk. Sorry."

On his way back to his desk, an angry Kaye was suddenly struck by an idea, then beat himself up for not thinking of it sooner.

Two minutes later he was on the phone with the Santa Barbara County jail.

"This is Detective Kaye at the LAPD." He gave his badge and callback number. "I heard from a source that you might have somebody I'm looking for in custody, and thought I'd call and check."

"What's the name?" the deputy on the other end asked.

"Augustina McMaster. White female, early thirties, tall, dark hair and eyes. Ink from left shoulder to left elbow. My source says she got popped up there last week for heroin possession with intent. It's a pretty unusual name, so I'm hoping it's the same woman I'm after."

"Hang on."

Kaye waited about two minutes before the deputy came back on.

"Detective Kaye, we had her, but, sorry, she bonded out last Friday."

"Well, crap, I guess I'll have to keep looking," Kaye said, then paused for effect before asking, "Hey, could you do me a favor?"

"Depends."

"Is there a chance you can e-mail me her mug shot? I can verify it's the same woman, and see if she's done anything major to change her appearance. The picture I have is pretty old."

"I guess I can do that," the deputy said. "What's your e-mail address?"

Kaye gave the deputy his department address and said, "Thanks. I appreciate it."

"No problem Detective. It's on its way. Good hunting."

Seconds later the e-mail dropped into Kaye's inbox. He opened it, contained his rage as his heart rate soared, sent it to the printer, grabbed the copy and headed back to Thompson's office. He walked in without knocking and dropped the photo on the Captain's desk.

"Kaye, what the hell? What is this?"

"That, Captain, is Auggie McMaster's booking photo from the Santa Barbara County jail. They just sent it to me. One problem. That's not Auggie McMaster."

"What?" Thompson said, snatching the photo off his desk and studying it.

"I'm guessing that the Chumash Oaks PD arrested her, arraigned her, held her for twenty-four hours, then sent a ringer to County in her place. The next day somebody bonds out the ringer, and before the next court date the Chumash Oaks prosecutor drops the charges. All nice and clean, and they still have Auggie. Cap, I really need help."

Thompson's gaze drifted past Kaye, then he looked his detective in the eye.

"Well, Lister just came in. I still can't officially endorse it, but if she's willing to help I'll try to cover your ass if something goes south. Let's ask her."

Kaye went and got her.

"What's this about?" she asked as she sat down next to Kaye. "Did I screw up?"

"No, you didn't screw up," Thompson told her, then looked as Kaye. "Go ahead."

Kaye spent ten minutes going over the situation again. Lister listened attentively, often nodding unconsciously.

"You say you have a plan?" Lister asked when he was done.

"I do," Kaye said, and outlined it for her. "This isn't technically our case, but –"

"Shut up, Kaye," she interrupted. "This woman is obviously important to you." She looked at Thompson and said, "Put me in, coach."

The three of them spent fifteen minutes working out logistics and timing. Thompson, though, refused to let Lister drive an unmarked department vehicle.

"No problem," Lister said. "I'll take my car."

"Okay, I think that'll do it," Kaye said, standing up. "Thanks Captain." He turned to Lister. "I'll see you later?"

"I'll be there."

Kaye pulled the new pickup into the Auggie's Wine'N'Diner parking lot just after 8:00 p:m.

The La Vina di Augustina van, dustier than it had been on Saturday, was still parked in the same spot. A small silver sedan was parked two spaces away. Cheri, Auggie's regular hostess, got out when she saw Kaye.

"Thanks for meeting me," Kaye said.

"Hey, if it helps us find Auggie, I'm all in," Cheri said.

"Did you find the keys?"

"I found the spare set in Auggie's desk."

"But not the ones she regularly carried?" Kaye asked.

"No," Cheri replied, holding up a set of keys. "There's no front door key on these."

Kaye took the keys and walked around the van. It was still somewhat light outside, but the back windows were too darkly tinted for him to see inside the cargo area. He walked to the front of the van and looked through all the windows, studying the passenger compartment and seeing nothing out of the ordinary.

He pushed the unlock button on the key fob. The parking lights flashed, two electronic chimes sounded from somewhere deep in the van and the door locks clunked as they disengaged.

"What are we looking for?" Cheri asked as Kaye opened the driver's door.

"Won't know until we see it," he replied. "Or don't see it, I guess."

The van was nice, Kaye guessed probably the top-of-the-line trim package. Tan leather, heated power seats, power everything else, large video display and premium sound system."

It was also very clean.

"I see something different already," Cheri said.

"What's that?"

"Auggie always has her favorite coffee travel cup in the van."

Kaye looked. No coffee cup in the cup holder.

Kaye had to move the seat back to get behind the wheel, which, given that Auggie was almost as tall and long-legged as he was, seemed odd.

He started with the glove box. A small flashlight, sunglasses – probably spares, he thought – a collapsible umbrella and several small packs of tissues rested atop a black leather case with a snap closure.

He grabbed the case, opened it, and found all the van's paperwork and manuals. The inside of the cover flap had clear plastic holders with business cards for the salesman, Auggie's insurance agent and a roadside assistance membership card. He grabbed the papers from inside the case pocket and sorted through them.

The MSRP sticker, tightly folded. Two years' worth of Auto Club membership cards. Insurance ID cards for six month policies written by the same agent whose card was in the holder, also going back almost two years. And an expired registration.

He checked the pocket again. It was empty. He sorted through the papers again, re-checking and comparing dates. No current registration.

He checked above the sun visors. Nothing.

He next checked the center console. Some CDs, more tissues, a phone charger, pocket knife, hair brush and a couple of loose pens and pencils.

He slid out of the van and walked to the back. The stickers on the license plate were current. He opened the back doors and the interior dome light came on. There was nothing, not even a scrap of cardboard or piece of crumpled paper, in the cargo area.

He went back to the driver's seat and sat there, hands on the wheel, thinking and looking.

"What's wrong, Ben?" Cheri asked.

"Was Auggie planning on getting rid of the van if her property purchase went through?"

"Not that I know of. Why?"

"It's just really…clean," he said. "I've only had my truck for a few days and it's already got more stuff in it than Auggie has in here."

"She's tidy," Cheri said. "But I wouldn't call her a neat freak."

Kaye nodded, then reached for the seat belt and pulled it out to fasten it. Even though he'd moved the seat back, he had to adjust the buckle position to click it closed. It suddenly occurred to him that Auggie might not have been the last person to drive the van.

"What's that?" Cheri asked, pointing at his chest.

On the seat belt webbing, just above the center of Kaye's chest, were two dark brown spots. One was tear-drop shaped, the other a broad smear.

"Looks like blood," Kaye said.

Cheri gasped and her hands flew to cover her mouth. "Oh,

my God!"

"It's dried," Kaye said. "Could've been here a long time."

"Still, that can't be… I mean, it's bad, right?"

Kaye looked at her, but didn't say anything, which answered the question.

He reached to unbuckle the seat belt and fumbled with the unfamiliar placement. He looked down to find the release button and saw the edge of a piece of paper where it had fallen deep between the seat and center console.

There was no chance he'd get his hand down there.

"There's a piece of paper down there," he said as he slid out. "See if you can get your hand down there and grab it."

Cheri slid in and pushed her hand down, grabbing the steering wheel with her other hand and contorting her body while she fished for the paper.

"Aha, got it!" she said triumphantly, straightening up with the paper trapped between two fingers.

"What is it?"

She looked at it for only a second and said, "Looks like the registration."

Kaye snatched it from her.

She was right. And it was current.

How did it get down there, he wondered. Why wouldn't it be…?

The answer hit him before he even finished asking himself the question.

Because a police officer asked to see it.

"Thanks for your help, Cheri. I'll take it from here."

\*\*\*

After Cheri left, Kaye called Lister from the truck.

"You close?"

"Five or ten minutes," she replied. "Find anything in the van?"

"Blood on the seatbelt."

Kaye ended the call.

"Shit," Lister muttered, pushing a little harder on the gas pedal. "Please don't let goddamn Macky be back in town."

\*\*\*

319

After Lister arrived at the diner, they spent time refining their strategy, devising cover stories and the appropriate responses to questions they both knew Lister would be asked.

"I brought a wire," Lister said. "Should I wear it?"

"No. These people know me, but they don't know you. If they find out you're on the job and you're wired, no telling what they might do. Besides, once I get my hands on one of them, your part in this is done and you're out of here."

"Oh, c'mon Kaye. Don't take the T-bird away. Let me have some fun."

"Just don't get shot," Kaye said. "Or tased."

"I'm all right," she said. "Don't worry about me."

Once it was full dark, Lister left first in Kaye's truck. He followed in her Outback. At the traffic circle junction they went east on San Marcos Pass Road.

Kaye had pulled the paper plate from the back of the truck and removed all the sale paperwork from the glove box. There was a manila envelope under the passenger floor mat with six thousand dollars cash inside, all twenties neatly rubber-banded into thin, tidy bundles.

Kaye held back, letting Lister get about a half-mile ahead as they drove east through the Village of Chumash Oaks. Lister ignored the 25 mph signs and drove fifty.

Kaye really wanted it to be Reid.

Their first pass came up empty. Weeknight traffic was sparse and they only passed one on-coming car.

They met at a historical marker turn-out two miles east of the Chumash Oaks city limits.

"If there's anybody taking care of business tonight," Lister said as Kaye slid into the truck's passenger seat, "I didn't see them and I was well over the limit."

"I didn't see a patrol unit, either," Kaye said, chagrined. "Let's give it thirty and try again."

Kaye fretted while Lister, ear buds in, listened to music and dozed.

The second pass proved fruitful.

Lister had barely passed the Chumash Oaks city limits when Kaye, about a half-mile behind, saw headlights come on in the trees up ahead and a vehicle head for the highway. As soon as it made the asphalt and Kaye saw its taillights, emergency overheads lit up and it took off after Lister.

Kaye backed off the gas and turned off the Outback's headlights.

That stretch of San Marcos Pass Road was almost straight, going through a shallow cut. Outside the fog line was about two feet of pavement before a crushed gravel shoulder. The graded and mowed ground then sloped slightly away for about another ten feet, giving Lister plenty of room to get off the road. The embankments, averaging maybe six feet high on the westbound side, sloped gently enough for native grass and scrub to grow, but were too steep to mow. Beyond the barbed wire right-of-way fence atop the embankments the trees were thick, looming in the darkness to form a false, mountainous horizon against the night sky.

As Kaye closed the gap he hoped it wasn't a K-9 unit making the stop. A dog would make it almost impossible for him to get close enough for his plan to work.

He coasted to a stop, using the emergency brake handle on the console to avoid lighting up the brake lights, about a hundred feet behind the patrol car just in time to see the officer approach the truck.

It was a Charger. Probably no dog, which meant that as long as he stayed behind the unit's spotlights he would be virtually invisible to anyone standing in their glare.

It was an advantage he could exploit.

Kaye swore when it took him what felt like an eternity to figure out how to disable the Subaru's dome lights, then quickly got out of the car, went to the base of the embankment and started moving cautiously forward.

When he was about twenty feet from the patrol car he almost stumbled into a small bush that had rooted near the bottom of the embankment. It was out of reach of the maintenance crew's mower deck, and not yet big enough to be deemed a hazard and cut down.

But it was big enough to offer Kaye a degree of concealment in case of passing headlights.

He crouched behind it and listened.

"…license is the only paperwork you have?" he heard the officer ask.

Adrenaline pumped into Kaye's system.

It was Reid.

"Yes," Lister replied. "I told you, it's not my truck. I borrowed it to carry some stuff. My friend said the paper plate on the back was all I needed, just in case."

"The problem, miss, is that there's no paper plate," Reid said, taking a step back and shining his flashlight in Lister's face. "Step out, please."

Lister slid out.

"Step around to the back of the truck," Reid said, using the flashlight beam to point.

Lister walked to the open space between the truck and the Charger. Without thinking, she automatically took the position where the spotlights would be in Reid's eyes, not hers.

Kaye hoped Reid wouldn't notice.

"No, you stand behind your truck and face me," Reid said, taking her by the shoulder and guiding her. "You said you just moved," Reid continued. "Is the address on your license current?"

"Uh, no," Lister said. "I'm sorry. I just haven't had time yet. Don't I have, like, thirty days or something?"

"Ten days," Reid said.

"Crap," Lister muttered. "Damn deadlines and commitments. Story of my life."

"Have you been drinking tonight?" Reid asked, again shining the light in Lister's face. "Or doing any illegal or recreational drugs?"

"No, sir."

Reid continued with the questions, most of which Kaye and Lister had anticipated: Where are you going? Where did you come from? Do you have any weapons on you? Anything in the truck you want to tell me about? Have you ever been arrested? A casual conversation disguised as an interrogation.

While Reid quizzed Lister, Kaye saw headlights approaching from the west.

If it was a back-up unit, things could get complicated, fast.

It wasn't. It was an older model crew cab dually pickup. As it slowed to pass by, the teenagers inside hung out the windows, hooting and hollering at Reid and Lister before speeding up again.

"...and because you don't have paperwork on the truck," Kaye heard Reid say as the noise faded, "I'm going to search it."

"You can't do that!" Lister protested. "Don't you need a warrant or something?"

"Are you an attorney?" Reid asked condescendingly. "You telling me how to do my job?"

Kaye saw Reid step forward and grab Lister's arm, steering her toward the passenger side back door of the Charger.

"What the hell?" Lister half-screamed. "Are you arresting me? I didn't do anything!"

Reid yanked her to a stop and said, "No, but I'm responsible for you. I can't have you wandering around out here in the dark and getting run over. It's for your safety and mine."

Knowing Reid would be behind the spotlights, Kaye made himself as small as possible behind the bush. He couldn't see very well, but he could still hear.

"Put your hands on the car and lean forward," Reid said.

"Hey!" Lister shouted a few seconds later. "Keep your hands to yourself, dude. That's over the line!"

"In your dreams, sweetheart," Reid said sarcastically as Kaye heard the sound of handcuffs ratcheting around Lister's wrists. "Now, watch your head."

Kaye heard the Charger's back door slam and peered around the bush to see Reid headed for the truck.

It took the cop only a minute to conduct the search. When he walked back to the Charger he carried the envelope of cash in his hand. He dropped it through the unit's open driver's window, then walked to the back of the car and opened the trunk.

Kaye's angle was bad and he couldn't see what Reid was doing.

"Hey, it's me," Reid said a moment later. "I've got a prospect. One fifty-four, east side."

Silence for a few seconds.

"Okay," the cop said.

Reid closed the trunk, walked back to the front of the Charger, put something down on the hood, then walked back and opened the back door.

"Step out," he said to Lister.

"Am I free to go?" she asked as she stood up.

"Afraid not," Reid said as he grabbed Lister and spun her around, then pinned her against the side of the Charger. "You're under arrest for possession of narcotics with intent to distribute."

"Narcotics?" Lister said. "Are you fucking crazy? I don't deal drugs."

"Then you can explain to a judge why you had a kilo of heroin in the truck," Reid said, "and six thousand dollars cash hidden under the floormat."

"Heroin?" Lister shouted. "That's not mine! That money is to pay for music equipment when I get to San Francisco. That's why I borrowed the truck. This is total bullshit!"

"I'm also seizing the truck and the cash," Reid said.

"You can't do this!" Lister screamed.

Had it not been for the loose gravel, Kaye would have taken Reid without a struggle.

But the crunch and bad traction betrayed him.

Reid heard him coming when he was still ten feet away. The cop's hand instantly went for his gun.

Kaye saw the pistol clear leather and the muzzle start to come up.

His left hand hit Reid's forearm just as the gun went off and he felt the shockwave as the bullet went past. He found purchase on Reid's wrist and yanked the cop down and forward.

Another shot, and pieces of gravel scattered.

Kaye grabbed the pistol with his right hand, reversed his momentum and drove his hands upward.

Reid was overbalanced and had no chance of avoiding the blow.

Kaye's hands and the pistol hit the cop square in the face and he crumpled to the pavement without making a sound.

"Holy shit, Kaye," Lister muttered. "You weren't supposed to kill him."

"If I wanted to kill him, he'd be dead," Kaye said as he knelt down and felt a strong pulse in Reid's neck. "Nice work, by the way."

"Thanks," Lister said. "Just working for a living and taking care of business. Now, if you don't mind, get these damn cuffs off me. I don't care for them at all."

Kaye removed the cuffs.

"What do we do now?" Lister asked, rubbing her wrists.

Kaye looked around.

"We've got to get off the highway before I can talk to our friend."

"He pulled out of a side road less than a half-mile back," Lister said. "North side."

"I saw," Kaye said. "I'll drive the patrol car and we'll leave it there. You follow in the truck and then I'll take you back to your car."

"But I —" Lister started to protest.

"No argument," Kaye snapped. "Until now the only offense you've committed is a traffic violation. Dumb shit here wanted to keep you a secret, so he never even ran you or the truck VIN. You're out of this."

"What about him?" Lister asked.

Kaye smiled and said, "He's with me."

"Did they ever status check him?"

"Not that I heard," Kaye said. "But he made a phone call while you were in the back seat. Called you a prospect."

"Miserable back stabber," Lister said. "Total set up. But if they do status check and he doesn't answer, they'll be looking for him pretty soon."

"If they find his unit, it'll be empty."

Lister turned and headed for the truck, stopped, picked up the bundle Reid had dropped on the hood and held it up.

"Think this is really heroin?"

"From what I've heard, they have a pretty reliable supply."

"Do you want this as evidence?"

Kaye nodded. "Put it under the driver's seat."

"Don't forget your cash," Lister reminded him.

Kaye put on gloves and used Reid's own cuffs to restrain the man. He found a Chief's Special in an ankle holster. That, and Reid's duty weapon, both went into the Charger's trunk. There he found a riot cuff and used that to bind Reid's ankles. The portable radio went in the front seat.

Then he put the still-unconscious cop into the Charger's back seat.

Where Reid had been parked prior to the stop turned out to be an access road into private property. Lister was waiting for him when he got there and followed him, blacked out, all the way to the locked gate deep in the trees. Beyond the gate, rows of grape vines stretched away into the night.

He hauled Reid, who was now regaining consciousness, from the Charger to the truck and put him on the floor in the back seat. He brought the envelope of cash and the portable radio, put the cash under the seat with the heroin, left the radio on the seat and signaled Lister to get out.

He led her some distance from the truck.

"No conversation on the way to your car," he told her, keeping his voice low and handing her the keys.

"Roger that," Lister agreed.

There was enough tree cover that Kaye was confident no one would find the black car in the dark.

By daylight, it wouldn't matter.

\*\*\*

Kaye dropped Lister at her car and watched her head eastbound until the Subaru's lights disappeared. Then he found another dirt side road that wound into the hills south of the highway.

He knew from Reid's breathing that the cop had regained consciousness, but had not yet uttered a word.

As Kaye drove deeper into the hills the portable police radio squawked.

"CO-six, status check."

There was no response and Kaye wondered if Reid was CO-6.

"CO-six, status check," the dispatcher repeated. "Reid, what's your status?"

That answered that question.

"CO-eight, Central."

"Go ahead Central." It was a woman's voice.

"CO-eight, CO-six isn't responding," the dispatcher said. "Can you clear and check on him?"

"Is he still out on one fifty-four?"

"Affirmative."

"CO-eight's in route."

Kaye grunted. At least somebody was paying attention.

He found a dark, secluded spot in a dense grove of oaks and parked.

"Get out," he ordered Reid after opening the back door.

Reid struggled to a sitting position and glared at Kaye, who saw blood on the cop's face.

"You broke my nose," Reid said, his voice different, more nasal.

"That's the least of your problems. Get out."

"My feet are tied."

"You'll manage," Kaye said.

"Fuck you."

Kaye reached in and grabbed a handful of Reid's uniform shirt, lifted him out of the truck and dropped him.

"Hey!" Reid shouted.

"I asked nicely," Kaye said. "That's how this is going to work, Reid. I ask nicely, once. If you don't answer, or I think you're lying, I hurt you until I find out what I want to know."

"I don't think so," Reid said. "I know you're a cop, Kaye. I'm not afraid of you. In fact, you're the one who's going to jail."

Kaye squatted down and locked eyes with Reid.

"I don't think you grasp the full implications of your predicament," he said, his voice low and even. "I chose the bitch over the job."

Even in the dark, lessened only by the dim glow of the truck's dome light, Kaye saw the first flicker of worry in Reid's eyes before the man looked away.

"I don't know what you're talking about," Reid said. "I'm a cop and –"

"You're not a cop," Kaye interrupted. "You work for Black Scimitar. You run phony drug interdiction for Gagnon and Renzo Maisano and you probably get a cut of whatever you seize."

Reid avoided eye contact and said, "Go to hell."

"But that's not why we're having this little talk," Kaye said. "I really only have one question. Answer it truthfully and we'll talk about getting you out of this alive."

Reid stayed quiet.

"Okay, I'll just ask." Kaye stood up and pushed the truck door closed, deepening the darkness, before squatting back down. "Don't forget the rules, Reid. One chance. Ready?"

Reid glared at Kaye but didn't respond.

"Where do you take the women?" Kaye asked.

"I don't know what you're talking about."

Kaye sighed, reached behind Reid, grabbed the man's left hand and began to squeeze. He heard Reid's sharp intake of breath as he increased the pressure, but the cop said nothing.

Five seconds later Kaye heard the sharp crack of breaking bone and released his grip.

"You broke my hand!" Reid half-screamed. "You fucker, you broke my hand."

"Probably just a metacarpal," Kaye said. "Easy fix. Want to answer the question now?"

"Kaye, you're crazy!"

"Not crazy. Just very determined to find...what did you call her? My bitch? Oh, yeah, that was it. My bitch."

"I didn't mean anything by that!" Reid shouted. "I was just trying to piss you off."

Kaye laughed and said, "Worked, didn't it?"

"Look, Kaye," Reid said between gasps, "there's gotta be a way we can work this out. I've got –"

"You've got nothing I could possibly want," Kaye said. "Except Auggie McMaster. I'll ask one more time. If you try to bullshit me, I'll leave your corpse out in the trees for the coyotes. Nobody will ever find you, Reid. Ever. Then I'll keep working my way through your entire crooked department until someone tells me. And someone will.

Might as well be you, right? So, one last time. Where do you take the women?"

"Renzo or his crazy bitch will kill me," Reid whispered, his breath ragged as he tried not to sob.

Kaye laughed again.

"I wouldn't be worried about Maisano right now if I were you. You have more pressing problems. Answer the question or you're coyote shit. Where do you take the women?"

"You won't do it," Reid said, again all bluster. "You're a cop. You won't do it."

"Have it your way," Kaye said as he stood up. He opened the back door of the truck again to get some light, then stepped around to Reid's feet and started removing the trussed-up cop's shoes.

"What the fuck?" Reid asked, trying unsuccessfully to squirm out of Kaye's iron grip.

"Shut up," Kaye said sharply. "I gave you your chance."

Kaye threw the shoes and socks into the back seat of the truck, then bent over and ripped Reid's shirt open, rolled the man onto his stomach and peeled the shirt off. The sound of ripping fabric filled the darkness as Kaye tore the shirt to get it past the handcuffs.

The ballistic vest came off next.

He started unsnapping the keepers that held Reid's gun belt to his trouser belt.

"Okay! Okay!" Reid shouted. "We take them to Maisano's house! He takes them and she pays me! I don't know what happens after that, I swear to God! Let me go and I'll tell you everything I know!"

"How much do you get?"

"Twenty-five grand."

"Each?"

"Yeah, cash."

"Who else is in on this?" Kaye asked.

"I don't know," Reid said. "She told me she'd kill me if she found out I talked to anyone else about it."

"How many women have you taken to Maisano?"

Reid hesitated and Kaye ripped the gun belt from around the man's waist.

"Six!" Reid screamed. "Your friend was number six."

That number meant Reid wasn't the only Black Scimitar contractor, maybe even Chumash Oaks PD regular cops, in on the kidnappings.

"Why Auggie McMaster?" Kaye asked. "She didn't fit the profile."

"She called me and told me to watch for your friend," Reid said. "Told me it would give her leverage on you."

"Leverage on me? Why?"

"She kept saying she wanted you to come to her. I told her I thought it was a bad idea. People would miss that chick. Come looking for her."

"You keep saying 'she' and 'her'," Kaye said. "Who is she?"

"Goschen," Reid replied, barely whispering. "Maisano's...I guess you could call her his girlfriend. She's one crazy bitch."

"Crazy how?"

"I mean bat shit crazy. Thinks she's some kind of fucking ninja or something."

"Do you take the women directly to Maisano's house?"

"Yeah."

"Is there a gate?"

"Yeah," Reid replied. "But there's no way to get through it, and there are guards."

"Is there another way in?"

"Not unless you can fly. Hey, if you're thinking of trying to rescue your friend, forget it. There ain't no way. Maybe FBI SWAT or a SEAL team, but they'd take heavy losses. Otherwise, no way."

"We'll see," Kaye said.

"Okay," Reid said. "I answered your question. Are you going to let me go?"

"I never said I would let you go. I said I'd try and get you out of this alive."

Kaye picked Reid up and put him back onto the floor in the truck's back seat, then stuffed the torn uniform shirt into his mouth to keep him quiet. Before he started back down to the highway he reaffixed the truck's temporary paper license plate.

Partway down, Reid's portable radio squawked again.

"Central, CO-eight."

"Go ahead, eight."

"I've been up and down one fifty-four. No sign of six. What did he give you when he made the stop?"

The dispatcher read back the make, model and color of the truck, that it had no plates, and that the driver was female.

"Did he run the driver?" Eight asked.

"Negative."

"Ten-four," CO-8 said. "Alert the Chief and surrounding agencies and put out a BOLO on the truck. I'll keep looking."

\*\*\*

A half-hour later Kaye pushed the buzzer outside the Solvang Sheriff's substation.

The same Lieutenant Barker was working, recognized Kaye and opened the door.

"Good evening, Lieutenant," Kaye said. "Would you hold the door for me?"

Barker watched quizzically as Kaye went back to the truck, lifted Reid and the cop's belongings out of the back seat, and walked back to the door.

"This better be good," Barker said as he stood out of the way, let Kaye pass and followed him in.

"Citizen's arrest pursuant to California Penal Code," Kaye said with a smile.

"The charge?"

"Kidnapping, multiple counts, for starters."

"No kidding?" Barker leaned over to look more closely at Reid. "Hey, isn't he…?"

"Yes, he is," Kaye said. "I need you to hold him in close custody, no outside contact. Get in touch with your Deputy Stephenson. Tell him this is about the Nicole Ingram case, and several others. We've talked. He'll get it."

"I can do that."

"Want me to carry him back for you?"

"Not necessary. We'll handle it," Barker said. "Where you headed now?"

A half-smile curled Kaye's lip.

"It's late, but I'm going out for Italian."

# DAY 25
## Thursday Week 4

It was just after midnight when Kaye drove past the western Welcome to the Village of Chumash Oaks sign at a sedate 25 miles per hour. He turned north on DaVinci Lane.

About a half-mile south of the village he met a patrol unit heading south. He watched the rearview mirror anxiously. The patrol car didn't go far before its brake lights lit up and it made a fast, shoulder-to-shoulder u-turn before the emergency lights lit up.

"Damn it," he muttered to himself, pulling over and hoping the patrol passed him by.

He'd kept Reid's portable radio and heard the stop call.

"Central, CO-eight, traffic."

"Go ahead."

"DaVinci half-mile south of the Village. Possible match on the BOLO vehicle. Paper plate," she read off the number, "start four this way."

Spotlights lit up the truck and Kaye heard the dispatcher send backup before he switched the radio off and stuffed it under the seat.

"Driver," he heard the officer's voice over the unit's loudspeaker, "step out with your hands up and face the front of your truck."

The image of Auggie the first time he'd met her flashed through his mind, and for an instant he considered not complying and taking his chances. He wanted her back. Anybody who stood in his way was simply somebody to be removed.

But he knew he couldn't remove anyone until he removed himself from the truck.

He followed the orders.

In the distance he saw another set of overheads coming fast from San Marcos Pass Road.

It was less than five seconds before the spotlights went off and he heard an approaching voice.

"Central, CO-eight. Code four. Not a match. Cancel backup."

The approaching lights went dark.

"Detective Kaye, fancy meeting you here. You can put your hands down."

Kaye turned toward the voice. Dressed in a Chumash Oaks PD uniform and holstering her pistol as she got closer was Elizabeth, the former Marine Captain he'd met at Black Scimitar.

"Good evening, Captain," he said. "Wish I could say this is a pleasant surprise."

"Yeah, well, sorry. But your truck's a close match for one we're looking for. You, though, are not."

"Good to know."

"What brings you to our fair city this time of night?"

"Looking for a friend."

"Anyone in particular?"

"Really none of your business, Officer," he looked at the name plate on her shirt pocket, "Latham."

An oncoming car slowed as it went by. It was the unit originally sent as backup, coming by just to make sure. Latham slightly raised her hand and flashed four fingers. The officer behind the wheel nodded, then looked Kaye over before continuing on.

"Another Black Scimitar hired gun?" Kaye asked.

"No," Latham replied. "Regular PD."

"How long have you worked here?"

"About a week," Latham replied. "Tomorrow is actually my first day off. I think Adrian got tired of paying me what he pays me to answer the phone, so here I am."

"You're okay with this?"

"Why wouldn't I be?"

"Met Lorenzo yet?" Kaye asked. "I think he goes by Renzo here in America."

"Who's that?" Latham asked, a little too quickly.

Kaye didn't buy it, convinced she was telling him what she thought he wanted to hear.

"Have a nice evening, Officer Latham," he said and turned back to the pickup.

"Kaye, hold on," Latham said.

He turned back. "What?"

"Go home. You're out of your jurisdiction and in way over your head. This will end badly for you."

"I told you," Kaye said, "I'm not working. I'm here to see a friend."

"That's not what I hear," Latham said.

"Who'd you hear that from?"

Latham didn't answer.

Kaye waited.

"You'll never get in," she said after a moment.

"Get in where?" Kaye asked.

Latham went quiet again for a moment, her lips pursed.

"Remember our conversation about Colonel Petrov?" she asked finally. "And you? About disobeying a direct order for the greater good?"

"I remember."

"Well," Latham said slowly, "I can help you."

"By disobeying a direct order from Gagnon?" Kaye asked.

"No."

"Lorenzo Maisano?"

"God, no."

"So, who's your...?" Kaye started to ask, then suddenly got it. Latham was a deep cover asset for somebody, probably the FBI, keeping track of Lorenzo Maisano's business interests in the United States.

"I can help," Latham repeated. "To a point. But you have to trust me."

"What point is that?" Kaye asked.

"You can't get to Maisano's house by car without going through the hotel parking structure and out a private exit on the other side. Everything is secured and controlled."

"And you can't get into the parking garage without being a guest," Kaye said, remembering being turned away.

"Or an employee, or Village cop."

"Can I get to Maisano's on foot?"

"You know what a ha-ha is?"

"A good laugh?"

"Not in this case. It's a kind of wall built below grade instead of above, then the ground is contoured to create a barrier. It doesn't obstruct the view, and in the old days it kept the sheep off the manor house lawn."

"I assume you're telling me that because Maisano's house is surrounded by them, right, and not as a history lesson?"

"Correct," Latham said. "I'm guessing close to fifteen feet. Pretty steep, even for someone with your capabilities. The satellite photos show a helipad."

"You've seen satellite photos?" Kaye asked.

"Check the internet, Kaye," she said, smiling slightly. "It's amazing."

"Have you been to the house?" Kaye asked.

"I've been here less than a week. I'm not high on anybody's trust list just yet."

"But you know what's going on."

"I wouldn't be here if there weren't rumors," Latham replied.

"It's more than rumors."

"So, you want my help?"

"Of course," Kaye replied.

"I have one question for you first," Latham said. "Is Reid alive?"

"Of course he's alive," Kaye said. "He's in county custody, close security."

"Did he plant drugs in your truck?"

"He did. A kilo of heroin. I have it."

"Good to know."

She took two quick steps back, drew her pistol and pointed it at Kaye's chest.

"Put your hands up and don't move. You're under arrest for possession of narcotics," she said before reaching for the microphone clipped to her shirt. "Central, CO-eight. One in custody. Request assistance."

Dumbfounded, Kaye stared at her.

"Relax, big guy," she said without lowering the pistol. "This is the fastest, and maybe the only, way for us both to get into Maisano's house and save your friend. So make it look good."

***

The holding cell was small, maybe six by eight feet. A closet, really. Except for the stainless steel toilet and sink, the small square of wire reinforced plexiglass in the door and the thin, red vinyl mat on the bunk bolted to the floor, the entire space was that color of pale green favored by hospitals and jails everywhere.

Kaye was stretched out on the poor excuse for a mattress, his right shoulder beyond the edge of the too-narrow bunk.

Latham had booked him, and during the process the on-duty supervisor had informed him that his truck and the envelope of cash were being seized as ill-gotten gains.

Not a word was said by Latham about him being an LAPD detective, but he had the uncomfortable feeling everybody knew who he was.

In the Corps he'd learned to sleep anywhere, anytime, and he took advantage of that ability now.

The loud buzzing of the door lock disengaging brought him instantly awake and he saw Latham's face through the plexiglass.

"Stand up and step away from the door," Latham ordered.

He did, his calves bumping against the rim of the toilet.

The door swung open and Latham stepped through. Behind her, a taser in one hand, stood Officer Hawkins.

"Rise and shine, Mr. Kaye," Latham said. "Time to go."

"Go where?"

"The next station down the line for the justice train," Latham replied. "Turn around and put your hands behind your back."

Kaye complied and felt a riot cuff tighten around his wrists.

"Use regular cuffs, Officer Latham," he heard Hawkins say.

"Can't," Latham said. "His wrists are too big."

"What time is it?" Kaye asked.

"Zero seven hundred," Latham said.

"Are we going to County?" Kaye asked.

"Shut-up, asshole," Hawkins growled, prodding Kaye in the back. "This isn't twenty questions. Just keep your mouth shut and do what you're told."

Kaye was put in the back seat of a unit already parked in the sally port.

"I'll drive," Hawkins said.

"Oh," Latham said, surprised. "Okay."

When Hawkins got to DaVinci Lane he turned north instead of south toward San Marcos Pass Road.

"Aren't we going to County?" Latham asked.

Hawkins glanced sideways at Latham but didn't say anything.

Kaye kept silent, looking out the window as they drove through the Village. He was struck by how his impression had changed from his first visit, when he'd found it festive, beautiful and inspired. Now, early in the day and the streets and walkways almost deserted, it seemed somehow ominous and Kaye felt a sudden sense of foreboding.

At the traffic circle beneath the hotel ramparts Hawkins went right, down the hill toward the parking garage.

The gate went up as they approached and the sleepy guard waved half-heartedly as the unit passed by.

Inside, Hawkins drove ahead to the row farthest from the entrance, turned right, and headed for the far corner.

Kaye noticed that even though they'd entered at ground level, each of the support columns bore a brightly painted '2' and a letter denoting the section.

There was a ramp heading down at the end of Section D. A metal gate barred the way and on the wall above the ramp was a sign.

## NO GUEST PARKING
### Hotel and Service Vehicles Only

Hawkins stopped at a keypad outside the gate, punched in a code and waited for the gate to rise before driving down the ramp. Then he simply ignored the lines painted on the concrete and steered the straightest possible course to a visible exit on the far side.

The columns now all bore the number '1', but the level was almost empty. There was a small knot of vehicles parked near the elevators and another group parked along the wall not far from the exit.

As Hawkins approached the exit and slowed, Kaye sat up straight and stared. The first vehicle in the line was a silver Jetta with no plates.

A surge of adrenaline-fueled rage coursed through Kaye as he scanned the other vehicles. He couldn't remember every car listed on the report Mitchell had forwarded, but he knew the dark green Jeep Cherokee, the blue Honda and a couple of the others.

His heart raced and his rage grew when he saw the vehicle parked last in the line.

Partly covered with a hastily tied blue tarp was Auggie McMaster's Street Glide.

Seconds later Hawkins pulled up to another keypad, entered the code and drove out into the bright morning sun.

It wasn't a direct drive. The road followed the rolling contours of the vineyards and Kaye frequently lost sight of the house. It dawned on him after the second sharp turn that the road had been built to slow approaching vehicles. After several minutes and several more turns the road crested a small rise and the house was directly ahead.

It was a spectacular modern interpretation of a traditional Italian farmhouse.

But it was the wall that got Kaye's immediate attention, and it was no laughing matter. Tip-up concrete panels at least fifteen feet tall formed an escarpment, atop which sat the house, that gradually curved out of sight on both sides. Many of the panels were adorned with low relief sculptures depicting life in old Italy and Roman times.

Kaye's first thought was that he could have climbed them. But when he looked at the top he saw downward curving steel barriers that protruded nearly five feet outward. Even he would have had a hard time with them.

The road went down the slope, straight to the wall and dead-ended.

Hawkins pulled up, stopped, and made a call on his cell phone.

"We're here," was all the cop said.

Seconds later the panel directly in front of the patrol car began to rise and Kaye realized it was a steel door, painted with a trompe l'oeil depiction of an ancient Roman bath.

Hawkins pulled into a sizable, well-lit, concrete-floored garage space. Several vehicles, ranging from four-wheelers to a Benz SLS AMG gullwing, were parked randomly.

Parked by the far wall, near the only opening out of the space Kaye could see, was a white Hayabusa.

"Stay in the car," Hawkins ordered Latham as he got out.

Two men in suits approached and conferred with Hawkins. After a moment, Hawkins came around and opened Latham's door.

"You can get out now," he said. "But your gun belt and weapon stay in the car."

"What?" Latham asked. "Why?"

"House rules," Hawkins said, shrugging. "It's your first visit. I had to do it, too."

"When do I get it back?" Latham asked.

"When you leave," Hawkins replied. "Look, relax. Mr. Maisano wants to meet you. These guys," he looked over his shoulder at the suits, "are ours."

Hawkins closed Latham's door behind her, turned to the two guards, and nodded. They advanced toward the unit, each now cradling an Uzi machine pistol, and the stockier of the two leaned in and opened the back door.

"Out," he ordered Kaye.

Kaye slid out and stood up.

"Step to the wall and put your nose against it."

Kaye complied, looking around as he stepped forward. He saw only the one exit, the wide hallway next to the Hayabusa, and it didn't go far before making a right turn.

The guard used an electronic wand to search Kaye.

"Elevator or stairs?" asked the second guard, taller and leaner.

"Stairs," the first guard said. "I don't fancy being in a confined space with this guy."

"Roger that," the second guard said.

"Okay, big guy," the stocky guard said, poking Kaye in the back with the muzzle of his Uzi. "Lead the way, that hallway you were checking out. And funny stuff gets you dead. Got it?"

Kaye turned and stared into the guard's eyes until the man broke eye contact, then started walking toward the hall. He didn't see Hawkins or Latham and assumed they had gone upstairs while he was against the wall.

The two guards trailed Kaye by a respectful distance after entering the hallway and making the turn. Almost immediately there was a slight bend to the left and Kaye saw the bottom of a wide set of stairs.

"Stop," the first guard ordered when Kaye reached the bottom of the stairs. "Nose against the wall."

Kaye again assumed the position and heard what sounded like the second guard hustling up the stairs.

"Turn around," the guard said. "Up you go, and play nice." He smiled a shark smile.

Kaye turned around. The second guard was, indeed gone. He looked up the stairs. It was wide, six feet or so, and curved. The top was not in sight.

"Move," the guard behind him ordered.

Kaye looked at the guard, looked up the stairs, and saw an opportunity. He took off, taking five steps at a time. On the way up he exerted all his strength against the riot cuff, breaking it.

"He's loose!" the guard at the bottom shouted.

The guard at the top wasn't ready. Kaye got to him before he could react, swatting the Uzi from his hands before grabbing him by the throat and spinning him around to use as a shield against the guard now rushing up the stairs.

For a brief moment, there was a stand-off.

Then Kaye heard a man's voice behind him.

"Let him go, or your friend dies."

Kaye glanced over his shoulder. Ten feet away, in an archway that opened to what looked like the house's main living area, stood a young, heavyset man with jet black hair. His right hand was clasped around

Auggie McMaster's upper left arm and in his left he had a pistol jammed against her ribs.

"After all, I assume she's why you're here," the man said.

"She is," Kaye said, releasing his grip in the guard. "Her, Nicole Ingram and, what, about a dozen other young women?"

The guard Kaye had overwhelmed immediately retrieved his weapon and lifted it toward Kaye.

"Stand down," the first guard said sharply from two steps down, then looked at the man holding Auggie. "Sorry, sir. He broke the riot cuff. I've never seen anybody do that."

"That's because you have never encountered a warrior like Benkei."

Heads turned. Kaye looked down to see Tamara Goschen mounting the stairs. Dressed in workout gear, she carried a kendo helmet under her left arm and a bamboo *shinai* in her right hand. Her shoulders were bare and the tattoo of the fierce Hayabusa *tengu* seemed to glow under the sheen of perspiration. Her lithe movements as she climbed made the *tengu* appear to fly.

"*Yokoso, Benkei.*" Goschen said as she topped the stairs. Welcome.

"I don't speak Japanese," Kaye said. "Or read Kanji."

Goshen smiled, raised the bamboo practice sword and placed its tip against Kaye's chest.

"You do, Benkei," she said, putting slight pressure on the sword. "You just choose not to remember. I was welcoming you to my home."

"The name is Kaye. Detective, Los Angeles Police Department. And you, lady, are insane."

Goschen laughed and lowered the *shinai*. She brushed past Kaye and walked to the man still holding Auggie.

"Good morning, Renzo my darling," she said and leaned in to kiss him on the cheek. "I see you've met Benkei."

"Good morning, my love, and you described him perfectly," Maisano said in return before turning to Kaye. "Please join us, Detective."

"You're Lorenzo Maisano?" Kaye asked, looking at Maisano as he walked into the spacious living room. "I was expecting...I don't know. A grown-up?"

Maisano instantly scowled and turned bright red. "Be careful. My grandfather put me in charge here for a reason."

Kaye kept walking toward Auggie, who had not yet acknowledged his presence or made any attempt to escape Maisano's grasp.

"Auggie," he said when he got close, "are you all right?"

She turned her head at the sound of her name. Kaye saw that her eyes were glazed and lacked focus.

"I'm better than that," she said, her words slow and slurred. "I'm flyin', man." She smiled.

"What did you give her?" Kaye asked, turning to Maisano.

"Just a little something to welcome her to the family," Maisano replied. He led Auggie to a chair near the expansive windows and sat her down. She immediately fixed on the view of the surrounding vineyards and ignored Kaye.

Maisano tucked his pistol into his waistband.

Goschen walked to a side table against the far wall and placed her *Ben* and practice sword on it. She tied an obi around her waist, picked up a long sword and dagger, and slid them into the obi.

The two guards stayed, taking up positions on opposite sides of the large room.

Kaye watched, studying the space at the same time. It was impressive, but to him it was now a prison with no clear avenue of escape.

"This was all your grandfather's idea?" Kaye asked. "The resort, the vineyards, everything?"

"It was," Maisano said. "He planned it for years as his retirement venture. It was all quite simple, really, once he found the right lawyers."

"And paid the right people," Kaye added.

"Of course," Maisano said, smiling. "Business is business on both sides of the Atlantic."

"What I don't get," Kaye said, "is why not leave it legit? You've got to be making a bundle. Why risk bringing heat on the whole place?"

Maisano smiled. "My grandfather failed to see the full potential of the enterprise. I'm simply taking advantage of the opportunities afforded by the laws of your wonderful country."

"I'm not so sure he'll see it that way when the whole place is taken away from him and you go to prison for life," Kaye said.

Maisano laughed and turned to Goschen. "Are you ready to take care of our business?"

"I am," she replied, then turned to one of the guards. "Please bring Elizabeth to the patio."

The guard nodded and headed for the stairs.

"Let's go outside, shall we?" Maisano said to Kaye. "You'll be astounded by the beauty of the falling sun."

The phrase instantly clicked in Kaye's mind. The nickname of Tomoe Gozen, *onna-musha*.

The remaining guard opened a wide, sliding glass panel the size of a barn door, then turned to Kaye and waved him through.

Goschen followed, then Maisano, again holding Auggie by the arm and steering her along.

It was a large space, paved with cobbles. The seating and plantings were all purposely low to the keep the view of the vineyards, undulating in the morning breeze like a rolling green sea, unobstructed. Maisano led Auggie to a bench near the edge of the space and sat her down. Kaye followed and stood only a few feet from her. She looked up at him and smiled vacantly.

"Hey, I know you. You're Johnny Strabler," she said. Then her attention was caught by a soaring hawk and she looked away to track its flight.

Kaye looked around. He could see the tail rotor and most of the fuselage of a helicopter beyond the corner of the house. But he could also tell that beyond the planters was nothing but air, the drop-off of the ha-ha fence Latham had described.

Goschen walked over and stood so close to him he could feel the heat emanating from her. The tip of her tanto pressed against his lower abdomen.

"Our business will be last, Benkei," she whispered. "I have some housekeeping to do first."

"You're not Tomoe Gozen," Kaye said. "You're a delusional –"

"Oh, but I am," she hissed back. "I have waited many lifetimes to avenge Yoshinaka, my Lord and husband. Now my *tengu* has answered my prayers and led me to you. Today you die again, Benkei, and this time you will fall."

"There is no honor in murder," Kaye said, changing tactics. "Your sword is legendary, *onna-musha*. The Hayabusa. But so is mine. I challenge you to a fair fight."

Goschen's gaze didn't falter as she said, "No, Benkei. Today I assert *tsujigiri* to honor my new katana and let it taste your blood."

Kaye had no idea what she meant, and before he could ask his attention was drawn to the guard leading Elizabeth Latham out onto the patio.

Goschen spun and walked to Latham.

"Elizabeth," she said. "Thank you for bringing Benkei to me. I

341

appreciate it very much. But things have changed."

"Changed?" Latham echoed. "How so?"

"I usually invite people to the house when they have gained my trust and I believe they are ready to join our enterprise," Goschen said. "Unfortunately, I will not be able to extend that opportunity to you."

"I don't understand," Latham said, looking from Goschen to Maisano and back. "I've been a loyal Black Scimitar asset for almost two years. Are you firing me?"

"Not exactly," Goschen said.

"I'm sorry, Elizabeth," Maisano spoke up as he walked toward Latham. "But we have discovered that your true loyalties lie elsewhere."

"Elsewhere?" Latham asked, and Kaye saw the first hint of panic in her eyes. "What are you talking about?"

"You work for the American federal government," Maisano said. "Such a shame. Adrian was devastated to find out."

"But, I... That's a lie... I don't..." Latham started to protest, looking to Kaye for help.

Kaye saw Goschen reach across her body with her right hand. He started forward, but the guard he'd overpowered on the stairs stepped in front of him, raised his Uzi and said, "Uh-uh."

Latham's protest stopped as Goschen's short blade slid easily through her ballistic vest and sunk into her abdomen.

Kaye saw Goschen elbow jerk backwards as the sideways cut was made, then Goschen stepped back.

Stunned, Latham was looking down as she tried to cover the gash with her hands, then she beseechingly looked again at Kaye.

Goschen moved quickly, stepping around Latham and drawing her long blade.

"Semper fi," Latham managed to squeak just as Goschen's vicious horizontal strike took off her head.

As Latham collapsed to the cobbles Goschen, and her blade, kept moving. Taking a long, sliding sideways step she reversed the stroke, looped the blade and, with a downward chop, severed the hand of the guard standing between her and Kaye.

The hand, still grasping the Uzi, fell to the patio. Blood squirted from the shocked guard's wrist as he turned and looked questioningly at Goschen.

"You brought dishonor to my house and yourself on the stairs," she said, then lunged forward and sunk her blade into his throat until a foot of bloody steel protruded from the back of his neck.

She was a millisecond slow withdrawing the blade and the weight of the falling dead man overbalanced her, causing her to stagger slightly and put a hand to the ground to keep her balance as the guard went down.

The second guard started to raise his Uzi toward Goschen, but Maisano stepped forward, pistol pointed at the man, and shouted, "Stand down!" Then he turned to Kaye and said, "I told you it would be beautiful," before starting toward Goschen.

While their backs were turned, Kaye saw his opportunity for escape.

He reached for Auggie, yanked her to her feet, wrapped one giant arm around her waist, took three quick steps to the planter that edged the patio, planted a foot on it, and leapt into space.

Auggie screamed.

***

It was about fifteen feet, plus the planter height. With Auggie's added weight it taxed even Kaye's legs.

There was a slight downgrade where he landed, and he used it to his advantage. With Auggie's added weight he wasn't able to stay on his feet, but did manage to avoid injury.

He quickly gathered himself and looked up.

An angry Goschen peered down from above.

"I will catch you, Benkei!" she screamed. "You cannot escape me!"

Maisano's head appeared and he pointed his pistol down at them.

Goschen stayed him with her arm and said something Kaye couldn't make out, then both disappeared.

Making sure he had a firm grip on Auggie, he took stock of his situation. From where he stood the ground sloped up, away from the ha-ha, to the grade of the vineyard.

He moved as quickly as he could with Auggie in tow. At the top of the slope he saw that the vines had been planted to run directly away from the house for about a quarter mile. Beyond that, the rows looked to Kaye to change direction by almost ninety degrees.

He'd be easily visible from the house until they reached the second planting area and could disappear between the rows.

Kaye couldn't see the hotel. The sun and shadows told him instantly that he had to be on the north side of the house.

343

The wrong direction, he thought, then corrected himself. South would be no better. There'd be no help for them in the Village of Chumash Oaks. Renzo Maisano owned it, and everybody in it.

There had to be other vineyards, other ranches in the hills, and they'd have phones. He'd just have to find one.

He hadn't gone fifty yards before he knew it would be faster if he just carried Auggie. He spun her around, bent down, put her across his back and shoulders in a fireman's carry and started jogging north. When he reached the change in vine row direction, Kaye turned around to look behind him. He was just in time to see a figure step onto the patio planter, pause, then step off the wall.

It had to be Goschen, and he knew she had likely seen them from atop the rampart before jumping. She, too, lost her footing, and he watched her gather herself and get reorganized.

Then she came, and Kaye knew instantly he'd never outdistance her as long as he carried Auggie and Goschen could see him.

He picked a row and started jogging again. The mature vines were slightly taller than he was, and he knew Goschen could no longer see them.

But now he was no longer going north. In fact, because the vines were planted to take advantage of the natural contours of the land, he realized he was slowly turning to the east.

"Shit," he muttered, but kept going.

A quarter mile later he came to a dirt road that crossed the rows of vines. He knew instantly that the vineyard wasn't just endless rows of grape vines. There had to be access for workers, implements and equipment, and that meant a basic grid, even if it was modified for the terrain.

The road led north and the hills looked tantalizingly closer, but Kaye knew he still had ground to cover.

He turned north and started jogging again, his spirits buoyed. He now felt he had the advantage. Goschen could chase him forever in this giant, green maze without finding him before he found a way out.

The key would be to not stay on the same road or row long enough to be seen from a distance. He counted ten rows, then turned left and headed west.

He followed the row around the shoulder of a slight hill. Just as he reached an intersecting road that headed north and decided to take it, he heard a noise and stopped.

It grew louder and Kaye instantly knew what it was.

344

The helicopter.

"Damn it," he cursed.

Game over.

He started toward the access road again and made some decisions. He would choose the place, and he would need to be rested and ready.

And he needed a weapon.

At the crest of a small rise, he stopped and looked in all four directions. Northward from where he stood the road sloped gently downward. A hundred yards away there was an irregular, jagged break in the vines before the road started up toward the next rise. A lone tree, the only one for miles, grew at the low point of the road and Kaye realized the jagged line of vine ends marked a creek.

That's as good a place as any, he thought as he headed down the hill. As he got closer he saw a bridge spanning the creek, next to which grew the giant, ancient oak offering shade and concealment.

The rudimentary bridge had no railing and the distance down to the creek was minimal, so Kaye carried Auggie into the oak's deep shade and carefully propped her against its giant trunk.

She stirred and her eyes fluttered open.

"Ben?" she barely whispered. "Is that you? Oh, God, I knew you would come. Help me, Ben. Get me away from these people, please."

"I will," he said, brushing her hair from her face. "I will. I promise."

"They drugged me," she whispered.

"I know. It's okay. We'll fix it."

"Where are we?" she asked, looking around.

"Safe," he replied, hearing the sound of the approaching helicopter.

"Where are we going?" she asked, then instantly added, "No, I don't care, as long as you're there and it's far away."

The helicopter flew directly overhead at an altitude of only a hundred feet and continued on its way.

The tree had kept them from being seen.

"Auggie, go back to sleep, okay? I'll come get you when it's time."

"Okay," she said breathlessly, then opened her eyes and looked into Kaye's. "I love you, Johnny Strabler," she whispered, then laughed and sank back into a stupor.

Kaye knew he had only minutes. He'd carried Auggie at least a mile and a half and his shirt was soaked. He clambered down the creek bank to see if there was water. A small trickle flowed over the rocky creek bottom. He studied it for a moment, then used his cupped hand to scoop it up and slake his thirst.

He needed a weapon. Goschen would surely come with two, maybe even three, blades. Wood would be useless against the layered steel of a katana. He needed metal, the stouter the better.

Kaye looked around. He stood on an island of shade in a sea of green. The end of a vine row caught his eye. It was anchored by a thick wooden pole that angled steeply away from the vines. A heavy cable, about ten feet long, was looped around the post near the top and anchored into the ground at a counter-angle. Two wires attached to the post disappeared into the vines at different heights, and Kaye saw what he thought was some kind of tensioning mechanism.

He looked down the row. There was no chance those two wires supported the entire weight of the vines over that kind of distance, no matter how taut you could make them.

There had to be more posts.

Please let them be metal, he thought as he stepped into the sun and trotted to the closest vine.

He found it only twenty feet in. A standard green and white metal t-post used by ranchers and farmers everywhere to string fence wire. The tensioned support wires passed through small grommets, attached between studs, that allowed the wires to slide, but still provide support. Kaye guessed that there was five feet of post, mostly obscured by vines, above ground.

It might work. If he could get it out of the ground.

Kaye started tearing away the vines. Soon the post stood exposed., surrounded by a circle of leafy green debris.

But he was immediately stymied. He had no way to cut the wires, and no way to remove the grommet attachments, which meant the post was still part of a larger structure, and the clock was ticking.

Frustrated, he grabbed the post with both hands and used all his strength in an attempt to loosen it from the soil. From the angles, he guessed it was sunk in some two feet, and he knew it had a barb near the bottom to keep it in.

When he felt the post was as loose as it would get by pulling and pushing it back and forth, Kaye stepped in, half-squatted, grabbed it with both hands as far down as he could, and pulled mightily. After a few seconds of resistance the post came loose.

But before it came completely out of the ground it came up against the tension of the wires and stopped.

"Damn, damn, damn," Kaye muttered, although he felt like screaming.

He'd have to break the attachments somehow or the entire effort would be a waste of time.

He tried his hands, but the hardware was too small for him to get a grip and too tightly attached for him to pry loose.

He needed a hammer. He thought how easy it would be if he was just in his shop overlooking the Pacific, and how absurd it would be to die in the middle of a bunch of grapes for lack of a hammer.

"Think, Ben," he said aloud, his hands wrapped around the top wire on either side of the t-post. "Think!"

He looked around. There wasn't even a decent-sized rock around.

He let go of the wire, ran to the bridge and scrambled down into the creek bed. Rocks everywhere, but they all seemed to be round, weathered smooth by eons of tumbling in the stream. He need one with an edge, something he could strike with.

He turned his attention away from the stream bed to the bank where it had been altered to support the bridge span. It only took him seconds to find a stone he hoped would work.

He ran back to the post, grabbed it with one hand and started pounding on the top attachment. It took only three blows to break it, the bottom one lasted only two.

Triumphantly, Kaye yanked the post from the ground. It was easily seven feet long, with the expected barb near the bottom end. The side that formed the top of the 'T' bore short studs designed to keep wire from sagging to the ground.

He hefted it with both hands, his mind going back to his pugil stick combat training in boot camp. He'd been good at it, his speed and overpowering strength besting even the instructors.

The barb slightly overbalanced one end, but a grip change compensated nicely.

"Okay," he said, "*onna-musha*, or *tengu*, or whatever the hell you think you are, bring it. Benkei is ready."

He turned and headed for the bridge, another drink, and some shade.

Two steps later her heard the sound of the helicopter. He scanned the sky and saw it off to the northwest, about a half-mile out.

Headed directly for him.

***

Less than a minute later the helicopter hovered one hundred feet above the tree. The rotor wash whipped the topmost branches, and even at ground level Kaye could feel the turbulence.

The noise disturbed Auggie. She rolled, sat up, saw Kaye, smiled and wordlessly sank back into the dark abyss visited only by addicts coming off a high.

Kaye walked to a point where he could look up and see which way the chopper cockpit was pointing, assuming that would be the direction Goschen would come from, and turned to watch.

He didn't wait long.

A figure crested the small rise to the south and headed down toward the bridge. The silhouette was odd, and from a distance Kaye couldn't really tell who it was.

As the figure got closer, though, Kaye recognized Goschen. She wore a tight-fitting cuirass of many small pieces lacquered a deep, blood red, a set of similarly constructed shoulder guards, thigh covers and a helmet shaped and painted into the image of the *tengu* tattooed on her shoulder.

When she was fifty feet away Kaye stepped from the shelter of the oak, fence post in one hand, strode to the middle of the bridge and stopped.

Goschen saw him and stopped. She waved to the helicopter, which peeled away and took up a new position some distance away.

Goschen came on, then stopped again just before stepping onto the bridge.

Kaye saw her smile beneath the nose guard of her helmet.

"Your irony honors me, Benkei," she said, nodding her head in a quick bow of acknowledgement.

"What irony would that be?" Kaye asked.

"That you will die on a bridge today as you did for your Lord, Yoshitune."

"I have no intention of dying today, on a bridge or anywhere else," Kaye said. "I'm a police officer. You, Tamara Goschen, are under arrest for kidnapping and murder. If you come after me with a sword I'm within my rights to kill you. Surrender now."

Goschen laughed.

"You study, Benkei," she said, "but you do not truly believe."

She echoed Roshi's words, and they stung Kaye.

348

"Believe what?"

"Eternal consciousness. We have each lived and died many times since Yoritomo became Shogun. Today will be the next re-birth for you."

Goschen withdrew her katana from its scabbard, grasped the long hilt with both hands, held it directly in front of her body, tip pointed at Kaye, and started forward with long, sliding steps.

As she advanced, Kaye developed a strategy. Goschen's katana blade was about two and a half feet long. With his two-handed grip, if he kept at least the equivalent of the blade length outside each hand and kept her hands outside the post, her blade couldn't reach him. The t-post was at least seven feet and change, giving him more than enough length.

He held the post so the studs faced Goschen, hoping they would provide some measure of protection should her blade slide down the post toward his exposed hands. She was clearly right-handed, so he held the barbed end of the post out to his left.

Kaye knew he was overthinking, and he also knew it was because he was afraid. He thought of his family, his often contentious relationship with his father, his time in the Corps, his life with Amy and how much he still missed her.

That caused him to steal a glance toward Auggie McMaster.

If he died, she died, too.

He wasn't about to let that happen.

He swung the t-post up into the two-hand grip and assumed a combat stance.

The move brought Goschen to a halt. She studied Kaye for a moment, shifted the katana to her right hand, and with her left drew the short sword. Then she again advanced warily.

Goschen's first attack was a blinding fury of feints and slashes with both blades, Kaye's head her primary target.

Kaye's speed and the length of the post countered each move. His hands stung from the impacts as the ringing of steel on steel filled the vineyard.

Goschen backed off to regroup. She fixed Kaye with the flat stare of a predator measuring its prey, then launched a second attack.

This time the target was Kaye's legs.

She came in with a low, crossing slash with the katana, which Kaye blocked. But she didn't withdraw the long sword, keeping it locked against the post as she lunged forward with the short blade directly at

Kaye's belly.

It almost ended Kaye's life. Swinging the post in a block of the short sword would have let the katana through, and only his amazing strength and body control allowed him to twist just enough to avoid the thrust. Still, the blade sliced through his shirt and left a shallow cut on his side.

Goschen retreated and smiled.

"Benkei, you bleed."

Kaye looked down. Blood stained his shirt, but he knew it wasn't enough to cost him the battle. But it did galvanize him, telling him he couldn't win by just playing defense. Eventually, one of Goschen's blades would find home.

He needed to kill her before she killed him, and he needed a psychological edge.

"You will bleed today, too, *onna-musha*," he said. "It took archers to kill me at Koronogama Castle, and I, alone, first killed three hundred of Yoritomo's samurai. You are only one."

She smiled and stared. "Ah, Benkei, you do remember. But I promise you that today the beauty of the falling sun will shine its light on your corpse."

Making small circles with the ends of the post, Kaye waited.

She came at him, blades flying. She led this time with the short sword, sweeping across at waist level while she held the katana over her head and behind her back.

Kaye saw the strategy instantly. If he stayed low with the post to block the short sword strike, Goschen would have a clear downward stroke at his head, no doubt cleaving him open all the way to his sternum.

Instead, he feinted with the left end of the post and took a half-step to his right. The short blade found only empty space where milliseconds before he'd stood. At the same time, Goschen brought the long sword up, over and down with the speed and ferocity of a striking cobra.

But Kaye was ready. He brought the t-post up at an angle, meeting the blade a foot outside his left hand and deflecting it downward, away from his hands. The blade played a high-pitched, staccato tune as it rode the studs toward the ground.

Goschen's own momentum overbalanced her just enough for Kaye to use the right side of the post to aim a vicious strike at her head. She deflected the blow with her short sword so it instead hit the armor of her shoulder covers, but it drove her to one knee.

Rather than advance, Kaye retreated, and it saved his life.

Goschen spun her katana in her hand and made an upward slash that would have taken Kaye's arm and ended the battle had it landed.

Kaye waited, watching Goschen. When she stood he saw a first, fleeting glimmer of doubt in her eyes, but she masked it instantly.

Instead of attacking head-on, Goschen now slowly circled Kaye, looking for an opening.

It gave Kaye time to strategize. The blow to her shoulder should have broken bone, but the ancient *rokugu* armor had absorbed much of the impact. Only Goschen's forearms and lower legs were not covered.

He weathered two more attacks, sustaining a slight cut to his forearm, before he anticipated correctly and finally found an opening.

Goschen came at him with the long sword and he again deflected the blow, but this time used all his strength to bounce her blade upward. Then, with lightning speed, he dropped into a spinning squat, letting the post slide through his hands until he held it near the barb-less end. The post carved a deadly arc, the barb catching Goschen in the lower left leg just as she stepped forward and put all her weight on it in preparation for a vicious, slicing blow directed at Kaye's head.

Kaye heard the sound of breaking bones as the barb tore flesh from her calf and blood misted the air.

Screaming in agony, Goschen went down onto her left knee, her leg grotesquely torn and twisted, but blades still raised and ready.

Kaye stood up. Careful to stay beyond the reach of the katana he stepped forward and forcefully placed the barbed end of the post against her neck. Twice she slashed viciously at the unyielding steel before looking down in defeat.

"Fight's over," he said. "You lose."

Goschen looked up, glaring at him, then tossed her long sword to the ground in front of his feet.

"We will meet again, Benkei," she said, then lowered her right knee to the ground and pulled her helmet off, tossing it aside. "My *tengu* will find you again, and you will fall."

Before Kaye saw it coming and could react, Goschen reversed her short blade, grabbed it with both hands and plunged it into her lower abdomen below the body armor. With one last, quick stroke she disemboweled herself while staring into Kaye's eyes.

"Do not let me die without honor," she whispered, her eyes

351

beginning to lose focus. "Take...my..."

She toppled forward and died.

As Kaye stood over the body and his focus widened, he became aware that the noise of the helicopter was growing.

He looked up and saw the chopper coming at him, low and fast. Standing halfway outside, his foot braced on the right side landing skid, was Renzo Maisano. He held a rifle in his hands.

Kaye waited, the t-post in his right hand, and hoped the pilot was daring.

At only fifty feet away, and less than fifteen feet altitude, the pilot flared the nose of the chopper up and spun it to the left, offering Maisano a clear field of fire toward Kaye.

As Maisano raised the rifle, Kaye took the t-post up and back, took two quick steps forward and with all his strength launched the post like a javelin.

Then, without waiting to see if he'd even hit the helicopter, he turned and ran to his right, across the nose of the aircraft, hoping to take away Maisano's angle.

The noise of the chopper was deafening and Kaye suddenly felt himself engulfed by the main rotor's downwash as it passed directly over him, gaining altitude and taking a south heading.

Confused, Kaye stopped and watched as the helicopter flew away, then turned and ran for the tree.

As he crossed the bridge he glanced to his right and stopped. Renzo Maisano, the barbed end of the post protruding from his back, lay dead in the creek.

"I don't think grandpa is going to be happy," Kaye said aloud, then headed for the tree again.

Auggie was still only semi-conscious. Kaye gently picked her up, cradled her in his arms, and started walking north.

\*\*\*

It took thirty minutes to reach the edge of the vineyard, and another twenty before Kaye spied a house in the distance. It was clearly a cattle operation, not a vineyard, and, Auggie still in his arms and hers wrapped around his neck, he jogged across the pasture.

They were met by a woman cradling a .30-.30 Winchester in her arms.

Less than a minute later he was on the phone to a 9-1-1 dispatcher, requesting an ambulance and the Sheriff's Office.

Less than an hour later he and Auggie were both in the ER at the Santa Ynez hospital. Kaye had stitches in his side and a dressing on his arm wound. Auggie's blood work came back and the doctor immediately arranged for critical inpatient care in Santa Barbara.

He watched as Auggie was loaded into an air ambulance for transport. She was conscious and aware enough that he gave her a kiss on the forehead before the paramedics pushed the gurney aboard.

"Ben, what happened?" she asked, her voice soft. "I remember some strange stuff, but..."

"I'll tell you later," he said. "Over a great glass of wine."

She smiled and said, "I'd like that. I'd like that a lot."

\*\*\*

Ten minutes later Deputy Stephenson walked around the exam room curtain. The man's jaw dropped when Kaye told him what had been going on at Valle delle Viti.

"Late yesterday I got an urgent bulletin from someone named Mitchell," Stephenson said, "but I had no idea."

"That's what happens when the bad guys dress up like the good guys," Kaye said.

Stephenson excused himself and returned about fifteen minutes later.

"Okay," he said. "I've spoken to the Sheriff. He's gathering our people and called the State for all the CHP officers they can spare." The deputy saw the look on Kaye's face, smiled, and added, "There's about to be a hostile takeover at the Village of Chumash Oaks municipal building. Care to come along?"

"Wouldn't miss it," Kaye said grimly as he stood up.

On the way Kaye called Kai Iwamura.

"The bad news," he told the FBI agent after filling him in, "is that Elizabeth Latham, or whoever she really was, is dead. I'm assuming she was Bureau."

There was a protracted silence.

"I can't confirm that, Ben," Iwamura said at last. "But can you tell me who killed her?"

"A woman named Tamara Goschen. Her body, and Maisano's, are in the vineyard north of the house, maybe a mile and a half."

"Thanks for that," Iwamura said. "And don't worry about Gagnon or Feinmann. We'll pick them up."

When Kaye and Stephenson arrived in Chumash Oaks things were firmly in the hands of State and County authorities, with officers in tactical gear and carrying long guns stationed at strategic locations. One of them directed Stephenson to the CHP Chief in charge.

Stephenson introduced himself and Kaye.

"Nice work, Deputy Stephenson," the Chief said.

"Don't thank me, sir. Detective Kaye from LAPD broke this open, not me."

"Really?" the Chief said, looking Kaye, bedraggled and bandaged, over. "I should think you'll be in line for a commendation."

"I don't want a commendation," Kaye said. "Right now I just want my truck so I can go home."

The Chief waved another trooper over and told him to help Kaye find his truck and the keys.

"Before you go, Detective," the Chief said, "is there anything else you can tell me to help me out? This is a mess and will take a while to sort out."

"One thing," Kaye replied. "Look close at all the people. They're not all regular cops, some are contractors, and I know some of them are in this up to their eyeballs. You might also want to check the surrounding counties and see if they contract with an outfit called Black Scimitar for drug interdiction."

Ten minutes later Kaye had his truck and keys.

Three hours later he'd called Santa Barbara to make sure Auggie was in good hands, and was asleep in his own bed.

# DAY 26

Friday Week 4

It was mid-morning when Kaye, still tired and sore, pushed through the doors into the Squad. Captain Thompson saw him and went to meet him.

"What are you doing here?"

"Working," Kaye replied. "I've still got a murderer to catch."

"Bettencourt?"

"Yes, sir."

"He's in the system. Somebody will pick him up."

"I don't want 'somebody' to pick him up, Captain. I want it to be me."

"You sure you're up to it? Are you taking anything not over-the-counter?"

"No."

"Okay, then," Thompson said skeptically. "Just don't do anything stupid because you're tired." He spun on his heels and headed back to his office.

Kaye started organizing his hunt for Dennis Bettencourt. It would take time to get up on the killer's phone and credit cards – he realized he didn't even know if Bettencourt had a cell phone, and if he did, what the number was. That made him sit back and re-think.

It had been four days since he'd arrested Megan Sullivan. She had certainly been arraigned, and odds were she'd posted bond and was no longer in custody. Unless she was smart. But Kaye knew that one night in jail had probably made her forget all about the threat Bettencourt posed.

He snatched his desk phone handset and called the DA's office.

"Good morning, Counselor," he said when Kayla Okafor answered. "Hey, can you tell me if Megan Sullivan is still in custody?"

"She is not. She bonded out day before yesterday. Fifty thousand dollars, to be exact."

"Who posted it?"

"You're going to love this," Okafor said, paused a beat, and added,

355

"Howard Feinmann."

"Seriously? Conditions?"

"None. No prior record. Solid citizen with a job, cooperating with the prosecution. Close ties to the community, so the judge didn't consider her a flight risk. For the record, I argued against bail at the arraignment, but…."

Kaye was stunned. In his mind, Megan Sullivan was probably in the wind, if not dead.

"We can probably kiss her good-bye."

"My thoughts, exactly," Okafor said. "Hey, her decision. We warned her. She didn't have to go with Feinmann. Any luck finding Bettencourt?"

Kaye knew Okafor must not have any idea where he'd been the last two days. "Not yet. I've been gone since Wednesday. Just getting back in the loop."

"Well, get up to speed quickly, please. If Sullivan is still alive and you can find Bettencourt soon, she just might make it to the witness stand."

"You'll be the first to know."

He had to look up Sullivan's number in the case file. All he got was the provider recording that the number was not available.

One more.

"Iwamura," the FBI agent answered.

"Kai, it's Ben. Have your people picked up Adrian Gagnon or Howard Feinmann yet?"

"Hello to you, too," Iwamura said jokingly. "The answer to your question is yes, and no."

"Meaning?"

"We arrested Gagnon at LAX yesterday afternoon before he could board a flight out of the country. We don't have Feinmann yet."

"Are you looking? Actively, I mean."

"Hell, yes, we're looking." Iwamura paused, then asked, "Is there a problem?"

"Not sure," Kaye replied. "He bonded out a suspect in the Geller murder and I'm worried about her."

"You think he'd hurt her?"

"Feinmann? Probably not. But my other suspect, the shooter, yeah. I don't think he'd hesitate to kill her if he finds out she rolled on him."

"Not good," Iwamura said. "Who is she?"

Kaye shared the particulars on Megan Sullivan.

"Okay. We have agents looking for Feinmann as we speak. I'll make sure they get this information and if they come across the Sullivan woman they'll take her into protective custody."

"Thanks, Kai."

"You bet." There was a pause. "Her real name was Stephanie Sherman. Ex-Naval Intelligence, three years with us, almost two of those deep cover on Maisano and company."

Kaye knew Iwamura was talking about the woman he'd known as Elizabeth Latham.

"She broke the case, Kai. Not me. She put herself in harm's way to get me face-to-face with Renzo Maisano."

"I'll make sure the Director knows that. Coming from you, that will mean a lot."

"Lonsbury was running the case?"

"He was."

"Tell him I said hello."

"Will do."

Kaye leaned back in his chair and idly spun from side to side. After a moment he got up, grabbed his riding jacket and headed for the door.

He had one half-decent connection to Bettencourt, and his gut told him to exploit it.

\*\*\*

Kaye braked the Road King to a stop outside the Paloma Canyon Country Club parking gate. The kid working recognized him and, without a word, raised the bar and let him pass.

He parked, walked into the clubhouse and looked around.

No sign of Carol Soares.

He spent another five minutes looking, then gave up and headed for the club offices.

"Can I help you?" asked the young woman at the front desk.

"Detective Kaye, LAPD," he said, pulling back his jacket to expose his badge. "I'd like to see Carol Soares."

"I'm sorry, but Carol is no longer with the club."

"Really? When did that happen?"

"Wednesday was her last day."

"Did she give notice?"

"No," the young woman replied, shaking her head. "She just

walked in, handed the general manager her badge and keys, told him to just mail her check, and left."

"Did she say why she was quitting?"

"I think there was maybe a family emergency or something."

Nice, Kaye thought. All the rats are jumping ship.

"I'm going to need her address," he said. "And any phone numbers you have for her."

The woman's expression changed to one of uncertainty as she said, "I'm not sure I can –"

"Trust me," Kaye cut her off. "You can, and you need to give them to me. Now."

Her expression changed again and she spun her chair around to face a filing cabinet behind her desk.

Less than a minute later, Kaye, the address and two phone numbers noted in his paper brains, was headed back to the Harley.

He recognized the address. It wasn't far.

*** 

The Tower had started life as high-end housing for UCLA students with well-heeled parents. Just off campus, and much more like a boutique hotel with suites than a dorm. For years the waiting list, and costs, had been daunting.

But as college costs soared and even reasonably well-heeled parents began to look for financial aid and student loans, The Tower found itself becoming the quintessential example of a solution in search of a problem.

So it became condominiums and expanded its market from spoiled college students to the larger client pool of the spoiled population in general, and their lessees.

Kaye rolled up and stopped under the building's lavish porte cochere, shut down, dismounted and looked around. Either an assistant country club manager made more than he thought, or her porn king ex-husband was paying considerable spousal and child support every month.

Both of which, he realized, were probably worth protecting.

"Hey," a hustling valet called as he trotted toward Kaye. "You can't leave your bike there."

"Sure I can," Kaye said as he hung his helmet on the handlebars. He turned around and showed his badge. "Police business. I won't be long."

The valet looked at him, shrugged his shoulders, and went back to his waiting spot behind the ever-present lectern.

Soares was listed in the directory as being on the 9th floor.

When Kaye stepped off the elevator there were no hallways, just a large lobby-like area, its carpet plush and the air redolent with the mixed fragrances from the floral arrangements on several side tables. Tasteful art hung on the walls. Ringing the space were two elevators, a door leading to a stairway exit, and five doors bearing unit numbers.

Kaye knocked on Soares's door and waited, and knocked again. Still no answer. He headed back down, wondering where else he might check.

As he walked out the front doors, he was about to try her cell number when he saw her, her back to him, standing near the driveway. Beside her was a little girl, her hand in her mother's. On the pavement on Soares's other side were a medium-sized soft suitcase and a diaper bag printed with Winnie the Pooh images.

"Fancy meeting you here," he said casually as he stopped next to the suitcase, hands in pockets and his gaze toward the street.

At the sound of his voice, her head spun toward Kaye. He glanced sideways and saw the color drain from her face. She instantly bent and scooped up the little girl.

"I was just upstairs looking for you," Kaye said.

"For me?" Soares asked. "Why would you...?"

"I need to know where to find your ex-husband."

"What makes you think I know where he is?"

Kaye raised his hands and gestured at the surroundings as he looked around. "Nice digs. Being a golf course gopher must pay better than I thought. But I heard you quit. Suddenly, too."

"Okay, yeah, Dennis pays the rent. But he doesn't live here. It's part of our settlement and custody arrangement. He lives in Venice somewhere and I've never even been to his house. And why I quit my job is none of your business."

"He comes here for visitation?"

"Yes, so I can keep an eye on him."

"Yeah, I heard he plays rough."

"You have no idea."

Movement caught Kaye's eye and he turned to see a silver Range Rover exit the parking garage and head toward them. It pulled up and stopped, and the valet jumped out, ran around the front of the car and held out a set of keys.

"Here you go, Ms. Soares," the kid said.

"Thank you, Frankie," she said, taking the keys, "I'll take care of you when we're done here, okay?"

The kid looked at Kaye, then nodded before turning to walk away.

"Going somewhere?" Kaye asked.

"My mother's, if you must know."

"Can I ask you a question?"

"I thought you were already asking questions," Soares shot back.

"Touche," Kaye said. "But I'm curious. Why haven't you asked me why I'm looking for Dennis?"

She hesitated slightly before replying, "Because I couldn't care less."

"Really? I'm thinking maybe it's because you already know."

"Know what?"

"That he killed Avi Geller and Nicole Ingram on your golf course," Kaye said. "Oh, excuse me, I guess that would be your former golf course."

"I don't know anything about that," Soares said, shifting the little girl's weight and bouncing her slightly.

"My problem," Kaye went on, "is that I think you do know. I think you fed Dennis information about when Geller would be on the course, and you found out that Nicole Ingram might be with Geller that day, and told Dennis that, too."

"You're crazy."

"In fact, I'm also thinking that when I check your phone records I'm going to find a call, maybe a bunch of them, from your phone to Dennis, or from his number to you, on the very day of the murders. Maybe the Tuesday the week before, too."

Soares stayed quiet. Kaye glanced sideways and saw a tear running down her cheek.

"You don't understand," she protested weakly.

"Carol, are you afraid of Dennis?" he asked softly. "Did he threaten you?"

"Not me, at least not this time," she whispered, then leaned and kissed the top of her daughter's head. "He's a monster sometimes. He used to beat me, bad, when we were married. I couldn't take the chance."

"Then let me help you. If you know where he is, tell me. I'll make sure he never threatens you or your daughter again, and your help will go a long way with the prosecutor."

360

"Prosecutor?"

"Yes," Kaye affirmed. "You're involved in two murders. I can't make any promises, but if what you're telling me is true, well, I might be able to help you keep your daughter."

Soares stayed silent.

"Tell me, Carol," Kaye prompted. "Where is he?"

She didn't turn to look at him, but when she spoke her voice was weary.

"You're as bad as he is, you know that? You threaten people that bad things will happen to them and tell them what you think they want to hear, just so they'll do what you want them to do and tell you what you want to know. Next thing I know you'll be pushing me around, and if I still don't tell you, you'll hit me. Just like he used to."

"I'm not like Dennis," Kaye said, but a voice in his head was whispering 'oh, yes you are' as the memory of Reid's bloodied face and broken hand flashed across his memory.

Soares went silent again.

Kaye waited, rocking slightly back and forth on his heels.

"I'm not sure exactly where he is," she said at last. "That's the truth. He's staying in a vacant house that's for sale. It was dark when I took him some groceries, and he didn't give me the address, just directions, and told me to look for the sign."

"Is it far from here?"

"No, it's really not that far. A few miles, maybe. It didn't take me long to get there."

"The real estate sign, did it say Classic Realty and have the name Megan Sullivan on it?"

She gave him a funny look and asked, "How do you know that?"

"Not important," Kaye said. "Did you see anybody else while you were there?"

"No, but I was only there long enough to drop stuff off, and Dennis didn't let me inside. He just took the food and told me to leave, and to keep my mouth shut or else."

"Thank you, Carol. That helps a lot."

"Am I going to jail?" Soares asked, her voice quaking.

"I thought you said you were going to your mother's." He smiled. Her relief was palpable.

\*\*\*

Soares tipped Frankie, loaded her bags and daughter into the Range Rover and drove away.

Kaye watched her go, hoping she wasn't stupid enough to call Bettencourt and warn him.

He pulled out his phone and made a call.

"Detective Lister."

"It's Kaye. You busy?"

"I've got twenty million things going, but that doesn't mean I can't be interrupted. What's up?"

"I think I know where Dennis Bettencourt is. I could use your help."

"When and where?"

"Now," he replied, and gave her a rendezvous location. "And hurry."

"Nothing outruns my V-8 Ford," Lister said and hung up.

***

When they made the first slow pass down the street Kaye thought he'd been overly optimistic to think Bettencourt could actually be hiding in the very house Sullivan had listed on the morning he'd run surveillance on her. It was too much of a coincidence, and he didn't believe in coincidences.

When he voiced his doubts, Lister pulled over and grabbed her phone. In two minutes she was able to determine that Megan Sullivan had no other listings in the area, and the house they were checking was the only one inside Carol Soares's time and distance estimate – if it was valid.

But the house, with no realtor key box hanging on the front door knob and a 'sold' placard atop the sign, looked woefully deserted and there was no sign of Bettencourt's vehicles.

"Makes sense, though, right?" Lister asked. "I mean, the guy's not in there taking a bath and making splish splash. He's hunkered down."

"I suppose," Kaye said. "Pull over and park, but not too close."

Lister glanced at Kaye and said, "Not too close? You mean don't park right in front? Gee, I'd never have thought of that."

"Sorry," Kaye said. "Just thinking out loud."

"Apology accepted." Lister looked at him and grinned. "Partner."

Lister scanned the area and ended up parking in almost the exact spot where Kaye had parked during his surveillance. He mentally gave her points for it as she called in their location to dispatch.

They'd been sitting for about fifteen minutes when Kaye noticed Lister didn't have her earbuds in.

"No music today?"

"I'm trying to break the habit. It interferes with my superhero-worthy powers of observation," she said without taking her eyes off the house. "Besides, I'm waiting for you to tell me what the hell happened in Valle delle Viti after you cut me loose."

"You didn't ask."

"I'm a big Hank Williams fan. I mind my own business." She smiled at him. "Mostly."

He told her everything, from how he'd extracted information from Reid to watching an undercover FBI agent be decapitated to his fight with Tamara Goschen and her death, the death of Renzo Maisano, and Auggie now being in inpatient detox in Santa Barbara.

"Holy shit," Lister muttered when Kaye finished. "She's going to be okay, though, right?"

"When I talked to the doctor this morning she told me Auggie was stable."

"Stable's good, right? I mean, she's not crashing or anything."

"Stable just means her condition is unchanged, for better or worse."

"She's staying alive, which means she's got Barry, Robin and Maurice covering her six. She'll be fine."

Things went quiet for a while as they watched the house. There were zero signs of activity. The mailman delivered to the houses on either side, but skipped the house they watched.

"I think that means it's vacant, right?" Lister said.

"Or they just didn't have mail today," Kaye observed.

But her comment jogged his memory and gave him an idea. He pulled out his cell, made a call, and put it on speaker.

"Gallegos Landscaping. This is Hernan."

"Hernan, Detective Kaye. How are you?"

"Hey, Detective, good to hear from you," Hernan said. "In my business, we say 'any day above the lawn is a good one', so I'm good."

"I've got a question for you."

"Ask away. Anything."

"You still take care of Classic Realty's vacant listings? Megan Sullivan?"

"We do."

Kaye gave Hernan the address of the house across the way and asked, "Are you taking care of that one?"

Hernan cursed and said, "I knew there would be a complaint."

"There's no complaint. But it's on your list, right?"

"Yes, but I was told not to send a crew this week."

"Who told you that?"

"Senora Sullivan," Hernan answered. "She called me, let's see, late Wednesday and told me she thought there was a buyer for the house, so we would be week-to-week now and she would let me know."

"Thanks, Hernan," Kaye said and disconnected before the landscaper could start asking questions.

"Seriously?" Lister asked. "Why would she...?"

"My guess is that Bettencourt threatened her if she didn't," Kaye said. "She said she was afraid he'd kill her if he found out she talked."

"Then why the fuck is she helping that dirtbag?"

"If I could answer that, I could solve one of society's very big problems."

"So what do we do now? Call SWAT?"

"No, we still don't even know if there's anybody in there. I don't want to call out the cavalry and traumatize the neighbors until we're sure it's not a dry hole."

"We need to find out, sooner better than later," Lister stated the obvious.

Kaye looked at the house for the thousandth time and considered their options.

"Drive around the neighborhood," Kaye told her. "When we come back, park down there." He pointed.

Ten minutes later she pulled into the spot and said, "Well, if nothing else, we know the evil prince's little red Corvette isn't parked nearby. What now? We can't really see the house from here."

"Which means nobody in the house can see us, either." Kaye opened the car door. "I'm going to see if the Corvette's in the garage."

"Whoa, whoa," Lister said. "When you get past the house next door you could be seen. Bettencourt's been face-to-face with you before. He's never laid eyes on me. Let me go."

"Not a bad idea," Kaye said. "Think you'll be able to see in the windows? They're pretty high."

"Watch it, buddy. Randy Newman was not singing about me, okay?"

"Then you go. And just look for the Vette or the van. No freelancing. Got it?"

Lister nodded, grabbed her portable radio, got out, and headed down the sidewalk toward the house while Kaye moved to the driver's seat.

They had parked three houses away. Kaye's view from the driver's seat was better, but his view of the garage door was still partly obstructed by the lush landscaping.

As Lister got closer, her pace slowed. As soon as she passed the last planter belonging to the house next door she left the sidewalk and cut across the small lawn area, stopped next to one of the tall Cypress trees that flanked the garage, and leaned forward. Kaye could just make her out through some intervening branches, and could tell she was listening.

After a moment Lister bent down slightly and crept onto the driveway.

Kaye lost sight of her. It made him nervous enough to get out of the car and step into the street for a better view.

He heard the muffled sound of the shots at the same instant he saw Lister spin and tumble backwards onto the driveway. He raced for her, drawing his Kimber.

After only a few strides he saw the garage door start to go up. At the same time he saw Lister roll off her back and start to scramble away. He heard her shout her call sign and then, "Officer needs help! Shots fired!"

When the door was about halfway up, Dennis Bettencourt, pistol in hand and arm extended, ducked under it and walked casually toward Lister.

"Bettencourt! Put it down!" Kaye roared as he stopped about fifty feet from the man and took aim.

Bettencourt heard and turned toward Kaye, taking aim.

Lister, alerted by Kaye's shout, rolled onto her back and drew her pistol just as the emergency traffic alert tone blared from her radio.

"Police! Drop the gun!" she shouted.

Bettencourt looked down at her and instantly changed targets again, aiming almost point blank at Lister's face.

All three fired at the same time. The noise was sharp and deafening.

Running forward, Kaye saw Lister's head snap back as she fired again.

Bettencourt staggered backwards a half-step, regained his balance and raised his pistol toward Lister again.

Kaye, closing fast and still running, raised the Kimber and started firing as fast as he could, over and over, trying to lay down fire that would take Bettencourt down.

He was almost on top of Bettencourt before the tall man started to topple. He lowered his shoulder and hit Bettencourt squarely in the chest, sending him airborne and crashing into the back of the red Corvette in the garage. Without stopping, Kaye kicked Bettencourt's pistol to get it beyond the man's reach, the adrenaline in his system propelling the weapon thirty feet across the driveway and into the middle of the front yard. He glanced down at Bettencourt. The front of the man's shirt was covered in blood, he was absolutely still and his open eyes stared at nothing.

Kaye rushed to Lister, knelt beside her, grabbed her radio and called in an 'officer down'.

Her eyes were open and her eyelids fluttered rapidly. Blood poured down the side of her neck, staining the grass.

"Mel, listen to me," he said urgently. "Where are you hit?"

"Leg, I think, but I don't know," she whispered slowly. "I can't feel anything except the side of my head. It hurts like hell."

Kaye quickly looked her over. Her pants were ripped and there was a flesh wound on the outside of her right thigh, below the hip. There was some blood on her cheek, and blood flowed freely from her neck area, staining the grass below. Not wanting to risk moving her head, he gently pushed her hair aside and bent low to try and get a better look at the wound. He saw a graze below and outside her right eye, and it looked like her right ear lobe was gone. That was where the blood was coming from.

By now, they could hear sirens converging on their location from all sides.

"Well, look on the bright side," he said, smiling.

She gave him a confused look that said 'bright side?'

"You'll save a lot of money on ear rings from here on out," Kaye said.

It took her a moment to comprehend what he'd said, then she tried a weak smile that turned into a grimace and retorted, "Very funny coming from my partner."

***

Within minutes the scene was crawling with cops and medics. The street was closed and crime scene tape encircled everything. The neighbors began to gather and gawk.

Lister was transported and Bettencourt's body covered to await the arrival of the coroner.

Kaye called Thompson and filled him in.

The Captain ordered him to remain at the scene and wait for the shooting investigation team, and he would head for the hospital to be with Lister.

Kaye used the time to search the house for any sign Sullivan had been there. The place was completely empty except for a sleeping bag on the living room floor and a few boxes and cans of groceries on the kitchen counter. He didn't find anything obvious, but with Sullivan's DNA now on file he decided to call forensics and have them check the house.

The forensics team and the coroner arrived at the same time.

Dr. Jaime Archuleta slid out of the coroner's van, saw Kaye, shook his head, and came up the driveway.

"Kaye, we've got to stop meeting like this."

"I hear you, Arch. As soon as you figure out how we can do that, let me in on it."

"What've you got?" Arch asked, reaching down and lifting the corner of the tarp. Eyes wide, he looked around at Kaye. "Holy shit, somebody shot Robert Mitchum's grandkid."

"His evil twin," Kaye said. "And the somebody is either Mel Lister or me, so do a first rate job on the slugs because the Board will want details."

"Got it, and sorry about the joke. Nobody told me this was officer-involved. Who is he? I mean, he's obviously not Robert Mitchum."

"Meet Dennis Bettencourt, the guy who shot Avi Geller and Nicole Ingram at Paloma Canyon Country Club."

Arch's eyes went wide. "You're shittin' me. You actually figured out who did that?"

"Arch, that's why I'm the detective."

Kaye next spoke with the forensics team, explaining the house was vacant, a woman was missing, and what he wanted them to specifically look for.

"Collect the sleeping bag for hair and bodily fluids, please," he said to wrap it up. "I know you'll do that, I just have to say it out loud. It might be the only real lead we have."

The team collected their gear and went to work.

Kaye spent the next half-hour being interviewed by the shooting investigation team detectives, thankful they weren't another George and Lennie team like Sloan and Leale.

About twenty minutes into the interview, the forensics team Supervisor approached and stood about ten feet away.

"What is it?" one of the investigator's asked.

"I need to ask Detective Kaye a question."

"What's up?" Kaye asked.

"I need to know if you want us to dig."

"Dig?" Kaye asked. "Where?"

"Out back," the supervisor replied. "We noticed what looks like a patch of freshly-turned dirt out by the pool house. Since you mentioned a missing woman, well…" He shrugged.

Kaye sighed. "Yeah, better check it. Keep your fingers crossed it's tulip bulbs."

"Amen to that," the supervisor said.

"Wow," the second shooting team investigator said, "sounds like you've got a real mess on your hands."

"This is only the tip of the iceberg," Kaye assured him.

"Well, then, we'll get out of your hair. With Lister in the hospital with gunshot wounds, this is all just a formality, anyway. We'll let your Captain know when the report is filed."

The investigators hadn't been gone for five minutes when the supervisor found Kaye again.

"Detective, you need to come see this."

"You found something?"

"We didn't have to go very deep."

The pile of dirt wasn't very big. People sometimes bury beloved pets in the back yard, and Kaye was hopeful as he walked up and stood over the hole.

He was disappointed.

He shook his head, pulled out his phone, punched in a number and put it on speaker.

"Kai, hey, it's Ben Kaye."

"What's up?"

"I wanted to let you know I've got Howard Feinmann."

"No kidding?" Iwamura asked excitedly. "Where are you? Is he talking?"

"I'm just east of Westwood, maybe fifteen minutes from your office," Kaye replied and gave Iwamura the address. "And, no, he's not talking. His mouth, nose and ears are full of dirt."

"Full of –" Iwamura started to ask, then tumbled to what Kaye was telling him. "You dug him up?"

"That we did. Found him in a shallow hole in the back yard, still wearing a very expensive suit. Looks like he's been here, maybe, a day or two."

"Think it was Maisano's guys?"

"No," Kaye replied, and quickly explained the circumstances. "I guess what I need to know is if the Bureau wants the cold leftovers or if you just want me to handle it."

"Would you mind? I know it's extra work."

"I'm already here, and it is my case. I'll send you copies of everything."

"Thanks, Ben. Oh, and hey, you'll be glad to hear that we found five of those missing women locked in another house on the Valle delle Viti property. But no sign of any others, at least so far. We'll keep searching."

"Five is better than none, I guess. Thanks, Kai."

"Thank you, Ben. Take a vacation, buddy. You've earned it."

After the call ended, Kaye turned to the supervisor. "You heard the man."

"We've got it, Detective. We'll find the shovel, maybe some DNA."

Kaye walked back to the front of the house. Arch was busy packing up.

"Where are you going?" he asked the deputy coroner.

"I'm done here."

Kaye laughed. "You wish. You have another customer in, well, actually under, the back yard."

"No joke?" Arch asked, raising his eyebrows. "Did you or Lister bury the body? I only ask because that would make it easy."

Kaye shook his head. "I'm pretty sure it was Bob," he said. "But not a hundred percent."

"I didn't really think it was you," Arch said, then reached down, picked up his over-sized red duffel bag and headed for the back. After a few steps he turned around. "Maybe Lister, but not you."

Kaye stood in the driveway. The shadows had moved across the street since he and Lister had arrived. Much had happened, very quickly. His mind flashed back to his very first day on the job, his first shift after graduating from the Academy, and the very first thing his training officer had said to him after they got into the patrol car.

"Ready, rookie? This is it, your first shift. If we're lucky, it'll be four hundred and seventy-five minutes of boredom and only five minutes of absolute terror. But don't hold your breath."

It was still the truest thing he'd ever heard from another cop.

But now, today, standing there in the driveway, he still had no idea where Megan Sullivan might be.

He no longer needed her as a witness, and her deal with Okafor might be null and void with Bettencourt's death, but he felt a responsibility to at least find her and make sure she was safe.

He'd been almost certain that when he found Bettencourt, if he didn't find Sullivan with him, he'd at least be able to lean on Bettencourt and find out where she was. But there'd been no sign of her in the house. Maybe she'd crawled back to her husband, or sought refuge with her cousin. Until he got forensics back on the sleeping bag he was stymied on even putting her here with Bettencourt.

He sighed deeply and decided he was done at the house and would go check on Lister.

That's what partners do, he thought, then grunted in self-deprecation.

As he turned to go tell Arch he was leaving a strong glint of reflected sunlight hit his eyes and made him turn his head. Instinctively, he turned to trace its origin.

The garage had a peaked roof with a gable above the door on the street-facing side. Centered in the gable was a round window; a cheap, miniature representation of the rose windows found in churches, this one maybe eighteen inches in diameter. Until the reflecting sun had betrayed its presence, Kaye hadn't really noticed it.

But he did now. A window usually means space on the other side of the wall.

Curious, Kaye walked into the garage. The walls were finished and painted, and looked to be standard drywall. He saw the bullet holes in the garage door from Bettencourt's first shots, and even pulled the door down partway to check above it, but couldn't see a hatch or any other method of access to a possible attic space.

He walked outside. The soffits had vents, and when he checked he saw a vent running the length of the roof's peak. He glanced inside, then again looked at the outside walls. They were several feet taller than the inside ceiling height.

He went back inside. Bettencourt's Corvette and van fit in the two-car-wide space, but the size of the van made it tight. Recessed can lights had been installed, along with a garage door opener. While the width was tight, the depth was not. There was at least ten feet of free space in front of the van, with two large fluorescent lights in the ceiling. A regular pattern of marks on the floor told Kaye that at some point a workbench, maybe two, had likely occupied the space.

The entire back wall was floor to ceiling storage cabinets, except for a door to the house between the first and second cabinets on the left. He randomly opened a couple of the cabinets. They were only about two feet deep, with shelving spaced to accommodate a variety of stuff, and no sign of an access panel.

Kaye opened the door to the house and peered inside. A hallway extended about ten feet, ending at the bottom of a short set of stairs. He could see enough to tell him they led up to the kitchen. Through an open door not far in on the right he could see a laundry room. On the left, the wall extended to the bottom of the steps, broken only by a set of folding doors near the far end.

He pulled the door shut as he stepped back into the garage, mentally fitting the puzzle pieces together.

He stepped sideways, opened the storage cabinet between the wall and the door and found what he was looking for. There was no false bottom in the cabinet. The concrete extended into a blind space maybe half the depth of the inside hallway's length. Centered in the ceiling was an access panel about two feet by five feet. The back edge was hinged, and from the front hang a stout piece of rope with a red plastic handle attached.

Kaye reached up, grabbed the handle, and pulled. At first the panel stuck a bit, but then it came free. The hinges and mechanism squeaked in protest as the panel swung down. Kaye could see what was either a ladder or set of folding steps mounted to the inside surface of the panel. As soon as he could reach it, he grabbed it and pulled. A set of steps unfolded as three pieces, the topmost attached to the access panel, and he used them to finish lowering the panel and ground the steps on the floor.

He looked up. Above the ceiling, the wall was unfinished and only about three feet tall before supporting the rafters. Light was scarce above the ladder, but he was able to make out a blue plastic electrical box nailed to one of the studs. It had wire running in and out, and the front was a light switch cover plate, complete with a toggle.

Aware that his weight was probably well in excess of the

manufacturer's recommended maximum load, Kaye climbed slowly and kept his feet at the very outside edge of the treads, testing each one before putting his full weight on it. He felt the treads flex, but they held.

He had to twist his shoulders to fit through the opening, and still several steps from the top he was able to reach up and try the light switch. Light; not enough to read by, but enough to keep him from bumping into things; filled the space above.

He took the last steps up, bending at the waist to avoid the rafters, and ended up standing on a piece of plywood laid atop the joists. Still bent over, he took a couple steps into the space before he straightened up, turned and looked around.

The entire space was unfinished and uninsulated, just exposed studs, rafters and roof decking perforated from above by thousands of nails. Much of the attic had been floored with plywood to create a platform, probably for boxes of treasured items never touched or used, but never discarded.

Megan Sullivan, her head turned toward Kaye, her open eyes dry and sightless, lay prone in the middle of the space.

She was naked. Her arms extended out to her sides, palms down, and her hands had been nailed to the platform. Her ankles were bound to a length of board that had been fixed between them to keep her from closing her legs. A chain, pulled tight enough to lift her ankles slightly and create an arch in her back, ran from the board to a collar around her neck. A ball gag was tied around her head, the red ball still in her mouth.

She had obviously been tortured. Her back, buttocks and the bottoms of her feet were half-congealed masses of lacerations and welts.

Her arms and legs bore dozens of cigarette burns.

But it was the drying blood that stained the backs and insides of her thighs and puddled under her hips, and the foot and a half of rusty rebar protruding from her vagina, that turned Kaye's stomach.

"Oh, my God," he muttered.

He stared until his numbed brain simply stopped receiving and decoding the nerve impulses his eyes were sending. His vision went fuzzy around the edges and he had to turn away and find support before he fell down.

Finally, he gathered himself, taking one more quick look to make sure he hadn't been hallucinating.

While he carefully went backwards down the steps, his rational mind asserted itself again, and he knew from the condition of the body and blood that he and Lister had likely been parked across the street, waiting, watching and talking while Dennis Bettencourt had brutalized and killed Megan Sullivan, and that Bettencourt had probably seen Lister window snooping through the little round window in the gable.

He also knew he now had to go find Arch again and tell him, 'Hey Arch! Come see! We hit the damn trifecta today!'

He reached the garage floor and took several deep breaths. He did need to find Arch.

But before he could move his feet, Carol Soares's words from earlier today...Had that really been today? It seemed like a lifetime ago...rang in his ears.

*"You're as bad as he is, you know that, right?"*

He couldn't move, and the little voice in his head kept saying, *'she's right, you know.'*

Instead of going to find Arch, he sat down on the second tread of the steps, put his head in his hands, and tried to fight back the guilt.

***

It was almost 9:00 p.m. when Kaye dragged himself back into the Squad. He was surprised to see the lights still on in the Captain's office and Thompson at his desk doing paperwork.

He went and knocked lightly on the door frame. "Captain, I'm back."

Thompson looked up, dropped his pen and said, "Come in, come in. Take a load off. You look beat, Detective."

Kaye collapsed into his usual chair.

"Wasn't sure I'd see you tonight," Thompson said. "You doing okay?"

"Had to bring the unit back. I've had better days, that's for sure."

"I imagine so. Too bad about Sullivan."

"You heard?"

"Dr. Archuleta called. He's worried about you."

"Why would he worry about me?"

"It wasn't your fault, Detective. You did your job, and you did it damn well. Dennis Bettencourt killed her, not you."

"Yeah, I just tied her to a stake in the middle of the jungle and walked away."

"Not true," Thompson said forcefully. "She could have refused to go with Feinmann, but she didn't. Her choice. Your judgment and actions in the Geller case were sound throughout, and your follow-up on Nicole Ingram was nothing short of brilliant police work. You saved a lot of lives today, too, Ben."

"And lost one."

"Don't beat yourself up. You exposed a major criminal enterprise that was operating right under everybody's noses and protected a lot of people from future harm. I'm proud of you."

"Speaking of victims," Kaye said, wanting to change the subject, "how's Mel?"

"You didn't go see her?" Thompson asked, a hint of reproach in his voice.

"I called before I came here. She'd already been released. I don't even know where she lives."

"That she was released should answer your question. She'll be fine. If she lets her hair grow a little nobody will ever know."

Kaye tried to laugh, but it died in his throat.

"So you'll close the Geller case on Monday?" Thompson, always the boss concerned about his numbers, asked the leading question.

"Might as well. Nobody left to prosecute. If I'm here Monday, that is. The shooting…"

"Already got the call. You and Lister are both cleared. There won't even be a formal Board. It wasn't just a good shooting. It was a goddamn public service. The guy was a monster."

"That he was," Kaye agreed, the image of Megan Sullivan burned in his mind and Ruthie Williams' words dancing across his memory.

"Go home. Get some rest."

"That's the plan. I've got to be in Santa Barbara tomorrow."

Thompson studied Kaye. He'd been truthful in court. He and Kaye were not friends. Still…

"She must really be something. Can't wait to meet her."

"Invite us for a barbecue," Kaye said, referring to a long-running joke between him and Thompson. "We'll be there."

"You're on."

Kaye smiled and stood up. "Thanks, Captain."

"For?"

"Being here. I appreciate it."

Thompson half-smiled and picked up his pen. "Okay, beat it. I still have work to do."

Kaye pushed through the Squad doors and headed for the Harley and home.

# LAST DAY
## Monday Week 5

The morning was devoted to finishing the reports and officially closing the case. Kaye made sure that the case heading in the system now read Ingram/Geller instead of just Geller.

He'd called the Ingrams the night before, figuring he had a better chance to reach them on a Sunday evening. He told them what had happened to Nicole those months ago, and he told them he had identified and found the man who had killed Nicole, why, and that it was the Storm Chase that had been on the list of Nicole's friends.

"He won't get bail, I hope," was the first thing Bradley Ingram said. "I'd like to attend the trial, whenever that is."

"There won't be a trial, Mr. Ingram. He didn't go to jail. He went to the morgue," Kaye said. "My partner and I had to shoot him when he tried to shoot us."

"Can't say I'm disappointed," Ingram said. "Thank you, Detective Kaye."

He called Mark Edler and gave him enough information to satisfy the firefighter's curiosity, again thanking the kid for being persistent.

He also called Anthony at the Ferrari dealer and explained that while he had no forensic evidence there had been a bomb in Howell's car, the overall circumstances of the case, including that his truck had been blown up during the investigation, certainly supported it. Anthony was grateful for Kaye's call and promised to relay the information to the engineers in Italy.

\*\*\*

Just after lunch, Kaye rolled up to the Century City high rise and parked the Flight Red '41 Knucklehead on the sidewalk.

The media was long gone. Less than a month had passed. Hollywood is a fickle town.

He grabbed the package from the saddlebag and headed up.

The offices of AZG Productions were still all about glitz and glamour, but a large portrait of Aviram Geller, Founder, now hung prominently in the lobby.

"How can I help you?" the new receptionist asked, not recognizing him.

"Ben Kaye," he replied. "I'm here to see Mr. Geller."

She picked up the phone and called back to announce him, hung up, smiled and said, "You can go back Mr. Kaye. They're expecting you. Mr. Geller's office is –"

"I know the way."

She smiled again and nodded encouragement. "Good luck."

Sam Geller greeted Kaye at his office door.

"Detective Kaye, how nice to see you. Come in, come in. You know my mother, right?" Sam waved him in and pointed him to a chair.

"I do," Kaye said. "Nice to see you again, Mrs. Geller."

Ziva Geller smiled and nodded.

When they were settled in and done with the chit chat, Sam steered the conversation to business.

"I must say, Detective, I was surprised to get your call asking for a meeting. I thought the case was closed."

"It is," Kaye acknowledged. "This is business of a more personal nature."

"Really?" Sam said. "What can we do for you?"

"Actually, it's what I can do for you," Kaye said, looking at Ziva Geller. "I owe you a favor, and –"

"Two," Ziva interrupted, smiling slightly. "You owe me two favors."

"Well, however many I owe you, I'm here to pay you back in full." Kaye lifted the package and put it on Sam's desk.

"What's that?" Sam asked.

"Nicole Ingram's screenplay," Kaye replied. "I got it from one of her neighbors during the investigation. You need to read it."

"You mean you want me to make a movie out of it?" Sam asked.

"Only if you think it's worth your time and money."

"Have you read it?" Ziva asked.

"I have," Kaye said. "I'm certainly no judge of screenwriting talent, but I know somebody who is, and she thinks it's worth a look. She called it Nicole's treasure."

"I have a question for you first," Ziva said.

"What's that?" Kaye asked.

"Did you ever find out if it was Les that this young lady went to Santa Barbara to see? I'd like to think he had nothing to do with her kidnapping."

"When I talked to him on the day he died, he swore to me he had nothing to do with that," Kaye said. "It wasn't in the part of his statement I was able to recover, but everything else he told me checked out. I believe him."

"Good to know," Ziva said somberly. "Thank you."

"I can't promise anything on the screenplay," Sam said.

"I'm not looking for a promise," Kaye said. "Just an objective evaluation. I think the Ingrams deserve that."

"I can do that, I guess," Sam said, glancing at his mother. "I'll let you know."

"You don't need to let me know," Kaye said. "In fact, I'd prefer the Ingrams not know you got it from me. Give the credit to your dad. He died trying to help their daughter."

"I'll read it," Ziva spoke up, reaching out and putting her hand on the bundle. "Papa told me about this girl." She turned to Kaye. "Thank you. We're even."

"What do I tell the Ingrams?" Sam asked.

"Sam, this is Hollywood," Kaye said, smiling as he stood up. "Land of make believe. I'm sure you'll think of something."

The '41 Flight Red Knucklehead was right where he'd left it.

It was about two hours to Santa Barbara. He was excited. Auggie hadn't seen the '41 yet.

**DON'T MISS A SINGLE EXCITING BEN KAYE CASE**

## THE BILBAO GAMBIT

Kaye finds himself caught in a web of intrigue, deceit and murder with roots dating back to 1937 Paris as he tries to stop an unspeakable act of terrorism.

## THE KUNDUZ PAYBACK

What first looks like a robbery gone bad leads Kaye into a morass of competing intelligence agencies, international diplomacy, guns, drugs and money as he searches for a ruthless killer.

## THE TRAIT

Kaye ventures to the glamorous ski town of Aspen, Colorado to help an old colleague and finds himself embroiled in the strangest case of his career as he deals with powerful political and religious interests. What he finds has the power to alter human history.

## MOURN THE INNOCENTS

When Kaye follows a single tenuous thread during a homicide investigation, it unravels to reveal secrets of his own past that shake the foundations of his very existence.